Treasure River

This is work of accurate historical events woven into the lives of fictional characters. All names, characters and incidents, depicted in this book are either totally the products of the author's imagination or actual historical characters or events recorded in the history of the area. Any other resemblance to actual events, locales, organizations, or persons, living or dead, is entirely coincidental.

ISBN: 0-9779680-2-2
Library of Congress Control Number: 2006931113
Published by Global Authors Publications

Filling the GAP in publishing

Edited by Barbara Sachs Sloan
Interior Design by KathleenWalls
Cover Design by Kathleen Walls
Interior Art by Jason L. Price
Expedition Map and R. B. Marcy Map credit to LSU Special Archives

Printed in USA for Global Authors Publications

WHAT OTHERS SAY ABOUT *TREASURE RIVER*

"'The Red River story has remained a best-kept secret, largely in part due to President Jefferson's embarrassment over the 1806 Freeman-Custis Expedition's failure at the hands of the Spanish; brought about by the Aaron Burr/Wilkinson conspiracy.' Every river has a story that can only be told by someone who knows her history and her heart. Red River was always "Treasure River." She just needed Wildwood Dean to tell her story."

Allen Rich, *North Texas e-News.*

"*Treasure River*, by Wildwood Dean, meanders along the Red River of the early 19th century with tales of trappers, whiskey dealers and treasure hunters. Yellow Beard, reared by his Wichita Indian mother, has not given up the dream of finding his treasure-hunting father. Jac Colter seeks to make his fortune, in part as recompense for an act of treachery against his father. Smuggling prohibited whiskey to the trappers proves a risky if profitable proposition. Want to know how to make frontier whiskey? Here you'll find the recipe, right down to the rattlesnake heads. In this saga the author lovingly chronicles the imperfect individuals who sought their destinies wherever the streams could take them."

Lydia Hawke, author of *Firetrail* and *Perfect Disguise*

Treasure River

by

Wildwood Dean

DEDICATION:

To the memory of Joe and Sybil Price who are responsible for the inherited disorder I have, properly diagnosed by my wife as "Red River in the veins."

ACKNOWLEDGMENTS:

In reading historical works of literature, I have found that most writers make the claim they have neither dramatized nor fictionalized their accounts of historical happenings, and in many works there is a total disregard for historical geography. Some, not all, come across as just another canned scholarly presentation with a host of references in hopes of making them authoritative. *Treasure River* goes back to the original publications of the early 1800s and recreates history and geography (histrography) the way the lay people of the early 1800s would have talked about it, around the campfire at night.

My sincere thanks to LSU Special Archives, Noel Memorial Library; their digital library containing many original manuscripts and maps dated around the Louisiana Purchase was invaluable. I thank them for their permission to publish the 1806 map of the Freeman and Custis Red River Expedition. I found especially useful: *Travels In The Interior Parts Of America* by Captains Lewis and Clark, Doctor Sibley And Mr. Dunbar and *An Account Of The Red River In Louisiana Drawn up From the Returns of Messr. Freeman and Custis.*

Thanks to Mrs. Frances A. Fuller and her great work: *The River of the West,* originally published by R. W. Bliss and Co. of Hartford, Connecticut, and Toledo, Ohio: 1870.

A special thank you goes to the pioneering newspaper reporters, and the companies for which they worked, who followed the frontier story wherever it took them. Thanks to the *Louisiana Gazette* of St. Louis and the *Louisiana Gazette Daily Advertiser* of New Orleans, the *Pittsburg Gazette, the Pennsylvania Gazette* of Philadelphia and the *New York Evening Post* all of which brought the day-to-day frontier life to their readers.

Thanks to *The Handbook of Texas Onlin*e and various historical societies for their dedicated efforts in preserving our history.

Last but not least, I must acknowledge that I owe Red River a debt of gratitude. She gave me the desire to tell her story and entrusted me to tell it in a manner befitting the Queenly river that she is. Thanks to the people of the Red River I have met along her shores and for their family chronicles which they so lovingly shared.

AUTHOR'S INTRODUCTION

"Civilization is a stream with banks. The stream is sometimes filled with blood from people killing, stealing, shouting and doing the things historians usually record, while on the banks, unnoticed, people build homes, make love, raise children, sing songs, write poetry, and even whittle statues. The story of civilization is the story of what happened on the banks. Historians, ignore the banks for the river." -- Will Durant

Treasure River is my attempt to record the things that happened along the banks of Red River. I could not record what transpired on the banks of the river, however, and ignore the things that happened in the river. By combining the things that happened along the banks with what transpired in the stream, I hope to have recorded the story of a civilization we have forgotten.

THE UNNOTICED RIVER

For eons Red River's quiet waters have run their course. Her satisfaction has come from her role in life, that of serving nations and humanity.

She has relented to man calling her whatever he wished. The French called her River Rouge. Rio Rojo is what the Spanish called her. Red River is the good old American name we know her by.

She has not run swift, falling from mountains, in order to obtain respect. She has not run wide and mighty, like the Mississippi, in order to obtain her glory. Glory has not been what she sought. She didn't transport famous explorers like Lewis and Clark; nor was she a highway to the trapping fields of the North and Northwest, like the Missouri River. She never became a link between the East Coast and the West Coast, as President Jefferson hoped she would.

What did she do, you ask? While famous rivers were doing all those things — she quietly kept nations at bay; she offered herself as a boundary line. The most honorable thing that a river can be, she thought.

Before the Louisiana Purchase of 1803, Red River was the boundary line between France and Spain. After the Louisiana Purchase, she became the boundary line between the United States and Spain.

In 1821, Mexico won her independence from Spain; then Red River became the boundary line between the United States and Mexico.

Red River proudly served as the boundary line between the United States and the Nation of Texas from 1836 till 1845.

Since 1845, Red River has served as the boundary line between two states: Texas and Oklahoma.

THE FORGOTTEN LIFESTYLE OF THE WHISKY BREWERS

The unconquerable thirst among the Indians and trappers for frontier whisky was brought about by competing fur companies for the soft gold of the Rockies, intensified with the creation of the rendezvous system, and created a great demand for the whisky being brewed along the banks of the rivers. The stills along the Mississippi and the Missouri rivers flourished from 1825 until 1832 when Congress passed a bill excluding spirituous liquors from Indian country. Whisky for the boatmen or whisky for the Indians — it no longer mattered — was illegal and subject to seizure. Government agents, inspecting shipments at Fort Leavenworth, seized every ounce of whisky they could find. Thus of the fourteen hundred gallons of whisky bound for the 1833 rendezvous, only two hundred fifty gallons made it through.

No one suspected that whisky could make its way from Red River to Indian country. The Donnegan still on Bois d' Arc Creek was in place. A smuggling operation sprang up to supply the want. Red River did her part to provide whisky for the rendezvous. Unpretentiously, though, she might add.

THE FORGOTTEN LIFESTYLE OF THE TREASURE HUNTERS

Sam Cooper knew better than most that Red River could provide a link to the treasures of Santa Fe. He knew very well what the Louisiana Purchase meant, and he was afraid that Red River would become a highway to Santa Fe — not meant to be — if the Spanish had their way. He was an explorer in the grandest manner, of his mind. He had digested all the reports that came in from Lewis and Clark, from Sibley and from Zebulon Pike. No one paid any attention to the ragged-misfit-eccentric trappers, hunters and explorers who came off Red River — with wild stories of hidden gold and Spanish treasures — told under breaths of strong hooch. No one, that is, except Sam Cooper. He riveted his attention to reports of the Spanish gold and silver in Santa Fe; and to reports of hidden gold in the Mexican province of Spain; and to the legend of the lost gold mines of Gran Quivira. He imagined that Red River would become his secret passage to the fortunes of the Taovaya Indians at San Teodoro — to the wealth of Santa Fe — and to the whisky stills along the banks of Red River.

FORGOTTEN IS THE TIME WHEN AMERICA'S RIVERS (NATURE'S HIGHWAYS) WERE THE ONLY HIGHWAYS

We have not always been people of the highways; we must remember we were once people of the river.

In the early 1800s most of the trade and exploration took the more conventional routes of the Missouri River, and the Arkansas River, and the Mississippi River. There was nothing conventional about Red River — she flowed to the song of the eccentric. Red River as a highway — for those in search of cheap whiskey; for those in search of treasures of the heart; and for those in search of Spanish gold and treasures of wealth — was a best-kept secret. Treasure River tells her story.

To settlers like the Donnegans, Red River became a highway to a new beginning — to free land. All they had to do was to settle it and hew a living from the treasures of the land, in their case the corn.

Red River became a spiritualistic river for Yellow Beard — it was the highway that led him in the search of his father.

Jac Colter found Red River to be a means to an end. To people like him, Red River would never be more than just a way to transport great miseries, in the form of whisky, to the Indians. To people like Sam Cooper, Red River provided a means by which he could transport Spanish treasures of gold and silver to New Orleans.

STORIES NEVER TOLD ARE NOT FORGOTTEN

The Red River story has remained a best-kept secret, largely in part due to President Jefferson's embarrassment over the 1806 Freeman-Custis Expedition's failure at the hands of the Spanish, brought about by the "Aaron Burr/Wilkinson conspiracy." Wilkinson, who signed the Louisiana Purchase, and Aaron Burr conspired to clue the Spanish government in to President Jefferson's plans for the Freeman-Custis Expedition up Red River in hopes of inciting a conflict that would lead to a war between the U.S. and Spain. They were in a position to profit greatly. The whole thing was squelched, and the Lewis and Clark expedition gained all the publicity. Red River was forgotten. Treasure River pays a tribute to Red River, which is long overdue.

Treasure River records the desires, the greed, the fantasies, the contentment and the fear found in the hearts of those who traveled her — of those who conquered her. It records how they used her and took advantage of her to create for themselves, and their families to come, great wealth. Recorded as well are stories of those who just eked out a living along her ways and byways. Treasure River records the stories of people she conquered and took advantage of in their frugal attempts to tame her.

LISTEN TO TREASURE RIVER'S STORIES

Stories of the birth of a baby on the wild frontier, without anyone to help; and of death without a funeral or anyone to care; of the raising of a newborn child without its mother. It will reveal to you the marriage of a daughter without a preacher or a proper wedding. Forgotten is the time when you had to kill your own supper, every day. It records what commerce was like before checks and debit cards. It will tell you of a time when it was more profitable to lose your own identity than it was to steal someone else's.

My desire is that you will live within this book, as you read it. I certainly did, as I wrote it.

LISTEN ... TO Treasure River!

OTHER BOOKS BY AUTHOR

Survival Value in Fannin County, Texas, published in *The Best of Texas Folklore, Vol. 1 and 2,* by the Texas Folklore Society.

Possum and Sweet 'Taters published in *The Family Saga: a Collection of Texas Family Legends* by the Texas Folklore Society.

Seeing Red published by North Texas e-News

THE CHARACTERS

COOPER FAMILY

SAMUEL COOPER, nickname (Sam) inherited one fortune and made another.

CATRINA COOPER, nickname (Cat), his wife.

Their child:

WILLIAM COOPER (Bill), Indian name is (Gold Seeker.)

DONNEGAN FAMILY

ROSCOE DONNEGAN, son of a Tennessee brewer working for Stiller Johnson.

GURDY (JOHNSON) DONNEGAN, his wife.

Their children:

EMMA VIOLET (Eve-e)

MARY ANNALEE (Annalee),

ROSCOE JUNIOR (Junior)

JOHNSON FAMILY

STILLER JOHNSON, a whisky brewer on Kiamichi River, wife was killed by Indians.

His children:

GURDY, Oldest

JEB, Youngest

LILLY FAMILY

PIERRE LILLY, a rich trader living in New Orleans, trades in St. Louis.

CHRISTINE (MEZIERES) LILLY, his wife.

Their children:

JACOB CLAY, Oldest son. His girlfriend, ANNABELLE

ABNER MANUEL, Youngest son.

MEZIERES FAMILY

MANUEL MEZIERES, head of State Mexican government.

MONA MEZIERES, his wife.

Their children:

CARISA, Oldest daughter.

CHRISTINE, Youngest daughter.

SANCHEZ FAMILY

ORTEGO SANCHEZ, rich trader in Vera Cruz, Mexico, trades in Santa Fe, Mexico.

OLGA SANCHEZ, his wife.

Their child:
PHILEPE SANCHEZ, moves to New Orleans and goes in business with Pierre Lilly.
CARISA (MEZIERES) SANCHEZ, Philepe's wife.
Their children:
RENEE ALBERTO SANCHEZ, Oldest
JUAN ORTEGO SANCHEZ, Youngest.

WICHITA INDIAN FAMILY

KETOX RUNNER , (Coyote Runner) Wichita Indian, medicine man and spirit keeper.
His child:
DANCING WATERS.
Her child:
SON OF GOLD SEEKER, illegitimate son of Bill Cooper.

ANTOINE GODIN, Instigator of the battle of Pierre's Hole.
BLACK JACK, The river boat captain of the West Wind.
BARLOW Mc KINSEY, A mountain man trapper for the Yellow Beard-Colter Red River Exploration.
BEN GAY, A traveler on his way to Cantonment Gibson.
BULL GRANDE, (El Toro Grande), Spanish/Indian (Mother was Comanche) A medicine man living at Pecan Point, on Red River.
COL. ARBUCKLE, In charge of construction at Cantonment Gibson.
COLTER, Jac Colter's name after he became a mountain man.
DANCING DOE, Jinx's Wichita Indian wife.
DUNK RIVERS, A trapper trapping for Yellow Beard.
EVERT HOLLMAN, A bounty hunter.
EZRA TROVER, Owner and captain of the Hattie, a Missouri Rivr Keelboat.
FISHY FORTNER, A fisherman on the Atchafalaya River.
GEEZER, An old, sourpuss trapper, trapped for Grizzly on Red River, and Yellow Beard in the mountains.
GRIZZLY, A trapper on Red River.
ROBERT HAMILTON, Bought Pecan Point Plantation from Jacob Black.
HENERY SHREVE, Cleared the Great Raft.
JAC COLTER, Alias for Jacob Lilly.
His mule, SQUIRT.
JACOB BLACK, First white person to own Pecan Point.
JACQUES, Yellow Beard's French/Taovaya Indian friend.
JINX, (Jink Townsend), trapper on Red River, The Cooper Exploration guide, habitual drunk.
KETCHUM, A trapper for Grizzly on Red River.

LITTLE FEATHER, Barlow's Wichita Indian wife. Jinx and Dancing Doe's daughter.
LANK, (Lankford Langston) a cowboy.
LUKE, First mate of the Hattie.
MOON WEAVER, A Shoshoni Indian seamstress.
NARY, A storekeeper in St. Louis.
NATHANIEL WYETH, Mountain man adventurer.
PUG, Pug Givens, a trapper for Yellow Beard.
REV, (Reverend Jonathan) a crazy Methodist circuit Preacher.
SHARP, (Jim Sharp) a white man living with Wichita Indians. Guided the Cooper exploration up Red River.
THOMAS LIVERMORE, A bugler in Nathaniel Wyeth's group.
TRICKY TONGUE, A Taovaya Indian at San Teodoro.
WIL-O, (WILL-O-WILLOW) Bill Cooper's care giver.
YELLOW BEARD, The name Grizzly gave SON OF GOLD SEEKER.
ZEKE, Ezekiel Netherly, a mountain man trapper for the Yellow Beard-Colter Red River Exploration.
His mule: OL' DOLLAR.

THE ROCKY MOUNTAIN FUR COMPANY

WILLIAM H. ASHLEY, A mountain man, founder of a fur company which was the forerunner of the Rocky Mountain Fur Company.

WILLIAM SUBLETTE,
JEDEDIAH SMITH, These three men bought Ashley's Fur Company
DAVID JACKSON,

MILTON SUBLETTE,
THOMAS FITZPATRICK, Purchased the fur company from William
JIM BRIDGER, Sublette, Jedediah Smith and David Jackson.
HENRY FRAEB,
JEAN GERVAIS,

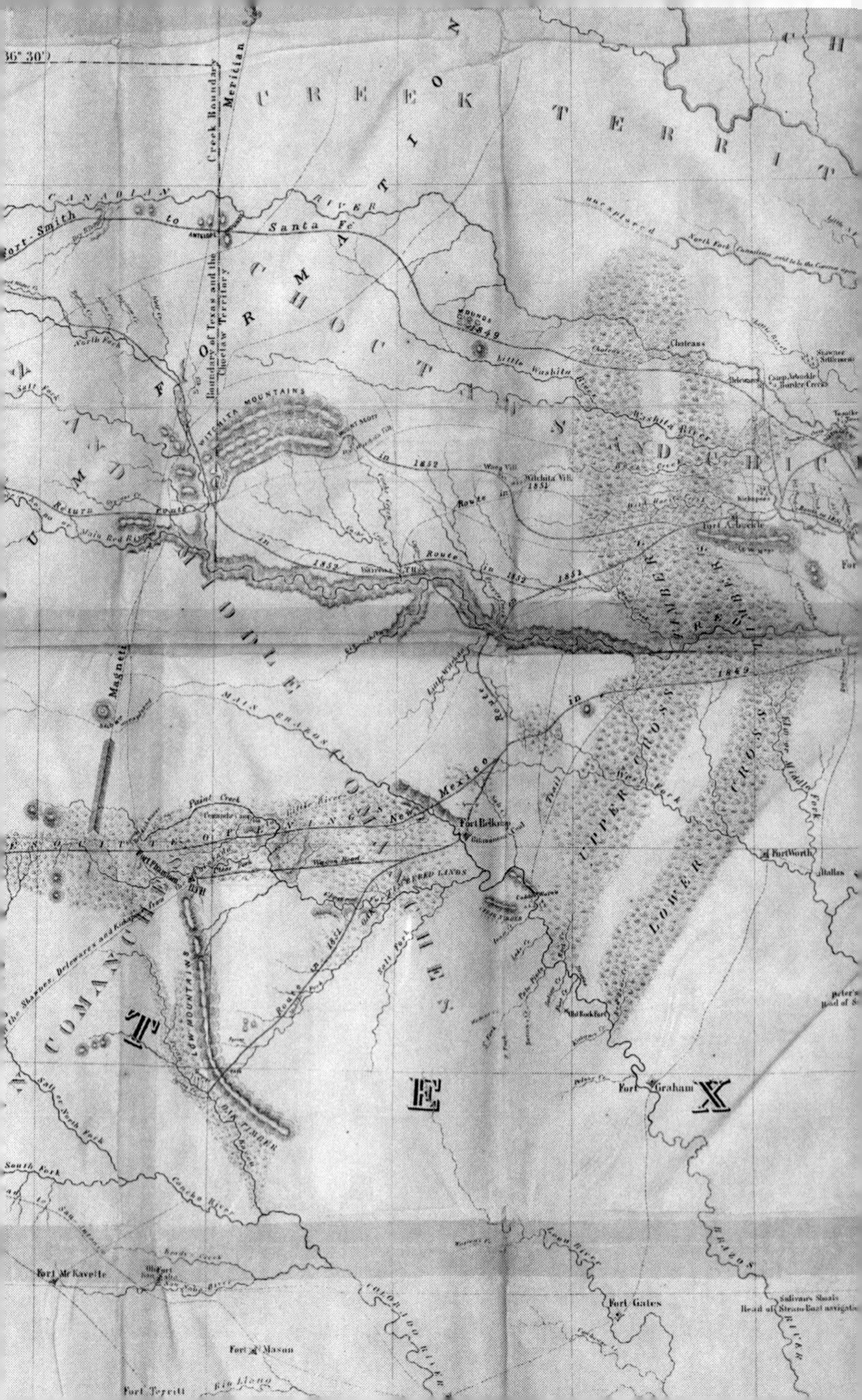
36° 30'
Creek Boundary
Meridian
C R E E K N A T I O N
T E R R I T
C A N A D I A N R I V E R
Fort Smith to Santa Fe
Boundary of Texas and the Choctaw Territory
unexplored
North Fork
Salt Fork
WITCHITA MOUNTAINS
Little Washita River
Washita River
Chateaus
Shawnee Settlement
Camp Arbuckle
Border Creeks
Fort Arbuckle
Witchita Vill. 1851
Route in 1852
Return Route
Main Red River
Route in 1849
Magnetic
Main Brazos
New Mexico
Fort Belknap
Paint Creek
Wagon Road
Fort Phantom
UPPER CROSS
LOWER CROSS
West Fork
Elm or Middle Fork
Fort Worth
Dallas
Route in 1851
Salt Fork
LOW MOUNTAINS
OAK TIMBER
the Shawnees, Delawares and Kickapoos
COMANCHES
T E X
Fort Graham
South Fork
Concho River
Fort McKavette
COLORADO RIVER
Fort Gates
Fort Mason
Fort Terrett
Rio Llano
Leon River
BRAZOS RIVER
Sullivans Shoals
Head of Steam Boat navigation

Fort Gibson
Grand River
Van Buren
Fort Smith
ARKANSAS
Little Rock
RIVER
White River
Napoleon
Fort Towson
Washington
Fulton
Sulphur Fork of Red River
Legrange
Conway
Big Cypress
Little Cypress
Marshall
Shreveport
Lake Providence
Providence
Vicksburg
Sabine River
Logan's Ferry
Spanish Lake
Natchitoches
Hamilton
Sabine
Angelina River
Neches River

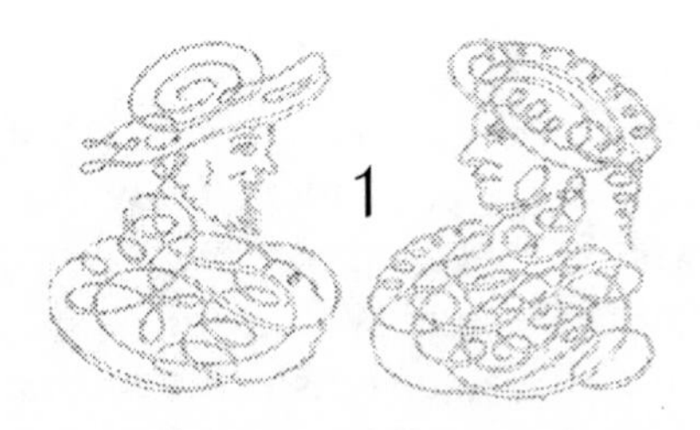

1

The dimly lit room in the cabildo, a former govnment building in the French Quarter of Orleans, filled with the rancid smoke of hand-rolled cigars. The scuffing sounds of chair legs scooting across hardwood floors broke the silence. The French delegation pulled their chairs up to the beautiful, crudely built round table. General James Wilkinson came into the room and was the last to be seated. France was about to sell the territory of Louisiana to the Americans ~ possibly for a great sum of money, for such God-forsaken land ~ they presumed. April 11, 1803, had finally arrived. Three documents that ceded Louisiana to the United States, antedated to April 30 in the year of our Lord 1803, lay on the table.

In the center of the table sat an open inkwell, full of black ink and ready for the signers. Two crystal vases filled with goose-feather quills stood, one on each side of the inkwell.

A French Parliamentarian was the first to sign. He lifted a quill from the vase, dibbled it briefly in the well of black ink, and eloquently scrolled his name onto the parchment. Governor William Claiborne of Orleans took a quill from the vase. He collected ink from the black inkwell and penned his name onto the document.

Now all that lacked was for General James Wilkinson to sign and close the deal. The excitement mounted. What was he waiting for? Surely he had the authority to sign for the United States. After all, President Jefferson had sent him to sign. Yet he stared at the document with an amused look on his face. What General James Wilkinson had found amusing was the way in which the feathery tip of the writing instrument danced in opposing arcs to the flow of the ink as the Frenchmen lay down their names. The delay on the General's part had only been a stall, not a refusal to sign, nor a lack of authority to sign. If he found their signing to be amusing, then what he found their beautiful penmanship to be was that it was amazing. *My pondering is holding up the show,* he thought.

He hurriedly extracted a quill from the crystal vase.

General Wilkinson rolled the quill in his mouth, dampening it with tobacco juices before he thrust it into the inkwell. Slowly and methodically he signed his name to the parchment. Only once did he re-dibble the quill into the inkwell so he could blot out a mistake. The purchase of Louisiana was done! As General Wilkinson's quill cleared the parchment, sighs filled the room. Some sighs came forth out of relief, some out of disbelief. General James Wilkinson had just purchased more than eight hundred thousand square miles for a measly fifteen million! Hurrahs and boos both filled the room. Everyone there realized that the United States had just doubled in size.

~

Back in Washington, President Jefferson ~ anticipating the successful purchase of the Louisiana territory ~ had called a meeting of his advisors and top aids, and they had begun to plan for explorations. The foremost task that faced the nation was to explore the vast lands the United States had just purchased. As a part of President Jefferson's master plan to explore the West, the Missouri and Arkansas rivers had been of utmost importance. Second only to them in importance, when it came to exploring the West, was the Red River. President Jefferson fondly called his plan to explore Red River "My Grand Excursion to the Southwest." His plan was that it would be the first major scientific probe into the American West.

A civilian scientist by the name of Thomas Freeman ~ President Jefferson insisted ~ was picked to be the Field Captain of the Dunbar exploration. Thomas Freeman then chose Peter Custis, an academically trained naturalist, to be his assistant. In spite of the scientific minds at the helm, the main goal for the exploration had remained intact: to prove whether or not Red River might be a commercially viable watercourse to Santa Fe.

~

General Wilkinson thought he might could stir up an international conflict between Spain and the United States. He knew if he could do that, he stood to gain greatly. It was with that purpose in mind that he tipped off Spanish Authorities. He sent an unsigned letter to Spain, and he addressed it to: Governor - General of Mexico. Sir: It comes to my attention that an expedition on behalf of the United States will enter Red River on 2 May 1806. They hold as their intentions to explore the total length of her to Santa Fe. Encroachment upon your soil may be forthcoming.

Spain held that Red River was their northern boundary. "Encroachment will not be tolerated," Spain declared. "Give them Americans an inch, and they will take a mile!" They dispatched two military units to Red River with orders to "Intercept and turn back!"

The Freeman-Custis expedition entered Red River on the anticipated date. They were six hundred fifteen miles up the river on July 28. There they met a Spanish force under the command of Francisco Viana, who ordered them to turn back. The Americans were retreating back down Red River by August 1. This turning point on Red River became known as Spanish Bluff. The scientific achievements the Freeman-Custis Expedition had accomplished ~ as dramatic as they might have been ~ had become obscured by the more dramatic and more publicized achievements of Lewis and Clark. Also obscuring its scientific achievements was its own failure at the hands of the Spanish forces.

The next attempt to explore the Red River came by lieutenant Zebulon Pike. He explored the Arkansas River and the upper Red River in 1807. The Pike exploration got foiled in much the same way as the Freeman-Custis Expedition. Lieutenant Pike, for some unknown reason, found himself on the wrong side of Red River and in Spanish territory. There Spanish authorities promptly seized him and escorted him back to Santa Fe. Pike published what he had seen, as well as what happened to him. Pike's accounts of those things aroused the interest of many Americans.

Red River certainly received its share of publicity, both bad and good. Interest in the reports that came back from explorations made on behalf of the United States of its newly acquired lands was extremely high. Newspapers back East filled their pages with stories of a land that teemed with fur and had natural resources galore. Some of the reports were true and accurate while some just filled their readers with gross misconceptions and flat-out untruths about easily obtained wealth and riches. A few people gleaned every tidbit of information that came from Red River, as if it was gospel. Sam Cooper was one of those.

~

Sam Cooper placed his smoldering pipe back into its cradle then reared back his armchair. He propped his feet upon his desk and lapsed into a daydreamy world of days gone by.

He remembered spending his younger days in the mountains trapping, then he wound up in Santa Fe before he returned ~ via the Red River and the mighty Mississippi ~ to Orleans with a trunkful of Spanish gold and silver specie. Who knew better than he about the potential there was to make a fortune bringing Santa Fe treasures and Red River whisky down Red River to New Orleans?

He had become rich when he inherited his Great Uncle's fortune. *I have made me a fortune in my own right. I have invested my profits from the Red River whisky and the Spanish treasure into the fur companies and trading expeditions.* He had lived in the French Province of Louisiana almost all his life. He lived in Orleans before the United States purchased the Louisiana Territory and changed her name to New Orleans. It was there Sam met his beautiful Katrina, "Cat." She was so beautiful and he so ordinary. What had Cat seen in his ruddy complexion, in his average size and in his little potbelly that had caused her to find him attractive? Could it have been his wiry, bristled Yellowish-red hair and his coal black eyes? He remembered that onlookers said he had hair like a pig and eyes like a chunk of coal.

Some of the women who frequented the French Quarter found his striking hair and black eyes appealing. All of them found his wealth appealing. Cat, though … she was different. She was a beautiful, blue eyed, Spanish/Indian maiden, and neither he nor she could have kept from falling in love with each other. He remembered their whirlwind courtship and the day they married. He dreamed of the times when Cat and he had frequented the French Quarter. They dined, listened to soulful music and danced. They were both too tight with their money for a honeymoon. They spent night on end in the French Quarter of Orleans after they married.

They were the most handsome couple of the French Quarter. He with wiry yellowish-red hair and beard along with his coal-black eyes and she with her olive complexion, raven-black hair and powder-blue eyes caught everyone's attention.

Their greatest joy came when they learned that Cat was with child. Then his dream went sour: Cat died giving birth to baby William. Then it was just him and baby William. Sam shuddered at the thought … *I can't raise a baby ... I'm all by myself!*

William stepped into Sam's office. The sun glinted through the isinglass windowpanes and struck him square in the eye almost causing him to spill the coffee he had brought Sam. William recovered and set the cup down amidst the pile of papers that covered Sam's desk. "What are you doing, daydreaming again, Pa?" William blurted out, scaring Sam almost out of his wits.

Sam cupped his hand around his ear. "Hanh, I didn't hear ya," he mumbled.

William frowned and retreated, leaving Sam to his own business.

~

Sam was a dreamer, and his first and foremost dream had come true. Sam had a son. Now, Sam's foremost dream was to explore Red River.

While most of the other wanderers and explorers of the day had squandered their money, Sam had invested his wisely. He never lost sight of his goal to explore Red River.

Sam was an old man now, by the order of the times ~ forty-nine years ~ but he still had the dreams of a man much younger.

William had grown into a fine young lad and was even more striking than his dad. He had inherited wiry hair from his father, but it was coal black like his mother's, and he had her piercing powder-blue eyes and olive complexion.

Sam and William were both uneducated ~ but they could read a little ~ as was the case with many citizens of the day. What they lacked in the way of education, they made up for with brilliance of mind.

Sam Cooper sat at his desk and gazed blankly out the window. He was daydreaming again, and this time ~ the same as usual ~ it was about Red River. *Someday I will explore Red River. Someday Red River will be my Treasure River.*

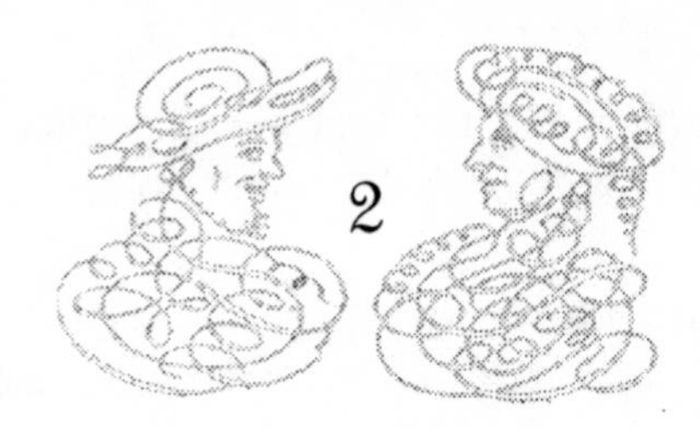

2

In a Catholic Church in Mexico City during a winter day in 1809, a very intriguing scene played out. The Mezieres family ~ one of Mexico City's most prominent families ~ had gathered for their daughter's wedding mass. Throngs of invited guests lined up outside the Metropolitan Cathedral to witness the exchange of vows ~ between Felipe Sanchez and Terisa Mezieres ~ and to hear the priest offer the nuptial blessing. They waited in line to dip their fingertips into the font of holy water and make the sign of the cross before they entered the Cathedral. The beautiful wedding and lavish ball lasted through the wee hours of the morning.

Felipe and Terisa had met at the National Autonomous University of Mexico ~ during their freshman year there ~ and their friendship had blossomed into something more. Upon their graduation, there was no question in either of their minds. They could not stand the thought of being separated by the difficult journey between Veracruz and Mexico City, so they were getting married.

Felipe's father and mother ~ Ortego and Olga Sanchez ~ lived in Veracruz, Nueva España*. They were criollos, meaning they were born in Nueva España but had Spanish parents. Ortego owned a successful trading company ~ Emporos de Nueva España** ~ which he had established before Olga and he married. He had spent his married life building it into an empire. Ortego had also spent all of his young son's life grooming him so, when he finished college, Ortego could turn the reins of the company over to him. Ortego Sanchez held a license ~ issued to him by Spain ~ that authorized him to buy slaves and horses from Nueva España and sell them to the King of Spain. It didn't matter to Ortego that the Taovaya Indians stole the horses, nor that they stole the children. That was their problem. He was making a fortune, and that

*It wasn't until 1821 that Nueva España gained independence from Spain and became Mexico.
**That was to say: traveling trader of New Spain.

was all that mattered. Olga ran the home with an iron fist and couldn't care less from where or how the money came, just as long as it kept coming.

Terisa and Christine's father and mother ~ Manuel and Mona Mezieres ~ were Gachupines: They were born in Spain of titled families. Manuel Mezieres held a high-ranking post within the government in Mexico City, having been appointed by King Ferdinand VII of Spain. Mona worked hard at being a socialite first. She left most of the homemaking to her staff.

~

Felipe and Terisa heard how lavish parties and masked

balls given by wealthy plantation owners spending their winters in New Orleans had gone on and how the Mardi Gras had been revived. They decided the Mardi Gras would be a perfect destination for their honeymoon. Their mistake was they let Christine know about their plans. Christine had been corresponding with a boyfriend in New Orleans. She begged her older sister continuously ~ before the wedding, during the wedding, after the wedding ~ that they would let her accompany them to New Orleans.

"After all, it is Mardi Gras, and my boyfriend will be there!"

Felipe and Terisa Sanchez engaged in their first argument, when Terisa asked him if Christine could go with them. Felipe went through the roof.

"She will be underfoot! We won't have any peace, nor any time to ourselves. You two will always be together! Honey, you know Christine will be, always, in our way!"

"But, honey! Christine and Pierre Lilly are in love! They will be courting! They will be no bother … I know my sister!" Terisa pled. "Out of sight and out of mind, they will stay, I assure you." Terisa won the argument although Felipe was none too happy with the arrangement.

Felipe and his bride began the trip to Veracruz early the morning after the wedding; it was there they were to make their home. Ortego, Olga and Christine gave them company ~ unwanted though it was ~ back to Veracruz.

Late in the evening the same day that they reached Veracruz, Felipe and Terisa along with Christine Mezieres, boarded Ortego Sanchez's schooner, The Trade Wind, bound for New Orleans and the Mardi Gras.

~

Felipe and Terisa didn't see hide nor hair of Pierre Lilly or Christine for the next two weeks after they arrived in New Orleans. Pierre and Christine carried on a whirlwind, week-long, Mardi Gras courtship that ended when Christine changed her last name to Lilly! True to Christine's promise and to Terisa's intuition, things worked out.

One morning, after they had played the whole night through, Felipe and Terisa retired to their hotel dining room to eat breakfast. They least expected to see Christine and Pierre, but there they sat at the other end of the room. What Terisa saw next came as total shock to her.

"Felipe! That is a wedding ring Christine has on!" Terisa exclaimed, once she recovered enough to open her mouth. She ran to their table, dragging Pierre behind her.

"Christine! You are married and you didn't invite us!" Terisa scolded.

"You made me give you my word that I wouldn't bother you, and I wasn't going to go back on it," Christine offered.

"Come to our home for dinner tomorrow evening." The four of them enjoyed a scrumptious dinner with very little small talk. Afterward Terisa set her sister Christine down and gave her a lecture she would not soon forget.

"Christine, do you know how much our daddy will disapprove of Pierre Lilly? That wedding you had, not even in a Catholic Church! Mother and Daddy will not only disapprove, they will disown you!" Terisa blushed from the fury she had just taken out on Christine. "Now tell me all about this Pierre fellow."

"Well, he really likes Felipe." Christine's voice was hollow when she said that.

"I know that, but that is not what I meant. Felipe likes Pierre also. What I meant is how can we sell him to Mother and Father?" Terisa giggled.

"He's not a member of one of those other Christian Churches. Christine's eyes lit up. "What if I could Catholicize him? He said he would start going to Mass with me. Maybe if we had a real wedding in our church in Mexico City."

"I think that's what it will take, before Mother and Father will not disown the two of you." Terisa was stern but had hope. *Their argument will be that Christine will not be able to convert Pierre Lilly.* Terisa thought.

~

Felipe and Pierre had withdrawn from the girls' conversation and had gone to the parlor. There they had their own discussions over fine Irish whiskey while they indulged in dollar cigars.

Felipe wanted to learn more about his new brother-in-law. So, after he had a few courage builders of bourbon on the rocks, he posed the question: "Pierre, what do you do? And tell me about that name … Lilly."

"Well, my folks are back in Ireland. Lilly is a common name there. I ran away from home when I was fourteen and worked my way to America." Pierre combed his fingers backwards through his sandy hair. "My Dad was a big burley potato farmer, and my mother was a warm-blooded French floozy." Pierre spoke without any kind of tone in his voice; he wasn't ashamed, nor did he brag. It was just a fact of life.

Felipe gasped at the frankness in Pierre's voice when he stated the fact regarding his mother. It was beyond Felipe's comprehension ~ being the devout Catholic that he was ~ how anyone could imply that their own mother was a prostitute.

"Is that the reason you ran away from home?" Felipe asked.

"It sure is. Then when I got to New Orleans I worked, went to school, and got an education. I went to work as a bookkeeper in the New Orleans office of a trading company that ran in and out of St. Louis." Pierre paused for a long time then spat on the floor.

"I began to buy trinkets, beads, mirrors, and the like and sell them to the trappers who had drunk and partied up all their money. They were returning to the mountains with nothing to trade to the Indians. I charged them excessively high duty for the use of my credit. I made myself a killing ~ got filthy rich I did. When they returned from the mountains with bundles of furs, I would confiscate their furs to cover their bill, or …." The look on Felipe's face as he gazed at the dirty spit ball on the floor was blank.

Pierre's education, if he has any, has never and will never, take the crudeness out of his ways, Felipe thought.

Pierre studied Felipe's face long and hard. "Or their lives then make it appear as if the Indians did it!"

That brought Felipe Sanchez's gaze squarely to the face of Pierre Lilly. "THEIR LIVES!"

"I was just checking you out," Pierre chided. "To see if you were watching spit or listening."

Felipe knew Pierre was uncouth ~ but was he a murderer? Felipe thought not.

One thing Felipe knew for sure was Pierre was wealthy beyond means. Pierre had become wealthy importing trade goods from far-away places, then trading them for furs he exported to France. Felipe knew his dad would like Pierre if only for that reason. He wasn't sure just how Olga would accept Pierre.

A heated debate developed between them as to whether or not Red River would prove to be a good route to the Wild West. The evening came to a close. Pierre convinced Felipe that Red River was indeed the way to the West.

The girls had finally reached an agreement as to what it would take to get their mother and daddy to accept Pierre, too.

~

Felipe and Terisa were on their way back to Veracruz, bearing the news that Christine had married Pierre Lilly. Whether or not their tidings were good or bad depended on which side of the family received it. For Felipe's parents, the news was good. They could care less whether Felipe had a Protestant brother-in-law or not, and Pierre's being wealthy didn't hurt things a bit. For Christine's parents, the news was bad. They possessed staunch views about their daughters' being married in the Catholic Church. They blatantly refused to accept the facts: One, their baby girl Christine had married a Protestant; nor two, she had married outside the Church.

"What are we to do?" Mona asked Manuel.

"Christine did not marry a Protestant," Manuel Mezieres declared. "That thing they had, that was not a marriage!"

"Pierre could convince Christine to become a Protestant." Terisa didn't help the situation in the least with her two bits' worth.

"Never! Terisa you and Felipe must convince Christine that we will disown her if she becomes a Protestant!" Mona declared.

"She's working on him, Momma ~ she's working on him ~ you must give her time. He will come around!" Terisa pleaded.

Ortego Sanchez embraced the news that Christine had married Pierre Lilly with a great deal of pleasure. Pierre was wealthy. Nothing mattered more to Ortego than that fact. Ortego had big plans. Felipe and Pierre would build a trading empire. *With my trade connections in Nueva España and Pierre's connections in St. Louis, how could they fail?*

Mail service was slow, but between Veracruz and New Orleans it seemed to stop. Pierre and Felipe stayed in touch, but that was about all. Pierre had always dreamed of opening a trade route between Santa Fe and New Orleans. *If we could only communicate, we could get the groundwork started for the new company,* Pierre thought. Then came the letter from Felipe:

"What about the profits? Are there any profits to make?" he wrote.

"What about a place to live until we can find a home?" Terisa wrote.

Now, he is biting, I will soon have him hooked into moving; then we can get serious about starting a new trading company, Pierre mused.

Pierre composed a letter and sent it to Felipe via hi-sail schooner. Pierre's letter was chock-full of exaggerated claims about how much profit they could make and how easy the route would be between New Orleans and Santa Fe. "Just up the Mississippi River, then up Red River straight to Santa Fe," the letter read. Finally there was a desperate attempt to beg Felipe and Terisa to move to New Orleans. The letter convinced them and they began to prepare for the move to New Orleans. The St. Louis-Santa Fe Trading Company was well on its way to becoming a reality. Felipe sent his answer.

The runner knocked on Pierre's door and announced that he had a letter for Pierre Lilly. Pierre held the envelope up to the lamp, then he hurriedly guided the blade of his silver letter opener under the flap. He lifted its contents then spread the letter out in the lamplight. Then he read it out loud.

"We're moving to New Orleans, but it will take some time to tie up loose ends here and raise my share of the collateral."

"Dad blast it!" Pierre uttered under a shushed breath as he read the short note. "Is that all there is?"

Christine entered Pierre's study just as he stuffed the letter back into its envelope. Pierre glanced up then volunteered; "The letter, what little there is of it, is from Felipe."

"How is everyone? How is Terisa and Mother and Daddy?"

"I don't know. That brother in law of yours is too clam-mouthed for his own good."

Days went by and no other correspondence came. Just the way Felipe and Terisa had it planned. Their wish was to surprise Pierre and Christine.

~

What happened next did catch Pierre and Christine by total surprise. They did not learn of the pending visit from Felipe and Terisa until it happened.

Felipe made arrangements with his father for the use of the Trade

Wind, the family's schooner. The very next day, they along with Ortego and Olga boarded the Trade Wind and set sail for New Orleans. It was late in the evening by the time they got underway. The setting sun sank behind their backs just as the full moon began to glow into their faces. Terisa's observation fit the occasion:

"Olga, why don't you sing us a lullaby? It's as if we're babies, cradled between the moon and the sun, and the ocean waves are rocking us to sleep," Terisa observed.

Ortego and Olga's reason for going along on the trip in the first place was that he intended to show Pierre Lilly just how much he desired to see them create the St. Louis-Santa Fe Trading Company; he wanted to offer Pierre start-up dinero.

Terisa's mother and dad didn't join them on the cruise. Manuel and Mona harbored less honorable intentions in that they wished to force Pierre to become a Catholic. Manuel prepared a letter toward that end and placed it in an envelope. Deliberately, he wrote on it ~ FROM: Manuel and Mona Mezieres. He finished addressing it TO: Pierre Lilly and in big capitol letters he wrote the word CONFIDENTIAL. He gave the letter to Ortego with instructions that he give it to Pierre Lilly. So they delegated their dirty work to Ortego and stayed home.

The surprise arrival of Felipe and Terisa almost gave cause for the smelling salts. Terisa's faintness and Pierre's wonderment over why Ortego and Olga had come quickly erased the surprise from their faces and replaced it with wrinkled brows. Christine asked Ortego:

"Do you and Olga plan to move to New Orleans, too?"

"Just here on business," was all Ortego said.

"We have not moved here yet," Felipe assured Pierre. "We're just here to tie up some loose ends before we move."

Pierre, Felipe, and Ortego retired to Pierre's study. Pierre slammed the door behind them. His suspiciousness was eating at him. What did Ortego mean by "business"?

Pierre lit a cigar. He needed to calm down. "Felipe I know why you are here, but Ortego why are you here?"

"I know about your and Felipe's plan to establish the St. Louis-Santa Fe Trading Company. Nothing thrills me more than to see my son continue in the trading business. I think your two-sided approach of an import-export business is a brilliant strategy.

"Now, let me see if I understand this right. You will bring the gold and silver from Santa Fe and the whisky you collect from Red River and deliver it to your Mississippi River post. Then you will send the whisky to St. Louis. The gold and silver from Santa Fe and the furs from St. Louis will come to New Orleans and be exported to France. That is a brilliant plan boys … just a brilliant strategy!"

"Now for the reason I'm here, Lilly. I'm here to give you dinero to start your business.

When it came to money, there wasn't a proud bone in Pierre Lilly's body. Money given, money loaned, or money earned, it was all the same to him.

Pierre had greedy bones and jimmied all the money he could from Ortego Sanchez. He promised Ortego in return that the St. Louis-Santa Fe Trading Company was a sealed deal.

"When Felipe and Terisa can get themselves moved to New Orleans, it will be operating," Pierre vowed. Felipe, Ortego, and he shook hands.

Ortego pulled the confidential letter from his coat pocket and placed it in Pierre's hand. "It is from Manuel and Mona. I advise you to read it in private!"

As soon as he and Felipe left, Pierre opened the letter and read.

> "We insist that you must do what is honorable toward Christine. If it becomes necessary: I, with Mona's full hearted approval, will bring to bear against you, government intervention ~ a trade embargo ~ that will block you from Santa Fe trade. To prevent you from having any doubt as to what I mean by honorable you must first become a Catholic and then marry Christine in the Church. If you fail to do that, we will consider that you and Christine have dishonored the Church and we will disown the both of you!"

Pierre mulled things over, then reached for his pen and composed his answer.

> "Christine and I will return to Mexico City as soon as I can make the arrangements. This thing about my becoming a Catholic has caused Christine and me much distress. I love my dear Christine more than anything in this world and will do whatever is necessary to keep me in her heart and keep us in your hearts. I will become a Catholic and Christine and I will marry in the church."

Pierre placed the letter into an envelope addressed TO: Manuel and Mona Mezieres and FROM: Pierre Lilly. He marked it CONFIDENTIAL and gave it to Ortego to deliver.

Pierre and Christine had already had many conversations regarding the Catholic wedding issue and had always wound up in a stalemate.

Now Christine had Pierre's word that he would become a Catholic and go through with the wedding. She knew it was all for show. Pierre was alive to make fortunes and would do whatever it took to accomplish that.

~

Felipe and Terisa could hardly wait to get moved to New Orleans. More than anything else they wanted to start a family and they knew that must not happen until they were settled in their new home.

Business plans were on hold. Felipe's trade route from New Orleans to Santa Fe would be by river up the Mississippi then up Red River. Felipe knew that required planning on his part and he felt he must be in New Orleans to do that planning. Felipe looked forward to an easy life of river travel. Pierre had pumped him full of stories about the lazy life of steamboat travel on the Mississippi.

Red River had no such idea of giving easy passage to Felipe or anyone else for that matter.

It seemed that everything was on hold. Plans to build a new home were held up pending the outcome of the new venture with Pierre. Having babies was on hold. Business plans were on hold. The only thing that was sure and settled was the fact that the move must take place as soon as possible. On that point they were in complete agreement.

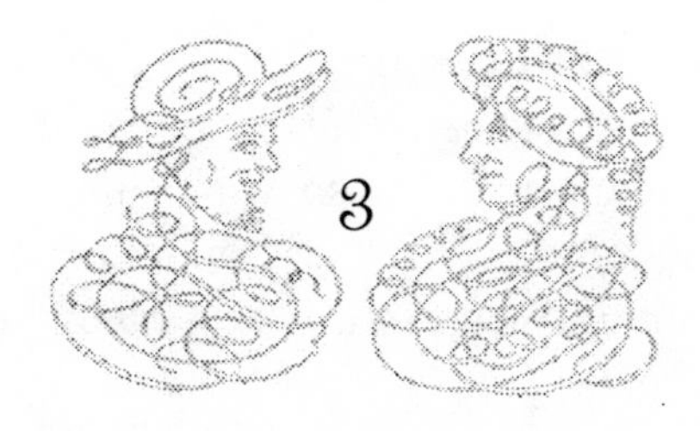

3

Just up Kiomitchie* River from its entrance far up Red River ~ amongst a grove of pecan trees ~ lived the Johnsons. Due to the fact that Mr. Johnson ran a whisky still, they had become known as the "Stiller Johnsons." Stiller had a daughter named Gurdy and a younger Son named Jeb. Also living on Stiller Johnson's place was a young migrant whisky brewer from Kentucky whose name was Roscoe Donnegan. Roscoe had descended from a long line of whisky brewers and despite his young age was a good brewer. Stiller hired Roscoe to teach him the finer points of whisky brewing and was paying him by furnishing him with room and board.

Neither one of them, Stiller nor Roscoe ~ unlike Sam Cooper or Pierre Lilly ~ gave a hoot as to whether or not Red River ever got explored. Besides, the only news they ever received came from hearsay, not from newspapers.

Nothing would please Gurdy's Pa more than if Gurdy were to hitch into the Donnegan family.

Gurdy Johnson was Stiller's only daughter. She was frail of frame and stood only four feet eleven inches tall. She possessed striking facial features ~ mainly buck teeth ~ that rendered her with a certain frontier beauty in Roscoe's eyes.

Roscoe had just turned twenty-one and Gurdy nineteen when Gurdy's Pa caught them out behind the barn kissing and decided their courting had gone on long enough. Stiller Johnson drew his double-barrel shotgun on Roscoe and Gurdy.

"Shucks, I'm leaving!" Roscoe protested.

"T'ain't so," Stiller insisted. "Get yerselves duded up. We're havin' us uh weddin'."

Roscoe, opportunist that he was, found his chance to get hitched

*Kiomitchie is the Indian name. It became Kiamichi in English, and in French it was La Ririere In Mine or Mine River

without having to pose the question. Roscoe eyed his dirty blue overalls and fastened his loose suspender. He tucked his blue dungaree shirt in and buttoned his side vents. He spat into his hand, ran his fingers backward through his tangled hair, and announced. "I'm duded up!" Roscoe's voice quivered, owing to the twin black holes staring at him from Stiller Johnson's shotgun.

Getting duded up for Gurdy was a bit more important. She went to the spring and fetched a bucket of fresh water. She washed the snuff from the corners of her mouth and erased the dirt necklace from underneath her chin before donning her cleanest apron. When she returned to the porch, Jeb greeted her with some sort of tune he was playing on a crock jug. Gurdy threw up her palmed hand in hopes that her gesture would make some silence. Jeb kept right on playing.

"Now ah'm duded up, too. Marry 'em to me, Pa!" Gurdy's voice quavered, but she wasn't afraid of the shotgun.

Stiller squealed like a pig hung under a gate. "Let the marryin' begin!" He raised his double barrel shotgun a notch so it was aimed directly at Roscoe's head.

"Do ya, Roscoe, take our Gurdy here ta be yer woman?"

"Yup … I guess I do!" Roscoe blurted. The double-barrel shotgun stayed steady aimed.

"Gurdy ~ do ya take Roscoe here ta makes a livin' fer ya ~ instead uh me?"

"Yup, but …." Gurdy began, but Stiller interrupted her. "There'll be no buts," he said.

Stiller pronounced the verdict. "Well, uh … awl right, now yer Gurdy Donnegan!

"You can take that dad-blame shotgun offa my head. If you're wantin' me ta kiss 'er, that is!" Roscoe's lip trembled.

Whether it was from his fear of the shotgun or his anxiety about getting to kiss her, Gurdy never knew. One thing she learned was Roscoe Donnegan wasn't afraid of anything. Gurdy felt warm and woozy inside as Roscoe put his arms around her and planted his lips on hers.

The only thing Roscoe and Gurdy had in common with Felipe and Terisa was that they had gotten married. The two weddings bore no semblance to each other whatsoever. One wedding forced and the other was of free will. One wedding was religious in nature while the other one was paganish. One wedding took place in a magnificent cathedral, the other one on the stoop of a log cabin.

Gurdy's Pa presented them with a spanking new whisky still and a flat-bottom boat. They loaded the still and their meager belongings onto the boat and floated them across Red River and up to Bois d' Arc Creek*. There was land for free in *Nueva España*. They had never thought of living in New Spain, but then how could they turn down free land just for settling. For a long time to come, getting the still cooking and building themselves a cabin would occupy every waking moment of Roscoe and Gurdy's lives.

~

Roscoe saw the bad storm brewing out in the southwest. Black clouds with tints of blue and hews of green indicated hail. More frightening than the possibility of hail, though, were the torrents of rain Roscoe could see falling from the clouds as if being poured from a bucket. The tremendous Red River flood, of 1809 rolled across Bois d' Arc Creek. Roscoe and "The Grays," his team of mules, had just drug up the last log for their cabin. The flood wreaked holy destruction on the Donnegans before it rolled on down Red River to free the Coopers. The Black Rock Bar had a death grip on them because of low water, and nothing short of a flood would free them. Roscoe and Gurdy watched in horror as the pile of logs they had cut for their new cabin floated down the creek, one log at a time ~ until there was not one log left. They watched the boat loaded with their whisky being torn from its safety. Then it too rushed swiftly out of sight. Roscoe and Gurdy huddled in the grasp of one another's arms and cried. They knew there was nothing they could do. The torrential flood was too much to overcome. They knew if they attempted to save their possessions, they would lose their lives.

Roscoe tried to console Gurdy.

"Shucks, honey … the whisky still won't go far. Ha Red'll spit er out, just ya wait and see. As for as them logs goes, I ken cut sum more."

Her crying turned to sobs.

"Laudy, I'm ahopin' Pa and Jeb'll be all right!" she managed to say.

"Stiller and Jeb …? Why shucks … Stiller prolly held that ol' double-barreled shotgun uh his on the thang and told it ta get on down the river," Roscoe quipped. "It's too late to do anything today, but tomor-

*Bois d' Arc is the French name; they many times called it bow-wood creek from the large quantities of that wood that grew upon it. The Indians called it Nahaucha; in English it was Kick Creek.

row will come."

Rain, lightning, and thunder continued all night, coming in waves from the south and southwest.

Daybreak brought a freshness to the air that spelled a new beginning for the young couple. Roscoe yawned, stretched and scratched.

"Today'd be a good day ta start buildin' us another cabin. But shucks, I better go find the Still and the boat first."

Gurdy took the shotgun so she could go up the bluff to fetch breakfast.

"Don't leave till I get back, Roscoe. You're lible ta be gone awhile and ya need something ta eat 'fore ya leave." She came back in a little while with a couple of young squirrels and fried them up.

~

The south bank of Red River below Bois d' Arc rises about ten feet straight up from the water's edge. Between the riverbank and the bluff that separates the bottom land from the upland lies rich sandy loam. This area is covered with dogwood, Bois d' Arc and vines, mostly grape and rattan. Scattered throughout are patches of cane. Roscoe kept a sharp look out for their boat and whisky still, as he wove his way through the vegetation. Three miles downstream, Red River took a sharp turn and headed east. It was here that Roscoe spotted a flash of light directly across the river on a long rock shelf. In the midmorning sunshine, he could make out the boat teeter-tottering on that ledge. The still's bright copper coil was reflecting the sun like a mirror. He knew what he must do, and he knew he must do it fast. It looked as though the unsteady boat could leave any second.

Roscoe hurried back upstream half a mile to get an advantage over the swift current. He eyed the raging river. *She's frothin' mad en icy cold ... she'll be perty nigh unbearable.* He threw his grub satchel down, shucked his overalls, and dove into the flooded river.

The first fifty yards, Roscoe made easily. The next fifty were much harder. Roscoe felt the clabber red, soupy river pull and churn at him as if it was trying to digest him. He rolled over on his back and could see the point where he began. The river was unbearable, but Roscoe's life would be even more so without his boat and still. *I'm too fur now ... I'm past the point uv no return!* He rolled back over, plunged his face into the murk and tossed his head from side to side, all the while making powerful overhand strokes. His energy soon waned. His mind clouded with thoughts of giving up. Just in front of him a giant cottonwood tree floated by. He reached for it and missed. He turned downstream and devoted all his remaining strength to two powerful overhand strokes that sent his head ramming into the log. Despite feeling addled, he was able to grab hold of the log and hold on.

Several long minutes passed, Roscoe floating down the river holding onto the log. He sucked air into his lungs and spewed muddy water back into the river. Wheezes replaced his coughs as his lungs cleared. *I'm gonna live*! A glance toward the boat told him he was even with it and it was still rocking precariously on the ledge. If he was to make landfall anywhere near the still he must let go … *now!* He shoved with all his might, freeing himself from the lifesaving log. He kept his head down and made powerful overhand strokes that propelled him quickly toward the down-river end of the rock outcropping. At last he touched the rocks and realized how near death he had come. He shivered. Then he crawled from the frothing mad river to safety. He lay there and sucked air into his lungs for a long while. It was but a short walk over the smooth rocks before he reached the boat and the still.

Now the question became how to take the boat upstream to Bois d' Arc Creek all by himself. One thing for sure: It would take three or four days. It never entered Roscoe's mind that Gurdy would worry about him or that he could tie the boat up and go for help. The only thing on his mind was taking the still back to its home. *First things first, I gotta cut me uh willer pole and pole this boat over and get my clothes, then I can eat supper 'fore it gets dark*!

Roscoe chewed on a piece of jerky for supper, while he tried to figure out the best way to take the boat back to Bois d' Arc Creek. *Polin' or paddlin' this contraption upstream is outta the question. What I gotta do is take er ta the sandbar side. Then drag er back up ta Bois d' Arc Creek. Red River'll be shallower over thar.*

By Sunup the next morning, Roscoe had poled the boat across the river and was dragging it in knee-deep water through flooded willows. When the water got too deep for him to wade, climbed into the boat and poled it, being careful to keep out of the main current. Night overtook him, and he tied the boat off to a safe place, settled down inside it and chewed on a piece of jerky until sleep came. The same old, same old held for the next day and the next until the boat, the still, and Roscoe were safely home.

Roscoe tied the boat off and scrambled up the bluff, and met the smell of frying eggs and ham wafting from their camp.

"Laudy, it took ya long enuf," Gurdy surmised. "Ya look hongry … are ya?"

"Shucks naugh, I have ett Jerky and ett Jerky and ett Jerky and then ett sum more Jerky. My belly is mostly full ~ but smellin' them ham en eggs acooking is acausin' my brain to tell my belly ~ naugh, you ain't full!"

"Laudy … laudy, if ya can wait long enuf, I'll whomp up uh batch uh biscuits fer ya." Gurdy opened the larder to fetch her flour bowl.

"Jest ya let me at them ham en eggs. Then ya go on an' whomp up them biscuits. I can drag 'em through the molasses later!" Roscoe dove into the breakfast Gurdy had prepared for herself.

They dug a slot into a high bank and put Bois d' Arc poles across the top of it, then piled the diggings on top. They left the front open for the time being, but come winter he would have to close it in. In due time, Roscoe cut more logs. They built themselves a nice cabin, high on a bluff that overlooked Bois d' Arc Creek. Their half dugout continued to serve them well as a root cellar. Roscoe and Gurdy survived the flood, and their hard frontier life went on.

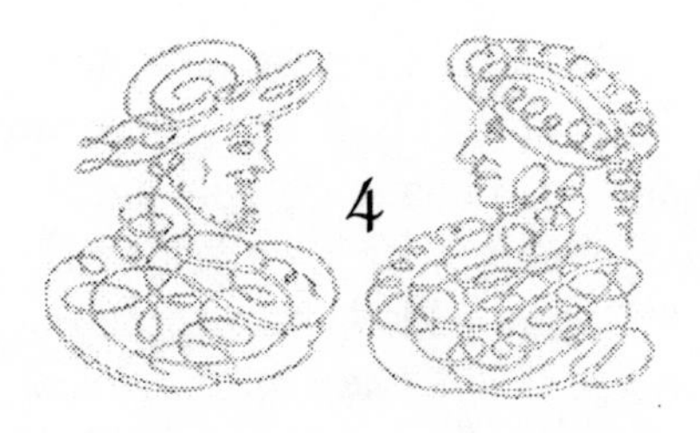

4

Sam Cooper pulled a box from underneath his roll-top desk. He lifted the lid and removed its contents then placed them in his lap. For the umpteenth time, he plowed through all his old newspaper clippings about Red River. He read the clipping that recorded Pike's findings. The atrocious deeds of the Comanches did not scare Sam Cooper in the least. He read again the newspaper account of the Freeman-Custis Expedition. The fact that Spanish soldiers intervened, turned them around and sent them home, did not dampen Sam's spirits. He placed those articles back into the box. Next on the pile was the clipping he was looking for. It was about the hidden gold of Nueva España. It told about the lost Gran Quivira gold mines and of a gold cross that a group of Catholic Spaniards had cached somewhere around Castle Gap.

Sam read the story of Gran Quivira and Castle Gap for the hundredth time.

The story was that Coronado had not found the lost gold mines of Gran Quivira. According to legend, the Gran Quivira mines had more gold than the Aztecs and Incas combined. The lost Gran Quivira gold mines reputedly contained more gold than had ever been found in one place, in the history of the world. Chief Montezuma had thousands of men ~ whose backs bent under heavy loads ~ carry the gold from the Gran Quivira mine and hide it in many underground caves nearby. Sam folded the clipping and put it in his breast pocket. He returned the rest of the papers to the box, replaced the lid, and shoved the box back under his desk.

Sam picked up the morning's newspaper. There was an article in it that had captivated his attention. He felt compelled to read it again, too. The headline read: *Sunken Keelboat Found on Red River Laden Down with Treasures and Whisky*. He quickly gleaned the facts. All that interested him was what the cargo was. There were five casks of wine, several barrels of whisky, and about one thousand dollars' worth of gold and silver coins. There was rare china and a goodly amount of silver plates. There was also an old sword, and carved on its blade were the words, "Duke of Wellington, G.B.A." There was a silver whisky flask trimmed in gold and an old battered gold decanter. The report read that a thimbleful of the whisky from the flask made one feel like they owned "Ye Ole Mint*!" Sam folded the clipping and placed it in his breast pocket with the other one. The reports of lost gold and Spanish treasures that had sunk on Red River fanned the flames of greed higher and higher in Sam Cooper's heart. He couldn't stand it any longer.

~

William entered the room. Sam pushed his chair back, lifted his spectacles and squinted under them at his son.

"I reckon we'd better be makin' that run up the Red River, William. I ain't gettin' any younger," Sam said. He removed his spectacles' and nibbled at the ear piece. "Do ya reckon we can be ready by the end uh the month?"

"Confound it, Pa … will ya quit calling me William! You know I like to be called Bill!"

"Huh, I didn't hear ya … son?" Samuel cupped his hand over his ear.

"I'm not Son, I'm not William, I'm not nothin' else. I'm Bill. Why, in tarnation, canst you just call me Bill?"

"Why … what If I don't call ya nothing?" Sam smirked at his little witticism.

"I reckon that nothin' ud be better 'en Son or William," Bill replied.

"Pa, ya thank that the river's somethin' ya aughta do, what with yer age en all?" William switched sides with his chaw of tobacco. *William Cooper sounds like some sort of person out of a novel. "Bill Cooper," now that sounds like a real Wild West name.*

"The way I got er figured, one day's good as the next … fer dyin', dont'cha reckon?" Sam refrained from addressing Bill by any name.

"Yeah, I reckon, but Pa …." Bill began, but Sam cut him off.

"Don't 'yeah but' me. If ya gonna have me adyin', my druthers'd be ta die on the ol' Red River, asearching for the lost Gran Quivira gold mine. Now, that's the end uh that … ya hear!"

Bill heard.

*The federal monetary system was established with the creation of the U.S. Mint in Philadelphia. The first American coins were struck in 1793. The mint was known as Ye Ole Mint.

~

Sam and Bill began in earnest to prepare for exploring Red River. First they mapped their course. They would follow Red River all the way to its head, or to Santa Fe, whichever came first. Next, they gathered the needed supplies.

Sam refused to face the facts as everyone else saw them; William too young and he too old. In his own eyes there would never be a more opportune time.

Bill looked at the facts differently. Sam at forty-nine was old in Bill's eyes and he knew that he himself had no experience living out of doors or in dealing with Indians. In addition to the age thing, Bill knew that Sam had plenty of money, but he refused to spend his life savings. He skimped on everything; the boats were second rate, and the provisions were barely adequate. Bill Cooper's assessment was that their private venture was poorly financed, under-staffed and hardly stood a chance.

Their indifference to each other, that had risen over their given names, was history. They had come to accept each other as simply Sam and Bill.

All the planning and preparation completed, they were ready to go. They set the date for Monday week.

~

Their friends lined the wharf to see them off. Fair-thee-wells echoed back and forth between them and those on the wharf. Finally, neither party could see each other any more.

Loaded to the hilt, their Keelboat floated low in the water. It carried guns, ammunition, trade goods, steel traps, and all the provisions required to live on Red River for the rest of their lives. The pirogue they loaded only with their daily necessities, so it floated high and dry. April showers were threatening, but there was no dampening of spirits.

The entourage rounded the first big bend in the Mississippi River. There was no looking back now. Beyond their ability of reckoning was the fact that today — All Fools Day, 1809 — would be the last time either of them would see New Orleans.

The first argument broke out between Sam and Bill after they left the Mississippi River and entered the mouth of Red River. They had been traveling almost three weeks, to the day, when they camped at the mouth of the Red River and began their search for a river guide. The days played on endlessly as Sam tried to hire a trapper to guide them up Red River. Bill grew restless; one guide was as good as the next was the way he saw it. He wanted to go. *Sam is way too picky,* Bill thought, and he told Sam just that.

"I reckon we need ta hire uh guide who ain't so hooched up that he knows where he's been," Sam replied.

"Why? If you wait ta hire a trapper who ain't all hooched up on corn squeezings, we won't ever get us a guide," Bill complained. Sam and Bill continued to bicker over the hiring of a guide. It seemed to Bill that Sam just looked for something he didn't like in about every prospect he interviewed.

The latest prospect looked promising. He was clean, and that was something the others had not been. He was also a smart-looking trapper, and rather than being boozy-legged drunk, he only smelled like a whisky still. Bill grew ever more confident that Sam was going to turn him down, as he had all the rest, but he kept his fingers crossed.

"What's yer name?" Sam asked, as the interview began.

"Jink Townsend is my name, but they calls me 'Jinx.' I've been atravelin' this here Red River fer nigh on ta a dozen years."

"Ya trappin' or adrankin'… which one?" Sam asked.

"Wahl, I'm mostly atrappin'." Jinx's eyes twinkled as if he wasn't sure which one he was doing the most of.

"Hanh, mostly trappin did ya say … Why'd they call ya Jinx?"

"Ferz I can tell, it's 'cause I don't put no lotta myself in ta trappin'. When it comes ta catchin' beavers and rackoons I'm the worst thar is. I can't even catch uh cold!" Jinx admitted. "But I make uh perty fair guide."

"I Reckon uh … we uh, can't use ya Jinx." Sam had stammered around, wanting to give the impression that this was a trapping party and nothing more.

Bill's Jaw gaped, and his lip drooped. "But, Pa!"

Jinx's eyes sparkled, and he fumbled with the buffalo scrotum bag that hung from around his neck. "Wahl, these here treasures er what makes my heart beat." From the bag, Jinx dumped some tiny gold nuggets into the palm of his hand.

Sam Cooper heard what he wanted to hear and saw what he wanted to see.

"Reckon I changed my mind. Yer on … yer hired, Jinx!" Sam shot his hand out for the sealing shake.

Bill felt relief. Jinx had good strong teeth, appeared to be healthy and didn't have any missing fingers, as many trappers did. He wondered, though, about Jinx's drunken state and just what meaning the name Jinx held.

~

With the dawning of a typical fall morning, heavy with dew and fog, Jinx woke up early and was sober. Jinx howled bits of advice as he scurried about.

"Wahl, boys, Natchitoches'll be the first chance we have ta rest up. We're gonna do sum huntin' there," Jinx advised. "Tis amazing how much fowl 'n' fish the lakes round Natchitoches holds. I 'spect we'll be there in a few."

"Days er weeks?" Bill asked.

"Could be days, could be weeks … depends on the weather," was the reply Jinx gave with a shrug of his shoulder.

~

Sure enough Bill Cooper could not believe how good the hunting was. He stood behind the same tree and reloaded his blunderbuss as fast as he could; the air filled with birds coming in to roost; he took no particular aim, just fired and fired, and the birds kept coming. In one afternoon he killed four hundred fowl between sundown and dark; included were several kinds of duck, geese, brant, and swan.

They were told by one of the few remaining Natchez Indians that fishing in the summertime was just as incredible.

"One Indian can, with a bow and arrow, sometimes kill 'em faster than another, with two horses, can bring 'em in," the Indian said.

Finally Sam put an end to Bill's hunting fun after hearing horror stories about the difficulties they would encounter going around the Great Raft. "After all," he reminded Bill, "you've kept us on leave from our travels nigh on to two weeks. You've had enough fun."

~

"Let's travel hard and fast boys 'cause in a few days we're gonna have to cut out around the Giant Raft. We'll be atakin' the Detche Bayou and Red Chute to get us 'round the raft. Slow goin' they are.

Going around the Giant Raft had proved to be a definite slow down. But it was nothing comparable to "The black rock bar" that poked through the heavy fog ahead.

What loomed in front of them was hardly discernible. It appeared to be black and stretched all the way across the waterway. The river looked as though it came to an end. Upon close examination, they figured out it was a bar of smooth black rocks blocking the channel almost completely. Only trickles of water escaped the rocks to feed the stream below.

"Here's where we stop en make camp till she rises," Jinx barked.

"Ya don't mean it … can't we tote everything around and get the boats over somehow?" Sam urged.

"Why, Pa, ya know we'd never get the keelboat over them rocks!" Bill switched sides with his chaw then glanced over toward Jinx. "How long uh wait ya talkin' 'bout?"

The oarsmen churned the water and aimed the keelboat toward a knoll of high ground on the south side of Red River. It was the first week of December when Sam and Bill Cooper stepped from the boat onto the rock-strewn sandy knoll. They began preparing for a stay of unknown duration. They had no idea that the black rock was lignite coal, and they simply referred to the outcropping as "the black rock bar."

The black rock bar was a good place for an extended camp. Besides, they couldn't get the keelboat past the bar until Red River got a rise on. A narrow gap with sufficient width for the pirogue to pass through ~ in the otherwise impenetrable rock fortress ~ flowed about six inches deep and with considerable swiftness. The keelboat needed at least two feet of water to navigate.

A few days' rest ~ without the short one-night bivouacs that the Cooper party had become accustomed to since leaving the Mississippi ~ would be a welcome change.

The Coopers' wait for Red River to rise proved to be time well spent. The famished party was able to get on a better diet and regain much-needed strength. They had harvested squirrels and rabbits, ducks and geese around camp while they were traveling. The small game kept starvation from knocking at the door. In their travels thus far, there had been no time wasted hunting for the more elusive, more nourishing big game animals. Jinx and Bill now had time to hunt deer and buffalo. Venison stew and big chunks of roasted buffalo were welcome supplements to the jerky and the small game they had been having. Sam didn't enjoy hunting, but he sure liked to sit on the bank of the river and fish. He caught plenty of nice catfish, and the Cooper exploration relished them as some of the best victuals their time could buy.

Their few days stretched into a week of rest and then into another week, of restlessness.

"I thought I had it scheduled to where we'd be along 'bout here when the spring rains hit." *Where en the world are they?* Sam wondered. Waiting for Red River to rise enough so that the keelboat could pass through the black rock bar had worn on all their nerves.

"Wahl, jest ya wait. They'll be here quicker en ya can skin uh skunk." Jinx studied the sky. "Ferz I can tell, them clouds er spinnin' off uh sumthin' way out west, right now. There's uh change in the air … a storm's abrewin' in the west." Jinx held his nose high to sniff the unsettled breeze. "Wildlife traffic's been extra heavy acrossin' the river all day. They're atravelin' to'rds the highlands from the low bottom land. The high water's uh coming!"

The sun had just set, and the sandbar had become twilit, adding to the eeriness of the flashing in the southwest. The western sky lit up, as if the sun were trying to rise back up from its grave. Every person, every creature for that matter, had been nervous since the first sign of lightning. The distant flashes brought an air of excitement to the men. It was invisible yet real, untouchable yet felt. By the time night had settled in around their camp, not a creature stirred, not a coyote howled, not a frog croaked, nor a cricket chirped. Leaves rustled one way then another. Every nerve was on edge.

Bill lay on his bedroll thinking about the only noise he heard. The snoring of Sam and Jinx ground on his nerves, until his mind blanked into sleep. In the wee hours of the morning the distant rumble of thunder began making music in Bill's ears. He roused from his slumber and stepped outside the firelight. He failed to notice the floating chunks of foam that are the first indicators of a rising river.

~

First light brought a new day, not to mention a new river. Torrents of rain followed each wave of thunderstorms, and lightning zigzagged the sky. The Cooper party had never seen Red River in a rage of fury caused by flash floods. Violent storms that began way out west on Red River rolled east down the river in wave after wave.

Red River's clear waters of yesterday had filled with red clay from the river's headwaters. Its crystal waters had been destroyed by clabbered mud. Chunks of dirty foam rode high on the current. The winds and waves wafted a foamy froth ashore and deposited it in a frothy mess. Whole Cottonwood trees were riding the current with their barren limbs standing out of the water. They rolled and tumbled, sending their limbs searching for something to grab hold of and hang onto.

The Cooper expedition had no way of knowing how much or how little the river would rise. All of a sudden the rising water was too dangerous and swift for them to attempt shooting through the gap in the black rock bar. Red River forced them to wait even longer.

"Wahl, at least now the wait is for the river to crest," Jinx consoled Sam. "The timing is crucial. When the flood waters crest and 'fore it can fall enough ta prevent the keelboat from squeezin' through the gap in the black rock bar … we go! Place a stick in the sand at the edge uv the water ta keep track uv Red River's rise," Jinx instructed. All the crew could do was anxiously wait for their chance to assault the black rock bar.

~

Jinx served as the patron and barked the timing orders. "Stand on the bow and man yer poles," he ordered. The keelboat inched toward the rock bar that had imprisoned them for too long. Under the full influence of the poles, the keelboat creaked and groaned. The men who manned the poles thrust her bow into the swift current and sent her headlong into the oncoming water.

"*A bas les perches* (down with the poles)," Jinx barked. The poles plunged into the water at exactly the same instant. The men pushed with all their strength and walked toward the stern. When the men arrived at the stern Jinx barked his orders again.

"*Levez les perches* (raise the poles)." The men raised their poles and scrambled to the bow. Jinx made steering corrections while the men rushed toward the bow. The men hurried as fast as they could before the keelboat started losing ground. Red River's swift current resisted the intrusion of the keelboat. Jinx's orders were barely audible above the din of the rushing, gurgling water and kept the men manning the poles in perfect harmony.

Fear flooded the mind of every crew member as the keelboat entered the strait in the black rock bar. The poles bent from the weight of the men leaning into them with such great force that they had to grab hold of the cleats on the deck to keep from going to their all fours.

The men panted from their exertion. Their panting grew louder than the roar of the current and were about to turn into sounds of panic. They weren't going to make it.

Suddenly and none too late, the keelboat cleared the black rock bar and burst into calm open water. Jinx's last command was cut short. His "*A bas…*" fell on deaf ears. Once the keelboat and the pirogue were above the black rock bar, they were in a lake of deep water and it was an easy matter to take them to the bank. There the men rested briefly before they began the run to Pecan Point* From the black rock bar to Pecan Point they didn't let anything slow them down, except for the

*In President Jefferson's report to Congress in February 1806, Mr. Dunbar and Doctor Sibley spelled pecan "packawn" and "paccawn" respectively.

first few days when they had flood water to contend with.

Early the next morning, after escaping the black rock bar, Bill stood up, pointed toward the south bank, and brought their attention to a flag flying from a tree.

"Reckon that's the Spanish flag flyin' over there?" He switched sides with his chaw. "I bet that's Spanish Bluff you were tellin' me bout."

"Hanh?" Sam said. "The report that I read in the Troy Sentinel referred to a place where the Spanish bluffed the Freeman Custis Expedition into turning around, then sent them scattin' back to the Mississippi. I don't recollect the place being called a bluff, though."

Bill sat back down and Sam twiddled his thumbs as they inched their way upriver.

~

"Paccawn Point! Paccawn Point! Thar she be, awaitin' me!" Jinx sang.

Sam and Bill Cooper and the rest of the crew sang along.

"Paccawn Point! Paccawn Point! Nary too soon 'cause my throat's dry 'n' my spirits er low!

"Paccawn Point! Paccawn Point! Thar she be, awaitin' me!"

They anchored the keelboat in the middle of the river and rowed the pirogue ashore.

Hoards of Indians ~ accompanied by their dogs and a small band of scruffy looking Americans ~ ran from the peninsula to greet them. Some came running with outstretched arms and others with open jugs. Among the Indians were some of the first American residents ~ troublemakers and fugitives from justice ~ to live at Pecan Point.

"Let's pitch in with them Injuns," Jinx advised Sam. "We don't wanta have nuthin' ta do with that bunch uv troublemaking fugitive Americans!" Jinx conversed with the Natchitoch well enough to obtain whisky and to talk trade talk with them. He was extremely fond of "El Toro Grande." Bull Grande, as Jinx called him, was their Spanish/Indian half-breed medicine man.

No sooner had they settled in with the Natchitoch than Jinx got drunk. To make matters worse, he proceeded to pull Sam under Beelzebub's influence with him. Bill Cooper and Bull Grande never drank a drop. They held themselves completely sober. Bill knew this was his opportunity to learn if Jinx would become a braggart under the influence of the devil's hooch. Bill needed to see if Jinx would give away his secret of where he found the gold nuggets. To Bill's surprise, not one time did Jinx nor Sam mention the gold nuggets. Instead, they both dissolved into a stupor. Bill Cooper's ideas of the kind of man Jinx was now included that Jinx could keep a secret.

Bull Grande and Bill became the best of friends. Bull even divulged a few common family secrets about medicine to him.

"Things ya might need ta know in yer frontier life," Bull told him. Bull showed him what skunk cabbage was and how to make a poultice from it, to put on the chest for bad coughing and such. Bill grabbed his throat in pain as Bull described the cure for "Much bad pale throat," as he called it. "First yuh mix up some honey and tallow into a sticky paste. Then yuh take cockleburs and tie a sinew to 'em and coat 'em in the paste. Take a stick and shove them down the throat, and when they get aholt of the pus, then pull it all out. There'll be blood with it, but it'll cure the pale throat."

They lost a week in getting drunk, sobering up and trading with the area's Indians. They traded with the Shawnee, Delaware, and Kickapoo and anyone else who would trade with them.

All of that weren't worth the headaches it caused, Bill thought.

"We lost too much time at the black rock bar. We gotta git goin', Pa!" Bill reminded Sam every day. Every day Sam gave Bill the same answer.

"Why, what's yer hurry? I'm gonna have me sum fun agoin' up the Red River. I ain't cumin' back, I reckon!"

"Pa, ya know ya will," Bill told him.

"I reckon I ain't … I'll be dead as a mackerel 'fore I see Paccawn Point again!" Sam made his feelings clear. The same conversation took place on a daily basis. Bill finally got fed up with trying to convince Sam that they should travel.

"Pa, I been thankin' 'bout it. We're leavin' in the morning. So, you and Jinx better sober up tanight!" Bill wasn't ready for the reply Sam gave him.

"Hanh … did ya say we wuz aleavin' in the mornin'? Why, aughright then!"

Bill felt relieved but annoyed. *Why in tarnation, didn't I set my foot down sooner?* he thought.

~

That night an extremely heavy fog settled in around Pecan Point and caused the moon to look as if it were shining through ice. They all sat in silence around the campfire as though they were in a trance. Bill quietly chewed on a piece of jerky. His mind wandered. *Sam's foggy,*

Jinx is foggy and it's foggy. Am I the only clear thing around here? Then Bill realized the jug had ceased being passed around. *Maybe things will clear by morning*!

From out of the fog, there appeared a rag tag old man with strange colorless white hair. He came crashing and falling toward the campfire. The old man was lank and starving, and he couldn't say anything but Rev, Rev.

Jinx questioned Bull Grande and interpreted for Bill Cooper. "Bull Grande say this: 'Crazy Rev, come first time many moons ago. Then he come and go, come and go. Finally he no come again till now. Bull Grande says the man much lost … he much crazy, too!' Reckon that's all Bull Grande knows 'bout crazy Rev."

Bill took it upon himself to nourish Rev. He spoonfed him coffee and turtle soup. To Bill's disgust the old man snuggled up to him, shivering and wild-eyed. The old man whispered in Bill's ear, "Reverend Jonathan is cold, Pa." Bill's disgust quickly turned to a sincere pity.

"Fer goodness sakes, I ain't yer Pa. Don't call me that." But Bill took off his coat and wrapped it around the old man's shoulders. Bill watched the old man's eyelids slowly shut. *Thank goodness I don't hafta look at those hazy wild eyeballs anymore,* Bill thought.

As the night passed, Rev roused up every couple of hours for more turtle soup and coffee. Each time, he revealed a few more tidbits about his identity, seasoned with wild-eyed expressions of "Holy Jehosaphat!" The facts Bill pieced together from it were Rev's real name was Jonathan and the Methodist Episcopal Church had sent him to the "Paccawn Point Circuit" to preach. Rev had become helplessly lost, and something awful had happened. Whatever it was had been so awful that it sent him into sporadic spells of amnesia and turned his hair colorless. *His hair is not white; it's just colorless, like your fingernails*, Bill thought.

"Holy Jumpin' Jehosaphat!" Rev screamed, sitting up. He jumped straight up in the air and came down running. He jumped the fire and howled at the full Moon. "I gotta git … I gotta git … I gotta git!" he hollered.

"Gotta git what?" Bill asked.

"Gotta git outta here, before they castr …." Rev passed out before he could finish the sentence and fell face down just outside the ring of light provided by the camp's fire.

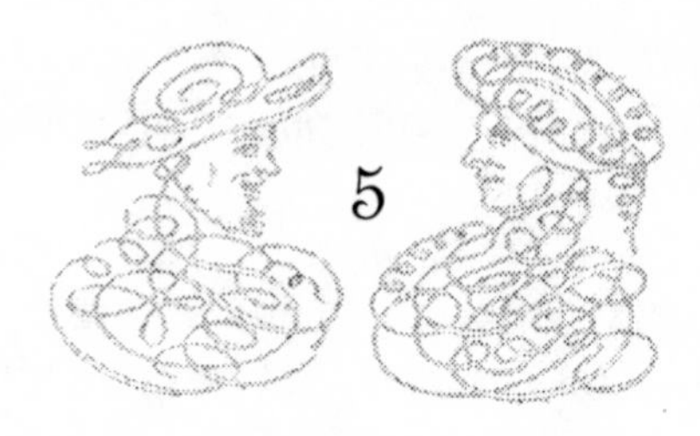

5

The Cooper Expedition left Pecan Point just like Bill Cooper planned they would ~ with all of them sober. They made good progress and arrived at the Kiomitchie River a couple of days later. Just as they rounded the last bend of Red River, before they could reach the Kiomitchie River, a storm hit, a blistering cold norther. Sleet, freezing rain and flitting snow flakes pelted them, wafted upon a thirty-mile-an-hour north wind.

Jinx recommended they take refuge up the Kiomitchie. "At least until the raging storm blows over."

Bill didn't want to waste any more time in someplace Jinx could get drunk and voiced his disapproval. Jinx and Sam overruled Bill. Jinx guided them up the Kiomitchie River to the Stiller Johnson place. Stiller lived on top of a high bluff, just up the Kiomitchie River from its junction with Red River. Traveling the quarter of a mile, which is what it was, between Red River and Stiller Johnson's ~ headed directly into the sleet-laden north wind ~ beat some sense into Bill by the time they got there.

The place looked deserted, the coon hounds didn't greet them, nor was there any smoke coming from the chimney.

"I'll check it anyway," Jinx said. He jumped out of the boat, climbed the riverbank, and trotted up to the cabin. He found a note Stiller had scribbled on a hand-split cedar plank with a chunk of charcoal and hung on the door.

"Gone to Bois d'Arc Creek, up in Nueva España, to see if flood got Gurdy, be back cum spring, make yerselves ta home."

"What did ya find?" Sam asked, after Jinx had gotten back in the boat.

"They're gone aughright … confusin' though." Jinx scratched his head "They're Gone like a bad hangover."

"What's so confound confusin' 'bout them bein' gone? What do ya mean 'gone like uh bad hangover'?" Bill asked.

Jinx laughed. "Gone like a hangover … I mean thar's evidence they'll be back. Their daughter Gurdy, now why on earth would she be up Bois d' Arc Creek? If the flood got her, she'd wash downstream, not upstream to'rd Bois d' Arc Creek. That's jest back'ards. Anyway Stiller's note said fer us ta make ourselves ta home. So, we'll do jest that 'til the storm passes; then we'll go on ta Bois d' Arc Creek.

"Just fer the record there ain't no Mrs. Johnson; she wuz killed by Injuns when they burned 'em out one time, fer their whisky."

After a week was lost waiting out the November storm, they finally left the Johnsons' and made their way toward Bois d' Arc Creek to aid in the search for Gurdy.

"Once the Gurdy mystery is solved, we'll probably come back with Stiller and winter over with him. It's late fall an' a body has no business abein' on the river in the winter," Jinx calculated.

~

They anchored the keelboat at the mouth of Bois d' Arc Creek and left the crew in charge of her safety. Sam, Bill, and Jinx piled into the smaller boat and started up Bois d' Arc Creek.

"I reckon we don't know what we'll find. Just look fer a little woman or a man in overhauls," Jinx instructed.

They were about two miles up Bois d' Arc Creek when faint sounds of people hollering came to Bill's ears.

"Shush … did ya hear that?" Bill cupped his hand around his right ear and listened intently.

"Hanh, I didn't hear anything," Sam said. "It's jest Jinx's infernal hummin' or the coyotes howlin' probably." Suddenly Bill stood up. The boat dilly dallied from side to side.

"Hold on!" Jinx screamed. The boat had nearly capsized and spilled them into Bois d' Arc Creek's icy waters.

"Don't ever give a boat a sudden notion. Yer lucky ya didn't drown us!" Jinx bellowed.

Roscoe and Gurdy had heard all the screaming and commotion and ran down the bluff to see what the problem was.

"Thar they be, up on that high bluff and here they come!" Bill hollered, pointing. Sam curled his paddle around the back of the boat, at the same time Jinx dug his paddle hard into the dingy water. They sent the boat into a sharp turn that plunged them toward the bank.

Roscoe ran down the bluff with Gurdy hot on his heels. Stiller Johnson stayed up on the bluff and waved furiously toward the visitors. Roscoe took the anchor line from Jinx and snubbed the boat to the big rock used for the purpose of tying off boats. Roscoe reached over the bow to give Jinx a hand and at the same time introduced himself.

"Hello, Jinx, I'm Roscoe Donnegan. I'm Gurdy's man. I figure ya know the rest of us 'cause Stiller Johnson knows ya."

"Wahl ... I know ever'body now that I know who you are. Sam and Bill there, they don't know who anybody is but you," Jinx answered.

"Shucks, ya'll foller me and Gurdy ta the top uv the bluff and I'll make ya'll known," Roscoe said. They were proud to have visitors.

Bill couldn't help laugh, as he observed Roscoe and Gurdy climb the bluff. One of Roscoe's overall suspenders had come unsnapped and was flying in the breeze, and Gurdy's apron flapped in the wind as she ran to keep up with him. The Black mud that had settled on the banks of Bois d' Arc Creek from the flood had squished up between Roscoe's toes and was being slung off in all directions. Gurdy had wrapped her feet in what appeared to be corn shucks and rawhide, and she was losing shucks.

"Shucks, if you'll tell me what yer laughin' at, we can both laugh," Roscoe said.

"You got it ... shucks is what we're laughin' at. Seein' Gurdy uh losin' her shucks while she's runnin' up the bluff. Maybe that's whar the 'spression cum from, ashuckin' yer shoes," Bill told Roscoe.

Bill Cooper quickly realized that there was going to be a problem with Sam and Jinx getting drunk. There was that same odor in the air that he had smelled at Pecan Point and there were corn shucks everywhere, even around Gurdy's feet. *There is a still somewhere*, Bill thought.

Jinx introduced Bill and Sam Cooper to Stiller Johnson.

"We never met the missus, formally that is," Sam offered.

"Shucks, everybody, that's Gurdy, and Gurdy meet Bill and Sam," Roscoe said.

Gurdy was taking time to snort a pinch of snuff. "Laudy it's a pleasure," she said.

Bill Cooper knew that sooner or later he would have to reveal his secret. *Right now is as good as time as any*! he thought.

"Back in the keelboat is someone I want ya'll ta meet," Bill announced. Bill glanced toward Sam and Jinx and read their disgust with him, at what he had done.

"Ya didn't stow away that Crazy Rev, Bill, now did Ya?" Sam Cooper asked. Bill went to the keelboat. He returned with Rev, who got so excited when he recognized his old friends that he went into a tizzy.

"Holy Jumpin' Jehosaphat, if it ain't Stiller and Gurdy. Rev pointed to Roscoe. "Who'dat?" Rev turned to Bill and continued talking before anyone could answer him who that was.

"These are the angels that I met on the road ta Damascus, Pa!"

"Confound it, Rev, I ain't yer Pa! I wish you'd quit callin' me that!" Bill scolded.

"Laudy, laudy, we ain't got much uv a home yet. We woulda had us a log cabin though, if the storm hadn't taken our logs away frum us. I'm sorry … but fer now this thang'll hafta do," Gurdy said. She was talking about the half dugout-half tent they lived in.

Roscoe popped the cork on a crock jug of whisky and offered drinks around before replacing the cork and returning the jug to its resting place in the wood box. Then he offered them a business deal.

"Sam how 'bout when you and Jinx come back down the river, ya'll buy some uh my whisky. Ya can sell it ta the fur traders, fer a tidy profit. Shucks, we can all get rich!" Roscoe dangled his enticing offer in front of Sam and Jinx.

"I don't think so. Why, Pa and Jinx'd drink up all uh the profits," Bill Cooper shot back, changing sides with his chaw.

"Pa wouldn't! Jinx might would, though," Sam corrected Bill. "I reckon I ain't acomin' back down the river, anyhow."

"Now don't start that Pa. Ya ain't agonna die, way up on Red River." Bill wondered why Sam thought his time was about up. "Back ta yer proposition, Roscoe. It ain't agonna happen. I know yer out ta makes profit from yer whiskey, either by sellin' it or by tradin' it for goods. The matter of the fact is that Jinx doesn't have any money nor goods. Pa and I got all the money and the goods. I refuse ta let Pa buy or trade for any whisky!"

During one of the worst blizzards of the winter so far, the Coopers and Jinx holed up with Roscoe, Gurdy, and Stiller Johnson. The weather was lousy for river travel, so they waited for better weather. Roscoe, Stiller, and Bill helped Roscoe tend to his long trap line to pass the time. Bill gained a lot of much needed knowledge about how to make sets for beaver and trapping in general. Bill even caught a few beavers with the traps he brought along.

One morning, they had been wading the black mud of Bois d' Arc Creek bottom for hours and were about halfway finished with checking and resetting traps when Stiller let it be known in certain terms that he was tuckered out and needed a rest. Roscoe and Bill left him to rest and went up Slough Branch to check traps.

"Bill, get Stiller ta tell ya 'bout the time when he cum ta the

Kiamichi River," Roscoe suggested. "Uh, it's a real interestin' story, 'bout when the Indians got 'is wife."

"I don't know 'bout that. It's a techy subject, wouldn't ya say?" Bill didn't *say* more. *Stiller might be uneasy atalking 'bout the Indians uh gettin' his wife*, he thought.

They were almost back to the Donnegan's half-dugout shelter. Roscoe had decided Bill was not going to ask Stiller about when he came there.

"Shucks, Stiller, tell Bill 'bout when the Indians got yer wife," Roscoe blurted out. Bill felt his face fire up.

Before Bill could make a plea that it was unnecessary for him to tell the story, Stiller had begun.

"Well, it wuz back 'bout nineteen er twenty years ago. I brung my family out here fer us ta get us a new beginnin'. We come out here with Josiah Doaks. He planned to start a small tradin' post at the mouth uv the Kiamichi River. He dropped my family and me off at the mouth uv the Kiamichi River. Then he took a group uv trappers to Blue River and left them there atrappin'. They were attacked by an Osage war party and all of 'em got kilt.

"Before Josiah and his men could get back here, that same blasted bunch uh Osage attacked us. The Missus went plum into hysteria and was dancin' round wringin' her hands. Next thang I know she went into labor and had Jeb. The blasted Injuns set fire to our house. The Missus burned up in the fire, but I got the young uns out. There I wuz left with two little uns ta raise. Jeb a new-born infant, born fore his time, and Gurdy wuz jest two years old.

"It wuz in the dead uv winter when it happened. I'd gather the hackberry seeds that the coons hadn't got, then make Jeb sugar teats with 'em. I tore Ma's dress up into little squares. Then I put hackberry seeds in the middle of 'em and give 'em a twist, then tie a string around the little ball and let Jeb suck on it. He wuz too little to eat table food 'cept if Gurdy and me'd chew it fer 'im. Jeb got so sick that none uv our chewed table food'd stay on 'is gut. I had ta make 'im drink tea that I made from slippery elam bark. Gurdy'd put a spoonful in 'is mouth, then I'd blow in 'is face and make 'im swallow it. Ya know that stuff is the slimiest thang that there is. It brung 'im through it though and we all made it by the Grace uh God!" Except fer Ma, that is, and she's in the Grace of God.

"How is Jeb now?" Bill asked.

"Jeb … why he's meaner than a Grizzly bear, and I aren't abraggin'." Stiller smiled broadly.

Sam and Jinx spent their time either nursing headaches ~ or trying to get one. If they couldn't find Roscoe's hiding place, they would smoothly talk him into letting them borrow a drink.

The crew back on the keelboat was content just to wait out the blizzard. They passed their time playing "hand" and other guessing games or fishing and hunting.

Rev regained some of his sanity, but he continued to hallucinate and have nightmares. He kept mumbling "I gotta get before they castr ...." in his sleep. Bill knew that beavers had castor glands, and he wondered if the Indians could have forced him to drink beaver castor. However, come hell or high water, he would not ask Rev what he meant. At the most inopportune times ~ usually in the middle of the night ~ Rev would jump up screaming.

Holy Jumpin' Jehosaphat, screamed in the quiet stillness of the night, is enough to wake the dead, they all thought.

During the long winter nights ~ by the light of their grease lamp ~ Roscoe devised a plan whereby he could sell all the whisky he could make. The catch was it depended upon his being able to get someone to haul his whisky to St. Louis. Bill's future son might be just the someone who would do that and make all of them rich beyond every imagination ~ but Roscoe had no way of knowing that.

~

Sure enough Jinx was right on when he told Sam Bois d' Arc Creek was as far as the keelboat could go. Leave it to Roscoe to come up with a plan.

"I'll tell ya what ya can do: The Injuns don't need a keelboat and I do; I don't need my whisky and they do, and they don't need their dugouts and ya'll do."

It is a brilliant idea, Sam thought.

So Sam traded the keelboat to Roscoe Donnegan for whisky. He gave the whisky to the Indians in exchange for dugout canoes. The Indians had camped across the river from Bois d' Arc Creek and for days on end it was apparent, from the hoopla that went on, that they thought they had made a good trade. *God only knows what will happen when the whisky runs out!* Gurdy thought.

After the deal that Roscoe contrived, he had to brag just a little.

"I knew if ya'll ud stay 'round long enuf I'd trade ya whisky for goods."

The keelboats' crew had gotten tired of fighting with the big keelboat and was proud to have small fast canoes.

Considering the extremely cold weather, the cramped quarters of the dugout, Jinx's and Sam's bouts with the jug, and a few minor conflicts with Rev, the Coopers had had a good visit with the Donnegans and Stiller Johnson.

The Coopers packed up and left the Donnegans' by the end of February. They left them with the impression that they would be back within a year. They were all glad to be on the river again.

"I was 'bout ready to go berserk there on Bois d' Arc Creek. If we hadn't exchanged her for the excitement of Red River I was afixin' to join Rev," Bill said.

~

Many days had passed since they left the Donnegans', and the uncommonly wet and cold spring had been hard on all of them. They were excited about arriving at San Teodoro.

A large band of Taovaya Indians had gathered up along the banks of Red River. They appeared as ghosts in the early morning fog, as they milled about. Some waved, while others just pointed; however, one rather stately looking white-haired man, that Bill presumed to be their leader, motioned for them to make landfall. Jinx's dugout made landfall first. The white-haired one reached to take his hand, then helped him from the boat. They walked shoulder to shoulder in the direction of San Teodoro. No one followed.

In a little while, Jinx returned and went straight over to the dugout Sam was in.

"What is his name and what did'e say?" Sam asked.

"I can't persactly say his name, but ferz I can tell it means Tricky Tongue." Jinx paused. "Anyway, they're Taovaya Indians and he wants ta trade us packhorses fer the dugouts."

"Now, reckon why on earth we would wanta do that?" Sam asked.

"We gotta have us some pack animals. Maybe we could trade with the Wichita Indians, but that'll be our last chance ta trade. It ain't very far ta the Wichita River where they live, if ya wanta chance it. After that Red River plays out. Then what'd we do? I'm atellin' ya we'd be up the river with boats and no packers.

"Reckon we aughta trade one uv the boats and keep the other uns till we get to the Wichita. You go make us a trade with em, Jinx."

Jinx and Tricky Tongue proceeded to sit down on the ground under a big cottonwood tree. Sam watched them through his looking glass.

He could see them gesture in sign language.

"Wahl, Tricky Tongue ~ I give you one dugout fer ten horses. What ya say?"

"Me say no."

Jinx held up nine fingers.

Tricky Tongue shook his head no.

Jinx held up eight fingers.

Tricky Tongue held up five fingers to which Jinx shook his head yes.

"And what else?" Tricky tongue asked.

"We'll throw in sum mirrors, sum tabaccy and a jug." The whisky sealed the deal.

Sam wasn't too happy with the deal. *I bet we could uv got ten horses if Jinx'd thrown in a jug ta begin with.* All he said though, was, "I don't wonder anymore how that Indian got the name of Tricky Tongue."

The horses under the care of the Indians had seemed docile. Under the care of the Coopers they seemed as wild as the Indians themselves. Being unsure as to the travel ahead, the Coopers kept their other boats. *We can always trade them to Wichita Indians,* Sam thought.

~

Jinx had lived with the Wichita Indians from time to time during his trapping forays on Red River. The thought of him soon being reunited with his old friends brought him a certain degree of excitement. Understandably then, Jinx made the announcement with a tremble in his voice.

"Wahl, we'll reach the coon eyes tomorrow!"

"Coon Eyes … who in the world are they?" Bill asked.

"They are the Wichita Indians ~ Kitikitisch ~ that's what they call themselves. We call 'em Coon Eyes because uv the tattoos the men wear 'round their eyes. If you're gonna trade with the Comanches, ya gotta do it through the Wichita. The Wichitas are the middlemen. They make Tricky Tongue look like a bunny rabbit." Jinx explained.

"They tend ta be friendly ta the strangers. Bill, did'ja know that their women don't usually wear clothes from the waist up?" Jinx loved to make Bill blush. Out of the corner of his eye he saw that Bill's face had begun to flush. Jinx stirred the fire a little more. "Bill there's apt ta find em a woman." Now, Bill's face was crimson scarlet. "Wahl, with yer face that red Bill, they are liable ta take ya in, athinkin' that yer one uv em!" Jinx gouged. Bill blushed even more, then spat a stream of tobacco juice into the grass. Then he turned and walked away from jinx and his disgusting conversation.

By full daylight the next morning, the Cooper expedition had been on the move for two hours. First sight of the Wichita village came shortly after that. Cone-shaped grass-thatched lodges, in neatly formed rows, lined the high ridge of ground between the Red and Wichita rivers.

Men, women and children came forth to greet them and, sure enough, just as Jinx had said, the young girls and women were scantly clad. The midmorning April sun was exceptionally warm ~ the sun's warmth along with Bill's shy nature caused his face to turn scarlet red.

Bill and one particularly beautiful maiden kept glancing at each other ~ she apparently as infatuated with him, as he with she ~ they couldn't keep their eyes off each other the rest of the day. The silken-maned maiden, in her mid-teens Bill guessed, finally picked up enough courage to come over and whisper in his ear, the words nor the sound of which he would soon forget. *I have gotta ask Jinx what she said. I gotta know.*

After a few days of drinking, smoking, eating, and trading, Bill knew that time for them to leave was coming soon. Jinx had noticed something wrong with Bill and didn't know what his problem was. *There is no way Bill knows what I am fixin' ta quit,* Jinx thought.

"Pick up yer lower lip Bill … afore ya step on it," Jinx warned.

Sam announced, "In the morning we leave fer Santa Fe and we have a new guide. Jim Sharp … he'll be here at five o'clock in the mornin'. Be ready ta float!"

Bill Cooper's heart sank and filled his mind full of questions.

"Confound it, what happened ta Jinx, Pa? He couldn't aquit … could'e? Pa, ain't Jinx coming with us? He's gotta come … dont'e?"

Sam Cooper's answer to his questions would sink his heart even further.

"No … he ain't uh coming!" Sam said. He looked into Bill's eyes and saw his anger. *Bill thinks I fired Jinx*, he thought. So he quickly added, "I reckon that Jinx has quit us."

"Why, confound it, what did'e quit us fer?"

"I reckon he's uh stayin' with his woman. Jinx says that he ain't ever been further up Red River than here. He says that Jim Sharp has been ta Santa Fe … once. Sam read the disappointment in Bill's face. "He's uh beaver trapper to, ya know." Sam knew that fact would weigh on Bill's acceptance of old Sharp.

"Once …! What good is once gonna do us?" Bill turned away from his Pa and headed toward the river. He walked along the well-worn river path hardly able to contain his disgust. He changed sides with his chaw and squirted tobacco juice into the clumps of Kentucky Blue Stem.

Then the words that the beautiful Indian maiden had whispered in his ear returned to his consciousness. *I gotta find Jinx 'fore we leave.*

~

The next morning five o'clock came and there was no sign of Sharp. Six o'clock came, then seven o'clock, and there was still no Sharp. Finally, about seven-thirty, Jim emerged from a cone-shaped grass hut scratching and rubbing his eyes. He broke up a big yawn to say, "How-de!" To Bill's surprise Jinx was right behind him.

Sam Cooper made introductions: "Jim Sharp this here's my son Bill." Sharp saluted. "Bill this here's Jim Sharp, he goes by Sharp."

"Ya ain't none too early Sharp," Bill jabbed

The young sprout ain't agonna daunt me any, no-sa-re bob, Sharp thought.

"Nope, guess not," Sharp countered. "But then I never signed on ta you. It is yer Pa I owed my presence to!"

Bill was canny when it came to reading the situation that he found himself in. So it was a rare moment when he couldn't think of anything to say. Jim Sharp had just put Bill into one of those rare moments. *Sharp is a good name fer em*, Bill thought. Bill realized Sharp didn't hanker to march to the tune of his unearned authority. Rather than let Sharp get the best of him, he changed the subject.

"I reckon a beaver man like yerself could teach a green horn like me ta catch beavers, Mr. Sharp. I brung me sum beaver traps." Bill put on his best snow job.

A glint in the squinted eyes of the old trapper revealed Sharp's satisfaction with being called, "A beaver man" and "Mr. Sharp" in the same sentence.

Jim Sharp's squinted eyes began at Bill's brogans. He slowly bathed Bill to the top of his head. Bill knew that Sharp was sizing him up and it made him feel uncomfortable.

"Yes-sa-re bob, I can teach ya beaver trappin'," Sharp said. "If ya can control the fever that's acausin' yer mouth ta shoot off, I can." Jim Sharp dragged his fingers through his tangled beard and stuck out his chest. He didn't know about Bill controlling his mouth, but he felt that he was in control. He had put Bill in his place.

The tension had evaporated from their meeting, or Bill had lost interest in what old Sharp had to say. Whichever was the case, it didn't matter. Bill went to find Jinx.

Bill and Jinx walked off toward the river, and Sam and Sharp began making small talk about Rev.

"Jinx … what, do you mean, aquittin' us?" Bill asked.

Before Jinx could answer, Bill pulled Jinx's head toward his mouth, then whispered in Jinx's ear. He whispered the words the beautiful Indian girl had whispered into his ear.

"What did she say, Jinx?"

"She say: 'My name is Dancing Waters. Ya be my man?' Bill, did'ja take er up on it? As fer as why I quit, ya get with Dancin' Waters and you'll know!"

Bill felt his face catch on fire and dropped his head and walked off. He returned to his pa's and Jim Sharp's conversation with a red face. He walked up just in time to get in on Sam's question about Rev.

"Do ya know anything 'bout the old coot that Bill's taken aliken to, Jim?" Sam was asking Jim Sharp.

"Yes-sa-re bob. Ol' Rev … I knew 'im way back 'fore the Comanches got ahold uv 'im.

He was agoing by the name uv Reverend Jonathan way back then."

"The Comanches, they got em!" Sam winced.

Bill gasped.

"Ya know, he has nightmares an' he talks in 'is sleep. He mumbles sumthin' about agettin' before they 'castr ….' Ya don't reckon they castrated him do ya?" Sam Cooper's voice trembled.

"Could uv!" Sharp paused long, as if in deep thought, then shivered. "They sure could uv!"

Bill cupped both hands and placed them over his mouth then shut his eyes and said a silent prayer on Rev's behalf.

A known fact about Sharp was that he liked to brag about himself just a little bit. Knowing that Bill was a willing student, Sharp dropped the subject of Rev and started bending his ear.

"Let me tell ya 'bout Sharp, Ol' Sharp, that's what they call me on the Red River. I been all the way up the Red a couple uh times, then on ta Santa Fe once." Sharp took Bill's arm, twisting him as if to make him see the words. "There ain't nothin ol' Sharp doesn't know 'bout them beavers. Ol' Sharp knows ever inch uh Red River; I can read 'er mind, and she's full uh trickery. Yer Pappy hired me for that. She's full uv 'erself too, jest like you."

~

Bill's heart sank for the second time since he learned that they were leaving. Dancing Waters and he looked into each other's eyes as they drifted farther and farther apart. He felt that they most likely would never see each other again, and he knew she felt the same ~ that sent him into despair.

Bill and Dancing Waters did all they could do in the way of departing good-byes. They held their hands high and waved vigorously. Bill was way too shy to throw any good-bye kisses.

Very late in the evening, August 1809, the Cooper Expedition reached the head of Red River. Immediately they made plans to leave for Santa Fe early the next morning. After eating a hurried supper of jerky, they stoked out the fire and hit the sack.

A wake-up call from a lone wolf reverberated across Red River's flat sandy bed and woke Bill Cooper up. He lay there and listened to the ever-decreasing echoes trail off down the river's bed, until they died down. Then he crawled out of his bedroll. Damp heavy air had settled in around the Cooper camp during the night. The carpet of grass that surrounded their camp glistened with dew and felt damp and cool to Bill's bare feet when they hit the ground.

"Hey, Pa, ya better come alive. We gotta long day ahead." Sam Cooper didn't make a move and that was very unusual.

"Hey, Pa, come on now … roll out!"

"Hanh, did I hear ya say roll out? Oh … well, if ah must." Sam mumbled out every word, as he threw the dew covered canvas from the den he had made for himself by the side of a giant cottonwood log. He drew his bare feet from the warm blankets and plunged them into the wet cold grass.

"Confound it, the ground's cold!" Sam hopped toward the fire and whistled, dragging his boots on over his wet feet.

Their overland march toward Santa Fe ~ unbeknownst to the Coopers at the moment ~ was about to become a fiasco.

~

Most of the river lubbers abandoned the Coopers and headed back down Red River. That left them short on manpower. It seemed they preferred unruly keelboats to unruly pack horses.

The Cooper party followed the Prairie Dog Town Fork of the Red River all the way through the Palo Duro Canyon until it shrank to just a creek, the Palo Duro Creek. Now after a couple of days the beautiful creek became a dry gulch that branched out in many directions, and so it was that they took the wrong branch. They should have kept a due-west heading and they would have eventually come to the Pecos River. Sharp chose to follow a branch that carried them too far south, in a course that was parallel with the Pecos River, and it took them deeper and deeper into Comancheria*.

Bill thought that in their march toward Santa Fe they had become misdirected. Misdirected wasn't the word for it; they had become flat-out lost.

"I know we're too fer south," Bill constantly reminded his pa and Sharp, but to no avail. The party stumbled upon a dry wash, then followed its course the wrong direction for half a mile before Samuel or Sharp would admit the error of their travel.

"I reckon a mile here and a mile there doesn't matter; we're lost anyways," Sam complained.

"I only been from the head uh Red River ta Santa Fe once … what do ya 'spect?" Sharp said. He had begun to admit that he might have led them wrong.

"Hey Sharp, I thought ya said ya knew ever inch uh Red River." Sam Cooper dumped the blame square into Sharp's lap.

"Why uh …," Bill butted in, "if ya know so much 'bout Red River, why don't ya take us back to 'er?"

Bill's interruption into Sharp and Sam's conversation was the final blow that set Sharp off.

"Well, Bill, you smart sprout uv a green horn kid, take the lead yerself if yer such a trail cutter!" Sharp threw up his hands in disgust, turned his horse and rode toward the back of the column, uttering under his breath, "Yes-sa-re bob, yer a cutter all right!"

Bill Cooper took the lead. He tried to take the expedition back to Red River by cutting cross country. He avoided following dry gulches; but with him guiding, they became even more lost.

"Yes-sa-re bob, yer a cutter all right, Sharpe jabbed. "If ya keep leadin' us 'round in circles, ya gonna cut us 'cross a Comanche trail."

"Confound it, we're helplessly lost!" Sam shouted.

Evening's shadows had grown long, and Sam and Sharp were still arguing about a good place to stop for the night. They finally agreed to camp on the edge of a deep ravine which seemed to be getting deeper and appeared headed in the right direction to get them back to Red River.

With camp struck, the cook prepared a big pot of jackrabbit stew.

*The land of the Comanche Indian.

The continual bickering about being lost and the salivating from being hungry was the main reason for the lack of caution on their part, their attention being focused upon the need of the moment, rather than the pending danger.

On a distant swell, a lone warrior, dressed in full war paint, sat atop his painted pony. Behind him in a slight draw, a band of warriors awaited his command.

"After they eat. We strike like a rattlesnake!" he told them. "White man give heap less fight on full belly."

Compliments to the cook were always in order, unless you wanted to be the one who had to wash the dishes. Sam leaned back against a rock, full of contentment, and expressed his praise over the victuals. Bill lay down on the grass, wiped his chin on his shirt sleeve, and pulled his hat down over his eyes. *Sure would uh been good soup if I had kilt another Jackrabbit*, he decided.

Rev was wide-eyed and alert, something he rarely was.

"What's amatter, Rev?" Sharp inquired.

"Uh, I don't know, but my hair just stood on end." Rev shuddered. "I gotta awful feeling in my gut, and it ain't from that Jackrabbit stew."

The cook gathered up the dirty dishes and utensils and had just finished washing the last dish. Half the Sun had ducked below the horizon, and the other half was disappearing fast.

He glanced over the dishpan in his extended hand. "We got company. Looky yonder!" He pointed toward the west. "Looks like they rode right out of the sun. Ain't that a purty sight."

"Jumpin Jehosaphat, it ain't purty, and it ain't gonna be purty. It would be Comanche acomin'!" Rev reached for the cook's butcher knife, grabbed it up by the handle, and stabbed the long razor-sharp blade through his own neck. "For God's sake don't let them take you alive!"

Rev's dying words pierced Bill's heart.

Bill rushed to Rev's side.

"Oh my God!" Bill cried. "Rev's cut his own throat!" A tear sprang from Bill's eye and dropped onto Rev's cheek. Bill wiped the tear with his forefinger. Sharp's voice brought him from remorse to the urgency of the moment.

"We're caught open, nothin' 'tween us 'n' God but mesquite!" Sharp screamed. A Comanche arrow pierced through his temple. "Yes-sa-re bob" were his dying words.

It was too late to bring their Hawken fire arms to bear on the battle. Things went from "here they come" to combat by hand in seconds. In moments all the members of the expedition, except Bill, met their maker.

Bill leapt on his horse and prodded him into action. The animal reared up as a Comanche arrow approached. Bill helplessly followed the glinting arrow with his eyes and watched it cut through his left arm's biceps. He slid over the rump of his horse and under a gnarly mesquite bush. He observed obscene things being inflicted on Sam more horrible than the lifting of Sam's scalp. They made him realize the reason Rev had colorless hair and hallucinations and took his own life. He shut his eyes, gritted his teeth and cried. Bill felt bound to the mesquite bush he was hid under, bound by the fear of losing his own life.

The thundering hooves of the raiding war party faded into the distance. A Comanche brave ~ instantly and seemingly from nowhere ~ grabbed Bill's arm and wrenched him from underneath the mesquite bush. The battle was swift and to death. Bill lifted the dead brave's necklace and placed it around his own neck, then stuffed it inside his shirt. He tore the brave's loin cloth from him and made himself a tourniquet. Painfully he wrapped it around his arm and twisted it as tight as he could get it. His blood loss slowed.

Bill's horse, shot through the neck, was lying on his only worldly possessions and had kept them from being seen by his attacker. Bill wrestled the animal over enough so he could collect his Hawken, knife, and a single steel trap. He hunkered down and waited for the sun to go down.

Darkness engulfed the high plains, sending the whippoorwills and wolves into their lonesome moaning. The sounds made Bill Cooper feel lonesome, but he had no time to be lonesome. *I must do my duty to the dead, then I must get away from this nightmarish hellhole!*

First things first. He dug a large hole, as deep as the rocky soil would allow, and rolled the bodies into it. The last one in was Rev, and Bill wanted to look. Bill wanted to see what the Comanches had done to Rev. He thought better of it and rolled Rev into the hole satisfied never to know. He piled rocks high over the grave to keep scavengers from digging the bodies out to eat. He stood back and said what he could remember of a prayer for them.

Confound it, I am glad that's done.

Bill's mourning for Sam and the things he saw committed against him would burn in his mind like fire for days to come.

~

Bill followed the brushy ravine toward what he hoped was Red River. Occasionally he stopped to check his arm, but for the most part he put steps behind him. *Space ~ I want space between that nightmarish hellhole and me!* he thought.

The stars had begun to fade as the sun washed them from the sky and foretold of a new day. Only one star, the Morning Star, remained now. There somewhere out in front of Bill a big river loomed up from the misty fog. *It has to be Red River!* he thought. *The big river is cutting its way through the morning fog toward the Morning Star. It's flowing East and its water is red. It has to be Red River.*

It was full daylight now and Bill wanted nothing more than to hide and rest. A big uprooted-Cottonwood tree had fallen across his path, and he decided the hollow underneath its root ball was the perfect place to hide. He knew he must rest and get some sleep. He crawled inside and drifted off into a feverish unfit sleep.

~

The cold dampness of late evening shadows seeped into Bill's bones. He woke from his garbled dreams, about the war prize, about Rev, and about his daddy. Bill reached inside his shirt sleeve and found that his arm was hot and crusted with blood. He pulled out his war prize to see just what he had retrieved from the Comanche warrior.

Bill Cooper examined the peculiar leather bag. It was some kind of opaque, very supple leather. The drawstring was long enough to hang around one's neck and made from pure-white sinew. He felt a lump loose inside the bag and wondered what it could be. He could tell it was heavy. The only thing Bill could imagine that anyone could have used to make such a supple and opaque bag might be the swimmer-bladder of a large fish. Several small items were in the bag along with something crunchy. *They're probably animal teeth. God only knows what is in there that is crunchy like dry grass.* He fidgeted with the white sinew drawstring but was too weak to open the bag. Then he slunk back into slumber.

~

Bill Cooper woke up just as the full moon peeked above the Eastern horizon ~ just as the last sliver of setting sun sank below the western one. The rising full moon cast a long trail of sparkles up the river that caused him to shiver. He took up his Hawken and slung his steel trap over his shoulder. His arm was feverish and swollen. He clenched his fist and rubbed his eyes with it. *It is almost dark. I must use the night to travel. I must get to the Wichita River and find the Wichita Indians ~ I must find Jinx soon.* He forced himself to go.

Bill plodded along all night, sometimes in a stupor, before he stumbled then fell headlong in the tall grass. He licked the early morning dew from the grass that was all around him. The dew quenched his thirst and revived him a little, and he pushed himself on. A new day had dawned before he gave in to complete exhaustion. His fever raged and consumed his energy. His thirst and hunger grew, and his bloody wound ached. *The Wichita Indian's aid, or lack of it, is the only thing between me ~ and death!*

Bill fought to keep his mind clear; fought back unconsciousness, but garbled thoughts overpowered him. *Wichita River! ~ Wichita Indians! ~ Jinx! ~ somebody!* He slumped forward and fell face down in the icy chill of the tall grass. When he roused, he was hot and feverish. The warmth from the overhead orb, striking him in the back, he recognized as coming from the sun. He rolled over and faced it then lay there for a long time and thought about his hunger. He grabbed hold of a log and tried to pull himself up, but the log overturned and spilled him back into a sitting position. *There!* Bill's vision was blurry, but he recognized the white things the overturned log exposed. They were some kind of roots. He grabbed them, tossed them into his mouth and chewed. *They taste wonderful! But they're not roots, they're not crunchy, they're soft and mushy.*

When he came to again he had a feeling that he was much better. He sat up and pulled his war prize from underneath his shirt and fumbled with the sinew drawstring until he got the opaque bag open. He dumped the contents into his lap. The contents themselves flabbergasted him, not to mention the unique beauty of the whole thing. There was a large, very heavy black walnut, yellow incisors from some sort of giant beaver and tassels of yellowish-red human hair. Utterly disgusted to the point of feeling puking-sick, he shut his eyes and flung the hair as far as he could send it. Bill fumbled with the walnut. There was something inside it that made it very heavy. Somehow a person could open the walnut because there was a seam between the two walnut-halves. He fumbled with it, but he couldn't get it open. His strength was failing. He returned the walnut and the giant beaver teeth to the bag, hung it back around his neck, and stuffed it down into his shirt. Slumping back into his hodgepodge world of semi-consciousness, he was unaware of his surroundings but painfully aware of his hunger and his parched dry lips ~ *Oh, my thirst!*

~

A beautiful Indian maiden, in the process of tending to his wounded arm, woke Bill. As their eyes met he knew it was Dancing Waters and he remembered the words she had whispered into his ear that warm April day. Everything was going to be all right. Their meeting had been only a few short weeks back, but in his feverish state it seemed as if it had been an eternity ago. Their attempts to converse were frugal. He was so weak he could hardly manage a whisper. He did manage a very weak "Where Jinx?" Dancing Waters managed to communicate the barest necessities to him, with some degree of luck, using sign language and broken English.

"Me can't be caught!

"I hide u!

"Me bring food … buffalo robe!

"Me be back!

"Jinx gone … trappin'."

The words, "Dancing Waters be back," were the only ones Bill Cooper deciphered.

Bill knew not how much time elapsed before Dancing Waters woke him again. She was feeding him with a soup of grain and fat bear meat. She dressed his wound with a poultice she'd made from bear grease, stone-ground garlic, and powdered Willow bark. *Something smells like a polecat*, he thought.

"Garlic and skunk cabbage'll keep green flies off. Willow bark ease pain." Dancing Waters tried to make Bill understand. He didn't care what she said or what she did; he just wanted her by his side. She gathered grass and made him a comfortable bed, then wrapped him in the warmth of a beautifully tanned buffalo robe. She gracefully slunk away without telling him bye. He felt more contented than he had been since the massacre.

Bill dozed in and out of consciousness until late the next day before he gained complete awareness. His arm was black, very swollen, and feverish. *I must travel ... I must go*. Then the stark realization pierced his heart. *Go where? It must be the first Norther of fall.* The thought made him shiver. He snuggled down into his buffalo robe. *The nights are so cold, and the days so hot*.

"Me Bill Cooper." He tried to tell her his name, but it was to no avail.

"Me not know white talk," she reminded Bill.

Bill slumbered back into unconsciousness, and Dancing Waters left him to his sleep.

Bill Cooper woke from a fearful dream, with mixed emotions that ran rampantly through his heart. First there was loneliness ~ *Where is jinx? Where is Dancing Waters?* Then fear whelped up inside him. Was he going to die? Bill Cooper never experienced such mixed emotions before in all his life. He wanted to leave and get back to civilization. He wanted to leave and find Jinx.

Suddenly Bill realized he was not shivering from the cold any more. Dancing Waters had crawled into his buffalo robe to keep him from freezing to death. He felt contentment engulf his body with warmth. His loneliness vanished and so did his fears. *The first fall freeze would have taken me out*, Bill thought, *if it hadn't been for Dancing Waters. Dancing Waters risked everything by getting into my robe to keep me from freezing to death.*

~

Bill Cooper thought less and less about leaving the Wichita and Dancing Waters, as fall turned to winter. They had accepted him as one of them. They had taught him their language and their customs.

Then, besides all that, Dancing Waters was carrying his child!

Once Bill and Dancing Waters could talk to each other they spent a lot of time just talking. Bill told Dancing Waters the nature and the intentions of his daddy's exploration party, how they had been on their way to Santa Fe and had become lost. He told her how they were in search of Gold and treasures and how the Comanche had attacked and killed all of them except him.

Jinx never returned from his trapping foray. Bill learned that wasn't uncommon for Jinx, especially when he got on the booze.

One day Bill Cooper was given the name of Gold Seeker. Dancing Waters' father, Ketox Runner ~ called that because he once ran down a coyote ~ gave Bill that name after hearing about Bill's past life searching for treasures. Ketox Runner was a Wisdom Keeper, a keeper of legends, for the Wichita tribe.

The Wichita spent many long days holed up in their domed grass huts, during the extremely severe Winter of 1809-10. They passed the time telling and re-telling Wichita legends. It was then that Gold Seeker learned about Castle Gap. Castle Gap, renamed Weick Pah by the Comanche, was on the Comanche war trail. Comanches, Kiowas, Rocky Mountain Utahs, and Plains Apaches used the trail to take them back and forth to their raiding grounds in Mexico.

"I will tell you *the Legend of Weick Pah* (Gap Water).

"It began over three thousand Moons ago," Ketox Runner began. "That would have been in 1510 your time, Gold Seeker."

Ketox Runner slowly dragged a puff from his clay pipe while he studied Bill's face.

"Beautiful yellow rocks, chunks that had fallen from the sun, were found and cached by a Spanish explorer by the name of Francisco Vazques de Coronado."

Ketox Runner took another puff from his clay pipe.

"Legend goes that the cache was found by spiritual leaders of the yellowish-red hair Spannishie Indians, from a distant land. They called themselves Catholic Spaniards. They made themselves a God, in the shape of a big cross from the sun rocks. The God was an evil God and the spiritual leaders cached the big cross because it caused many battles and much blood shed."

Ketox Runner took another puff.

"From that moon till this moon, sun rocks have been feared by our people. The spiritual leaders from the yellowish-red hair Spannishie Indians are evil because they created their own evil God."

Coyote runner wrinkled his forehead and closed his eyes as if retelling the ancient legend brought him fear. He lay his pipe in his lap, expelled a sigh, pursed his lips and remained silent.

Gold Seeker's curiosity about his black walnut necklace in its peculiar leather bag had grown more and more with each day that passed, but when he heard the Wichita's legends about the sun rocks, it grew by leaps and bounds. He imagined that one of those yellow rocks was in the black walnut making it heavy. He had tried untiringly to open the black walnut. He had tried everything he could think of, short of bursting it with a rock.

Gold Seeker convinced himself that his black walnut had a Gold nugget inside. *The legends about gold being cached at Castle Gap by Coronado and then about the cache of the Catholic Cross are pretty convincing.* He promised himself he would not destroy the black walnut just to find out what was inside. He would open the black walnut the way the maker intended, or he would never know what was inside. He decided that opening the black walnut had something to do with turning it end on end. The key to opening it was in the sequence he rotated the walnut. Once to the right, twice back to the left, then three times right, sometimes he could see the crack between the walnut-halves, open a little!

It remained locked.

~

A shiver of fear went through Gold Seeker's body when he remembered his daddy's hair. It was wiry and yellowish-red. Questions entered his mind.

What kind of hair might our baby have? What if our baby's hair is yellowish-red, will the Wichita Spiritual leaders consider it an evil God? Will they banish the baby from the tribe? Will they banish Dancing Waters? Tonight, I must talk with Dancing Waters ~ I must tell her!

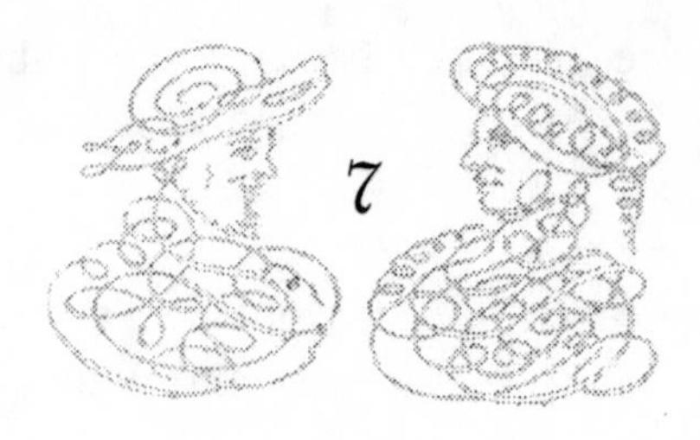

Nighttime came and Gold Seeker couldn't bring himself to have the conversation about his Daddy with dancing Waters ~ at least not that night. The nights accumulated and the moons passed. His indecision tore at him. Should he tell her ~ or ~ should he just leave? He decided he must tell her if for no other reason than just for the baby's sake. Gold Seeker came to the conclusion that he had let his imagination run wild. Dancing Waters' baby would probably have black hair. Even if the baby was born with yellowish-red locks, they would cross that path when they came to it. He loved Dancing Waters too much to abandon her, at least without good reason. He would tell her, tonight.

"Can we go down to the river 'n' talk?" Gold Seeker asked Dancing Waters. "I gotta tell ya somethin."

The night was extra warm for April and as Gold Seeker and Dancing Waters strolled arm in arm toward Red River, the light southern breeze blew her long black locks over her shoulder and they brushed against his cheek. Her hair took on a blue hue as the light from the full moon reflected from it. Gold Seeker looked into Dancing Waters eyes and saw her concern. *She must be thinking that I am leaving her in search of yellow sun rocks.*

Gold Seeker sat down on the bank of the river and leaned back against a cottonwood tree. Their hands met as they reached for each other. He pulled her down to sit beside him, and he pulled his necklace over his head and handed it to her.

"Do you remember the legend of Weick Pah, Dancing Waters?" Gold Seeker asked.

"Yes." Dancing Waters told him.

"Do you remember the yellowish-red hair spiritual leaders of the Spannishie? They called themselves Catholics. Long ago they created themselves a God in the form of a cross they made the God from sun rocks, and it was an evil God."

"Yes, I remember," Dancing Waters said, wincing. "Yellowish hair

Catholics strike much fear into my people!"

A long silence ensued while Gold Seeker held Dancing Waters tight in his arms. "My Daddy had yellowish-red hair. He was not a spiritual leader, nor a Catholic. Our baby might have hair just like his."

"Oh … No!" Dancing Waters shrieked. "You must go! You will be tortured and killed!"

"But … baby is still three moons away from being born," Gold Seeker pleaded. "I can't go now. I must see our baby first!"

"If you stay, we must hide our fear well. Father has strong medicine; he will know something is wrong. He will cause us to tell him."

"You're right … during all the excitement over our new baby ~ if baby have yellow hair ~ I will flee immediately!" Gold Seeker pledged.

"And if he has black hair … you stay?" Dancing Waters pried.

"Yes, Dancing Waters, I love ya … if baby have black hair … I stay!" Gold Seeker felt relieved that everything was out in the open.

~

The moons passed quickly. During the new moon of July 1810, Dancing Waters gave birth to a handsome baby boy. Every Wichita marveled that the baby boy had no hair, that he was baldheaded. Wichita babies were born with lots of black hair. Dancing Waters and Gold Seeker didn't marvel ~ they knew the reason.

Gold Seeker couldn't afford to wait for the boy's hair to come in. He removed the war prize from around his neck and handed it to Dancing Waters.

"Give it to our baby when he reaches his tenth birthday. There is a gold nugget inside the walnut shell, I'm sure of it. I haven't been able to open it yet, but it does open if someone can figure out how its maker intended for it to be opened. My strictest orders are that the shell not be ruined to remove the gold nugget. Instruct our boy when you give the shell to him that he must figure out how its maker intended for someone to open it. The necklace will show my boy how to find me; it will be our spiritual link."

Gold Seeker hugged and kissed Dancing Waters; then he held his new son briefly and kissed him on the forehead. He fled into the dark night, running toward Red River and choking back tears of sorrow. He realized his love for Red River would have to replace his beloved Dancing Waters and his baby Son. Would he ever get to see his Son again? Would he ever see Dancing Waters again? He wondered. Those two questions flooded Bill's heart, and he choked on the salty tears that rushed down his cheeks and into his mouth. He wished tomorrow would never come. When he reached Red River he glanced toward New Orleans, but he never gave it a second thought. He turned toward the setting sun, toward Santa Fe. He shivered at the thought that, beyond a doubt, he would never see Dancing Waters again.

In the days that followed, Gold Seeker found the quiet deep waters of Red River soothing to his broken heart. The only solace he could find for his aching heart was to erase Gold Seeker's world from his mind. He reverted back to being "Bill Cooper."

He decided he would chase his daddy's dream. He would find the lost Gran Quivira gold mine for Sam. *Anyway, I don't have much of a reason to do anything else,* he thought. Bill took the neatly folded newspaper clippings that had belonged to his daddy and read them again.

Hunh, the Quivirans had more gold than the Aztecs and Incas combined. It was more than had ever been found in all the history of the world. It was cached in caves around Gran Quivira. I will find it for Dad, he thought, *and I will not give up till I do!*

~

Dancing Waters cached the gold necklace under a giant rock. If she ever let Father know about the necklace he would make her throw it in the river. She knew it would become the only spiritual link between her son and his father. She feared that she had seen Gold Seeker for the last time. *I have his steel trap that he left behind, and that will be my link to his spirit.*

Dancing Waters' baby was now three moons old. She knew that her son's hair would come in soon and that she must tell her father about Gold Seeker's daddy having wiry yellowish-red hair. She knew her father could concoct a story that would protect her son from the fear the Wichita had of yellow hair. Ketox Runner was the spiritual leader of the Wichita, and in Dancing Waters' eyes he possessed strong medicine. She convincingly persuaded her Father that Son of Gold Seeker was a gift from the good spirits. So it was, at a specially called meeting of the Wichita elders, that Coyote Runner spoke.

> "The Gold Seeker is gone. He kind and good to Dancing Waters. The God of victory give Gold Seeker power over Comanche. The God of victory revealed to Gold Seeker his son will have yellow hair. Gold Seeker ran away. He feared he would bring persecution upon his baby, Dancing Waters and himself. My grandson is sent to us by Gold Seeker's spirit, on

behalf of the God of victory, to teach us not to fear yellow-hair people.

"My Grandson will be called Son of Gold Seeker until his guiding spirit give him name. He will soon have hair; strong wiry hair, of reddish yellow. He will become Wichita spiritual leader ~ he will declare unto you forgiveness ~ for he will face many hardships as a Wichita child. When Son of Gold Seeker reaches ten dozen moons he will have no father to go to; he will be on his own. I present unto you Son of Gold Seeker."

Ketox Runner held Son of Gold Seeker high above his head for the elders to see. Ketox Runner saw a smidgen of yellowish-red fuzz on top of Son of Gold Seeker's head as he held him high in the noonday Sun. Dancing Waters had not noticed that Son of Gold Seeker had this yellowish-red fuzz. It had gone unnoticed by everyone. Ketox Runner was the first to know for sure that Son of Gold Seeker's hair would be yellowish-red. Coyote Runner decided he would let everyone find out on their own; even Dancing Waters.

After she heard her father's speech, Dancing Waters felt sad. *Either way I lose. If baby's hair comes in normal and black, my father faces ridicule; if it comes in yellowish-red, Son of Gold Seeker faces ridicule.*

Without Gold Seeker to help her, Dancing Waters knew that the job of raising her son was going to be a difficult one. It was a thankless job that she gladly accepted, however.

Wichita boys, after being raised by their mothers until they reached ten dozen moons of age, became the responsibility of their fathers. *Then when he is supposed to go to his father, what will I do?* Dancing Waters wondered. She was afraid he would run away if made an outcast by his peers, before he ever reached a hundred twenty Moons.

Having been raised in the Wichita culture, Dancing Waters hadn't given their kinship system a second thought. But now she thought about Son of Gold Seeker's family. *He would not have a lot of fathers and mothers like other Wichita children; because his Father had no brothers or sisters and his father ran away. He will not have any cousins; therefore, he will not have a lot of brothers and sisters like other Wichita children.* She felt a pain of sorrow for Son of Gold Seeker.

Son of Gold Seeker ~ although looked upon by the tribal elders as one with special powers ~ became an outcast among his own peers. Tearing at every fiber of Son of Gold Seeker's personality ~ as he grew up ~ were his feelings of duty toward his people on the one hand and on the other hand his overwhelming desire to find his father.

A little over a year passed after Felipe and Terisa's wedding before they finally made their move to New Orleans. Felipe and Terisa Sanchez landed in New Orleans on March 1, 1810. Pierre and Christine Lilly met them on the wharf. "You are welcome to live with us as long as it takes to find a decent home for yourselves," Pierre said. Terisa and Christine had a lot of sister talk to catch up on. Pierre and Felipe discussed the operation of The St. Louis-Santa Fe Trading Company.

The company's charter had a stamped date of April 15, 1810. They had not begun operations, due to the fact that Felipe was absent from the country. The company's mode of operation would be sort of a revolving-door scheme. They would buy gold and silver treasures and slaves in Santa Fe and bring them to New Orleans and sell them for a profit. With part of their profits, they would buy supplies and whisky to take to St. Louis and trade for furs they could export to France.

For the next ten months, Christine and Terisa saw little of their husbands. Likewise, little did Felipe and Pierre see of each other.

Pierre Lilly's part of the company was the New Orleans-to-St. Louis division. This was the old Lilly Trading Company ~ that fact had not changed. Pierre had a rather easy trade route, due in part to the fact that he had the trust of the Indians along the Mississippi River. Pierre's division made extremely large profits ~ a fact not shared by the New Orleans-to-Santa Fe division. Pierre also had a good riverboat crew. His riverboat captain's name was Black Jack. Pierre referred to him as being trustworthy as the sun rising and as hard as pig iron. He ran the "West Wind" with an iron fist. Black Jack didn't allow his crew to get drunk or complain, and there was absolutely no trading on the side.

The preponderance of those facts ~ the company's large profits and Black Jack's abilities to run Pierre's boat ~ prompted Christine to insist that her husband slow down. More than anything else, Christine wanted a baby. With Pierre so preoccupied ~ well, that just hadn't happened; nor was it likely to happen.

"When we start our family you're going to turn the trading over to Black Jack and stay home," Christine told Pierre, in those certain terms. "You have your hands full with the books and with purchasing."

"I agree, I agree, my darling. The excitement of river travel and the camaraderie with the Indians and trappers will be hard to give up ~ but for you I will do it!" Pierre was adamant.

~

Felipe's share of the new venture, the New Orleans-to-Santa Fe trade route, ran into trouble from the start.

Felipe and Pierre's original plan was to use Red River as their route to Santa Fe. The lack of a guide who knew Red River combined with the insurmountable features of the river, like the Great Raft, blocked Felipe's efforts. He abandoned that route. Hostile Comanches and Spanish Soldiers patrolled Nueva España; thus far, one or the other had foiled all his overland attempts to establish a trade route to Santa Fe. Felipe wished at times that he had never moved to New Orleans. He found that his portion of the company demanded more from him than he had bargained for. On a rare occasion when Felipe was home, Terisa cornered him. "You are being gone for months at a time, Felipe. That is no way to start a family." Terisa longed for children ~ the same as Christine ~ and a stay-at-home husband. Christine and Terisa both hated the fact that their husbands gave all of themselves to the company and didn't have any time for their wives. The sisters began to scheme as to what they could do to alleviate the unjust treatment they felt they were getting from their husbands.

"Our absentee husbands have got to slow down, Christine said. "Don't you agree? What if we planned a cruise to Mexico City, together, and left them out of our plans, as if we thought they'd be too busy to accompany us?" Their eyes sparkled with the thought of the devious plan.

"It will work! If I know Pierre and Felipe, it will work!" Terisa agreed.

Christine glowed, revealing her pride that she had come up with such a good plan. *If and when they ever came home, we can tell them*, Terisa thought.

~

To Christine and Terisa's surprise their husbands returned home in late December. Pierre announced that they were going to stay awhile. They expressed their desires: They wanted to be home for their upcoming anniversaries and to take in the Mardi Gras.

"Well, we're still going through with our plan because when Mardi Gras is over, they will be out of here for another year," Christine told Terisa.

Terisa took pains as she set the table. She covered it with a white appliquéd tablecloth and placed a beautiful candle arrangement in the center. Next she set out the chinaware, the silverware and then the crystal. Christine iced down the champagne. They lit the candles. They were all ready to make their announcement about going on the cruise by themselves.

Then Pierre came in and announced, "We have dinner reservations for the four of us at New Orleans' finest new dinner-house ~ The Providence House."

"What are we to do?" Christine asked Terisa.

"We can't ask them to cancel the reservation," Terisa said, placing her forefinger on her temple as if it would help her think of a solution.

"No … if they did that we might be blackballed from The Providence House forever." Christine agreed. They finally arrived at the perfect solution. They accepted with pretend joy and made plans to tell them later.

"Let's just do it after dinner. That way we won't spoil our meal at The Providence House." Terisa giggled. "They can't get ahead of us, can they?"

~

The white linen table cloth, the silver service, the fine china and crystal are not nearly as pretty as ours, Christine thought. What she didn't know was that was only a prelude to what the night held. Candlelight and vintage champagne and a band playing romantic songs lent a special atmosphere to the magic of the New Orleans night ~ then from there things went downhill. Pierre ordered an appetizer, something he had eaten in St. Louis and relished, but the sight of the smoked buffalo tongue on the platter gagged both Felipe and the girls.

Felipe and Pierre lifted their long-stemmed crystal wine glasses high in the air and locked their free arms. Then Felipe announced:

"Hear ye, hear ye … we have a special toast to make!" Felipe nodded toward Pierre and sat down.

Pierre finished: "Here is to the love and devotion of our special wives. May we all have a glorious time on the cruise, all four of us are about to take ~ to Nueva España! This very moment the Trade Wind is awaiting our arrival, down at the wharf!"

Terisa and Christine didn't fall out of their chairs because of surprise, but they could have. Instead they both just looked at each other in total shock. Terisa said, "hmm," as she reached out and rolled her hands palm up. Christine, at the same time, said "whee," as she twirled her forefinger around in the air.

~

The trip to Nueva España was exhilarating to say the least. The Trade Wind's crew carried the high-sail schooner across the Gulf of Mexico. They sailed at a leisurely pace down the coastline to Veracruz. By mid-afternoon each day, the glint of the sun refracted from the glassy waters and transformed the Gulf into a carpet of diamonds. The rays of brilliant light sent needling points of pain into the crew's eyes.

Late evenings brought a rainbow of colors to the otherwise white cottony clouds as the sun painted itself into the distant horizon. When the greenish blue water, the puffy white clouds, and the azure blue sky lost sight of the sun, their world turned black. Then the heavens filled with millions of stars and a lover's moon; but try as hard as they might, they could not replace the glory of the sun.

The excursion was a dream for Pierre and Christine Lilly who had never taken time for a honeymoon.

Felipe's parents along with a whole host of their friends welcomed the four of them with open arms.

The trip from Veracruz to Mexico City ~ to Christine and Terisa's parents ~ was not as pleasurable. The pass over the mountains proved to be very tiring, even for Pierre. Christine and Terisa's parents welcomed them, but "with open arms" would be an overstatement. Pierre Lilly felt a coldness displayed to him by Christine's parents.

Pierre knew what he had to do. If the St. Louis-Santa Fe Trading Company was to become successful, he must first of all become a Catholic; then Christine and he must get married in the church. He had to have the cooperation of the Spanish government ~ to do that he had to get Manuel and Mona Mezieres to accept him as their son-in-law ~ and to do that he had to do as Manuel and Mona wished. *It is as simple as that. I have no choice*, he thought.

Christine knew just how Pierre felt about becoming a Catholic. They had had the same conversation so many times before. Pierre made it clear, one more time, to Christine. "Even though I'm going to announce to the family that I am becoming a Catholic, when we get back to New Orleans you should not expect me to attend Mass or do anything that will take me away from the company."

~

Ortego and Olga threw a lavish party to welcome the Lillys and their son and daughter-in-law. The Sanchez party was the social event of the year. It seemed that every well-to-do in Mexico City and Nueva España was there. Officials from the government, from the church, and from his company all were there. They dined, drank, and danced. It was well after midnight when Manuel Mezieres made the announcement:

"Your attention, may I have. Quiet please! Pierre has made it known to me that he intends to become a Catholic! Mona and I beg your attendance to their forthcoming church wedding." All the guests lined up to congratulate them, and planted upon them their hugs and kisses.

Pierre's and Christine's wedding, more than likely, was the most extravagant event of the year in Mexico City. Pierre had accomplished what he had planned to do and that was to bring the family together. Of course, the only purpose he had in mind for bringing the family together was for the betterment of the St. Louis-Santa Fe Trading Company. They left port when the wedding was over. There was no reason that Pierre could see for them to extend their stay in Mexico City. Pierre couldn't wait to get back to New Orleans and the fortunes of the gold, whisky, and fur trade.

~

The girls knew that their husbands had put one over on them. They agreed, though, that they had accomplished what they set out to do. They got them to slow down long enough to begin families. Christine and Terisa arrived back in New Orleans knowing they both were with child.

"When they find that out, they might wish they had never planned the cruise," Terisa said.

"Somehow, we must figure out a way to break the news to our husbands. Not just any way to break the news, but something that will pay them back for the way they surprised us," Christine said.

"Yes, I agree. Their cruise plans hit us like a whirlwind didn't they?" Terisa said.

~

After they returned to New Orleans, Felipe and Pierre put their nose back to the grindstone.

They were not only busy with the St. Louis-Santa Fe Trading Company, they devoted their free time to affecting the outcome of the War of 1812. Pierre and Felipe volunteered every spare moment of their time to that cause. They both suspected that the battle for New Orleans would become a pivotal battle in the war. They also felt the patriotic thing to do was help turn the British back.

Terisa and Christine were lonely. It used to be that when their husbands had any spare time they got it. Now the war got their husbands' spare time. The two women insisted that Felipe and Pierre not volunteer their spare time to the war effort and devote more time to them.

"We're sure that the real army can handle the situation. We want you home with us. You need to quit playing army!" They insisted. Adding to Terisa and Christine's loneliness was the fact that hey began to feel not only lonely but ignored as well.

"I'm beginning to show swelling, and did you know that Pierre doesn't even know I am with child?" Christine asked Terisa.

"You don't mean it! Felipe doesn't know I'm with child either. "I'm exasperated as to what to do. How about you?" Terisa replied. They began to conspire together as to how they could get some respect. Their conniving led to a most dramatic and devious plan sure to command Felipe and Pierre's fullest attention.

"This time we won't be outdone. I'll make sure of that." Terisa was resolute about that fact.

"Christine and I are planning a special dinner party for Friday night, just for the four of us," Terisa told Felipe. Then she made it vehemently clear:

"Neither you nor Pierre will be late, and neither will you forget! Furthermore, do you understand that neither of you will make other plans for us!"

Pierre and Christine had been sharing their home in Chalmette, in the St. Bernard Parish, with her sister and brother-in-law. The special dinner party brought no suspicion to the guys since both the girls liked to entertain. The only thing Pierre had to say about the matter was, "Wonder what they mean by a special dinner party?"

~

The girls planned and prepared all week, and Friday night finally arrived.

Again they covered the large dining table with a white linen tablecloth. Candles adorned the beautiful centerpiece. The light from them bathed the china dishes, crystal stemware, and silverware in a soft sheen of light. Christine had engaged the best chef in all New Orleans to cook the most succulent gumbo one's palate ever tasted. Served on a bed of fluffy white rice, the gumbo looked fit for the king. To complement the main dish, Terisa brought chocolate éclairs from the French quarter.

"We have bourbon and fine cigars for you," Terisa told Felipe and

Pierre to tantalize them.

"And fine wine for us!" Christine added.

A Creole band was playing in the courtyard of the Lillys' mansion. A Jim Crow* tapped to their hauntingly romantic music**.

The sisters donned beautiful new maternity frocks and waited for Felipe and Pierre to come home. Pierre stepped through the door first, Felipe entering right behind him.

"Look, Christine, they're here and they're not late. I hope this sets a new trend for the both of you," Terisa said to the men.

"Now, will you two kindly go upstairs and get yourselves cleaned up. Get dressed for dinner and hurry back down here … we're starved," Christine ordered them.

This was going to be a fun evening. They both giggled.

Pierre grumbled something as he ascended the staircase, Christine thought. She was sure it was *"One time doesn't make a trend."*

Felipe and Pierre came downstairs in a little while dressed in their finest and ready to play their wives' game. When both men had their feet firmly planted on the landing at the foot of the stairs, Terisa and Christine both spoke at the same time: "We regret to tell you that we are both searching for new husbands!"

Pierre and Felipe looked at each other in astonishment. They could tell the girls were dead serious. Felipe looked straight at Christine and asked, "But why … what on earth for?"

"We cannot say," Terisa answered as Christine waved some pre-arranged papers at the speechless men. "If you two do not figure out what is going on by the time this evening is over, we want a divorce. Spell that with capitols, D-I-V-O-R-C-E!" They both chanted as they spelled it out. Just what the girls suspected, even hoped would happen … happened. Their announcement ruined the ambiance of the evening, for Pierre and Felipe, but not for them.

The four quietly ate their dinner. They spent the evening after dinner without the men ever venturing a guess as to what the problem might be.

Pierre and Felipe discussed the matter in the privacy of Pierre's study.

"I know what the problem is, Felipe," Pierre ventured. "Yeah, me

*Early 1800s, Stereotype Negro in a song-and-dance act.
**The music that came from the Lillys' courtyard had its roots in the 1790s when the slave uprising in Haiti brought an influx of whites and blacks to "Orleans," from the West Indies. It eventually became known as jazz.

too," Felipe replied. "They want more of our time, and I can't say that I blame them."

"Not a word!" Pierre said. "Not a word … at some point we are going to force them to talk about the problem; then it won't appear like we didn't know what it was. We'll just let the thorn fester."

~

The evening began to wind down. Unable to stand the men's non-chalance any longer, the girls went to the parlor where the men had retired and were drinking bourbon and smoking fine cigars.

"Well, what will it be?" both women asked in unison.

Boldly, Felipe blurted out. "Well you girls have one on us ~ don't they Pierre. We cannot tell anything is going on!"

"These are maternity frocks we're wearing. How could you be such stupendous idiots! We are with child!" Christine's composure crumbled. She began another spelling lesson and Terisa joined right in, with her. "That is spelled with capitols, P-R-E-G-N-A-N-T!" Christine still wasn't through making the men feel bad. "And if that is not plain enough, we are having a baby. That is B-A-B …."

"Stop!" Pierre stormed out. "We can spell."

Terisa applauded ~ then as an afterthought she added ~ "Baby is plural, as in we are both having babies!"

Felipe's and Pierre's mouths gaped open in disbelief. *How could we not have known?* they wondered.

Pierre always seeming to know exactly what to say and when to say it, offered in his own way an apology for him and Felipe.

"First, you both are beautiful in those frocks. Second, I can say you sure went to a lot of trouble to make Felipe and me feel like dirt. Third, we want to make it known to the both of you that you have failed! You've made us the happiest two men in the world!"

The divorce didn't happen.

Time passed quickly. In October of 1812 both Terisa and Christine gave birth to bouncing baby boys. Jacob Clay Lilly was born October 3rd, 1812, and the day following, October 4, 1812, Renee Alberto Sanchez was born.

"You can bet your bottom dollar, honey, the second time around I'll be much more observant!" Pierre said as he hugged Christine. Felipe assured Terisa also. "Next time, honey, I will not miss it. I know it would cause a divorce if I missed it the second time around."

"You got that right, Felipe!" Terisa said.

The second time around happened quickly. Exactly thirteen months to the day, November 1813, Abner Manuel Lilly was born; one month later, in December, Juan Ortego Sanchez was born.

~

The war with the British had escalated. Major General Andrew Jackson and his troops arrived in New Orleans by January 8, 1815, just in time to defend the city from British attack. Pirates, Creoles, and blacks ~ all volunteers ready to fight the British ~ quickly joined his forces. What he wound up with was a ragtag force of mismatched soldiers, who prided themselves on their hardiness, courage, and recklessness when held to the fight. British losses were approximately seven hundred killed and fourteen hundred wounded; American losses were only eight killed and thirteen wounded.

"The year of 1815 will go down in history as the most disappointing year of my life!" Pierre Lilly lamented. With the "Battle of New Orleans" over, Pierre and Christine assessed their losses.

When the British "kept acoming," Jackson's forces held them to their position with a devastating artillery and musket assault; however, something went badly wrong. Some stray ordnance or some British arsonist destroyed the Lilly mansion.

Terisa, although not exactly happy about Pierre and Christine's mansion being destroyed, knew that because it burned, she and Felipe would have to get their own place.

"You know, Felipe, we would have never got out of that place if the battle hadn't destroyed it."

Felipe and Terisa soon built themselves a mansion in the French Quarter. Pierre and Christine bought a few acres of land on the outskirts of town and built their new mansion.

"Even though we all got along fine living in one house, it is such a relief for me to live in my own home," Terisa told Christine.

~

Terisa and Christine sat on the verandah of Sanchez mansion chit-chatting. They discussed family matters, the weather and whatever else entered their minds.

"I'm so proud of our men," Christine said. "They're refraining more and more from taking long voyages away from home. They're learning to leave the trading up to their Field Captains."

"Can you believe Pierre is already insisting that Jacob get an education? He already has plans for him to become the company's lawyer! We can't even talk about it. I tell Pierre that Jacob is only three years old, and it goes right over the top of his head. He just keeps saying,

'After all, what this company needs is a good lawyer.' Pierre never lets up!" Christine complained.

"Well, we're not putting any pressure on Renee one way or the other. There will be plenty of time for that," Terisa said.

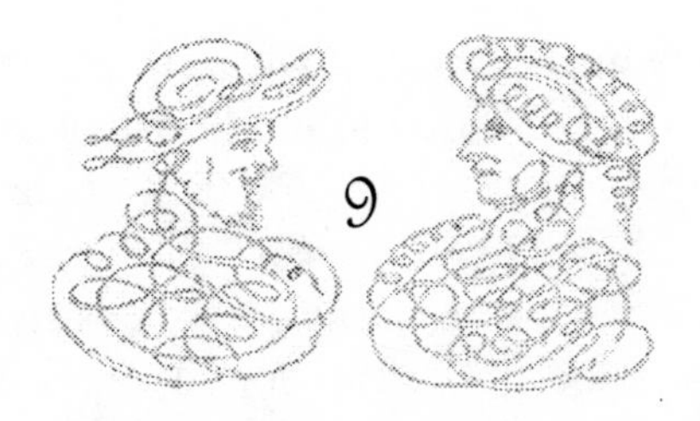

9

Spring had brought new life to Bois d'Arc creek bottom. The Bois d' Arc trees' leaves had finally reached the size of a squirrel's ear and had triggered Roscoe to plant corn.

"Ten acres is perty near all I can handle, with jest one team uh mules. We gotta get another team, for you to plow with Gurdy, or ya gotta have me a boy," Roscoe complained.

Demand for their corn whisky was so high, they couldn't meet it. Even though their creek-bottom cornfield had produced a bumper crop, they were running out of corn. Every day it seemed that some traveler came by, headed up or down Red River, and needed to buy whisky. For Roscoe and Gurdy Donnegan, living on Bois d' Arc Creek never brought them a dull moment.

The Donnegans could finally afford some of the luxuries of life that they desired. Roscoe now owned two pairs of overalls. He owned one solid blue pair and one pinstripe pair. *Like the train conductors back east wear*, he thought.

Gurdy had become tired of smoking Mullein (Rabbit Tobacco) in corn-cob pipes. She had ordered her a case of snuff from a riverboat peddler who passed by on his way to New Orleans. "The kind in the little tins," she adamantly told the old hawker. "I don't want me none uh the snuff in them glasses."

After the riverboat peddler left, Roscoe and Gurdy sat on the porch. They watched the beautiful sunset and discussed their plans to start a family.

"We're amakin' enuf money ta have us some young uns, honey." Roscoe spat his chaw off the end of the porch. "I need me a boy ta teach the brewin' business to. I need help afarmin' all this corn, and I need me a boy ta handle hisself a team uh mules."

"Laudy … laudy, I need me a girl ta help with the chores 'round here. I ain't gonna have ya no boy, Roscoe Donnegan."

As summer gave way to the crispness of autumn, Gurdy began showing. Their plans for the family's expansion had indeed taken root.

Every day, after Gurdy finished washing dishes and Roscoe finished his night chores, they retired to the front porch to watch the sunset. There they discussed baby names and contemplated whether or not the new arrival would be a boy or a girl.

"It's a boy and I thank a good name'd be Roscoe Junior. It'd do me proud. Besides, Roscoe Junior just sounds like a 'Stiller." Roscoe's face lit up with pride.

"It ain't no boy 'n' we gotta quit callin it a it. Frum now on it's a her ta you and 'er name's Emma." Gurdy had a women's intuition, a gut feeling as she called it, that the baby was a girl.

The strenuous living on Bois d' Arc Creek had taken its toll on Gurdy. Her being light of frame and frail gave one the impression that she couldn't stand the harsh frontier life. Morning sickness of the worst kind wreaked havoc on Gurdy's ability to keep her food down. No sooner would she down her breakfast than she would run to the back stoop and spew it out. Roscoe thought Gurdy had lost her mind because she craved the weirdest things. She loved the crushed coffee beans and would dig them out of the coffee pot and eat them. To watch her do that gagged Roscoe. Gurdy managed, after she got through those terrible mornings, to milk the cow, feed the chickens, slop the hogs, cook three meals a day, do the darning, and then shell corn for the brewing. Then the next morning, the same usual sickness and the same old chores would greet Gurdy again.

~

Emma Violet Donnegan arrived in September of 1809. She came during one of the coldest days of fall they had had so far. *Her name's too hard fer me ta spit out,* Roscoe thought. He never did like the name Emma Violet, and he began calling her by her initials, E. V.

"I don't like E. V. That's too hard on my tongue," Gurdy complained. "Eve wuz the first women in the Bible; why don't we call 'er Eve?" That name lasted for a while, but neither of them liked the name Eve.

"Roscoe do ya 'member that Eve deceived Adam in the Bible? Deceitful, is not our little Emma's way," Gurdy said. Roscoe agreed with her. They settled on Eve-e.

~

Before Eve-e started to crawl, Gurdy was with child again. The first indication was her severe cravings, this time for Poke sallet. Roscoe insisted that this time she was going to have a boy, and Gurdy agreed with him.

"This time it's a boy, honey. Start picking ya a name!" Gurdy told Roscoe.

Gurdy set in on Roscoe to go get her some poke sallet. "I'll be glad to, if you'll stay off uh them crushed coffee beans," Roscoe answered.

"Daddy use to send me and Jeb alookin' fer poke sallet just as soon as the frogs started to croak in the spring," Gurdy said. "He'd cook me and Jeb up sum ever spring. He claimed it was a good blood cleanser. The best way I like it cooked is to boil it down low then fry it in sum bacon grease 'n' then mix sum scrambled eggs in it. I sure wish ya would bring me home sum."

"I promise ya I'll bring some home when I find it. Poke ain't put its shoots up yet. It'll be the first thing that pokes its head up, though. That's fit ta eat, that is." Roscoe said. They both had a long laugh.

"Maybe that's how poke got its name 'cause it's the first thang fit ta eat that pokes its head up in the spring," Gurdy commented.

Roscoe spent his time trapping, fishing, and brewing or shinin' as he called it. The Donnegans' modest income came from selling whisky, furs, and fish, but they both dreamed of more.

"If we could just get our whisky down to the Mississippi River, then we could sell it to one uv those fur tradin' companies. Shucks then we'd really be livin' high on the hog," Roscoe explained to Gurdy.

"Well ya know that them Coopers'll be acomin' back. Maybe they'll start buyin' our whisky and takin' it ta the Mississippi River and sellin' it, like they said they would," Gurdy reminded Roscoe.

"Yeah, I been athanking; when they came back I'd dump the keelboat on 'em fer a tidy profit." Roscoe calculated. "They're apt ta need it ta tote all them treasures they wuz aplannin' ta buy in Santa Fe."

"Laudy, laudy, ya know what, Roscoe? It's been too long. Somethin's happened to the Coopers!" Gurdy shivered as she thought, *I gotta 'tuition that the Comanche got 'em or something*!

Roscoe plowed the chaw of tobacco out of his mouth with his forefinger and slung the wad off the end of the porch. "Shucks, they couldn't uv let the Comanche get 'em. That Jinx is way too savvy to uv let that happen."

"Ya've got that stupid keelboat that ya bought off them Coopers. Why don't ya just take a load uv brew ta the Mississippi yerself?" Gurdy asked.

"What? With you havin' one young un asuckin' 'n' one on the way? No!" Roscoe thought a minute. "It'll wait. Sumbody'll come long. If not, after we get our family raised, who knows then, maybe I'll go inta the tradin' business."

~

The next day, Gurdy got up with the morning sickness. *The first I've had with the new baby*, she thought.

Roscoe reluctantly got out of bed. He yawned, stretched, and scratched before going about tending chores, as if nothing was wrong with Gurdy. About midmorning Roscoe left to run his trapline. He decided he would pull his traps because with warmer weather arriving, fur would no longer be prime. He pulled his last trap and headed home. Roscoe spotted something in the shadow of a distant cedar tree. There it was, the prettiest patch of poke he'd ever seen, there on the south slope of a cedar ridge.

Gurdy spied Roscoe trotting toward the cabin with a pack over his back, and she could see poke sticking out the top of it.

"Guess what I brung ya, honey?" Roscoe's grin stretched from ear to ear.

Gurdy flung herself around Roscoe's neck and at the same time chanted. "We're gonna have poke sallet fer supper! We're gonna have poke sallet fer breakfast! Hallelujah, I'm gonna have all the poke sallet I can eat!"

~

August 1, 1810, was a typical fall day. The morning began cool and with everything covered by a heavy dew, but the day warmed and transformed into a warm crisp evening. Annalee arrived upon the scene just before suppertime. If her first night was to be anything like the rest of her life, there would not be a peaceful moment in the Donnegan house for years to come. It was glaringly apparent by morning that Miss Annalee knew how to get her way. From the time that Roscoe slapped her butt until daylight the next morning, she did not stop crying unless she was nursing or being cooed to.

Roscoe and Gurdy were not in the least bit disappointed that the baby was a girl, just surprised. They had been so sure the baby was a boy.

"We'll have us a Roscoe Jr. next time," Roscoe said.

~

During the spring of 1813, Roscoe and Gurdy's problems began. The spring had been an unusually wet one; every puddle and every swamp was infested with mosquitoes. The result was an awful outbreak of the "Swamp Fever." The fever hit Gurdy just about the time the summer heat began. She lay on their straw bed all summer and into early fall with a raging fever, chills and shakes. By the time the cool nights of September set in, Gurdy had shaken the fever. Annalee turned three in August and Eve-e four in September, and they hadn't a worry in the world. Roscoe had seen to that. He had been so preoccupied with taking care of Gurdy and the girls, though, that he hadn't laid enough supplies up for the winter. Now it was getting too late in the season. Instead of getting better, things got worse.

The lack of stored goods made the winter of 1813-14 extremely brutal for Roscoe and Gurdy. Now starvation knocked at the door, but Roscoe saw that his little girls had full bellies. They tried to be of help but were just too young.

The Donnegans ran out of corn for the Jersey cow, for squiggles the sow, and for the still. They were out of firewood, and their larder was empty. There was no coffee, sugar, flour, or beans. Roscoe was a good provider, but scrounging from the land was taking its toll on Gurdy and him.

Hoping this was the last cold-snap, Roscoe spent the blustery, damp morning of the 1814 Ides of March chopping wood with the ax and keeping the fireplace fed.

He took his shotgun off the rack above the front door and went to the slough to kill enough ducks for the family's supper. When he stepped up on the porch proudly bearing a poke full of ducks, Gurdy complained.

"Laudy, laudy, the girls, and that includes me, are gettin' tired uh duck. I have fried duck, I've boiled duck and I've baked 'em. I've roasted duck, and I've made jerky frum 'em. They ain't any good any way I've cooked 'em. We're through eat'n 'em. Ya can go kill us rabbits or possums or anything but coyotes!"

After yet another supper of duck, Gurdy and Roscoe left the kitchen table in a hurry to get their night chores done up so they could sit on the front porch and watch the sunset. Gurdy gathered up the eggs and fed the chickens, with the help of Eve-e and Annalee. She and the kids then headed to the front porch. Eve-e and Annalee were busy playing with their cornshuck dolls when Roscoe came around the corner of the porch.

"Laudy, what took ya so long?" Gurdy wanted to know.

"Shucks, I been ajuicing the Jersey, and she pulled one uh her contrary fits and kicked the stool out frum under me." Roscoe was none too happy.

"What does juicing the Jersey mean, Daddy?" Annalee asked.

"That's milking, honey," Roscoe told her.

Silence prevailed for a long time. Roscoe and Gurdy just sat and watched the kids play and didn't say a word. The wind rushed through the willows that grew along Bois d' Arc Creek and provided harmony for nature's symphony. Lime-green tree frogs were trilling in soprano while the whaling whippoorwills sang alto. Bully, the livestock-watering-hole bullfrog, lent his hoarse raucous bass voice to the production. He seemed to keep time with the squeaking and tweaking of Roscoe's and Gurdy's rocking chairs. Rounding out nature's song was a whole host of crickets and locust singing back up.

Gurdy interrupted the concert. "I still wanta have you that boy, honey, but I jest can't seem ta gets swelled. I reckon I'm over frum havin' that swamp fever that went around." Gurdy wrinkled her forehead as if she couldn't understand.

"Shucks, spring's right 'round the corner, and everything is matey, tain't uh bit atellin' you're lible to start making Roscoe Junior any day now," Roscoe said.

"Now, don't start countin' yer chickens 'fore they hatch, Roscoe." Gurdy wasn't sure she would ever have another baby.

~

Spring was welcome for many reasons. The boat peddler came by, and Roscoe and Gurdy filled their larder brim to the top with the necessities for good eating. Roscoe borrowed seed corn from Stiller Johnson and planted twice as many acres as in years past.

Eve-e and Annalee were swinging from the grapevine that hung in the yard. Roscoe and Gurdy sat on the front porch and watched the sun set.

"Ya know, Gurdy, we wuz jest abeginnin' when them Coopers showed up here with their expedition. We didn't even have Eve-e, if my memory serves me correctly." Roscoe began.

"Nah, it wuz some'ers round the end uh February 1809 when the Coopers left. Eve-e wuz born in September," Gurdy said. Gurdy's memory was good, so Roscoe always depended on her for the dates that things happened.

"Them Coopers never did return like they said they would. What d'you 'spose happened to em?" Gurdy asked.

"Shucks, I don't have the foggiest idea. Do ya 'member Sam Cooper always asayin' he wudn't comin' back. I guess he thought he wuz uh gonna die er something?" Roscoe remembered.

"Adyin', laudy, laudy, let's change the subject; I don't like that morbid stuff." Gurdy shivered. "Anyway, I wuz adoin' purty good ahavin' us kids until after Annalee come along, and then last year the swamp fever hit me."

Gurdy thought a long time about Eve-e. *She's so quiet and requires such little attention that she rarely gets any. We need ta pay 'er more attention.* Gurdy's thoughts made her restless. She got up and moved to a straight chair and cocked it back against the wall. *That Annalee ~ laudy, laudy she is sure gonna cause a lot uh trouble with the boys. She is always uh teasin' and uh goin' on.*

"Roscoe ya know I sure have been afeelin' tired lately. My chores are a botheration ta me. I catch myself awantin' ta cry 'bout everything. I don't know what's amatter with me," Gurdy confided. Gurdy soon learned her problem ; within a couple of weeks, her time of the month came and went without anything happening. That and the lousy way she felt, everything seemed to get her goat. Suddenly, she knew! She was with child again … finally! When she told Roscoe, he was beside himself.

"This time the baby's name will be Roscoe Junior, so ya better have a boy, Gurdy." Roscoe made himself clear. Things went exceptionally well this time. There was no morning sickness and no craving of poke sallet or coffee beans. Instead, Gurdy craved everything she could get her hands on. If it was edible, she craved it. The best she could figure the baby would be due in the early part of November.

The summer had been a scorcher, especially down in Bois d' Arc Creek bottom where it seemed a breath of air was uncommon. Gurdy had survived. October brought cool nights and the first real Norther of the season, and they were both welcomed by her. Standing only four feet eleven inches, Gurdy was almost as big around. Not only had she gorged herself, but she was carrying a big baby.

November 5, 1814, would be the day Roscoe and Gurdy would always remember. Roscoe had gone with the team of mules to skid up another jag of firewood. He hadn't been able to get a wagon yet but had built himself a sled the mules could pull. He used it to move corn from the field to the corncrib and to the still and for hauling things around the farm. Eve-e and Annalee loved to play in the corncrib, especially on cool days and were there playing. Gurdy washed the dishes and had just sat down in the rocking chair when the pain of birthing hit her. She went to the door and hollered for Eve-e to go get Roscoe, but the girls apparently couldn't hear her. *This is not somethin' that is going to drag out for a while!* Gurdy thought. Better reasoning told her not to go to the barn and get the girls herself. *I'm thirsty, and the sweats have gotten me,* she thought. She went to the back porch and got her a dipper of water. What she didn't drink she poured over her head. She made it back inside and lay down on their straw bed. She lay on her back and got into position for the baby to come, but she couldn't stay comfortable for long. She screamed for the girls and she screamed for Roscoe ~ no one came.

She shifted her weight to her other side and pushed with all her might. She sucked her lungs full of air. Uncomfortable again, she shifted her position; she pushed, she sucked air, then she just screamed. This time not for the girls, not for Roscoe ~ this time for herself. *I need water ... I'm so thirsty*. She wiped her sweaty face on the blanket. Then she sucked for air again. *I need air ~ the baby needs ...*! She screamed and pushed with every fiber in her body. There was not room in her mind for anything except giving birth ~ her mind centered on that. Then, Roscoe Junior was there!

She sat up and picked him up in her arms. She tenderly brought him toward her breast ~ the cord was long enough ~ she placed little Roscoe on her breast and lay down. As she rubbed his back, he started to cry. *We're cold*, she thought, and snuggled the blankets up over them. *I can't cut the cord; maybe Roscoe will be here soon.* The warmth of their bodies soothed each other, and they began to forget the struggle of birth.

Roscoe pulled the grays up beside the woodpile. "Whoa," he hollered. *I better check on Gurdy 'fore ah unload*, he thought. When Roscoe stepped up on the front stoop, Roscoe Junior let out a cry. Roscoe's fear of what might have happened to Gurdy because he wasn't there collided with his happiness at hearing a baby cry. "You okay, honey? Is it a boy?"

"His name is Roscoe Junior!" Gurdy exclaimed.

He whooped as the door slammed behind him. "It's a Roscoe Jr. … It's a Roscoe Jr.!" he yelled at the top of his lungs. He reached to pick little Roscoe up.

"Whoa!" Gurdy protested. "Not 'fore ya cut 'im loose frum me. I couldn't cut the cord." Roscoe reached for his knife.

"Laudy … laudy, wash that thing off first!" Gurdy burst out.

~

Roscoe and Gurdy continued doing what they did best. They grew corn, raised kids, and sold whisky to the local citizens and to the Red River travelers who were passing by.

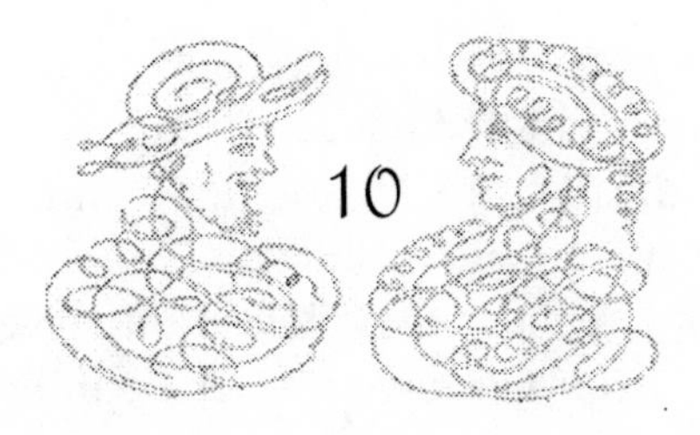

10

The year of 1819 had proved to be exceptionally trying for Dancing waters and the son of Gold Seeker. Next year, Son of Gold Seeker would become ten years old, the time when Wichita children leave the care of their mothers and begin learning from their fathers. He had already begun to try everyone's patience with his revolting pranks. He ran away from home and went to San Teodoro. The Taovaya Indians lived there, and he felt more at home with them than with his own tribe.

The French came from New Orleans to trade with the Taovaya and with the Spanish in Santa Fe. Many stayed behind and took wives from the Taovayas. Son of Gold Seeker made friends with and played with half-breed children. He became especially close to Jacques who was the son of a French trapper and whose mother was a Taovaya. In their playing with each other, Jacques taught Son of Gold Seeker broken French.

Dancing Waters had refrained thus far from seeking help outside the family with raising Son of Gold Seeker. She was well-versed with regard to Wichita custom. Her father, Ketox Runner, was the wisdom keeper of the tribe. She knew that if she asked for help from outside the family to punish her rotten child, they could use whatever form of punishment they deemed necessary. She was also painfully aware that after she had asked for outside help she could not interfere in any way. *Son of Gold Seeker will revolt against my authority when he turns ten, then he will become like the wild stallion that roams the Wichita River bottom.* She shuddered at the thought. She knew she would need outside help then.

During the summer when Son of Gold Seeker turned ten, Dancing Waters' problems compounded. A group of American trappers who had camped on Red River took a liking to Son of Gold Seeker and kind of took him in. He couldn't resist running away to visit them, too.

Dancing Waters tried to explain to Son of Gold Seeker that he could not run away. She explained that when he ran away it caused her too much worry. Reasoning didn't seem to have any effect on him. Son of Gold Seeker always countered her reasoning.

"You ain't my father" ~ or ~ "Now that I'm ten, my father must be the one to tell me what to do." She was afraid to apply force. She was afraid Son of Gold Seeker would leave and never return. She was afraid to seek outside help and have no say-so in his punishment. So the problem persisted.

Gold Seeker made her promise she would give him his war prize on his tenth birthday. She didn't want to, but she had given her promise.

"Son of Gold Seeker," she said, "there is something I want to give you from your father." Dancing Waters showed him the opaque leather bag. She took hold of the white sinew drawstring, opened the bag, and extracted the black walnut. "Feel how heavy this is." She handed her son the walnut. "Your father gave me specific instructions to give to you. He said for me to tell you if you figure out how to open the walnut shell, what is inside will lead you to him. Do not force the shell to break open. You must figure out how to open it the way its maker intended for it to open. That is what Gold Seeker said tell you." She held out her hand, accepted the black walnut necklace from him, and returned it to its peculiar bag. Dancing Waters placed the drawstring around his neck and stuffed the bag down inside his shirt, then warned him: "Do not ever show the black walnut necklace to anyone, unless you are pretty sure the person is your father. Men will kill you for the contents of that bag or steal the necklace from you."

Son of Gold Seeker just shrugged his shoulders and spat on the ground. "Not nun uh me they won't. I'll kill 'em first!" He stomped through the lodge flap and returned to the encampment of trappers on Red River. He was good friends with Grizzly, the trapper's leader. He became more convinced than ever his father was a trapper. Grizzly always referred to beaver as the soft gold of the Rockies. Son of Gold Seeker knew real gold as sun rocks. His father would not be out chasing rocks. His father would be out seeking the soft gold of the Rockies.

Son of Gold Seeker almost begged Grizzly to take him with them and teach him how to trap beavers.

Grizzly refused. "Sonny, yer jest a kid. When ya can grow a beard ta match that Yellowish-red, wiry, tangled mop uh yern and when ya can grow up enough ta quit givin' yer Mammy so much trouble, I'll reconsider."

"I don't like troublemaking kids that can't talk good enough English so I can understand them," the trapper named Deacon said. Grizzly tossed a couple of rusty traps ashore and slung a bit of advice at Son of Gold Seeker as they left.

"Here ya are. Learn yer'sef sumthin' 'fore we cum back."

Son of Gold Seeker waved good-bye to Grizzly's party. They cast off down Red River to take their pelts to the Mississippi River. The trappers waved at Son of Gold Seeker, and he waved at them until they were out of sight. Son of Gold Seeker headed back toward the Wichita River with his head hung low and his spirits hung even lower. *How'um I ever gonna find my father?* he thought. After a brief spell of feeling sorry for himself, he centered his thoughts around what he must do.

I'm agonna becomst a better beaver trapper 'en any white man... ever! When Grizzly cumz back, I'll show 'em! And I'll talk so good Deacon won't be able'ta figure out what I'm asayin'.

There was an immediate change in Son of Gold Seeker's demeanor. The whole clan welcomed the new Son of Gold Seeker, especially Dancing Waters.

"Mother," he said, "I want ya ta keep Father's war necklace fer me. When I'm ready ta leave 'n' find Father, I will come for it." He removed the opaque bag and handed it to Dancing Waters. I haven't figured out how ta open it, but I will, just you wait 'n' see."

"I know you will," Dancing Waters said, encouraging him.

"Mother, I wanna 'pologize fer all the trouble I've caused ya." Son of Gold Seeker hugged his mother. "May I go ta San Teodoro 'n' stay awhile and learn trappin' frum Jacques? I wanna learn trappin' and then someday I'm gonna go ta the mountains 'n' find my father. They have a teacher there, at San Teodoro, what can teach me how ta talk white talk, and I'm gonna learn ta talk educated!"

Dancing Waters knew she could not do anything to keep her son from going. She was so thankful to see him growing out of his childhood troublemaking and into a fine respectable man. How could she refuse her consent?

"You are free to go, my son. Your attitude tells me you're a man now. You'll make a fine trapper. You'll find your Father. Just promise me that if I am not gone to the spirit world when you find him, you will bring him back to me."

"I do, Momma, I promise ya as if I wuz on my deathbed. I'll brung 'im ta ya! I haven't left yet, Momma. I'll just be away awhile learnin' trappin'. I will return 'fore I leave fer the Mountains," Son of Gold Seeker promised.

Dancing Waters hugged him and sent him on his way. She felt proud to be his mother, and she finally had a good feeling that everything was going to be all right.

Son of Gold Seeker stayed at San Teodoro for weeks on end. He trapped with Jacques, his French/Indian friend, and studied English French and Spanish.

When Son of Gold Seeker did come home, he astonished his mother with his politeness. Dancing Waters never knew what caused the change of attitude in her son, but it was welcome. From that day forward, Son of Gold Seeker quickly grew into manhood.

~

Son of Gold Seeker was fourteen now. He practiced his French, English, and Spanish religiously. He had grown into an extremely astute trapper. Plus, he had the beginnings of a wiry reddish yellow beard that soon would do any trapper justice.

It was the summer of 1824 before Grizzly's trapping party camped in the vicinity of the Wichita village again. His big party of trappers, that Son of Gold Seeker knew, had dissolved. Grizzly was there along with three new trappers, and Son of Gold Seeker took right up with them.

Son of Gold Seeker had rehearsed this moment many times in his mind and knew exactly what to do. He went to Dancing Waters and asked for his necklace, then went straight to Grizzly's camp. This time Son of Gold Seeker didn't plead. He forcefully stated.

"I am going to winter with you and trap beavers, then I am going to Henry's Fork with you, to the first rendezvous ever … come spring." His transformation shocked Grizzly. Not only had the boy grown tall, but he now sported an amazing yellowish-red beard. He had polished his English into something their ignorance would hardly let them understand. Not only did he speak English and Wichita, he now spoke French and Spanish! *And the kid ain't but fourteen*, Grizzly thought.

"What can ah say?" Grizzly told Son of Gold Seeker. "A man who has a bristle-hair beard like yourn … you're in. One thang, you'll have ta change yer name ~ you'll be Yellow Beard."

Grizzly turned to the other trappers and introduced Yellow Beard.

"We've taken on a new green horn. He doesn't know trappin, but I'll teach 'im. This here's Yellow Beard," Grizzly said.

Yellow Beard held his peace. He knew trapping and he knew he could trap better than any of them. He would just let time teach Grizzly that.

The tall lanky gray-bearded trapper spoke first. "I'm Ketchum and ah'm pleased ta know ya, Yellow Beard."

"I'm Geezer," an old sourpuss of a trapper grumbled.

A man of medium build and of average features was sitting on a cotton wood log sipping from a jug of whisky. He had been observing the whole affair as if he couldn't care less.

"Wahl, 'tis here es uh...Donnegan whisky. Do ya wanna swig uv it?"

"Uh, no, I believe not. Thank you, though."

"Wahl, it's the best thar is. It's brewed by Roscoe Donnegan hisself, with Bois d' Arc apples, he claims. By the way ah'm glad ta makes yer 'quaintance, Yellow Beard. I'm Jinx. And I want ya ta know that 'fore ya wuz born, I lived with one uv yer own!"

Yellow Beard's heart almost quit beating, and a lump as big as his fist came into his throat.

"What was her name?" Yellow Beard asked.

"Dancin' ... dancin' ... dancin' sumthin' uh can't 'xactly 'member who." Jinx's mind blurred.

Yellow Beard's heart raced wildly as he plunged his hand into his smoke-stained leather shirt. Memories of warnings flooded his mind, and his thoughts caused him to leave the necklace where it was.

Yellow Beard remembered what his grandfather, Coyote Runner, had said. *White man turn greedy when he sees Sun Rocks*! He remembered what his mother had told him. *Do not ever show the black walnut necklace to anyone unless you are pretty sure the person is your father. Men will kill you for the contents of that bag, or they will steal the necklace from you.* Yellow Beard decided it would be best for him to wait until Jinx and he could be alone.

Jinx looked puzzled when Yellow Beard asked him to go for a walk.

"What in the world for?"

"I wanta show you something, Jinx," Yellow Beard answered.

The men approached a fallen cottonwood tree on the river bank. After the weight of rattan vines had uprooted it, it had plunged down the caving river bluff. It was a perfect place to sit, in privacy, hidden by the rattan vines.

Yellow Beard reached into his shirt and retrieved the opaque bag from his bosom. He had never seen anyone's eyeballs come so close to popping out. Jinx reached for the bag. Yellow Beard withdrew it.

"What's in the funny leather bag?" Jinx asked.

"Never you mind. Have you ever seen it before?" Yellow Beard dangled the bag before Jinx's whisky-dazed eyes.

"Wahl …." Jinx stopped.

Jinx hesitated, as if he was fixing to say yes, Yellow Beard thought.

"Uh …." Jinx lost his train of thought again, then changed the subject. "I got me a funny lookin' bag too." Jinx fumbled with the buffalo scrotum bag that hung around his neck. "I'll show you what's in my bag if'n you'll show me what's in yern." Jinx dumped his bag's contents into his hand. "Sum Gold nuggets is what I got."

"I don't care what you've got. What I want to know is if you've ever seen this bag before?" Yellow Beard dangled the bag into Jinx's face again.

"Can't say as ever I have. But I do recollect the maiden's name ya asked me 'bout … Dancin' Doe ~ her name was Dancin' Doe." Jinx winked. "The pertiest thang ya nearly ever did see."

Yellow Beard almost fell off the log his heart dropped so fast. Jinx's memory plunged him into despair!

Yellow Beard suddenly remembered; he would be leaving first thing in the morning. He must visit his mother and tell her good-bye. *I may never see her again!*

"Grizzly, I have all my belongings packed and ready. I must go tell Mother bye. I'll be back before daybreak and I'll be ready to go."

~

The last rays of daylight cast fingers of light through the cottonwoods as Yellow Beard arrived at his mother's thatched lodge.

Somehow, the wailing of a whippoorwill sent a shiver of loneliness down his spine. He ducked into Dancing Waters' grass hut. The thought of maybe never seeing her again haunted him more than the whippoorwill.

"Mother, I've joined a band of trappers, and I'm going to go to the mountains to trap and find my father. I have come to say good-bye!" Yellow Beard felt mixed emotions about leaving his home and his mother.

Son of Gold Seeker's revelation broke Dancing Waters' heart. She had dreaded the day he would leave in search of Gold Seeker and now the time had come.

"Maybe, Son of Gold Seeker, just maybe, you can find your father. If I could only remember his white name, that would be such a great help."

"My name is not Son of Gold Seeker anymore, Mother. The white Spirit Keeper has given me my real name. My name is now Yellow Beard."

"Oh, Son …ugh , I mean Yellow Beard, that is a fitting name. You wear it well. Your Father would be proud of that name." Dancing Waters' eyes glimmered.

Dancing Waters leaned back against her ground chair and pulled her sleeping robe over her feet. *The feeling I have lost my son is making me shiver*, she thought. She asked Yellow Beard to tell her all about the trappers. She was groping for some way to keep a connection between herself and her son.

"Their names, at least the main ones, are Grizzly, Ketchum, and Jinx and there is one old grumpy man named Geezer."

"Jinx … Jinx!" Dancing Waters began screaming the name. She placed her hands up in front of her face and shook her arms violently. "Oh, Jinx … he was your father's best friend. Please have him to come visit me!" She suddenly remembered. "Jinx can tell you your father's white name!"

~

Yellow Beard returned to the trappers' camp just as a new day washed the stars out of the sky. He crept into his blanket and lay on the dry sand bar thinking about the beauty of his war necklace. *I will always wear it under my shirt, reserving its beauty for no other eyes than Father's,* he thought. Could Jinx possibly know where his father was? One thing for certain, Jinx knew his father's white name. Yellow Beard's consciousness gave way to dreams of distant lands and the soft gold of the Rockies.

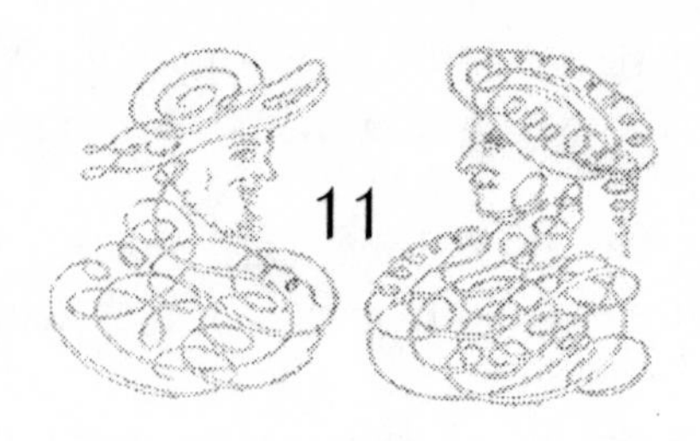

The October morn dawned bright, clear and frosty. Grizzly rousted the sleepy-eyed Yellow Beard to life by reminding him: Today is the day we're pulling out. You gonna go?"

"Uh, what do you think?" Yellow Beard replied, but first he must talk to Jinx.

Yellow Beard had a thousand questions in his mind.

"Mother knows you, Jinx. She says you were Father's best friend and that you know his white name. Do you know it?"

"Wahl, jest who'd be yer mammy?"

"Dancing Waters is my mother. I don't have a mammy. Puppies have mammies, and I'm no pup. Now, does that answer your question?"

"Wahl, yeah it's true … Bill Cooper 'n' me shared sum glorious times on the ol' Red River!" Jinx gleamed, as he fondly remembered back on those times. *They seemed so long ago.* "Ferz yer mammy goes, that thar Dancin' Waters is one dandy woman!"

"Mother really wants to see you, Jinx. Could you pay her a visit before we go?"

"Sure thang … Ya fill in fer me till I get back?"

"I'll be glad to. Bill Cooper is my father's white name!" Yellow Beard proudly proclaimed his fathers' name. Now, he felt a renewed determination.

"Wahl, yeah 'n' Sam Cooper wuz yer granpappy. He had hair just like yourn. It wuz the wiriest mop that ya nearly ever did see. Just like a hog's hair. Yeller-red, it wuz, jest like yourn, too." Jinx's eyes twinkled. He thought back to the time that Bill Cooper asked him what Dancing Waters had whispered in his ear.

Jinx turned to leave, but Yellow Beard had an afterthought and interrupted him.

"Before you go, I have to ask you one thing. When we make camp at night and aren't too busy skinning beavers, will you tell me all about my grandfather and father. Will you do that?"

"Wahl yeah, I'd be glad to. Yer granpappy was more like me, I can tell ya that. He took alikin' ta huntin' treasures more 'n' he did ta trappin'. Bill Cooper was real levelheaded. I 'spect he stuck ta his trappin' jest like I did."

That was just what Yellow Beard wanted to hear.

~

Grizzly's plans were to trap down Red River to the Donnegans where they would trade some of their pelts for whisky. Then they would trap down Red River to "Pawcon Point" and trade some of their Donnegan whisky for supplies. From Pecan Point, Grizzly planned to continue trapping down Red River to the Mississippi River and catch a steam boat to St. Louis. After they sold their furs, they would leave for the mouth of Henry's Fork. There they planned to attend the first rendezvous ever. The appointed place of the rendezvous was about twenty miles up Henry's Fork from its junction with Green River and was to take place July 1, 1825.

~

Yellow Beard thought he had learned all there was to know about trapping from Jacques. He soon realized that much of what he and Jacques had learned together was just childhood play.

Grizzly taught Yellow Beard a lot about beaver trapping in the months to come. Yellow Beard was tough as a buffalo bull. He waded the cold Red River water, setting and running traps as if it were summertime. By the time Grizzly and them reached the Donnegans on Bois d' Arc Creek, Yellow Beard, a very astute learner, was trapping as many beavers as Grizzly.

Jinx taught Yellow Beard the ways of Red River, lessons that would prove invaluable to him in his search for his daddy.

~

When they reached Bois d' Arc Creek, Jinx pointed it out to them; then he directed them up the creek to the Donnegans. It was mid-December, and gray clouds hung low. The clouds spat sleet pellets that bounced from the trapper's backs as they poled their boats up the creek. The Donnegans welcomed Grizzly's trapping party with open arms. They were especially proud to meet Yellow Beard, whom Jinx quickly introduced as Bill Cooper's son.

"Ya look just like yer granpappy," Gurdy said.

Roscoe plowed a juiceless cud of tobacco out of his jaw with his forefinger. "Shore nuf ya do."

~

Dusk closed in on Bois d' Arc Creek bottom and caught the Donnegans and the trappers sitting on the front porch jaw-yakking.

"We have been awonderin' what happened ta the Cooper expedition. You'll hav'ta bring us up'ta date on 'em, one uh these nights," Roscoe said, as if right now all he had time to do was to bring Yellow Beard up to date on the Donnegans.

"There ain't much to tell," Yellow Beard said. "They got lost between the head of Red River and Santa Fe. The Comanche killed all of them except my father." Yellow Beard was about to go into detail, but Roscoe interrupted him.

Roscoe began to tell Yellow Beard the Donnegan story. "We wuz just abeginnin' when yer granpappy showed up here with 'is expedition. We didn't even have Eve-e, there." Roscoe pointed to Emma Violet, "did we, Ma?"

Gurdy reached in her apron pocket and brought out her snuff box, took a little snort of snuff, and took over the conversation.

"Eve-e wuz born after they left. It wuz sum'ers round the end uh February, back in aught nine when the Coopers left, if my memory serves me c'rectly. Eve-e wuz born the followin' September." *Why does Roscoe always depend on me to date everything?* "Annalee wuz born in October uh 1810 ~ there wuz uh dry spell ~ then Roscoe Junior came in November 1813."

"Uh, 1810 … that's when I was born. I'm older than Annalee; I was born in July," Yellow Beard calculated. Yellow Beard's thoughts wandered: *I feel a special fondness for Annalee I can't explain. Possibly the reason is the fact that Annalee is her mother's helper just like I was. Maybe it's because she is always the center of attraction. I always watched everything from the sideline. That Annalee is right in the middle of everything. For Whatever reason, I feel a warmth inside unlike anything I've ever felt before.*

Gurdy's straight chair creaked as she cocked it back against the log wall.

"Uh, where is Roscoe Junior?" Yellow Beard asked. I ain't met him."

"Laudy, he took the boat and went to his grandpa Stiller's ta check on 'em. Jeb, my brother that stayed with 'em, went ta the mountains trappin' and never has cum back. Anyways ever since I had Junior, I ain't been able ta get swelled again," Gurdy said.

~

Roscoe and Gurdy persuaded the trappers to stay and finish the winter with them, at least until after Christmas, was the way they put it.

"Shucks, ya just gotta eat sum uv Gurdy's Christmas dinner; she goes all out," Roscoe proclaimed.

"Laudy, laudy, I'll cook wild goose and wild turkey with dressing and all the trimmings. Roscoe'll roast one uh squiggles' shoats." Gurdy was persuasive.

"The beavers are plentiful on Bois d' Arc Creek and so's the whisky," Roscoe added. Lots of beaver convinced Grizzly, and lots of whisky convinced Jinx that they should linger.

Skinning the day's catch, then stretching them on willow-hoop-drying-frames filled the days' labors. They would hang them in the log barn then help the Donnegans do up the night chores.

After they finished that, everyone listened for the ding-dong of Gurdy's dinner bell. As the ringing died down, her clear-as-a-bell voice called, "Everyone wash your faces and hands, then come and get it!" It was time for everyone to indulge in Gurdy's scrumptious cooking.

Roscoe always grew a patch of popcorn along with his field corn. Usually after supper was finished he would help Gurdy wash the dishes, then pop a dishpan full of fluffy white popcorn. He loved popping popcorn in the fireplace and did so most nights.

Roscoe would heavily salt it and then drizzle butter, that Gurdy churned from the rich heavy cream their Jersey cow Brownie provided, into the popcorn. He would holler, "Don't break yer necks agettin' here!"

The Donnegans and the trappers whiled away many long winter evenings. They sat around the fireplace and visited while they ate popcorn and watched the kids play "hide the thimble."

Jinx, after hiding the thimble, directed the girls while they searched for it.

"Yer gettin' warm!" he told Annalee who was approaching the corner whatnot shelf. Yellow Beard had hidden the thimble behind Junior's beaver skull. Annalee looked at the beaver skull. "You're warmer," he told her. All the girls rushed to Annalee's side. She became excited and stuffed popcorn into her mouth faster than she was eating it. "Keep alookin' up ta the shelf," Jinx said. Before the other girls could see where Annalee looked, she stepped to one side and saw a glint from the thimble hiding behind the skull.

"I spy!" Annalee screamed, spewing popcorn from her stuffed mouth all over them.

"How many times have ah told you girls don't talk with yer mouths full?" That order, repeated over and over, served a constant reminder to the girls ~ especially the vivacious Annalee.

~

Yellow Beard was persistent: He had a thousand questions about his father and grandfather. He wanted to know what they looked like, were they educated, why they came up Red River ~ the list went on and on. Roscoe, with Gurdy's help, patiently answered all his questions. The Donnegans' desire to learn more about the demise of the Cooper exploration controlled much of the conversation. Yellow Beard, though, always seemed to change the topic back to his father and grandfather. The Donnegans had a lot of respect for Sam and Bill Cooper. It saddened them to learn about the demise of the Cooper expedition at the hands of the Comanche. It did not surprise them that Bill Cooper had survived the ordeal.

"When ya come in to Bois d' Arc Creek did you see that ol' keelboat at the mouth, Yellow Beard?" Roscoe asked.

"Yes, but it's mostly sunk." Yellow Beard wondered where Roscoe's question was going.

"I traded sum whisky ta yer pa 'n' yer grandpa fer it. Then they traded the whisky ta the Choctaw Indians that lived across the river there, fer sum dugouts." Roscoe was proud of that deal.

"You don't mean it. I sure would like to prowl around in her and see if I can find anything that belonged to my pa. Would you mind?"

"Shucks, naugh. Hep yersef, Yellow Beard," Roscoe said.

"Okay, I'll go first thing in the morning then."

~

The sun had just touched the top of the tall cottonwood tree on the yonder side of Bois d' Arc Creek. Everyone knew when that happened it was a couple of hours till sundown. The girls burst through the front door and announced that Junior had come home and he had Grandpa Stiller with him.

"Laudy, laudy, Junior made it back fer Christmas and bless 'is heart, he brought Pa with 'im. I wuz atrustin' that Junior'd get back fore ya'll left so that ya'll could meet 'im. Well, that is just hunky-dory!" Gurdy sighed. They all went out on the porch and watched Junior help Stiller climb the long bluff up to the cabin. After Gurdy made the introductions all around, Junior poured the questions to Yellow Beard. Having never seen a real Indian up close, he was full of them. Roscoe Junior loved hearing Yellow Beard spin stories. He would sit squat on the floor, chin in his cupped hands and elbows on his knees, and listen as long as Yellow Beard would talk.

They all sat spellbound listening to Yellow Beard enthrall them with Wichita legends. He told them that the ones the Wichita Wisdom Keepers had passed down for thousands and thousands of moons. *If Grandfather Ketox Runner could see me now, he'd be proud of me*, Yellow Beard thought.

Yellow Beard told the story Grandfather Ketox Runner had told him so often, *"The legend of Weick Pah."*

"What does Weick Pah mean in my talk?" Roscoe Junior asked.

"Gap Water," Yellow Beard said.

"My grandfather told me the legend like this: 'Beautiful yellow rocks, chunks off the sun, fell to Mother Earth. A Spanish explorer by the name of Francisco Vazques de Coronado found them and cached them, over three thousand moons ago. Spiritual leaders of the yellowish-red hair Spannishie Indians ~ Catholic Spaniards ~ from a distant land found the cache. They made a god in the shape of a cross from the sun rocks. The God was an evil God, and the spiritual leaders cached it because it caused many battles and much blood spill. The good God keeps the evil god from ever being found.' That is why my father had to leave when I was born. He knew that I was apt to inherit Grandfather's yellowish-red hair and that my people would think he was an evil god."

"Wahl, if ever I get back up ta the Wichita River, I'm gonna look up Ketox Runner. I sure'd like ta hear 'bout that big gold cross! I might even try ta find 'er myself." Jinx crossed his heart, as if to promise himself that he would do it.

Yellow Beard thought, *I have said enough.* He refrained from talking anymore.

One thing that puzzled Jinx and Roscoe was, if Bill Cooper had gone to St. Louie to sign on as a trapper, why in the world hadn't he stopped at the Donnegans?

"There ain't no explanation fer it. My money's still on Bill Cooper abein' a trapper; he wuz too level-headed ta go off ahuntin' a gold cross!" Jinx told Roscoe.

"Shucks, my money is on 'im abein' a trapper too," Roscoe agreed.

Jinx looked over at Roscoe and winked. "What uh you think, Yellow Beard?"

"My mind was made up when I joined up with the likes of you

beaver skinners. Father is a trapper, and I'm going to find him, that is if we ever get on the move again!"

Yellow Beard realized that his patience was wearing thin. *I will not miss the drinking nor the small talk in the least. This thing about Christmas that everyone is talking about ~ I didn't even know Christmas and I wouldn't care anyway ~ except that the kids sure seem excited.*

~

Yellow Beard headed to the mouth of Bois d' Arc Creek. He couldn't believe he had finally found something that belonged to his grandpa. He crawled around over the top of the keelboat trying to pick up enough courage to dive down among the ruins. His foot slipped off the muddy board he was standing on, and he made the dive ~ want to or not. He felt along the muddy bottom for something, anything, that might have belonged to his folks. Then he saw the monster, a flathead catfish of a hundred pounds or more. He turned toward the top. There in the sun's rays was an old rusty steel trap ~ he grabbed it on his way up, busted through the surface, and swam to the creek bank. He sat on the bank and studied the trap. *It is just like the one Mother has that belonged to Father*. He threw it over his shoulder and headed back to the cabin.

Roscoe had put up a cedar tree. Gurdy and the kids had strung popcorn on it. They couldn't afford Christmas tinsel, and besides, even if they could, the riverboat peddler didn't have any. The excitement among the kids came from the fact they had made each other something special, not that Ol' St. Nicholas was coming. Gurdy had made special dresses, from her and Roscoe, for the girls ~ to be saved in case they ever got married. She and Roscoe had made Roscoe Junior a coonskin cap. The kids had crafted a hammer for Daddy to bust hickory nuts and pecans with, from a Bois d' Arc limb they'd found buried in the creek. They strung Mother a necklace from the iridescent mussel shells that lined the creekbanks. Roscoe Junior, knowing how much Yellow Beard liked his beaver skull, offered to give it to him, from the whole family. They all were going to give Jinx a crock of whisky. They hadn't come up with gifts for Grizzly, Ketchum, and Geezer as of yet.

Suddenly Yellow Beard had a sinking feeling in the pit of his stomach. *I will miss Annalee. Someday, after I find my father, I'll come back ta Bois d'Arc Creek and see her again. I promise myself that.*

~

Yellow Beard expected them to pull out the next morning after Christmas. To his astonishment, Grizzly decided that they would not leave until after the first of the new year.

"We'll pull out January 2, 1825," Grizzly announced. "Yellow Beard thinks we've spent way too much time at the Donnegans, but we sure have caught lots uv beavers."

It's true. Ketchum and I have caught lots of beavers. All that Grizzly and Jinx caught was a jug of whisky, Yellow Beard thought.

January second came in facing the disgust of Yellow Beard. *Everyone's drunk or sick and hung over. Travel is out of the question. The only good thing to come from that is, with all the old folks drunk and sick, I can spend some time with Annalee without Roscoe butting in.*

Yellow Beard and Annalee spent the morning together in the corncrib of the hand-hewn log barn. Roscoe put an end to that shortly before noon. "Shucks," Annalee said when Roscoe hollered for her to come in and help Gurdy get dinner on the table.

The old folks spent the afternoon drinking from a crock jug. They bragged about things they'd done and embarrassing situations they'd been in. Yellow Beard thought how terrible whisky must be that it could make a person brag about past embarrassments.

Yellow Beard and Annalee sat on the bank of Bois d' Arc Creek and watched the sun set. They were wordless, just taking in the beauty of the colored sky. Yellow Beard felt peaceful away from the belligerence the whisky caused in the old folks. *The only thing that I want right now,* he thought, *is to see the setting sun and be with Annalee.*

They, for an instant, took their gaze from the sunset and looked into each other's eyes. Yellow Beard blushed for his thoughts about Annalee. Then he felt restlessness replace his longings. He thought about what he wanted. *I want to be traveling. I want to go to St. Louis and abandon this bunch of losers. I want to join a real trapping company. I want to find my father!*

Grizzly's rough drunken voice startled them. "Hey, Yellow Beard, in the mornin' we gotta pull er traps 'n' pack 'em up. We'll be amovin' out today-after-tomorrow. We are gonna stay afloatin' 'cause we're 'hind time. We've been here way too long as it is."

"You have that right. Packing won't take all that long though," Yellow Beard observed. "All we have to pack is fur and whisky. We could leave in the morning."

"Nope … we can't leave till Ketchum and Geezer gets back. They're up the creek atrappin' and'er 'spose ta be back in the mornin'." As an afterthought Grizzly added. "With a lotta pelts."

Ketchum returned loaded with Beaver pelts and a buffalo hind quarter. He promptly cut the meat into jerky-sized pieces which he hung over a bed of smoldering pecan wood. The smell of the smoke curing the raw meat into jerky was mouth-watering.

~

Yellow Beard woke up early, five o'clock to be exact. He was raring and ready to float the Red River. He watched Eve-e whomp up a big batch of biscuits. She fried slices of sugar-cured ham and made a huge bowl of red-eye gravy.

Things got quiet while everyone filled their stomachs with Eve-e's savory breakfast. The eating wound down to the tune of spoons scraping empty plates. The sounds of straight chair legs scooting across the hard-pack clay floor announced that stomachs were full.

"My gut feelin's we oughta stay on fer awhile," Grizzly said. "I dreamt uv a fearful flood on Red River, and I got kilt. Yellow Beard's got ants in 'is pants ta travel, though."

"A man's dreams are powerful medicine," Yellow Beard volunteered. "We can stay on a while if you want."

"I spect that ever'one's ready ta get the show on the road, me too … I guess." Grizzly was hesitant.

With fare-ye-wells exchanged, they cut the dug-out canoes loose from their ties and cast out into Bois d'Arc Creek. The Grizzly trapping party was finally on their way to "Peecan Point."

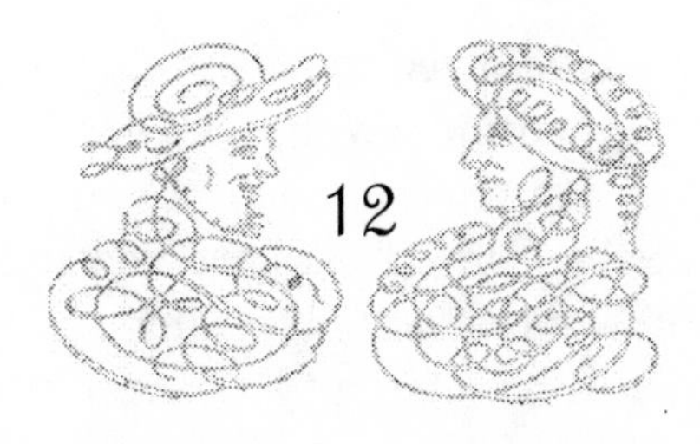

12

Christmas in New Orleans was a one-of-a-kind affair, made so by long-standing French and Spanish influence that mixed with the evolving customs of the United States and then was shaped and reshaped by Catholic and Protestant immigrants from all over the world.

The Christmas of 1824 was a time of great change, as far as celebrations went. Pierre and Christine were especially fond of the Christmas Eve candlelight service held at midnight at the Saint Louis Cathedral. It depicted Joseph's search for lodging before the birth of Jesus. Jacob's and Renee's performance in the sacred ceremony was impressive, and Christine was proud of them.

On Christmas day, Felipe and Terisa woke up at dawn to prepare for the Feast of the Nativity. Terisa baked breads and cakes before she made her special holiday plum pudding.

The Roman Catholic Church had chosen December 25th as the day for the feast, and Saint Louis Cathedral would hold their first feast. The Catholic Church replaced festivities honoring the birth of Mithra, the god of light, with festivities to commemorate the birth of Jesus ~ the Feast of the Nativity ~ whom the Bible calls the light of the world.

In that way, the Catholic Church accomplished two goals: They got rid of their paganish god of light festivities; yet they allowed the revelry of the feast.

Saint Louis Cathedral held three masses on Christmas Day. The mass held at dawn was the one Felipe and Terisa chose to attend. Felipe always liked getting up at the crack of dawn on Christmas day. Christine couldn't drag Pierre out of bed before noon on Christmas day. She put her foot down when it came to going to mass, so they attended the sunset service.

The French community was also feasting and celebrating. Their Christmas, called Noel, reached its peak Christmas Eve with a lavish midnight meal. Pierre, against Christine's wishes, went to the Noel feast, but he left long before midnight. The event turned into a boisterous affair because the wine flowed so freely. He felt it was inappropriate, for some reason, to get drunk on such a solemn occasion.

In many of the Spanish communities 'round about New Orleans, pagan celebrations like the "Urn of fate" were in full swing. Christine had always found them exciting and intriguing.

Christine had learned about Urn of Fate ceremonies while growing up in Mexico City and as a child had always wished to attend one. Her parents had taught her that these festivals were paganism in its rawest form and had refused her permission to attend one.

"You don't need to be around that kind of flamboyant public behavior," her Father insisted.

Christine begged Pierre. "Please, can we go down to Esplanade Avenue. They have an urn of fate there and I want to put our names into it?"

His answer was short. "No!"

"Why, no?"

"I've been to them before and I've seen what goes on there. Your name would get drawn out with someone else's name. Then my name would get drawn with someone else's name. Then where would we be? Do you really think we should take little Jacob and Abner down there among all that gambling? They'll be overindulging in drink; and God only knows what else."

Christmas time in New Orleans was not only a spectacular time for Christians and churches; children got caught up in the festivities as well. Christmas times they were achanging. New customs came and old ones went, while many customs got reworked to fit the times. The end result was Christmas became more and more a children's affair.

Sinter Klaas, a tall dignified religious figure riding a white horse through the air ~ as known by Pierre Lilly, who was from Holland ~ become known as a fat jolly old Saint for the children of the United States. Pierre Lilly found it hard to let go of the Sinter Klaas legend from his growing-up days in Holland.

The children's side of Christmas was the topic of discussion. The Lilly and Sanchez Children were products of the culture of the United States. Neither Pierre nor Felipe liked the paganism associated with Christmas; it was Christ's birthday; why couldn't it be left well enough alone?

"Pierre, are you and Christine going to keep telling the kids that Sinter Klaas is a tall dignified religious Saint that rides a white horse through the air?" Felipe asked.

"I don't know. Christine and I have talked about it. It sure seems like a lot of parents are telling their kids about this new Saint Nicholas fellow," Pierre said.

Christine picked her clipping up from the side table. "Have you read this wonderful little poem that came out in the *Troy Sentinel* last year on Christmas Eve?"

"Yes!" Terisa's eyes twinkled. "You're talking about *Twas the Night Before Christmas*. I wish I knew who wrote it. It's a wonderful poem!"

Here comes Christine's opinion, Pierre thought.

"I think the idea of a fat jolly old gentleman flying over housetops in a reindeer-drawn sleigh is much more appealing than a skinny old saint riding a white horse. I haven't been able to convince Pierre of that, though," Christine said.

~

Terisa and Christine had grown up influenced by the Spanish/Mexican culture. They had gone all out decorating their homes for the Christmas season, like their parents had.

Felipe Sanchez thought Terisa and Christine had gone to extremes. *We don't need a tree in the house and evergreen boughs and colored paper lanterns hanging everywhere to help us remember the birth of Jesus,* he thought.

Pierre Lilly, being of Irish descent, had grown up having a Christmas tree in the house at Christmas time. He was also familiar with the German tradition of decorating the tree with silver tinsel. Pierre accepted the tree in their parlor with the silver threads hanging from its branches. He believed, though, that it was unnecessary.

Not so with Felipe ~ "There will be no tree in my house," he declared to his wife.

Felipe and Pierre agreed that the *"Presebras,"* the replicas of the manger scene where Jesus was born, were sufficient in the way of decorations.

~

The reenactments that commemorated Mary's and Joseph's search for lodging were what the Sanchezes and Lillys liked to participate in most of all. From December 16 until Christmas Eve, they went on nightly *Posadas*. They would not miss a single one. Felipe and Terisa or Pierre and Christine would dress up as Mary and Joseph. Then friends and relatives would accompany them house to house. They carried candles and sang songs. Mary and Joseph knocked on doors and asked to stay. Each house refused them entry; but eventually a household invited them in to pray at their *presebra*. After they prayed, everyone danced and sang, then ate a large meal.

The children anxiously waited for their turn to have fun once everyone had sufficiently dined. The children tried to break clay or paper-mache *piñatas* filled with sweets and small gifts. *Piñatas* in the shape of donkeys, birds or other kinds of animals hung from a tree branch or other high place. The blindfolded children lined up and waited their turn with the long stick. The grown-ups stood around watching and clapping for their child to be successful in their attempt to break the *piñata*. The child whose turn had come took the long stick and gave the *piñata* his best whack. Eventually the *piñata* burst open and spewed its contents on the ground. The children dove in with squeals of delight. The goodies that had spilled out onto the ground vanished almost as fast as they had poured out.

Felipe, being the devout Catholic Christian that he was, made himself a New Year's resolution. He vowed with himself: *Next Year, I will ban from my family anything that remotely resembles pagan practices: the Urn of fate, piñatas, the thing about a jolly old fat man flying over houses in a sleigh drawn by reindeer. They all have to go! Everyone will call me a scrooge, but paganism has no place in my house.*

New Orleans, the Sanchezes, and the Lillys returned to the everyday swing of things after the festivities were over and the New Year came in.

"Right now, I'm so tired of all the festivities, but as soon as I can get rested up, I'll be ready for Mardi Gras," Christine Said.

"Yeah," Terisa agreed, "ain't New Orleans a ball!

~

Time seemed to fly after the New Year came in, and before anyone knew it, Jacob's birthday was upon them.

"Jacob will turn thirteen in a few days, and I haven't made any plans for his party," Christine agonized.

"I know, I know," Terisa said. "It's incredible how time flies. Felipe says, 'It seems only yesterday we moved here from Mexico City.' Renee's birthday has slipped up on me as well."

"Jacob Lilly is just like his daddy," Christine lamented. "Pierre is spoiling him rotten. Whatever Jacob wants, Jacob gets! It's not good for him, and I cannot convince Pierre he's ruining our son. What's a mother supposed to do?"

Christine asked Terisa that question ~ not really wanting her suggestions, but she would get them anyway.

Terisa seized her opportunity and lit in on Christine. "Felipe and I have talked about the problem you're having with Jacob being spoiled. Jacob is milking Pierre for every cent he can get. By the time he gets into college, you won't be able to afford him. Jacob is ruthless when it comes to getting what he wants. You and Pierre had better crack down on him now, while he's still young."

"Are you through now? My little Jacob is not ruthless!" Christine said. She couldn't stand Terisa's critical eye.

"Just one more thing. Everyone knows, except you and Pierre Lilly, that Jacob will bring you heartaches and many of them when he reaches college age," Terisa added.

"We know that. It's just that Pierre and I can't agree on what to do about it."

"I'm fixing to get to the real heart of the matter," Terisa said. "I'll give you two reasons that you'll have trouble with Jacob. Pierre is going to insist that Jacob become a lawyer when he enters college. I have you cornered now, and I'm going to tell you the main reason you'll have trouble with Jacob. You're always complaining: 'Jacob is just like his father.' Well, let me tell you … he is just like you! You love to party, and so does Jacob. He only thinks of college as a reason to party."

Christine knew it was true … *I do love to party. Jacob is just like me. Abner is just like Pierre, thank God; he adores his father and will do anything to please him.*

~

Felipe with Terisa's help raised Renee and Juan in the church, in the strictest Catholic manner; and they did not spoil them by letting them always have their way.

"Another thing that we have going for us is that we support each other's decisions fully when it comes to matters of discipline," Terisa told Felipe.

Pierre, without Christine's help, raised Jacob, and Christine, without Pierre's help, raised Abner. They seemed never to arrive at the same conclusion when it came to matters of discipline. As a result, discipline ranged from little to none. Pierre always had something for Jacob to do on Sundays. Abner always went to church with Christine and spent the day with Renee and Juan.

~

As the summer of 1830 came to a close and autumn began, Pierre Lilly and Jacob were more and more at each other's throat. Jacob would turn eighteen in October. What he wanted in life was to become a Field Captain for the Lilly Trading Company. Pierre wanted more than for Jacob to just be a laborer. What Pierre wanted for Jacob was that he would go to Miami University then on to law school and become a lawyer. Pierre wanted that more than anything else in the world, or so he thought.

Jacob had other thoughts. *I am not going to move to Oxford, Ohio, and leave my girlfriend, leave Annabelle.*

The day before he was to leave for college, Jacob stormed into Pierre's office.

"I will not leave here and go to Oxford. That Butler County is uninhabited backwoods. I would be cut off from everyone. I'll not go there!"

Pierre swiveled his chair away from his roll-top desk to face Jacob square on. "If you want to become a Field Captain for this company, you will do as I say. You have to give up your partying and show some interest in things around here, and get yourself an education."

Christine heard the ruckus between Jacob and Pierre and came from the kitchen.

"I will not give up partying. Annabelle loves to party, and I love Annabelle," Jacob returned. He had scarcely gotten the statement out of his mouth before Christine walked in.

"Party, party, party! That is all I ever hear around here anymore. That Annabelle is evil! You must break it off with her!" Christine's temper flared.

"I'll tell you how it is going to be, Jacob." Pierre had never laid the law down; but now he was, and Jacob listened. "If you refuse to go to Miami University, you will no longer work for the company, and in addition, your mother and I refuse to support yours and Annabelle's party habits. In plainer words ~ we will cut your money off!"

"Well, if that's the way it's going to be, Dad, I guess I might as well go to college." Jacob turned and stumbled out of his dad's study. *It's different with Dad this time. I might as well let em cool off; then he will come around.* Jacob headed down the street toward Annabelle's house.

"You know that Jacob is not going to apply himself. You're just going to throw away good money after bad!" Christine advised Pierre.

"He might; he just might apply himself. Two things that he cherishes are his job and our money," Pierre said, with hope in his voice. Pierre had hopes that Jacob would go to college and apply himself, but his thoughts were contrary to his hopes. *If I was his age, with that beautiful floozy hanging around my neck, I'd be just like him. I'd be wasting everything too!*

~

By the time the fall semester began, Jacob had long since given up that he could change his dad's mind. He moved into a dorm room at Miami University and began his studies. Thoughts of Annabelle took up most of his class time.

He soon found that wrestling and boxing were very indulging sports and helped him keep his mind off his other sport, his beloved Annabelle. Wrestling and Boxing took up most of his free time at the university. He practiced the techniques used in them. He walked around sparring everywhere he went. Jacob had not an inkling why. For some reason, though, he found himself being more captivated by the training than by the actual boxing or wrestling. *If I ever get to pursue a real job, the agility and the muscles will come in handy.*

Jacob became the star of the team. Midterm had come and gone, and he hadn't lost a single fight. He became known by his wrestling and boxing friends as "Jac the Ranter" because of the way he ranted and raved in the ring. No one got under their opponent's skin like Jac the Ranter!

By the end of Jacob's first year in Oxford, Ohio, Pierre and Christine Lilly knew they had thrown their money to the wind. His grades were deplorable.

Pierre and Christine invited Felipe and Terisa to their home to discuss the problem they had with Jacob. They had just about come to their row's end and felt that they had to talk to someone. *Whom else could we talk to that would be better than family,* Christine thought.

A gentle coastal sea breeze was blowing. It caressed the papery leaves of the gnarly magnolia trees that lined the Lilly courtyard. The branches waved and the leaves fluttered as they cast an ever-changing dappled shade onto their faces. They reclined in the cool evening shade and sipped iced tea. The silence was deafening, each of them waiting on the other to attack the touchy subject at hand.

"Well, I guess I might as well break the ice," Terisa volunteered.

Pierre's thoughts had his ears stopped up, and he didn't hear what he thought he had. "Yeah, bring me some ice, too." He said.

That was all it took to get Christine started. "Why don't you pay attention Pierre, You're not deaf.

"What a pleasant atmosphere in which to discuss a most unpleasant problem," she lamented. "'The Jacob problem,' that is what Pierre calls it." Christine cringed.

"We've had about all of Jacob that we can stomach," Pierre opened up. "Or so we think. Jacob is spending every penny he can beg from us to pay Annabelle's way back and forth from here to there." Pierre grimaced, and everyone could tell that grappling with the problem had worn on him.

"Felipe and I both concur," Teresa said. "The kid's a real botheration to you — isn't he? We wish there was something we could do." Terisa's sympathy was genuine.

"The only thing that our money has bought us, after a whole year of him going to college, is that Jacob has really become a good fighter. As if that will ever help him become a lawyer," Pierre complained.

"Well, it might. A lawyer needs to be a pretty good fighter when he gets in the courtroom." Felipe tried to take some of the edge off the conversation.

Christine swelled with pride. "Now, there's something that I can be proud off. After all, I am his mother, and I will find the good in Jacob. Jacob went a whole year having never lost a fight, neither boxing nor wrestling. That's something that no other student has ever accomplished."

"Well, he should have won every fight. Twenty-four hours a day, seven days a week, he either practiced his fighting or practiced his loving." Pierre displayed his infrequent wry humor, and everyone laughed.

After the laughter subsided, Christine remarked, "Well, it won't be long before school is out, and then Pierre and I are going to come up with a plan to whip Jacob into line before the summer is over."

"If he was my kid, thank God he isn't, I'd tell him to shape up or I'd kick him out of the family," Felipe said.

"Hmm." That's all Pierre said.

~

The long-awaited day, of June 7, 1831, finally came for Jacob. He had made arrangements for Annabelle to be there when he got out of school, so they could ride back to New Orleans together. Jacob chanted the old favorite school's-out song. "School is out! School is out! The teacher has turned her mules out!"

Jacob's thoughts were running wild. *Oh, we're going to spend the whole summer, the glorious fun-filled days of summer, having fun together*. In their excitement they hardly felt the bumps being transmitted to them from the stiff spring buggy. Jacob drove the horse as fast as it could pull the buggy over the chug-hole-filled road toward New Orleans. They both thought, *How sweet and wonderful it will be!* They neither thought, *How terrible it will be when one of us dumps the other one!*

~

Pierre and Christine put up with Jacob's and Annabelle's foolishness all summer long. August came, and the new school year was approaching fast. It was after many discussions about the subject that they came to an agreement. They had had all that they were going to tolerate from Jacob. Pierre and Christine devised a plan whereby they would end the problem. *Guaranteed!* they thought.

Pierre summoned Jacob, sending him a note by Abner, to make his presence known in his study at ten o'clock the next morning.

Jacob felt the hammer about to drop, as he opened the door and stepped across the threshold into his dad's study. *Mother is here, too! Why are they both here?* he wondered. Jacob came into the study with his head hung low.

"You better have a seat, Son," his mother told him.

His heart raced.

"Jacob, your mother and I concur," Pierre stated. "We are not paying another cent for the education that you are not receiving!"

Jacob glanced toward his mother. She was nodding her head in agreement. Jacob dropped his eyes back to the floor.

Pierre continued. He was firm and to the point. "The company has a job for you."

Jacob's thoughts trailed off. *Ah, easy money*, he thought.

"Listen to me … Jacob! The St. Louis-Santa Fe Trading Company has a bill of goods for you to deliver to our customer on the Grand River. You will make the delivery, then you will collect a sum of five thousand dollars for those goods and return to New Orleans pronto!"

Jacob thought, Or ... *go to college and learn something*. He waited for Pierre's "Or." Pierre's "Or" never came.

The three of them sat in silence. Pierre and Christine waited for Jacob's answer, he waited for their "Or."

After an eternity of silence ~ it seemed to Jacob ~ he asked. "Or?"

"There isn't an or ~ as in, or go to college ~ to it. You either take the job ~ or ~ you are on your own. Those are your only choices!"

Pierre looked straight into his son's eyes with a wry scowl on his face and fired the needle-sharp dart that cut straight through Jacob's heart. "Jacob, you have disgraced the name Lilly."

"But … D-a-d," Jacob whined.

"No buts. You have a few days to think it over. By the way … you will not be paid until you successfully complete the job." Pierre folded his hands on his desk. "That's it, take it or leave it. You are dismissed."

Jacob left Pierre's study in a state of delirium. He swabbed at the tears in his eyes with balled up fists. *I must find Annabelle*! That thought rolled over and over in his mind. *I must find Annabelle ~ I must find Annabelle*. Momentarily he pushed Annabelle to the back of his mind. There she was again, in the front of his mind. *I must find Annabelle and tell her about the dire strait that I am in!*

For a while now, Jacob had imagined that Renee had feelings for Annabelle, but he couldn't put his finger on it; somehow, Renee was different when Annabelle was in their presence.

I am letting my imagination run away with me. I'm imagining more than there really is to it. Even if Renee is in love with Annabelle, it will do him no good. Annabelle loves me.

Annabelle had realized that she had enjoyed about all the luxuries Jacob's mother and father were willing to hand out. She had had her eyes set on Renee Sanchez, Jacob's cousin, for some time now.

~

Ah, there you are. What is Annabelle doing at Renee's house? Jacob ducked behind a hedge to keep them from seeing him. *Renee and Annabelle are busy enjoying a flirtatious escapade. Right out on the front porch! Right there in the porch swing, for all the world and me to see! It is very apparent that she's enjoying it much more than Renee ... I see!* Jacob saw ~ but his sight was beginning to blur. He clenched his eyelids shut. He attempted futilely to hold back the swelling tears. During the brief moment between blurry vision and clenched eyelids ~ Jacob saw more than he had ever imagined.

Jacob's thoughts were beginning to blur, except for the thought of running. He ran.

He churned his arms and pumped his legs until his mouth gaped open. His brain wanted more air, but his lungs refused and a piercing pain stabbed his side. He ran until the taste of his hot salty tears made him want to vomit. He ran until his understanding cleared. He didn't think his eyes would ever be free of tears. The thought returned of his Annabelle in the arms of Renee. That thought sent his heart plunging ~

down, down, down. A lump as big as a hen egg hung in his Adam's apple. Jacob suddenly remembered when his mother took him to France, after he graduated from Twelve. He rode "The Aerial Walk," a French rollercoaster. *The feeling that it gave me when it plunged off its loftiest pinnacle, that's how I feel! In my wildest imagination would I have ever suspected a woman could give me that kind of feeling!*

That thought made up Jacob's mind. *I will just disappear without telling Annabelle anything. She will just have to find out from Renee.*

~

Jacob burst into Pierre's study and announced that he would take the job. Pierre's fiery dart, "Jacob, you have disgraced the name, Lilly," crystallized in his mind, when he saw Pierre. Jacob then left politely, whispering under his breath: "Me, disgrace the Lilly name. Well, if that is the way that you and Mother feel about it, I'll just see what I can do about that." He hurried up the spiral staircase to his bedroom and lay down across his bed. He planned what he could do about that.

Pierre called for Christine to come to his study: "Guess what, honey? Jacob just told me he accepted the job."

"That's wonderful. Maybe by the time he gets back from Cantonment Gibson, Annabelle will have dumped him for someone else!" Christine said that in a wishful thinking sort of way, not knowing Annabelle had already dumped Jacob for someone else and that someone else was Renee.

Jacob came down from his room briefly and asked Pierre how soon he could depart.

"The trunks are packed and the bill of lading is made out. They're in our warehouse on the wharf. All you have to do is book round-trip passage on a steamer bound for Cantonment Gibson. I suggest you do that first thing in the morning."

Pierre was extremely business-like with his instructions. "The recipient of the goods is on the bill of lading." He looked up from his desk, then held out his hand with an envelope in it. "Here, I'll advance you money for a round-trip ticket."

Jacob took the envelope. "Where in the world is Cantonment Gibson?"

"About three miles up the Grand River from its junction with the Arkansas River. Three rivers converge together there, at almost the same place. The Arkansas River veers off toward the left. The Verdigris is the river in the center, and the Grand River is the one on the right. Take the Grand River and go about three miles. You can't miss Cantonment Gibson. It is the busiest place on the America's southwestern frontier right now. A new military post is under construction there."

With Jacob's curiosity satisfied, he returned to his room and made his plans. *In the morning I'll leave, before Mother and Daddy get up, and they'll never see me again! As far as Annabelle goes, I never want to see her again either. As long as I live ... that is, if I do live*!

13

It was early spring by the time the Grizzly Trapping Party reached the Kiomitchie Red River. *We spent way too much time visiting with the Donnegans, or we could have been here before now*, Yellow Beard thought.

"If I were ta say Kiomitchie in English, jest how'd I say it?" Grizzly asked.

"It's about the same, except you would replace the o with an a, leave out the t and leave the e off the end. It means Little Red River.

"Don't go givin' me all them letters ta deal with." Grizzly scowled.

"Uh, say it more like Ki-me-she then."

We don't need another Red River to deal with, Grizzly thought. From then on he called the Kiomitchie Red River the Kiamichi River.

He knew how anxious Yellow Beard was to get to St. Louis. So Grizzly refrained from telling him they would be camping a couple of days there. Now that they had entered the mouth of the Kiomitchie, Grizzly knew he had to tell Yellow Beard. He just couldn't bring himself to tell him, though, and see the disgust in his face.

Grizzly was aware of the facts ~ the Kiomitchie River headed in the mountains and was prone to dumping huge amounts of water quickly into Red River from mountain thunder storms. If the clouds gathering in the north had their way, the Kiomitchie River would be an accident waiting for a place to happen before they were on their way again.

Grizzly had selected a stand of big pecan trees on the west bank for their campsite. The river made a big bend there, and Grizzly called the place Kiamichi bend.

Yellow Beard climbed to the top of the shallow bluff that rose from the river to the pecan trees. He found Grizzly, Ketchum, and Jinx striking a permanent camp.

"What in the world is going on here? We're not fixing to stay on here awhile, are we?" Yellow Beard demanded.

"I'm awantin' ta catch Stiller Johnson and get Jinx sum more whisky!" Grizzly answered. He knew that was a cover up. It was the first thing that popped into his mind, though.

"You know that's a lie. You're wanting to get drunk and laze around here, you old coot," Yellow Beard shot back. *I have him cornered.*

"I don't want to get drunk. I 'spect I got my reasons, though." Grizzly said. "Man, you got an attitude like uh alligator. Yer all mouth and no ears!"

"I got ears all right. It's just what they're hearing ain't making sense." Yellow Beard decided Grizzly was about to get him riled.

"I 'spect I'll just cum outright and tell ya." Grizzly knew Yellow Beard had an explanation coming.

"I wish somebody would." Yellow Beard was getting tired of playing Grizzly's game.

"You wuz uh cooin' ta Annalee. Just like uh 'gator ya had yer mouth open and didn't hear uh word I said about the dream I dreamt. Did ya?"

"No … Yeah." Yellow Beard had suddenly remembered. "I guess I did hear ya."

"Which is it … did ya or didn't ya hear me?"

"I heard you all right. Don't you remember me telling you that your dreams are powerful medicine and that we could stay on at the Donnegans if you wanted to? You must be the one with the alligator attitude!" Yellow Beard bristled.

"Anyways, I dreamt that a big storm cum on the upper Kiamichi and somehow I was kilt in the flood. I ain't aleavin' here 'til, if there is a storm, it passes us over." Grizzly was serious.

"Grizzly, you mean to tell me that you're going to stay here and wait for 'if there is a storm,' before we go on? Just because you're afraid of your dreams don't give you the right to hold us all up. I'll give it two days; then if there's not a storm, I'm moving on." Yellow Beard felt put out with having to wait. "Your dreams are powerful medicine but not when you are afraid of them."

Dark settled in. Jinx kindled the fire and sat down across from Grizzly. There would be no moon tonight. The campfire would provide the landscape's only light. Firelight flickering against Grizzly's face revealed the only visible signs of his worries. The skin above his eyebrows wrinkled, and the muscles in his cheeks twitched every once in a while.

Fireflies beckoned with pulsating taillights in hopes that they would attract a mate. No one uttered a word. Jinx yawned, and everyone yawned. Soon everyone was asleep except Grizzly. It was pitch dark, but he watched for lightning. Deafening silence filled the air, but he listened for thunder. *All the thunder I can hear is them asnorin' like thunder. The only lightning I can see is them lightning bugs.* His thoughts made him chuckle. At some point his chuckles turned to snores.

~

Daybreak brought heavy damp air. The winds spent the day building clouds in the north which, as the day progressed, grew into an ugly mass. They turned from a beautiful blue to a blue black, then completely black and finally as night approached, blackish green.

"We arn't aleavin' here until that blue or black or green bank in the north passes us over," Grizzly commanded.

"Whatever color it is, I 'spect it's the ugliest thang I ever saw," Jinx said.

When night came again, there was plenty of lightning and thunder for Grizzly to watch and listen to. The clouds rolled across the lower Kiomitchie in wave after wave, brought about by a fresh cold Norther.

There was no rain. All the rain-filled clouds split their seams and dumped their load on the upper Kiomitchie River. Severe thunderstorms and drenching downpouring rain plagued the Kiomitchie Mountains all night long. There had not been a drop of rain all night, though, on Grizzly's camp.

~

The next morning Grizzly was the first up, and he awoke grinning from ear to ear. Yellow Beard roused shortly and Grizzly told him, "I 'spect she's past us. That's the one I wuz adreamin' about, 'n' she didn't do me in … hallelujahr!"

They packed up. When they got into the boats to head toward Red River, Jinx noticed small chunks of foam and un-lodged sticks floating by.

"We better hold up!" Jinx warned. "The Kiamichi's gettin' a rise on!"

"Not you too, Jinx." Yellow Beard declared.

"'Spect we're gonna go ta St. Louie boys … whoopee! I arn't afeared uh floodin'. It's the storms that I'm afeard uv." Grizzly sounded brave now, but it would not be for long.

The Kiomitchie River gushed toward Red River, a violent torrent. Within a matter of minutes she forced herself upon the calm Red River.

Grizzly was in the bow and Yellow Beard was in the stern of the lead dugout. Ketchum, Jinx, and Geezer followed in the trailing dugout, Ketchum in the bow and Geezer in the stern. Jinx sat flat down in the middle and nursed on his jug.

There was a sandbar at the mouth of the Kiomitchie River that had her blocked from making a direct hit on Red River. The sandbar took the two rivers in a parallel course for more than a mile before it let them join each other. One will never know whether the sandbar was nature's way of protecting Red River from Kiomitchie's violent attacks or just her way of letting the two rivers get used to each other. The Kiomitchie, in all her gusto, ate at the sand bar that had her cut off from Red River. The boiling sand, the giant swirls of turbulent water, and the huge round sinkholes vehemently clawed at the dugouts.

The lead dugout dove into one of the huge round sinkholes. The bow plunged down, and the stern bucked up. Then the opposite happened, and they bucked out the other side of the sinkhole. Just as the stern of the dugout cleared the sinkhole, it entered a giant swirl. The force of the opposing currents was too much for the craft. The dugout jerked sideways to the flow of the current. Their forward progress stopped for too long. Grizzly rose to his hunkers to look back at the trailing dugout. It was just coming out of the same wild ride through the sinkhole. The bow shot into the air as the boat bucked out of the sinkhole. Then it crashed down and into Grizzly's dugout and rammed a gaping-hole in its side. The unexpected collision stood Grizzly to his feet ~ rather than set him down in the bottom of the dugout. He lost his balance and sprawled head over heels into the frothing soupy water. He flounced a couple of times, only to holler that he couldn't swim. Ketchum dove headfirst into the side of Grizzly's dugout and fell into the roily river. Red River's grinding swirling waters sucked Ketchum under right in front of their eyes. He never surfaced again.

Jinx, in his stupor, remained slumped in the belly of the dugout with Geezer. Geezer's face was white as snow, as were his knuckles from holding onto the side of the dugout. Yellow Beard had somehow managed to grab hold of their dugout. He abandoned his sinking boat and crawled over into theirs. He shucked his buckskins in preparation to try and save the two victims.

"Yellow Beard, what da ya thank yer adoin'?" Jinx hollered.

"I ha-have got t-ta …!"

"No … no!" Jinx screamed over the roar of the rushing water. "Red River's got'um now! You can't take back what Red's got. If ya try, Red'll get you, too" Jinx grabbed Yellow Beard's arm. "Let 'em go, let 'em go … there ain't nothin we can do. The river swallowed both uv 'em. Now, she'll pass 'em through her bowels to meet their maker!"

Yellow Beard lay there, breathing heavily. The color returned to his face.

"The river'll spit 'em out when she gets through with 'em." Geezer hung his head. "Ya'll can paddle me ta shore. I'm gonna take the land trail from here to St. Louis.

They all three struck camp and waited for the river to settle down.

"I'll stay with ya tonight, and ya'll decide what yer gonna do," Geezer offered.

"What ya'll 'spose we aughta do 'bout a proper burial? We couldn't ever find any bodies ta give a proper burial to. The turtles'll have their bones picked clean as a whistle. I ain't ahuntin' dem bones!" Jinx shivered.

"One time before I could understand white man talk I heard a man that called himself a preacher say something over some dead bodies before they buried them. I guess I could say something for them," Yellow Beard suggested.

They looked toward the setting sun, bowed their heads, and shut their eyes.

"God, help 'em …! Yellow Beard paused ~ he couldn't think of the word.

"Augh Men!" Jinx said.

They all felt better knowing they had done all they knew how to do.

"Geezer, I'm going to take this tried and true boat and myself to St. Louie," Yellow Beard sternly proclaimed. "Anyone that wants to join me, they can."

"Wahl, I'm agoin' with ya. I gotta make it ta Peecan Point." Jinx still had the jug he had weathered the disaster with under his arm, but it was almost empty. "This 'citement calls fer ol' Jinx ta bust out his last jug uh whisky."

"Oh no ya don't. I'm in charge now, and there won't be any more indulging. At least not till we get ta Peecan Point … ya hear!" Yellow Beard seized command.

Jinx heard but thought, *What's ta keep me frum slippin' a sip once en uh while.* He swelled up like a big toad frog.

That's fine, Yellow Beard thought. *The drunk skunk wasn't much to talk to anyway. Jinx in command might be our doom.* By Yellow Beard's calculations Jinx caused the death of Grizzly and Ketchum.

They were dead because of his drunkenness. If he wasn't drunk and in such a hurry to get to Pecan Point, he would have been more persistent in warning them about waiting the flood out.

Yellow Beard made an oath with himself and with Jinx. "Only because you saved my life, Jinx, am I willing to keep company with you till we get to St. Louie. Furthermore, if the two of us ever get there, you and me are parting company!"

~

In a few days Jinx sobered up and for the first time in a long time, Yellow Beard thought, *Jinx might not be half bad.*

Immediately after the Red River catastrophe, Yellow Beard's thinking ~ was there would be no more trapping. They were getting themselves to St. Louis as fast as possible.

However, Jinx set traps every night after they struck camp, and he caught a remarkable amount of beavers. Yellow Beard considered this and Jinx's change in attitude. He decided if Jinx would stay sober he might not be in such a hurry to part company with him. In the days to come, Jinx talked less and less about getting drunk and more and more about Bill and Sam Cooper. Jinx and Yellow Beard were getting to be good friends. *He's the best friend I ever had when he's sober and the worst that I've ever had when he's drunk*, Yellow Beard decided.

~

They had made good time; it had only been a couple of days since they left Kiomitchie River. Jinx woke Yellow Beard from a doze off when he began singing his Pecan Point song. Yellow Beard quickly learned the lyrics and joined right in.

"Paccawn Point! Paccawn Point! Thar she be, awaitin' me."

"None too soon cause my throat's dry 'n' my spirits er low."

"Paccawn Point! Paccawn Point! Thar she be, awaitin' me."

Pecan Point was a big chunk of land within a loop of Red River. It was a peninsula that had formed when Pecan Bayou cut the land off by slicing across the base of the peninsula.

When Jinx had last visited Pecan Point, there were five Indian traders and twelve families living there. Jacob Black had acquired the land within the loop for his own private use. The individual traders who had always been there were no longer welcome. Black controlled the trading at Pecan Point; from staple goods to hardware, he had it all. If whisky was what the customer wanted, he had that, too; but it would be Donnegan or Stiller Johnson whisky.

When Jinx and Yellow Beard arrived there in 1825, they found that

Pecan Point was no longer an exciting place of hustle and bustle. Jinx hid his disappointment well. He didn't live for hustle and bustle. What he lived for was the whisky, and it still flowed like water. To Yellow Beard's surprise, though, Jinx hadn't touched a drop ~ yet.

~

"The best way, and the fastest way, ta go ta St. Louie is ta cut across land from here. There's uh lot of obstacles down the Red River the way Grizzly had planned on going," Jacob Black informed Yellow Beard. "If you go down the Red River, you'll have to portage around the black rock bar, because there hasn't been enough rain ta keep the river up. Then you'll hit the Great Raft, as Henry Shreve calls it. It's nothing more than a gigantic logjam. She stretches maybe a hundred miles. She starts just below the mouth of Twelve Mile Bayou. You have to portage around her; there ain't any other way."

"Just how would I go if I went across land?" Yellow Beard asked.

Jacob Black squatted down on Red River's white grainy sand and picked up a stick and sharpened a point on it with his knife. He swirled the stick around in the sand and made a starting point. "From here." He drew a line northward. "You cross Red River." He slashed a line in the sand to indicate a river. Then he extended his northward line across it. "Now you're in Miller County of the Arkansaw*Territory." He stood up and straightened his back. He tossed the stick aside and described the remainder of the trip.

"Cut a dew north heading, then the first big river you come to will be the Little River."

Jacob Black took time out from his directions giving to have a big laugh. Yellow Beard didn't catch on.

"Get it? The big river is the Little River."

Yellow Beard kept a solemn look on his face as if he thought the joke wasn't funny.

"Anyway, keep acuttin' dew north ~ you'll cross the Quachita Mountains ~ then you'll come to a big river. She will be the Arkansaw. She's a lot bigger than the Little River."

"Belle Point is in a ten-mile-wide and ten-mile-deep bend of the Arkansaw River. So, if you have kept a good dew-north heading, you should hit somewhere in the bend of the Arkansaw River. You should hit pretty close ta Belle Point. When you hit the Arkansaw River, if her water is aflowin' north you should turn and go downstream. If she is

*Named after the French interpretation of a Quapaw Indian word "Acansa," meaning "Downstream place." It is now spelled Arkansas.

aflowin' south, turn and go upstream. That'll carry you directly to Belle Point. A few days there will heal your weary traveling bones.

"When you leave Belle Point hang more northeast. There is a perty good trail. It'll be several days of hard going, but you'll finally get to the Missouri River. Cut into her and follow her current. She'll take ya right to St. Louis. You might be so lucky as to pitch in with a keelboat and hitch a ride to St. Louis. If you want to go across land, I'll swap you some mules for your dugout and throw in some supplies to replace those you lost on the Kiamichi."

Jacob Black provided Yellow Beard and Jinx with meager supplies, enough to get them to St. Louis. There they planned to sign up with a trading and fur company. Yellow Beard was grateful and promised Jacob Black, "If I ever get back here to Paccawn Point, I'll repay you. Your kindness and my debt to you will forever be on my mind until you are repaid."

~

Yellow Beard and Jinx left Pecan Point to follow the map Jacob Black had scratched in the sand.

"Ya 'member the map?" Jinx asked.

"Sure I do. Jacob Black scratched it in the sands of my brain," Yellow Beard assured him.

Jinx had never mentioned whisky nor drinking in any manner while they were at Pecan Point or since they had left. Once he had sobered up after the Kiomitchie flood, he was a different man.

Yellow Beard made an assumption: *That the prolonged abstinence from whisky, albeit involuntary, broke Jinx's will to get drunk.* Not so!

The overland trip was long and difficult. During the full moons they traveled day and night, aided by the light of the moon. Despite the difficulty of travel they were able to make St. Louis after four moons, thanks to Black's excellent directions.

~

Yellow Beard and Jinx walked along the stone wharf on the mighty Mississippi River in St. Louis. The steamboats' being loaded and unloaded intrigued Yellow Beard.

The throngs of travelers ~ in their fancy attire and their bustling activity ~ amazed him.

Jinx, unbeknownst to Yellow Beard, was also admiring the many saloons and brothels that lined the wharf.

Yellow Beard pointed toward a motley group. "That there looks like a trapping party. Let's go ask them about the rendezvous." When he turned to look at Jinx, Jinx had disappeared. He had a sneaky feeling that Jinx was in one of the saloons. He felt compelled to keep peeking behind every swinging door he came upon. *I must find Jinx*, he thought. *Or must I?* Yellow Beard's apprehensions tugged at him. He knew his strange appearance, his yellowish-red hair and beard, his piercing cobalt eyes and dark bronze skin, caused stares everywhere he went.

Yellow Beard remembered stories told around nighttime campfires. They told about what went on behind swinging doors in St. Louie. *One more door ... I'll look behind one more door. Then I'll forget the whisky-mongering loser.* He shuddered at his thought. He stood underneath the sign, that, unbeknownst to him, read Last Chance Saloon. He gawked into the smoke-filled den as anxious and thirsty patrons brushed him aside to enter.

"Thar ya be, Jinx!" Yellow Beard said aloud to himself. Jinx had a plump woman wound under his arm, and he waved a half-empty bottle of whisky toward a long spiral staircase. Yellow Beard heard Jinx's gravely bullfrog voice. "Cum on, honey." He coaxed her toward the stairs.

Yellow Beard realized he didn't feel any of the cravings Jinx displayed. *It is horrific what a whisky-loving codger can do to beautiful girls,* he thought. The thought of Jinx with his beautiful Annalee flashed before his eyes ~ he saw Jinx forcing her up the stairs ~ then his heart felt disgust. *If Jinx ever bothers my Annalee, I will kill him!* He shook his head trying to dismiss the ugly cobweb-like thoughts from his mind, but they persisted.

Yellow Beard found Jinx's actions so repulsive, he stepped inside the saloon and hollered at Jinx.

"Uh, you … inx! You ha-ha-have, pu-pu-pulled, one t-ta … uh one too many drunks," Yellow Beard stammered. After he finally got that said, he stumbled away from the Last Chance Saloon. He wandered along the wharf trying to locate the scraggly group of trappers he'd seen earlier.

Yellow Beard waited around for a few days and looked for his father. He soon learned that all the trappers who were worth their salt ~ of whom he knew his father was one ~ were up in the mountains trapping.

William H. Ashley, Yellow Beard learned, had back in 1822 advertised for a hundred young men to ascend the Missouri River to its source. They were to accept employment for one, two, or three years. He further learned that Ashley was in the Rocky Mountains and would not return to St. Louis until after the rendezvous he had helped organize took place. That rendezvous would be held around the first of July, 1825, on Henry's Fork of the Green River. *That is where Father is likely to be*, he decided.

He made up his mind: He wanted to trap for William Ashley, so in the early morning hours he pulled out, headed to the rendezvous without Jinx.

Knowing Jinx's inclination to drink, Yellow Beard figured he'd better hurry. *No one in their right mind will hire Jinx, and he's apt to keep Ashley from wanting to hire me. I'll get to the rendezvous before it breaks up, and I'll hire myself to Ashley.* Yellow Beard, in his mind's eye, had no choice.

~

Yellow Beard made good progress. He followed the Missouri River for what seemed like a thousand miles, and entered the mouth of the Yellowstone River. He knew he couldn't be far from the Green River. He figured the rendezvous would last at least a couple of weeks. For the first time since he left Pecan Point, he knew he was going to arrive at the rendezvous before it was over. What he had not known nor had he planned on was that William Ashley would leave early. Ashley had left the rendezvous days earlier ~ only two bends of the Yellowstone River lay between Yellow Beard and William Ashley. They were on a collision course. Destiny or fate, whichever or both, they were about to meet on the Yellowstone River.

~

The first rendezvous had gotten underway as planned. It was proving a huge success. Ashley had departed early with nearly eighty-eight hundred pounds of beaver pelts he had obtained at two to three dollars a pound. Jedediah Smith accompanied him, and by July 7, 1825, they had reached the navigable waters of the Yellowstone River. There they rested for a short time before heading down the Yellowstone toward the Missouri River, bound for St. Louis with their bounty.

~

Yellow Beard impressed Ashley with his life's story. He told him about his father and grandfather from New Orleans and how he had come about his wiry yellowish red hair and beard. He told him how he had learned to speak French and Spanish from Taovaya half-breed children at San Teodoro. He explained how he had studied hard to polish his "white-man talk" into something far better than most white men could speak. Ashley listened intently to how Ketox Runner had taught Yellow Beard all about nature's medicines. Yellow Beard really spread it on thick. Ashley loved a good storyteller, but none of that really mattered. What really got his attention was the number of beavers Yellow Beard had caught since he left St. Louis. Ashley hired Yellow Beard on the spot and told him he could find his trappers at the Rendezvous if he hurried. He then gave Yellow Beard directions how to go to Henry's Fork on the Green River. Ashley scribbled on a piece of parchment from his field book and handed it to Yellow Beard.

"Give this to Thomas Fitzpatrick," Ashley said. "It says," 'Yellow Beard is my trapper. Jinx is his friend. I hired 'em both.'

"Jinx! Wa-wa-waugh ... I ain't got uh Jinx with m-m-me!" Yellow Beard couldn't find the words.

"You do now. Jinx, come on out." Jinx showed his face, and Ashley shoved him at Yellow Beard. "If you wanta trap for me, you gotta to take Jinx with you."

How in thunder 'd Jinx beat me here? I have a zillion questions. I will reserve them for Jinx, though. They'll have to wait for now, Yellow Beard decided.

~

Yellow Beard and Jinx were extremely grateful for the jobs Ashley had given them. *I guess we'll hang together; we're both in dire straits,* Yellow Beard thought. The meager provisions Jacob Black had so graciously provided them had played out. Their clothes, rag tag and filthy, had served their purpose. All their hardware, except for their worn-out guns, had been eaten by Red River in the wreck at the mouth of Kiomitchie. Now, Yellow Beard felt good about his situation for the first time ever. He owned new clothes, new beaver traps, and a new gun. *I got all the trimmings it takes to be a mountain man.*

Yellow Beard felt certain he could find his father now. He assessed the information he knew. *His name is Bill Cooper. He loves trapping. He will recognize the gold pendant that he gave Dancing Waters to give to me.*

He knew that Jinx and he had to trap hard. *We owe our soul to William Ashley. Come next rendezvous, our bill will come due.*

~

For the next six years, until fate would take him back to Red River, Yellow Beard roamed the Rocky Mountains, searched for his father, and trapped for the soft gold of the Rockies.

Jinx only lasted one year. He became resigned to the fact he was getting too old to take the Rocky Mountain winters any more.

"I'm agonna go back ta Bois d' Arc Creek. I'm agonna go back ta Red River 'n' to the Donnegans' whisky," Jinx announced.

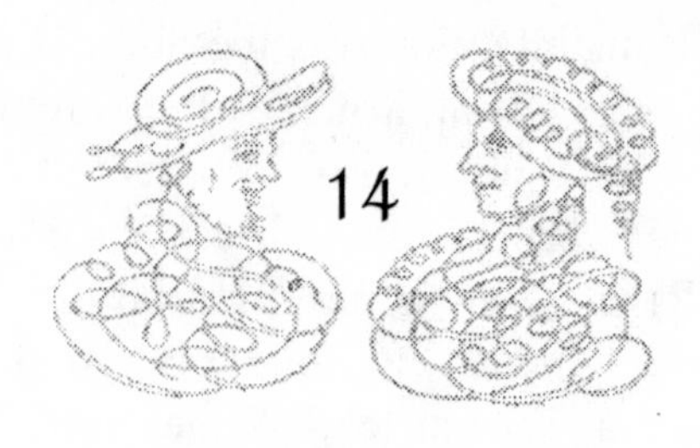

14

Jacob was awake all night. Around four o'clock in the morning he got dressed and slipped down the stairs. After he opened the front door he turned to capture one last glimpse of his childhood home. He looked at his goose-down bed. Indelibly, he wrote the memory of its fluffy softness in his mind. He knew he might never sleep there again. He felt some kind of inkling, but he couldn't put a finger on what it was. *It's not fear. It isn't elation or regret. Maybe crying has washed out all my feelings*, he thought. Then he thought about Annabelle and knew he felt lonely, he was by himself. *Without Mother and Daddy and without Annabelle ... I have no one.*

The night had been a typical hot and sultry August one. Daylight was only a couple of hours away, and the air was still unbearably warm. There was no reason to shiver, but shiver he did. He walked briskly toward his daddy's warehouse. *I have to hurry if I want to be out of here before Daddy gets here.* When he opened the warehouse door, there in front of it sat several wooden crates loaded onto steel-wheeled flatbed cargo carts.

Each crate had a label. Cantonment Gibson
Grand River, Indian Territory
Attention: Col. Matthew Arbuckle

He hurriedly pulled them down the wharf to the steamboat O'Hara. She was back in New Orleans after taking a cargo of goods, recruits, and Cherokee emigrants to Belle Point on the Arkansas River. Now she was ready to make a trip to Cantonment Gibson. Jacob paid his fare and checked his cargo with the loadmaster and boarded the O'Hara.

Every time Jacob heard the mournful sound of the steam whistle cut through the eerie darkness of the early morning dawn, loneliness tugged at his heart. The whistle sounded so final. It spurred his thoughts. *Oh, my beautiful Annabelle, why did you abandon me?* He felt her glimmering eyes looking into his. He felt her bouncy black hair brush against his cheek. That dreadful morning of August 18, 1831, he would never forget.

For the next several days Jacob thought about nothing but his future. Every waking moment he planned and schemed. Things had finally come together; he had it all figured out; he had a plan formulated in his mind. *I will change my name and abscond with Daddy's money. I will run away to the mountains and become a trapper. I never want to see Annabelle nor Daddy again, for the rest of my life. Mother ... I don't know.*

The only thing he knew for sure at this point was that he was not going by the name of Lilly.

Naturally, Jacob liked the name of Jac the Ranter. Everyone had called him that in college, but he thought it not a fitting name for a trapper. He thought Colter sounded like a good mountain-man name. He also liked Barlow and Buck.

Montoya, that sounds like a good name for a trapper. Then he remembered that Montoya was Annabelle's last name, so he ruled it out real quick. He wanted to cut all ties with Annabelle. He settled for just plain Jac, like his college name. He said the name Jac over and over, putting it with all the other names he had thought of.

"Jac Barlow, naugh. Jac Buck, naugh, definitely not. Jac Montoya, not bad. Jac Colter ... ah, that's it!" *Yes! Jac Colter sounds like a trapper's name. I'm going to become a mountain man and from here on out I am Jac Colter*!

~

Jac felt a tap on his shoulder and heard a jovial voice ask him, "Talkin' ta yer'sef are ya, Jac. Ya need a friend?"

"Unh huh!" Jac blushed at the thought that he had been talking out loud to himself. He had answered the man before he even knew who had addressed him. He turned about and saw a withy sort of man with a plain beardless face and dressed in overalls.

"Ugh then, in that case I'm yer man. I lost all uh my family ta the Injuns. I'm uh gonna go ta Cantonment Gibson and start all over. The name's Ben ... Ben Gay. I didn't rightly get yer name?"

"I'm pleased to make your acquaintance, Mr. Gay. I'm Jac Colter, and I lost all my family, also. I am enroute to Cantonment Gibson, as well."

Ben and Jac sat silently as if they were sizing each other up. Jac had his doubts about Ben Gay. There was something about him that Jac couldn't put his finger on. He could tell Ben was ignorant, just listening to him talk, but that his intentions seemed most honorable.

Jac had reserved feelings about telling Ben Gay anything about his past or anyone else for that matter.

"Ya go by Jac or Colter?" Ben broke the silence first.

Jac mulled over his choice for a second. "Jac." *Somehow Colter seemed too brazen.*

Neither man spoke for a long moment.

"Do you know a Col. Matthew Arbuckle, Mr. Gay?" Jac asked.

"I've heerd uv 'im; he wuz at Belle Point in March uv 1822 when I wuz there. He wuz there in twenty-three and twenty-four too, but I don't know what happened to 'im after that. He's uh 'structin' uh new Fort at the site uv Cantonment Gibson. Did'ja know that?"

Jac Colter gleaned all the information he could from Ben Gay. Then he politely dismissed himself. "I need to go tend to some book-work." What he really wanted to do was to think about his future. Jac knew that when Pierre discovered he was not returning with the money, he would hire the meanest-orneriest bounty hunter in New Orleans to track him down. *The last thing I want to happen is for a bounty hunter to find out that a Jac Colter delivered the Lilly Company's shipment.* He mulled everything over in his mind and decided that when he got to Cantonment Gibson he would use his real name.

~

Immediately after Jac arrived at Cantonment Gibson he made his way to Col. Arbuckle's office. He knocked on his door and announced, "Sir, I'm Jacob Lilly, and I'm here with your shipment."

"Whom from? May I ask, Sir Lilly?"

"May I come in, sir?" Jac asked. "The Lilly Company, sir. The shipment's from my daddy, Pierre Lilly."

"Spit your quid out first. Then take your own chances about coming in."

How did he know I had a chaw. Jac spat his chaw out and stepped through Col. Arbuckle's door.

"'Spose, you're a might latish, don't you think?" Col. Arbuckle had a name for staying on the offense.

"I had to get out of college before I could bring the shipment to you, sir. We regret the delay. If you will be so kind as to inspect your shipment, sir, then I can be on my way back to New Orleans with my daddy's money."

"Will you quit sir'ing me, you young whippersnapper. Cut your smearing-the-niceties campaign and let me see what I got."

Col. Arbuckle inspected the shipment; satisfied, he gave Jac/Jacob an A-okay. He signed that everything was present and in good condition. With the inspection completed, they went back to the office. Col. Arbuckle reached into his roll-top desk and withdrew his ledger; he composed a certificate of deposit for five thousand dollars.

Jac fidgeted. It hadn't crossed his mind about to whom Col. Arbuckle would make the Certificate of deposit payable.

Col. Arbuckle glanced up over his spectacles and saw Jacob twiddling his thumbs and knew something was awry. "Do you want this drawn to The Lilly Company, Pierre Lilly, or Jacob Lilly?" he asked.

Ah, I'm in a pickle; no matter which one of the three he makes it out to, it doesn't matter, because I'll be going around calling myself Jac Colter.

"It's like this," Jac began. "The money belongs to the Lilly Company, but if you make it payable to the Lilly Company or Pierre Lilly, I won't get my half till I get home. Sir … you see a man who is in dire straits. I'm kaput, I am destitute! It would sure be nice if you could draw it to me. When I get back to New Orleans I'll give daddy his half.

"Didn't you get an advance?" Col. Arbuckle pried.

"Well, unh huh." Jac hung his head. *He's trapping me*, Jac thought.

"Were you up to too much hanky-panky on the Mississippi steamer and spent all your advance … hunh?" Col. Arbuckle scribbled in his Ledger. "You seem honest enough, son." He tore the completed certificate from the ledger and handed it to Jacob.

Jac took a quick glance at the certificate. He didn't want to seem pretentious about the amount or the "to whom."

"It's made out to you." Col. Arbuckle stood up from his chair and stepped up close to Jacob. "Put PAID IN FULL and your JOHN HENERY on the bill!" He looked solidly into Jac's eyes. Jac went through all the formalities. He had Col. Arbuckle sign each copy of the bill of lading as having received the shipment. Then Jac printed PAID IN FULL across both copies of the invoice. Jac Colter penned Jacob Lilly across the bottoms of all the papers and handed them to Col. Arbuckle. *Why did he watch me so close when I signed my name?* Jac folded Pierre Lilly's copies of the paperwork and placed them into his parfleche ~ along with the certificate of deposit ~ which he stuffed into his breast pocket.

"Thank you, sir. It's been a pleasure doing business with you. I hope we can do more in the future." Jac Colter had lied, more than once, during the transaction. *That serves Pierre right.*

Jacob headed toward the door, but Col. Arbuckle stopped him.

"You have just one problem, Jacob, and that's how to convert that certificate into some real money. St. Louis doesn't have a bank as of yet."

Hmm, I haven't said a thing about going to St. Louis. How in thunder did he know? Jac thought.

Col. Arbuckle returned to his chair and raised the roll top from his desk. He pulled something from a drawer. He scribbled on a piece of paper and talked at the same time. "Give this to William Sublette when you catch up to him. Upon my recommendation, he'll give you credit on the books for your certificate." Col. Arbuckle wrapped the note in a piece of parchment. He printed CONFIDENTIAL FOR WILLIAM SUBLETTE across the front of it and melted beeswax across the closure. "If this has been tampered with in any way, you will not get your money from William. Is that clear?" Col. Arbuckle handed Jacob the note along with a bag with some coins in it. "Here's enough money to get you to St. Louis. You can repay me next time I see you."

Jac Colter had never in his life felt so humiliated. Col. Arbuckle knew he was lying. Did Arbuckle know he was going by the name of Jac Colter? Could his daddy and Arbuckle have been corresponding? Could it be that Col. Arbuckle was keeping track of him for his daddy? For some reason he had had Arbuckle's sympathy … why? When he reached the river, he promptly tore the bill of lading to shreds. He threw it into the muddy Grand River and returned the parfleche to his coat pocket. *Now I can be Jac Colter for good. I don't want to ever hear the name Jacob Lilly again. I know exactly what I want to do for the first time in my life.* Jac thought about the rest of his life, at least as he saw it. *When I get to the Mississippi River, I'll book passage on a steamer bound for St. Louis. I'll find the best fur company in all of St. Louis and sign on as a trapper. If I have to, I'll hire my own trappers and be my own brigade leader. It will be as if Jacob Lilly disappeared from the face of the earth!*

~

In early January 1832 Jac Colter arrived in St. Louis. Catching up to William Sublette to get credit for the certificate of deposit would be his first task. When the steamer docked and Jac Colter stepped onto the plank that led to the wharf, the first thing he saw was a sign that read Exchange Square. He stepped onto St. Louis soil and his legs went wonky, but he soon regained his land-legs. He followed North Market Street up the bluff to Jackson Place.

St. Louis was a bustling place full of people dressed in every manner of attire. There were trappers in grimy buckskins, fresh from the mountains. There were doctors and lawyers and undertakers wearing the clothes of their trade. Commoners were dressed in their everyday clothes ~ some wore vile, filthy raiment while others wore freshly laundered, starched and pressed clothes. Then there were plumpish ladies of questionable reputation dressed in frills and lace and full petticoats.

Jac recognized several languages ~ French, Spanish, and Indian ~ that he did not understand. They could all be heard, rising from the little groups of people gathered around on street corners. St. Louis was just like New Orleans, a hodgepodge of language, seasoned with dialects from every region and ethnic class. Some of the foreign words were soothing. Some of the vulgar dialects burned his ears, though.

He needed to find Mr. Sublette. How to find him became a quagmire in his mind. Then he remembered something he had learned in college. The first thing you have to do when you want to learn something new is learn its history. Jac had never thought of himself as being a bounty hunter, but in order to track down his man he set out to learn everything there was to know about William Sublette. That soon led him to the Rocky Mountain Fur Company.

William Ashley's fur company was the grandfather of this Rocky Mountain Fur Company.

Ashley had operated a fur trade business in 1822 and '23 with the help of his old friend Andrew Henry as his Field Commander. He had left Andrew Henry in charge of his fur business in the fall of 1823 and entered politics. Ashley's bid for governor of Missouri in 1824 was unsuccessful, so he set out for the Rocky Mountains. In the meantime Henry pulled out of the partnership. Ashley wound up on the Green River in April of 1825. He dispatched three brigade leaders with small trapping parties in various directions, then he set out down the Green River with seven trappers of his own. They had made arrangements to meet around the first of July where the Green River forked, up above the Uinta Range (Henry's Fork). Ashley set up the second rendezvous to take place in the Cache Valley in 1826, and it also went off without a hitch.

Ashley encountered William Sublette and David Jackson on the Bear River ~ shortly after the two-week rendezvous of 1826 was over ~ then and there, he sold out to them and their absentee partner Jedediah Smith.

I have finally put my finger on a trail that will lead me to William Sublette, Jac believed. Then the trail took another turn.

During the 1830 rendezvous, William Sublette and his co-owners had sold out. His brother, Milton Sublette, was one of the new owners, and they had changed the name to the Rocky Mountain Fur Company. When William Sublette sold his share of the company, it was a given that he would be the new company's supplier of trade goods. *Except for him being a supplier of their goods, the company is a dead-end street as far as me being able to find William*, Jac suspected.

What Jac learned next was of great interest to him. He remembered that his daddy and his Uncle Felipe had had wild dreams of trading in Santa Fe.

Early in the spring of 1831, William Sublette bought seven hundred seventy-nine acres of excellent land a few miles west of St. Louis and made it his home. In an attempt to obtain trade goods for the Rocky Mountain Fur Company, William Sublette, Jedediah Smith, and David Jackson, along with several small investors, gathered together twenty-three wagonloads of goods to carry to Santa Fe. They had found the trail to and from Santa Fe long hot and dry.

"Too dangerous for man or beast," William said later.

Hostile Comanche Indians threatened the caravan frequently. They killed Smith; Jackson abandoned the party in Santa Fe. Their failed attempt at the Santa Fe trade in 1831 bred rampant stories around St. Louis.

Jac learned William Sublette's plan: He was to leave Independence, Missouri, in May of 1832 bound for Teton country and the July rendezvous. He would have wagonloads of merchandise, but he planned to beat the American Fur Company to the rendezvous. The American Fur Company kept to the rivers with their supplies. Overland vs. river ~ it would be a race to the finish.

If I am to catch William in Independence, I have to rush, Jac realized. *He'll be slow with that big caravan, though. If I miss him in Independence, I'll catch him on the trail. Now I have him cornered!*

By 1832, the Rocky Mountain Fur Company had reached its height of glory. The rendezvous had grown into the social event of the year for the trappers and the Indians. For the fur companies it had become a time for sending their profits soaring through the roof. The best year for the Rocky Mountain Fur Company they reported they took in eighty-five thousand dollars in furs alone. The 1832 Rendezvous set for Pierre's Hole in the Teton country was fast approaching.

News of the ice breakup in the north country had expelled a great migration. It was as if everyone who was fit headed to the mountains. *Would there be anyone left in St. Louis or Missouri, for that matter?* Jac wondered. Mountain men headed to the mountains to trap beavers. Artists in hopes that they could capture the Wild West on canvas headed to the mountains. Explorers just trying to capture fame or fortune headed up the rivers to the mountains. Jac had spent a most enjoyable winter in St. Louis, but he was ready to travel.

~

The steamboat Otter was taking on a load to go to Independence, and she was Jac's first choice. *She is first class and I am first class*, he thought. Traveling first class wasn't to be. Jac got turned down when he tried to book passage on the Otter.

"We're booked solid. Nathaniel Wyeth and his group of adventurers have reserved every available berth," the captain of the Otter informed him.

It was mid-April 1832 when Jac set out for Independence in a keelboat named Hattie. He frowned as the captain took his money. "She might look a shamble, but she is second class." the captain bragged.

Second class, I doubt ... fourth class maybe. Someone has fitted her out with cabins for passengers, and if they were carpenters, they were none too bright, Jac observed.

"How did she get the name Hattie and what is your name, Captain?" Jac asked.

"I'm Ezra Trover, and gee whiz, I hattie name her sumthing," Ezra joked.

Ezra gloated over the fact that he had a thrall* who was such an able-bodied young man like Jac.

"Can ya believe that Jac has 'greed ta be a workin' passenger 'n' he paid fer the privilege?" Ezra asked his mate, Luke. "Albeit he is a greenhorn. Notice, Luke, I said that Jac is a greenhorn. By the time we get through with 'im, he'll be a river man."

Luke countered, "Or he'll hire on ta Milton Sublette ~ head ta the mountains and gets as fer 'way frum keelboats as beaver trappin' ul take 'im. Luke laughed. "Either way, he won't be our green hand any more."

~

When Jac boarded the keelboat Hattie, the first thing he heard was Ezra's shrill voice barking out orders.

"Jac! Chin up the mast 'n' tie off the cordelle rope."

Jac shucked his brogans so he could grip the mast with his bare toes, grabbed the rope in his teeth, and chinned up the pole. About two

*A person in moral or mental servitude, rather than a person owned by another.

thirds of the way to the top, he heard Ezra bark out: "Jac … tie 'er off there, then pitch the end down ta Luke." Luke reached out and grabbed the rope with one hand as its end back-lashed by his head. He half-hitched the rope into the big steel ring on the loose end of the bridle. The other end of the bridle remained permanently attached to the bow of the Hattie.

Ezra's shrill voice cut through the air. "We're ready to pull 'er now ~ overboard, men!"

Jac and about a dozen other thralls jumped into the water. Luke, as fast as he could, fed the cordelling rope to them. They grabbed hold of it and struggled toward the shore, stumbling and splashing water in their own faces. The rope that was over a thousand feet long tightened when the men placed it over their shoulders and leaned into it. They began their tug of war against the ten-ton Hattie. The war lasted sunup till sundown, and they moved the Hattie up the Missouri River five miles. *Not bad progress for the first day and considering that we were cordelling the whole way*, Ezra noted.

Jac Colter found himself catching the brunt of the labor. *Ezra is French and most likely hates the Spanish race.* Jac being Irish/Spanish felt he was sort of an outcast. *Maybe I'm just letting my imagination run wild.*

The Hattie and its crew continued to make good progress for the next five days. They depended on the wind and the sails, they polled, they oared and they cordelled. All-in-all, they had averaged about ten miles a day. So far they hadn't had to rely on warping, but their luck ran out.

Deep water beside a shoreline was ideal for cordelling; deep calm water was ideal for sail or oar. If the water was on the verge of being too shallow, whether calm or swift, the poles got the nod. When the water was too shallow, they stuck and had to push and heave or wait for the river to rise. Sometimes, the water was almost too shallow and entirely too swift; then warping was the only thing left. The second of May they came to such a place. The water became too shallow and swift for the poles.

"Overboard, men, and dig yer feet into the sand! Anchor yersevs and hold 'er. Don't let 'er slip back downstream! Jac, take the cordelle rope way up yonder."

Jac plodded through the boiling current as fast as he could.

"Now, tie it ta that snag over there by the bluff." Ezra Trover pointed to a big snag sticking out of the river. Jac tied the rope off and waded over to the sandbar and collapsed. He lay there panting and watched the men on board the Hattie line up and place the rope under their arms. The men pulled hand over hand on the cordelle rope, and the keelboat inched closer and closer toward the snag. The anchor man took up the slack. Luke chanted the orders that kept the men in time. "Pull! Take up slack! Pull! Take up slack!" Warping was slow arduous work, but when everything else failed, it moved them forward.

Jac liked the sail more than any other means of propulsion, as did all the other boatmen.

Cordelling will be the end of my life, Jac thought. *Wading waist-deep in ice water with knee-deep mud sucking my liver out and that manila-sisal cordelle line sawing me asunder will kill my soul. The tangled vegetation along the shoreline, ice-covered fingers of death, has already clawed and snagged my clothes half off me. Warping the keelboat is almost as arduous. Pulling the rope hand over hand gives me raw-sore-bleeding hands. But at least it's dry work and within the safety of the keelboat.*

About mid-afternoon the second week of May, they reached the shoals. Sandbars jutted out into the water from both sides of the river bank. The Missouri's current was shallow and swift, but Ezra judged that the depth was sufficient for the poles.

Man, the pole is coming. The oars in shallow water will do very little to advance our progress, Jac decided.

Jac hadn't finished the thought when Ezra barked the command. "All you men en the river load yersevs into the boat and grab yer poles." They all flounced over the side, like so many fish, ready to do whatever it took.

"Cut 'er ta the middle boys. Thar's shoals up ahead. Ya gotta fight 'er hard. If 'n ya don't, we're gonna go back'ards instead uh for'ards." He was snapping orders as fast as he could think. "We'll have ta shoot 'er through that deep-lookin' spot and fast. Prepare yersevs! We can't run the risk of Hattie asticking!"

Jac took his place on the walk plank, pole in hand, and waited for the command.

"Man yer poles!" Ezra screeched.

They all placed the knobs of their poles into the hollows of their shoulders and nervously waited for Ezra's chant that would keep them working with perfect timing.

"A bas les perches!" came the order. They thrust their pole into the sandy bottom and pushed with all their strength. Then they began

their laborious walk down the walking plank toward the stern. Under the weight of the push, they leaned into their poles and groaned. They literally caught the cleats of the *Passe avant* (walking plank) with one hand, then pulled themselves along, as they crawled on tip-toes to the stern.

"Levez les perches!" Raise your poles ~ was the order this time. They scampered back to the bow to repeat the process all over again. While they scampered, Luke corrected their course.

Jac was good with the poles as well as the oars. He was young and muscular, and on top of that, polling and rowing with the oars was clean work. He lay exhausted with the others around the campfire that night, thinking. *Keelboat travel is the hardest way that I ever did get anywhere. But with the workouts I'm getting, there is not an Indian anywhere that I can't undo.*

The wind came up during the night, gave the fog a good blow, and sent it vanishing. When the winds blew hard enough to use the sails, it was always a welcome occasion. The sufficient wind of the coming day would give rest to the weary boatmen. As the day warmed, Jac became increasingly aware that the mosquitoes that had been plaguing them during the past few warm days had also vanished.

"The wind 'as blew 'em ta kingdom come," Luke observed.

~

"The Hattie can progress upstream under the influence of the wind with a skeleton crew and a helmsman today," Ezra announced. "Sum uh ya'll go see if ya can kill us some meat."

"Now this is my way of traveling," Jac said. Everyone was in full agreement. Some of the puny boatmen spent the day lounging, while the others spent the day scrounging for eatables that would give them a much-needed change in diet. By the next day, May tenth, the wind had laid, and it was back to the old grindstone.

May 11, 1832, was blustery, one of those kinds of days when the sun even felt cool because of the wind. Frothy waves lapped against the shore and against the keelboat and made it seem like winter lingered. The rowers heaved, and their oars creaked at the very moment the helmsman swung the rudder around sharp. He sent the bow of the Hattie headlong into the shore. Shrieks and waves came from the welcoming party on the shore of the Missouri River. The sound of lapping waves, melodic mingling voices, and the whistling of the wind played a river march for the weary travelers.

Jac jumped overboard on command and splashed toward the sandy bank. He pounded a mooring spike into the shore to secure the boat. He never once gave thought to the icy water of the Missouri River.

There was no mistaking who the fellow standing on the shore was.

"Do we have any travelers interested in assaulting the mountains in search uh furs?" he bellowed out. The man was William Sublette. Jac could tell by the way the man dressed, by his demeanor, and by his question. It was pure supposition on Jac's part that the man with Sublette was Nathaniel Wyeth.

Jac's heart throbbed faster and faster. He felt it climb his gullet to the top of his throat as he approached William Sublette. "Yes," Jac said. He didn't say anything else out of fear that his voice would tremble.

"And who might you be?" Sublette asked.

"Jac, sir … Jac Colter, sir."

"You look fit and capable although a little wet behind the ears. I'll take you on, Jac." Sublette eyed Jac from head to toe.

"My brother Milton will be at the rendezvous and needs all the able-bodied trappers he can get his hands on. I'm warning you, though, marching in a caravan is much tougher than just riding in a boat!"

"Who's been riding? I've been working!" Jac shot back.

"You can pick you out a mule from the corral over there to tote yer belongings."

"Ah sir, I have some business I must take up with you before I accept your offer," Jac said.

Sublette was taken aback. "Unh, okay … then let's go to my office." He led the way, with Nathaniel Wyeth right by his side. When they reached William's tent, Jac shocked him again.

"You are dismissed, Mr. Wyeth; my business is with Mr. Sublette," Jac said firmly.

William Sublette had gotten caught completely off guard by this sprout of a kid. He wondered who in the world this kid was and where did he come from.

They stepped inside the tent and sat down. "What can I do for you, Jac sprout?"

The fury easily seen in the red flush of Jac's face caught William's eye as did the way Jac refrained from flying off the handle.

Jac reached in his coat pocket and took the envelope out, never taking his gaze from William Sublette. He removed the certificate of deposit from the envelope and laid it on the table. He watched William Sublette plow over the drawn-to line ~ he saw his mouth gape open ~

then he heard him sucking extra air into his lungs.

"This here certificate of deposit of yourn ~ if it is yourn ~ it doesn't impress me. I gotta hunch you probably stole it. It's made out to Jacob Lilly, and you said your name was Jac Colter."

William Sublette had him trapped. Jac knew that. Things were fishy with Col. Arbuckle. He had hoped he wouldn't have to use the confidential letter Col. Arbuckle had given him. He was afraid the letter might reveal that he was a runaway. Now, he had no choice.

"Here, sir … this letter from Col. Arbuckle will explain everything." Jac handed the sealed letter to William Sublette and crossed his fingers.

William Sublette, a look of quandary on his face, broke the seal and opened the letter. He slowly read the letter to himself.

> 'If the young lad who presents you with a certificate of deposit made out to Jacob Lilly has told you that his name is any other than Jacob Lilly; then you will know that he is a run-a-way. I know the lad's Father and he is meaner than old Lucifer hisself. The kid has a lot of gumption to run away from home and take money from the likes of Pierre Lilly. If you will give the kid a break, I will stand behind your generosity and see to it that you do not lose any money.'

Sublette lay the letter on the table face down and looked square into Jac's eyes.

I have been seeing the kid's gumption. He is purty brazen all right, and there he sets, calmer than it gets before a tornado. I'll just let 'im stew in his own juice. Sublette propped his feet up on his desk and set to packing his pipe.

Jac never moved, even to blink his eyes, but his fingers were getting numb. He wanted to un-clench his fist and uncross his fingers. He sat there for what seemed like an eternity.

Sublette took the grease lamp and held his pipe up to the sooty flame. He inhaled deeply to get the pipe fired up and blew a huge billow of smoke in Jac's direction. He knew that would make Jac move, and it did. Jac clawed at the thick smoke trying to find fresh air.

"How do you want yer money, Jac sprout?" Sublette asked.

"First off don't call me that again!" Jac choked out through a strangled cough. Jac let that thought soak into Sublette's head a long moment. *The numbskull!*

"I want you to issue me credit with the Rocky Mountain Fur Company in the amount of four thousand dollars."

"Fair enough, I can do that. What about the other thousand?" William asked.

"I want to bet you one thousand dollars!" Jac laid it on the table.

"I'm a betting man. What is your game, Jac?"

"I want your word that if my trapping doesn't work out, you will hire me to go to Santa Fe with you. If you hire me, you can keep my thousand. Ah, if you don't, then return my thousand and you owe me a thousand."

"Let me get this straight. You arn't betting me anything, are ya? You just want to buy yourself a job in case you're too puny to be a mountain man. Am I right?"

"Well, unh huh ...." *Will he ever let up on me?*

William figured Jac was squirming like a worm in hot ashes now.

"I guess since you put it that way, it does sound rather like I am hedging my bets. You can take the one thousand as my investment into your company."

"Now, I'll gladly take your investment, and it will be well used. If you can keep your mouth from getting yourself stabbed in the back or shot twix the eyes for a whole year, and you still want to go to Santa Fe with me next year, come see me. Now is that all, Jac?" William knew he was not going to repeat the Santa Fe fiasco, but then he wasn't about to risk losing Jac's investment by telling him that.

"Unh huh, I reckon so." Jac felt relief. *Maybe this sticky transaction is over ...* But he was wrong. It wasn't quite over yet.

William Sublette turned the certificate of deposit over and drew a line across the piece of parchment. "Sign here, Jac." He shoved it across the desk.

"Do you want me to sign Jac Colter or Jacob Lilly?"

"You have to sign Jacob Lilly. That's whom it is made out to."

While Jac was penning his name, Sublette scribbled across the top of a piece of parchment the name "Rocky Mountain Fur Company." Underneath he wrote "Credit duly given Jac Colter, this day May 12, 1832, is in the amount of four thousand dollars with the Rocky Mountain Fur Company." He signed the voucher and handed it to Jac. He took the certificate of deposit from Jac, folded it, and put it in his vest pocket.

"I penned my name to your credit voucher, but you better have Milton Sublette pen it as well," he advised Jac. He issued Jac Colter a receipt for the thousand dollars Jac had invested in his trading company. "You got it, Jac … you're on!"

"Shake on it?" Jac reached to shake William's hand.

Sublette dismissed Jac with a "be ready to travel in the morning" and left. Sublette shook his head. He could not believe what had just transpired.

~

Jac looked forward to pulling out across land the next morning and heading for the 1832 Rendezvous. He lay on his blanket and stared at the night sky. *The stars are so close! Where is the North Star? He searched until he found it. It's over the rendezvous site right now.* He held his hand at arm's length and aligned the North Star between his thumb and forefinger. Jac pinched the star between his fingers, as if to pluck it from the heavens, then placed his fingers upon his forehead and released his imaginary star. His thoughts became increasingly garbled. *Nathaniel Wyeth's adventurers ~ they probably paid a lot. Not me ... I'm going free. R-e-n-d-e-z* …. He lapsed into a sleep of exhaustion.

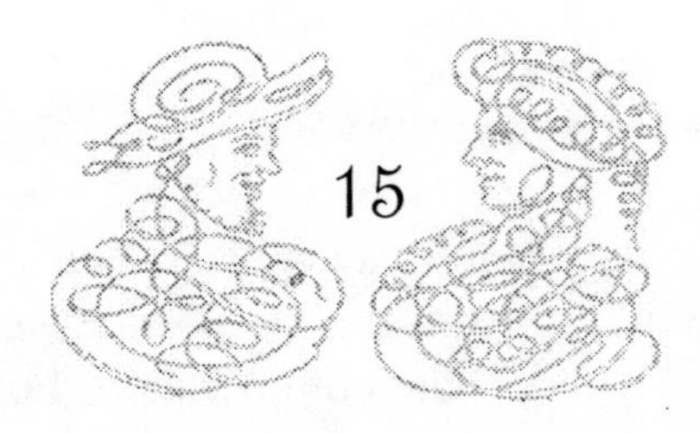

15

William Sublette was punctual in every aspect of his behavior; consequently, when he said, "We leave at five a. m. for the Rocky Mountains," everyone knew what that meant. Exactly at five o'clock the morning of May 13 Jac woke up. At five after five he stood and watched Sublette's caravan depart.

He hobbled around with one leg in and one leg out of his breeches until he got them on both legs. *Where are my Balmorals*?* he asked himself. Suddenly, he remembered he had gone to sleep with them in his bedroll. He threw his cover back, grabbed them, and stabbed his feet into them. *I haven't got time to lace them up*, he thought. He threw his muslin shirt on, half-stuffed it into his breeches, cinched his belt tight, grabbed his coat and blankets, and dashed to the corral.

Jac never noticed his unkempt appearance. He had cinched his belt too tight around his waist, scrunching his muslin shirt around his skinny belly. His unfastened shirt was on wrong side out, his shoe laces followed behind him, and the loose end of his belt flapped as he ran.

Jac had picked out the smallest mule in the bunch for his own. *Did they leave him behind?* he wondered. He ran to the corral with his smutty coat in tow over his shoulder. The little mule was still there. Jac hurriedly unhobbled him, threw the bridle on him, and made a beeline to catch up with the caravan.

The trail left by men and beast was very easy for Jac to follow. They were headed toward the Rocky Mountains and about as easy to track as a small army. They had trampled the grass in their path, leaving the ground behind almost barren. William Sublette's supply train alone had more than one hundred men and a hundred-fifty pack mules in it, not to mention two horses per man. Nathaniel Wyeth's party of misfits consisted of approximately twenty men ~ for whom Wyeth had purchased three horses each ~ as well as a herd of fifteen sheep and two yokes of oxen.

*A laced boot of the early 1800s.

Jac Colter soon overtook the march.

"It's about time and just look at you!" William scowled.

Jac had not taken the time to look at himself. He knew by the tone of William's voice that he'd better have a look. Sure enough, his shoe's laces were untied and his shirt was on wrong-side out.

"Tidy yerself up, Jac," William commanded. "For goodness sakes, you look like an orphan!"

Jac dragged his open fingers backwards through his mop of hair. After that, he bent over and tied his laces. Then he jerked his shirt off, turned it right side out, then put it back on and stuffed it in properly. "Now, is that better?"

"I reckon so. At least you don't look like ragamuffin*."

"You're much obliged for your vote of approval."

~

By the end of the first day the caravan had reached a spot where they could leave the Santa Fe Trail the next morning. The pace had begun to show on Wyeth's greenhorns as they headed northwest. Three of Wyeth's greenhorns ~ Livermore the bugle player and two others ~ had taken "French leave,"** before they even crossed the Kansas River.

Jac reveled in the fact that Thomas Livermore had taken French leave. *I'd rather march to a rattlesnake rattling than to Livermore's bugle. The sound of that thing is awful.*

The caravan crossed the Kansas River and followed it north. When they came to the Blue River they crossed over between the Little Blue and the Big Blue and made camp. They had been averaging about twenty-five miles a day, but that was about to change.

"From here until we cross the South Fork of the Platte River, the water will be awful and there won't be many, if any, buffalo. Get ready and get used to it," William Sublette warned.

By the time the caravan reached the putrid muddy waters of the Platte River they had slaughtered the last of their sheep and begun to experience sharp, gnawing hunger pains. Drinking the warm, soupy water from the Platte River brought about its own form of sharp pains, called diarrhea. Jac wondered what was worse: hunger, thirst, and the scours or travel by working on a keelboat. His hunger pains turned to weakness and his thirst turned into nightmares in the daytime; and then he knew which was worse. Jac had progressed through all the stages of the Platte Botheration, as they called it. It had begun with hunger and

*Ragamoffyn, a demon in Piers Plowman (1393), attributed to William Langland..
**A secret departure.

thirst, then had turned into diarrhea and nausea. *Now, I am vomiting my toenails up,* Jac lamented.

William encouraged his men to keep pushing on. "We'll reach the South Platte River in a few days, and there are usually buffaloes there. Can you men choke down the hungers that long?"

Camp broke up early the next morning. Just as soon as they reached the South Platte River they began seeing an occasional buffalo grazing on the other side. The sight of food, on the hoof, almost sent the men into slavering hysteria.

I promised Col. Arbuckle I'd give Jac a break, and I sorta like the kid. I'm gonna teach him how to hunt buffaloes. William decided. He dispatched Nathan Wyeth and Jac with orders to ford the South Platte River and bring in meat for the caravan.

Lush verdant meadows were in abundance between the South Platte and the North Platte rivers. Tall grass waved in the breeze and stretched as far as the eye could see and so did the buffalo. The main herd spanned almost as wide as the view, and there were little groups scattered here and there.

"Ah, just look at them. There are at least a googol of buffaloes in that herd!" Jac exaggerated.

Nathaniel Wyeth questioned Jac's guestimation. "I ain't ever heard of a googol, but naugh there couldn't be that many. I bet there is not even a million. Why don't we quit arguing about it and go shoot some of them!"

"Just for the record, some of my college buddies came up with a googol. You put a hundred zeros after a one ~ that's a googol," Jac explained.

When Jac and Nathaniel got back across the river, they had all the huge chucks of buffalo meat with them that they could wag. Several big roasting fires were blazing, but there was no evidence of a camp, nor that there was going to be a camp. The hunger-stricken men barely let the meat roast long enough to get hot before they grabbed the sticks from the fire and tore the meat from them. They gorged themselves like ravenous wolves.

"I bet those yokels would complain if they had silver forks to eat with," William told Wyeth.

All the men full of stomach and with jerky in their saddlebags were in much better spirits. Yawns and moans filled the air. They had stuffed themselves beyond capacity with half-cooked meat and putrid water.

"Move 'em out," William ordered. "Ya got thirty minutes to get un-drowsy. We're not stopping till we cross the South Platte River and get on up the North Platte and find some decent water to drink."

Jac was so ill, he couldn't keep up with the march. He fell even farther behind from taking leave to relieve his bowels.

"For as long as I live, I will always have a phobia when I see Platte River water," Jac told William Sublette.

They soon found a place just below Lodgepole Creek where they could all ford the South Platte. Upon reaching the North Platte the men were overjoyed and relieved to find good water to drink. Jac and the rest of the men quickly felt much better.

The trek west up the North Platte River, for the last week, had been a pleasant one, but now they had reached the Laramie River. The first of June was two days past. Were they going to make rendezvous by July one, Jac wondered. Jac looked out across the Laramie and surmised that it was at the same time wide, swift and deep. How could they ever cross such a powerful stream? They would most certainly lose all their animals and supplies. He could not imagine how they could keep from losing themselves, either.

"Bull boats are called for here." William Sublette made the perfect call. "The Laramie is a cantankerous old cuss of a river. I ain't never seen me a river I couldn't tame with a bull boat, though," Sublette bragged. Neither Jac Colter nor Nathaniel Wyeth had ever seen a bull boat.

"Will you tell me what in tarnation a bull boat is?" Nathaniel asked William. "Tell me why it's so special as to be able to fetch us across that appalling river, while yer at it!"

"Well, a bull boat is just buffalo hides stretched over a framework of pliable willow branches; then the seams are greased down with buffalo tallow. They're like a giant bowl, and they'll float a ton. They're the only thing I know of that will get all your blacksmith equipment and all those kegs of gun powder across the Laramie. Without dunking them in the river that is!"

William Sublette gave directions to his men ~ telling them exactly how he wanted the bull boats constructed then waterproofed with buffalo tallow and loaded.

He advised Wyeth to give up his crazy idea of building rafts. But Wyeth was stubborn, and William became disgusted with him. "I see that you are not a man easily diverted by the advice of others!" Sublette told him.

"I'm not easily diverted when I know that I'm right," Wyeth said firmly. Wyeth ordered his men to construct a raft. "Do so exactly as I tell you. If you follow my directions to the T, we'll show him who knows what." While the work was in progress, Wyeth dispatched a man on horseback.

"Take the end of this rope and go tie it on yonder shore." His plan was to guide the raft across the swift current with the rope. The rope broke, and the raft drifted toward an ugly snag. The roar of the current drowned out Wyeth's cursing.

William Sublette screamed at Wyeth with all the voice his lungs would give.

"I told you so! I told you so! You never listen to anyone!" Sublette scowled. "A one-legged man had a better chance uh swimming across that river than your raft had," he chided.

Just then, Wyeth's raft hit the strategically placed snag.

The blacksmith equipment and the kegs of gunpowder teeter tottered. They were on the edge of disaster for a long moment while the raging current and the snag fought a ferocious battle with the raft. Each demanded that they wanted to destroy the raft. The boiling current rammed and sucked at the raft and tried to take it away from the snag. Then it happened … the contents of the raft slid into the swirling waters and sank irretrievably to the bottom.

Sublette screamed one last time. "I told you so. You should uh listened!"

"No lives lost, only property; so collect yourselves together, we're agoin' on," Wyeth told his men.

"There arn't a good reason why we shouldn't camp here a few days at the junction of the Sweetwater and the Platte … are there?" William asked. "Does anyone object? We've got good water, and meat is plentiful, and we've been making good time." No one objected. They spent two glorious days there. They swam in the river, hunted, and caught up on their rest.

After they broke camp, they traveled hard. In a couple of days they arrived at the Sweetwater River. From the Sweetwater they continued northward until they came to the head of the Popo Agie. When they left the Popo Agie camp, they followed the Wind River and the Wind River Range. They crossed the Wind River Range by way of Togwotee Pass into Jackson Hole where they camped briefly. From there they continued to the foot of the Three Tetons. That would be their last camp before going through the Teton pass and down into Pierre's Hole. They sat around the cold fireless camp that night, listening to the hominy snow pelt down, and reminisced about the hardships and thrills the trip had brought them.

Crossing the Wind River Range had caused them much anguish. Fireless camps ~ because of fear of Indian attacks ~ had been the order of the day. They had lost a dozen horses in one waylay. Some of them had gotten sick, nigh unto death. Others lost their prized possessions in the river. "But all in all, we made it." William Sublette declared*.

"Thanks be to God Almighty! In the morning we'll descend directly into Pierre's Hole for a two week rendezvous!" Nathaniel Wyeth proclaimed.

~

Jac Colter sighed with relief, apprehension, and joy. He was arriving at a rendezvous. He was going to be a mountain man and a trapper. The sight of Pierre's Hole struck him with awe. It stretched for miles, it seemed to him, lush grass waving in the gentle breeze and snow capped mountain peaks framing it. *Even in July, there's snow, yet it's hot here*! he marveled. Rendezvous brimmed over with frolicking trappers, traders, and Indians.

William Sublette had begun with a supply train the size of a small army. They had dwindled very little in size by the time they arrived in Pierre's Hole. Because of dire circumstances ~ their own starvation to name one ~ they had lost some of their animals. Furthermore, Nathaniel Wyeth's group of Eastern tenderfoot adventurers had dwindled from twenty to seventeen, and now there were only eleven. They hadn't been killed; they had deserted.

Jac heard the firing of rifle shots announcing their arrival; then he saw clouds of smoke from the smoking guns. He cut himself out of the march. In all the excitement he took himself to the front of the line where he strode up beside William Sublette. He hoped he was unnoticed; and indeed he probably would have gone unnoticed, except his little mule bounced along stiff-legged behind him, resisting being towed.

"Jac, fall behind!" William Sublette scolded. "You'll get your chance to meet Milton. Just you hold on, strike a march; this is not a free-for-all!" Jac ducked his head and fell back in line. He may have been cowed for a moment, but not longer.

Out of all the smoke from the gunfire, Jac saw five men riding abreast on Indian ponies. They approached the caravan and held their hands palm up, in a hello salute. Jac Colter's heartbeat quickened. The

*The path that they blazed others followed and it became known as the Oregon Trail.

owners of the Rocky Mountain Fur Company were not more than fifty yards in front of him and were approaching fast. He recognized Milton Sublette on the left. *He looks a lot like William*, Jac thought. The other four he knew by name but not by their faces. They were Thomas Fitzpatrick, James Bridger, Henry Fraeb, and Jean Gervais. The sight of the approaching legends mounted on their handsome Indian ponies ~ back-dropped by the snow-capped mountains surrounding Pierre's Hole ~ was almost more than his fluttering heart could stand.

The owners of the Rocky Mountain Fur Company spurred their mounts onward. They pulled up face to face with William Sublette, not 20 yards from Jac. They straightened in their saddles, in a stiff-backed manner, and saluted each other. Then William Sublette dropped his hand from his forehead and turned back toward his men.

"You're dismissed. Have yerselves some fun."

William Sublette's men scattered like a covey of quail. Some sought out old friends, while others sought whisky and merriment. Jac knew there would be time for that later. Right now he had business to tend to.

William and Milton hadn't visited since William's failed attempt at the Santa Fe trade; so they had a lot of visiting to catch up on. They were making an attempt to retire to Milton's tent and do some serious visiting when Jac sidled up to them. They tried to avoid Jac, but his questions erupted fast.

"When am I going to meet Milton Sublette? You said I would get my chance. Can I have it now?" Jac rudely interrupted.

"There he is, Jac … meet him," William Sublette said, with an air of disgruntlement. Then he walked off and left Milton and Jac, face to face, with their own introductions to make.

Milton felt disdain for Jac's rude manners although the tenacity of the young Colter impressed him. *Yep, that is the way it is with these young whippersnappers; they want everything right now*, Milton thought.

"William told me that you'll make a fine trapper, Jac. You'll be reporting to Yellow Beard. He'll take you in and teach you all 'bout the beaver. He's one of the finest trappers the Rocky Mountain Fur company has. You best get you some proper duds for mountain living. Yellow Beard knows all the Indians who make buckskins. He'll help you get some good ones. It was nice meeting you, Jac. Now scat … I got business to tend to!"

Milton turned away from Jac to meet Jim Bridger and William

Sublette who had just walked up, but he felt Jac's hand grab his arm. "What, Jac? I though I told you to scat." Milton scowled.

"But … sir! I have something of utmost importance ~ a proposition for you ~ may we retire to your quarters where we can have some privacy?" Jac pleaded.

William indicated with a nod to Milton that he needed to hear Jac out. "Go easy on the Kid. I'll show you his letter later," William whispered into Milton's ear then winked.

"Follow me, Jac." Milton pointed to a tent pitched in a grove of willows near a small stream. Jim Bridger fell in behind Milton and Jac, and the three of them headed toward the tent. William knew their business was about the money, so he went his own way.

"Not him!" Jac said. He held up the pace and thumbed over his shoulder toward Jim Bridger.

"What's good enough for me is good enough for Jim. Jim Bridger's my old friend and companion in battle," Milton said firmly.

Jac stood staunchly in his tracks. He thought back, for a split-second, to his dad's ability to negotiate and his quick wit; both these qualities came to the forefront of his own personality.

"What is good enough for Mr. Bridger just might not be good enough for me." Jac made no offer to continue ~ he intended to call Milton's bluff. It seemed to Jac that moments turned into minutes. He knew Milton was trying to think of a way to dismiss Jim Bridger and save face.

"Jim, this here greenhorn thinks he has something that he doesn't want anyone else to hear. Could you let us be for a few minutes, till I find out what it is?"

"Sure enuf, what I had can wait." Jim Bridger immediately struck a brisk stride that carried him to his own tent.

The disgruntled attitude that Milton displayed made Jac think he had leveled the playing field.

"I don't have much time fer you lad, so lay it on the table." Milton Sublette was short and to the point.

It was very plain to Jac that he had bent Milton's feelings out of shape. Jac was short with his actions, as well. He reached into the breast pocket of his smutty jacket.

"It's not what I don't want anyone ta hear. It's what I don't want anyone to see." He removed his credit voucher and placed it upon the table in front of Milton. Milton's eyes bulged as did the muscles in his neck as he tried to see into the envelope from whence the credit voucher came.

Jac quickly stuffed the envelope back into his pocket as if there might be something else in it. "I need you to sign this, then put my name in the company's ledger for four thousand dollars' credit. Then, sir, I want to make a wager with you. You can knock a thousand off of my credit if I don't make a good mountain man and catch my share of beavers this coming season for you."

"And if you do?"

"If I do … you leave my thousand on the books and make me a field captain, then assign me a river to trap." Jac saw in Milton's eyes that he was close to closing the deal.

"That's all … that's it, Colter!" Milton Sublette reached for the company ledger and entered the credit. Right under that, he wrote in "Minus one thousand" with the notation "(For a Wager)." Then he showed it to Jac. "Is that what you wanted? Then at next rendezvous, if you have made a good trapper, we put a thousand dollars back on the books?"

"Unh huh, and make me a field captain." Jac made that clear.

"And if you don't come through, what then?" Milton wasn't quite sure what kind of deal this was.

"If I don't come through for you, then you can have the thousand and you can re-supply me from my credit on the ledger and I will be outta here. Is that fair enough?"

"You got it, Jac. You're on!" Milton agreed. He rose to his feet and extended his hand across the table. "Shake on it?" he asked. Their hands met across Milton Sublette's table, and they shook on the deal.

Jac turned and walked to the tent fly. He threw the fly open and as he walked out, he said, "Keep it quiet. I don't want anyone to know that I've got money!"

Jac heard Milton Sublette's shushed voice trail after him as he walked away.

"Hey, kid you're sure 'nuff a brassy one. You'll make it. You'll make a mountain man, and you'll get your trapping party."

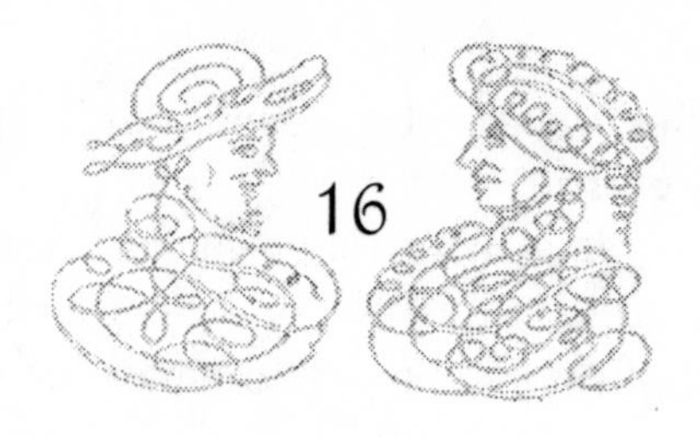

16

Yellow Beard had signed on as a trapper with William Ashley before the rendezvous of 1825. He and the other greenhorns had borne the brunt of many practical jokes during that first rendezvous, but they had survived. Grizzly had taught him well, and he had made Ashley a good greenhorn trapper his first year. That first year was a hard one, and he was ready for the July rendezvous of 1826. He found that even though he was a full-fledged mountain man in his second rendezvous, he was quite a misfit. He didn't curse, gamble or drink. There was no curse words in his native Wichita language, so he never took the time to learn any. Things happened quickly for Yellow Beard after the 1826 rendezvous. First, Jinx pulled out and headed for the Donnegans and their Bois d' Arc Creek whisky. Ashley sold his fur company, so Yellow Beard found himself working for new owners. Ashley had pointed out his skills to William Sublette, one of the new owners, and as a result after the 1826 rendezvous Yellow Beard became the leader of a small trapping party. For the next four years, Yellow Beard led small trapping parties for William Sublette and searched for his father. Then the company changed hands again.

During the rendezvous of 1830 held at the junction of the Popo Agie Creek with Wind River, Yellow Beard found himself not only employed by a new group of mountain men but by a new Company. He now worked for the Rocky Mountain Fur Company. When William Sublette sold his share of the company to Milton Sublette and the new Rocky Mountain Fur Company was formed, it was understood that William would become the supplier of goods to the new company. Yellow Beard now worked for Milton, but William had grown quite fond of him.

Before departing, William Sublette had taken Yellow Beard aside and made him an offer, though, that brought Yellow Beard to an important crossroads in his life. "Yellow Beard, now that I've sold out, I'm moving to St. Louis. I'm gonna buy me a farm and settle down for a while. Then I plan on putting together a trading expedition to Santa

Fe. Would you like to join me and go look for your daddy somewhere else?"

Since Yellow Beard became a trapper in 1825 there had been nothing else for him to do. He had trapped and he had searched for his father, but now he had a new opportunity. He had a decision to make. One fact that weighed heavily on him was he had been trapping for five years and hadn't found hide nor hair of his father. He lay on his blanket and gazed up at the star-sprinkled heavens and wondered what his future held. *Maybe Father is in Santa Fe chasing real gold. Must I go with William Sublette ~ or ~ must I stay with Milton Sublette and continue trapping for the soft gold of the Rockies?* Yellow Beard knew he was at a turning point in his life. His love of the mountains, his love of trapping, and the fact that he hadn't fully given up on his father's being a trapper swayed his decision. He would stay and trap with Milton Sublette.

The rendezvous of 1831 had come and gone and was rather uneventful for Yellow Beard. The year just past had been a holy terror, though. The Indians felt that the trappers were stealing their beaver. That drove them into a warring frenzy, and they attacked almost nightly. More so than in previous years, the trappers were proud to be at the 1832 rendezvous. The valley might be full of rattlesnakes, but no Indian war party would disturb so many armed men; so for a few days the trappers could sleep with both eyes shut, as their old saying went.

Yellow Beard had been trapping seven years but hadn't uncovered a shred of evidence that his father was a trapper. He was still a loner, but he wished for a good partner; furthermore, he had longing to go home and see his mother. *One more year ... I'll stick it out one more year; then I'm going home,* he decided.

~

Jac left Milton Sublette's tent and wove his way through the willows that grew alongside the Teton River. Milton's trappers lounged along the riverbank. Some of them just sat quietly while they drowned their loneliness in tin cups of frontier whisky. Some of them indulged in games of chance; still others pitted themselves against each other in games of strength. A few of the trappers had succumbed to the festivities of the rendezvous and were sleeping it off. One young man, just a boy Jac thought, was crawling to the river being pushed along by the dry-heaves. *The boy can't hold his liquor. I bet he ain't had whisky before. That won't happen to me.*

Jac wandered through the many encampments of trappers and admired their trade goods. He wound up back at the trade store William Sublette had set up. There he purchased a tin cup of frontier whisky and observed some of the fur trading. He couldn't resist eyeing the long rifles on display. After almost a year of hard labor and living the party-less life, he was finally having some fun. Jac soon found, just as the old trappers did, that indeed the compliant Indian women and the frontier whisky was each as intoxicating as the other.

Seeing trappers with submissive raven-haired Indian maidens close by their sides, as they strolled through the grassy paths, sent warm memories of his beautiful Annabelle coursing through his red-blooded veins. Jac thought about her beautiful hair, her constant smile, and her flirtatious ways. His brain became so impregnated by the thoughts of her that he could hardly think of anything else. Except for the whisky.

I either want Annabelle ~ or ~ I want another cup of that whisky! After that brief thought, Jac decided. *Unh hunh ... I'll just have to settle for another cup of that whisky!* He went back to the barrel and told the barrel tender, "Gim-gimmy uh … nuther." He drank that cup down in a couple of swigs. *Hunh ... that was better than the other one*. Jac went back to the barrel tender and handed him his cup. But before the barrel tender could fill it, Jac insisted that he wanted the good-tasting stuff out of the other barrel.

"I ain't got but one barrel. Do ya want it or not?"

"Ah, I guess so … if you're out of the good st-stu-stuff." Jac tossed it down in one gulp and left. *To go find Annabelle*.

Jac watched the increasingly beautiful Flathead maidens weave their graceful arms and legs to the throbbing sounds of the flutes and drums and banjos. Suddenly there was no room for Annabelle in his thoughts. He never knew why she quit haunting him, whether it was the scantily clad writhing bodies of the Indian maidens dancing to the unnerving music, the frontier whisky and his throbbing head, or all of them put together. Ever so slowly, Jac felt the warm fuzzy feeling in the pit of his stomach turn into a torch that only the frontier whisky could quell. But for reasons unknown to him, the Indian maidens refused his advances. In Jac's mind the reason the beautiful Flathead girls wouldn't pay attention to him was his New Orleans duds. It never occurred to him that being drunk out of his mind was the reason.

I gotta find Yellow Beard 'n' get him to get me some proper duds. Jac wobbled over to Yellow Beard's camp. Along the way, Jac stumbled and fell across a vile-smelling, vile-looking old trapper. The old fellow apparently was nowhere near as drunk as Jac. After a brief scramble the old trapper regained his legs and managed to stand. Jac flounced around from his backside to his bellyside trying to get up. Then he just lay there.

"Ah, where's Yellow Beard … hu-hunh?" Jac moaned.

"Ya askin' me?" the old trapper quipped.

"If ya … know where-e is I am!" Jac felt pickle-tongued.

"Ya be the spunky greenhorn what stood yer ground with Milton Sublette 'n' Bridger?"

"Unh huh, Ya-ya ol' coot uv uh trapper. What does 'at have ta do with whar Yellow Beard es?"

"The name's Geezer 'n' ya better get hold uh that cantankerous tongue uh yourn. This old geezer doesn't take ta loose tongue greenhorns acallin' 'em ol' coot. Those on hooch that is! Me 'n' Yellow Beard goes back aways. Back ta when he was just a pup. If they's one thing I know 'bout 'em, it's that he hates drunks. You better sober up 'n' come back later. You can find 'im over at the Flathead Indian camp, though, if yer so mind to."

"Unh, you talkin' 'bout Yellow Beard?"

"Naw, now who we been atalkin' about anyways? Now git!" Geezer snapped.

Jac didn't know quite how to take ol' Geezer. He moseyed off toward the Flathead camp. Behind him, the old man laughed deep from within and mumbled to himself. "Yellow Beard'll chew that drunk greenhorn up 'n' spit 'im out!"

~

Jac approached the group of Indians with caution. Several of them he recognized as being Flatheads. The big trapper, however, with the yellowish-red wiry hair and tangled yellowish-red beard had to be Yellow Beard.

The unmistakable qualities of Yellow Beard's tall straight physique not only included his hair but his hard eyes of cobalt blue. They seemingly looked straight through you.

Jac took one look at Yellow Beard and remembered what Geezer had mumbled. The thoughts of Yellow Beard chewing him up and spitting him out were enough to shake him into appearing judge-cold sober.

Jac walked toward Yellow Beard, held out his hand and, without the slightest slur to his speech, introduced himself.

"I'm Jac … Jac Colter and I've not been drinking. Milton Sublette hired me to become a trapper for you. He sent me to you for proper duds." Jac felt the stutters coming on and hushed.

"Uh, I'm not Yellow Beard if you haven't been drinking. Your words smell like beaver castor, Jac! Go tell Geezer that I said to let you sleep it off. Then we'll get you some proper duds." Yellow Beard's first impression wasn't much.

Jac made his way back to where Geezer was. He'd never heard an Indian talk like Yellow Beard. He wondered where he got educated.

Sleep it off Jac did. He swore to never touch the stuff again. *I've drunk corn liquor before. It was nothing like that frontier whisky William Sublette sells*. Jac contemplated where he could go to relieve his stomach. *That stuff was muddy. It was bitter and fiery hot. It was awful and aside from making me drunk, it set my stomach to wambling, loosened my bowls and gave me a sore throat*! He didn't want to think about the awful stuff any more but couldn't get it out of his mind. After a couple of days, the sharp pains subsided. His stomach finally accepted some of the bear fat broth Yellow Beard fed him. And he could keep it down, just as long as he could keep from thinking about or smelling that rot gut frontier whisky.

~

Some people are just different ~ cast from a different mold. Colter is one of them, Yellow Beard observed. *He speaks with education and he is confident with his place in life.* Yellow Beard knew Jac had backbone, judging from the way he held his own with Milton Sublette and Jim Bridger. Somehow he believed Jac, when he swore that he would never touch the whisky again. He believed that Jac and him would make real good partners. There was the thing, though, about his necklace, the black walnut with the gold nugget inside. Could he trust Jac to keep his secret? Trapping partners didn't keep secrets. Yellow Beard's suspicion was that Jac, just as well as he, had a secret of his own.

Within a few days, Yellow Beard deemed Jac well enough to take the next step. "Uh, Jac you've shriveled since that whisky gave you the squirts, but I think Moon Weaver can fix you up with some duds. That is, if you're ready. Moon Weaver's a Shoshoni, the best leather tanner there is. She saves her water. Says it makes the leather soft and tough and gives it a pretty color. Besides all that, she'll give you a fitting you won't soon forget!"

"Ah, you mean she uses her urine to make leather? Whewee," Jac said, feeling his insides flip flop. He wasn't that long over the wambling stomach, and he gagged at the thought.

"Hmm, her urine," Yellow Beard mused. "Is that what it is ...

urine? I've heard it called many things but never really knew what it was." Yellow Beard changed the subject. "Do you have any wampum to pay her with?"

Jac faced away from Yellow Beard and fumbled with the leather envelope in his coat pocket. He presented Yellow Beard with a look at his credit voucher from the Rocky Mountain Fur Company. "I don't have wampum. I pay cashum!" he joked.

Yellow Beard couldn't resist joining in. "Indian no wantum cashum they only wantum wampum or no tradeum." They both had a big laugh.

"Well," Yellow Beard finally said, "you'll need something to trade to Moon Weaver for your clothes. Come on, let's go buy you some gewgaws." Yellow Beard led the way to the trade store.

Jac bought some mirrors, beads and Santa Fe jewelry, and Yellow Beard helped him buy the rest of the necessities he needed. These were things Milton Sublette hadn't furnished him with already.

Jac felt naked. For the first time in his life, all he had was credit, a few simple things he needed to become a mountain man, and one measly little mule. The mule had marched with a pack on its back from Independence to Pierre's Hole. He had eaten very little on the trip except for roughage along the trail. Now the little fellow was gorging himself on the lush grass around Pierre's Hole and getting bloated.

"You're just like me." Jac Colter rubbed the little mule's belly. "Rendezvous is too much for you … gave you the squirts, just like it did me. You little scrawny thing, you're no bigger than a squirt. Ah, that'll be your name, Squirt."

~

Jac stood deadbolt still while Moon Weaver held the knotted sinew on his ankle with one hand and slowly pulled it up his inseam with her other hand. She reached around him from behind and pinched the taut skin of his stomach to hold the sinew in place, then guided her measuring string around his waist. Jac could hear Yellow Beard and Moon Weaver talking. Their voices mingled with his thoughts, but Moon Weaver's voice sure had a teasing taunt to it.

When Moon Weaver bent to her all fours to measure Jac's foot, his eyes fixed square into Yellow Beard's eyes. Yellow Beard winked at him, and Jac felt his face flame with a scarlet blush. Finally, Moon Weaver stood up, took a step back, and studied Jac for a long while before giving the hand sign for finished. Jac sighed in relief. *Ah, that embarrassing job is over with. Thank goodness*! Moon Weaver held up her hand, palm facing Jac as if to wave goodbye.

~

Rendezvous was just about over before Moon Weaver sent a runner bearing the message for Jac to come see her.

Jac ran to Moon Weaver's teepee in the pre-dawn darkness and rushed inside. Draped across a bundle of Buffalo hides were his new duds. They were everything he had hoped they would be. He took a quick inventory: breechcloth, leggings, a long-tailed fringed shirt, a buffalo robe for warmth and sleeping, and a beautiful pair of hi-top moccasins; everything was there. He quickly cast his old clothes aside and pulled on the new fringed-leather outfit. Moon Weaver stepped into the teepee from outside. So instantaneous was her entry, Jac thought she must have been watching. He blushed.

"U like?"

"Unh huh, very much, but …!" *This feels like robbery*. He handed Moon Weaver a buckskin pouch containing the trinkets, which was all she had asked for. Then he pulled from his breast pocket a pure white linen appliquéd handkerchief and draped it across her hand.

Her mouth gaped open.

"You like?" he asked.

She shook her head yes. Her eyes twinkled.

She draped herself about his neck and he turned scarlet hot from the blood rushing into his cheeks.

"Me like, too, very much!" he stammered. Jac Colter's pains of thievery vanished upon seeing the sparkle in Moon Weaver's eyes. She spread the contents of the buckskin pouch on a pure white Ermine skin, as her smile spread from ear to ear. Her joy told all. She did like very much!

Jac brushed the fly aside and stepped outside. The mark of another day had peeked over the pass with a vermilion smile. He headed back to Yellow Beard's camp walking tall in his new buckskins. He felt like he owned the mountains. He felt like he could stand up to the Indians and live as they did, wild and free.

Jac Colter didn't feel like a Jac anymore. The fact was he had hated the name Jac ever since Col. Arbuckle had called him 'Jac Sprout' back at Cantonment Gibson. *I feel like COLTER!* he thought. He gazed at the setting moon then pounded both clenched fists upon his chest and declared for all the world to hear — "I am COLTER!"

The Indians headed deep into the mountains from whence they came. The artist and journalist returned to the big cities. They were ready to paint their renditions of the Wild West and to sell their stories about rendezvous life. The mountain men were ready to get back to the raw excitement of living in the mountains and trapping beaver. The fur companies were ready to export their bounty and reap their profits. Everyone was looking forward to getting on with the year's work that lay ahead of them.

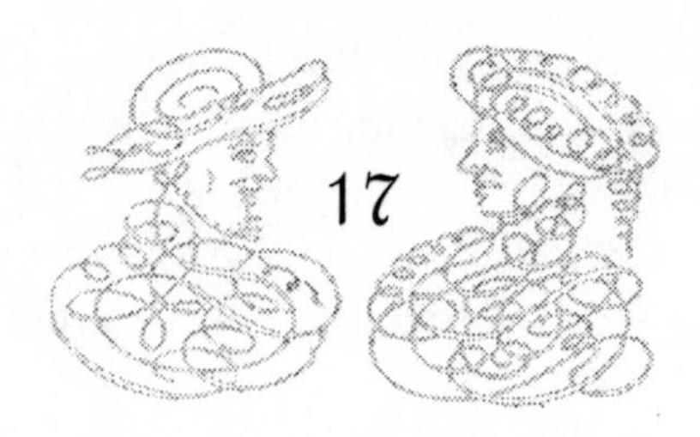

17

Yellow Beard, after eye balling Jac's new duds, announced, "We're ready to pull out of rendezvous. Milton Sublette is taking his Rocky Mountain Fur Company division, which we're a part of, to the Snake River area. When we get to the head of the Salmon River, we're going down it to the Lemhi River. We'll spend our winter trapping it. Be prepared to depart in the morning, bright and early."

"Yellow Beard, who exactly are 'we'?" Colter asked.

"We … uh, we are you and Geezer, Dunk Rivers and Pug Givens, and me."

"There's something I have to tell you. I don't like everyone calling me Jac. Jack is what a Jack Ass is and I ain't a Jack Ass. I'm not a Jack sprout either. Besides, with these Moon Weaver duds on I feel like a real mountain man. I want everyone to quit calling me Jac."

"Well then, Jac … what do you want us to call you?"

"Colter … that's my last name anyway. It won't hurt for you to call me by my last name, will it?"

"In that case then, listen up, all you men. Jac here wants us to call him Colter. He says he ain't no Jac Ass." Yellow Beard winked.

Jac felt a red tinge of embarrassment creep into his face. *My name is my business, and I can change it if I want to. It's the thing I have that I can be proudest of.*

"Uh, Colter … you ready to leave Rendezvous and get down to some serious trapping and mountain roaming?" Yellow Beard asked.

Yellow Beard used my new name, and I like the sound of it. Colter nodded.

~

Yellow Beard's trapping party had been up since pitch black and were ready to go. The sun had painted a salmon color to the sky in the east. *The rising sun always seems to push me,* Yellow Beard reflected.

Due to all the captivating events that had taken place since Colter arrived at the rendezvous, he had lost track of time ~ at least, the number of the day. He finally got his bearings when he overheard Captain Wyeth whispering to one of his men.

"It's July seventeen," Captain Wyeth whispered, "of Eighteen Thirty-Two."

"I know the yeer it'd be. I ain't no dummy!" the man said with a disgusted frown on his brow. Captain Wyeth made a few circles around his ear with his forefinger, then turned and walked away from the man.

"Antoine Godin here will be our guide," Milton Sublette announced. "He'll guide us through Blackfoot country then deliver us to the Salmon River in Idaho. Unh, fall in the lot of you!"

Colter knew that 'the lot of you' meant man and beast alike; so he and Squirt fell in behind Yellow Beard.

They did not get far, perhaps from too much rendezvous hoopla. They camped a mere eight miles south of Pierre's Hole. They struck camp overlooking a palisade, through which a trapper's trail wound down into the valley.

The morning following ~ just as they were raising their camp and before sunrise lit the pass ~ they observed a long thread of people making their way down the trail. Wyeth cast his spyglass on them: "My perception is that they are Blackfeet and there are around two hundred of them."

What remained of their festive mood vanished as the trappers reached for their Hawken rifles. The trappers readied themselves and watched the column unwind down the pass.

The Indian braves came on.

Every Hawken hammer had a thumb on it.

They are Gros Ventre (Big Belly), Milton surmised. "Unh, they're still acoming … stay ready!" he advised.

Yellow Beard checked to be sure his knife was in its place and advised Colter to do the same.

As if they sensed something, the Gros Ventres stopped in their tracks. Baihoh, a Big Belly war chief, left the band and made his way forward. He was unarmed and carried only a red blanket and a medicine pipe.

Milton Sublette was too wary of a mountain man to wholly trust the Big Belly envoy. He was willing to parley, though. However, he chose the wrong two men to do the parleying. He chose Antoine Godin and a Flathead Indian.

Antoine Godin hated the Blackfeet ~ they had killed his father. In Antoine's eyes, Baihoh, chief or no chief, was no more than any other

Blackfoot. The Flathead that accompanied him harbored much hatred in his heart toward the Blackfeet and Gros Ventre. He had seen them commit much savagery against his tribe. Antoine Godin and the Flathead urged their mounts forward. They rode up beside Baihoh, one of them on either side of him.

What Antoine did next would catch Milton Sublet and the trappers completely by surprise. Baihoh extended his hand to Antoine Godin in a gesture of friendship. Antoine gripped his hand hard and shouted to the Flathead. "Fire!" The Flathead's rifle belched smoke! The Gros Ventre had no time to react before Antoine jerked Baihoh to the ground and snatched the red blanket from him. Antoine and the Flathead galloped back to the trappers' barricade, whooping and waving the red blanket as if they had done something honorable.

The women and children are leaving. That's not good. Milton thought. *What are our odds ... they arn't good?* Milton began barking orders.

"Look to your priming … thumb back your hammers!" He issued commands as fast as he had inventoried their plight. "Send for reinforcements. Send back to the rendezvous for William!"

Mountain men, if successful at saving their necks, stayed prepared and ready for surprises, but Wyeth and his men offered no assistance. Being ready and prepared was not their long suit.

Help arrived from the main camp in what amounted to a whole army. William Sublette brought two hundred white trappers, two hundred Flathead and three hundred Nez Perce warriors. They were eager, every one of them, to wipe out the hated Gros Ventre. Taking command, William got Wyeth's greenhorns out of the line of fire. Then he led a force of some sixty volunteers into the willow-filled swamp where the Gros Ventre had taken a stand. The Gros Ventre later admitted they lost twenty to thirty horses dead and twenty-six of their people killed.

"The fight is over!" Wyeth recorded in his own flamboyant words. "The din of arms has now changed into the noise of the vulture and the howling of masterless dogs," he wrote.

Milton Sublette and his men, along with Wyeth's men, retreated to the site of the Rendezvous. They carried with them William Sublette who had taken a ball to his shoulder.

The ball broke his shoulder and caused him to bleed severely. They knew they would be there a while; there were many wounds to heal. Five men dead and six wounded was the toll on the fur company's side.

William Sublette recorded in his log: "It will be necessary to remain some time in this neighborhood, that both men and horses might repose, and recruit our strength."

There was work to do on every hand. First they had to bury the dead and care for the injured. The seriousness of the battle had required the expenditure of most of their lead; so the able-bodied returned to the battlefield to scrounge up spent lead. They dug it from the trees and from dead animals and picked it up anywhere they could find it.

Yellow Beard and Colter had fought bravely together and received not a scratch. They had a lot of spare time while they waited for the wounded to recuperate. They used their time to relive the battle and talk about what had brought them to this point in their lives. Colter could see the pain and bewilderment in Yellow Beard's eyes and on his face when he told him that he had run away from home. Yellow Beard could not comprehend how a person could run away from his father and change his name ~ nor could he fathom what it would be like to have wealth and live like the Lillys and the Sanchezes.

Yellow Beard revealed the many hardships he had faced, growing up without a father and how he longed to find his father. As Yellow Beard's story unfolded, Colter's heart mellowed. Yellow Beard made being cut off from one's father sound so terrible. Colter shared his pain. Colter had not an inkling what it would be like to be poor and live from the land where the dollar meant nothing. To escape that destiny became a sudden and utmost desire of his. Furthermore he realized for the first time that he most likely would live out the rest of his life poor. Neither Colter nor Yellow Beard revealed to each other their deepest secrets. Yellow Beard never mentioned his father's war prize, the opaque bag that contained the black walnut pendant that hung around his neck. Colter never mentioned the thing that hung around his neck, that dastardly deed he had perpetrated against his father.

Trust in each other would have to develop before they could reveal their dark innermost secrets to each other. That kind of trust grew out of fighting and surviving, side-by-side, as trappers and mountain men.

The battle of Pierre's Hole had caused them considerable delay. Out of the delay, though, a flicker of friendship glowed between the two men although they did not, could not, and would not understand each other's motives … ever.

Finally on the twenty-fourth they were able to move off once more toward the Salmon River.

From the moment Yellow Beard's story struck his heart, Colter's remorse had grown and grown. Soon it was almost more than he could bear, and until he found a way to make amends with his dad, nothing or anyone could quell it. For Colter to see the fortitude and the perseverance with which Yellow Beard pursued his father opened his eyes. His heart ached to find a way to make amends with his daddy for what he had done. Colter could not imagine how he could ever save up five thousand dollars working as a hired trapper. *I must find a way to become a free trapper; only then will I have a chance to make amends with Daddy.*

Yellow Beard's desire to find his father, and Colter's desire to repay his father, would lead Colter and Yellow Beard down many a trail together. Their pursuit of the soft gold of the Rockies would not last all their lifelong days. But their common desires, like glue, bound them into a lifelong partnership. A partnership that would become much, much more than merely a friendship.

~

After having removed themselves from Pierre's Hole, Milton Sublette's party along with Fraeb's party, Joe Meek and his party and Yellow Beard's party arrived in Snake River country during the early fall of 1832. Milton Sublette took his men and went to the Salmon River. That is where he had planned to set up the Rocky Mountain Fur Company's winter camp. Yellow Beard and his trappers went down the Salmon River to the Lemhi River and spent the winter trapping up it.

Colter was turning into a pretty good beaver trapper, thanks to Yellow Beard's teaching ability and to his own ability to learn fast when he applied himself.

Even so, he wasn't catching his "share" yet, according to Yellow Beard. "You're coming along real good, though." Yellow Beard assured him.

Colter couldn't stand to find a gnawed-off foot left behind by some desperate beaver, so he always tried to make drowning sets. He would brave waist-deep water if necessary to tie his trap in sufficient depths for dispatching the beaver quickly. He also was a natural when it came to taking care of the pelts. He loved to comb and dress the furs. When it came time to skin and stretch the day's catch of beavers, he loved that, too.

Colter impressed Yellow Beard the most with his ability to keep a watch on his backside. He had a natural instinct of what went on in his surroundings. It was impossible for any of them to slip up on him, no matter what he was doing, and they all tried.

Colter bent over the fleshing-beam and deftly prepared a pelt for the stretcher. Despite his progress, he worried. *I know I'm making a good mountain man. I just hope Milton Sublette doesn't renege on our deal.*

~

Things were about to change drastically for the worse, as far as the rendezvous went. In July of 1832, Congress passed a bill that excluded spirituous liquors from being sold to the Indians. By August, government agents in Fort Leavenworth were enforcing the newly passed bill, ensuring that the upcoming 1833 rendezvous would be as dry as a bone. However, news about the new law and its enforcement had not made it to the field commanders yet.

~

As winter wore on, the Blackfeet grew more hostile. It was if they thrived on extremely harsh weather. Every day the trappers got jumped by Blackfeet and if not by them then the Nez Perce was always there to provide them with a skirmish. Both the Nez Perce and the Blackfeet blamed the fur companies for steeling their beaver pelts. They looked on the stiff competition between the Rocky Mountain and the American Fur Companies not as competition between each other but as pure and simple thievery of what belonged to them.

Working through skirmish after skirmish together helped Yellow Beard and Colter develop a trust in each other. They learned what the other would do in a pinch. They came to know each other so well, many times they knew how the other one would react or what the other one would say before it happened. They came to accept that anything in their past was just that, in the past.

By halfway through the season, Colter was catching his share of pelts. He had become as good a trapper as the Rocky Mountain Fur Company had. He was as hard as frozen steel, as temperamental as a loaded trap, and as lightning fast as the snapping jaws of a sprung trap. He was cautious to a degree and ready to lead his own trapping party.

It just might be that Colter would be of more value to the Rocky Mountain Fur Company as a supplier of goods, though.

~

In January of 1833 the Rocky Mountain Fur Company moved their winter camp to the Snake River. Milton Sublette moved again in early spring, this time to the Big Lost River. Trappers returning from their winter trapping areas went to the Big Lost River camp. There they staged up in the warm comfortable camp of the Rocky Mountain Fur

Company and waited for the deep snow to melt from the passes. Yellow Beard and his trappers arrived there around the first of April.

Another successful trapping season had come and gone. The trappers removed the pelts from their stretchers and placed them in bales. They cleaned and cached the traps. As soon as the snow melted off the pass, they could transport the furs to Rendezvous. The wait consumed their time and began to take its toll on Yellow Beard and Colter.

"Come on, Colter. Let's you and me get out of here and go hunting. I could use some kind of meat in my stew besides Jerky, couldn't you?" Yellow Beard rubbed his stomach.

"Fine. I've stood all this chicken coup that I care too."

They went up the river following the edge of the bluff, then followed a line of stark-naked cottonwood trees up a draw. As they approached the head of the draw, their path was blocked by a fallen tree grown over with brambles. Colter carefully parted the vegetation only to discover it was hiding a surprise. "Lo and behold, look what I found, Yellow Beard!" he hollered. It was a cave, and someone had occupied it at some point. There was evidence of a campfire, chips of flint and some figures carved in the walls. Yellow Beard and Colter returned to the little cave every day while they waited for the snow to melt off the pass.

No one offered to follow them. The trappers were so proud to have deer in their diet after a month of eating stewed beaver, they remained satisfied just to let Yellow Beard and Colter bring in the meat.

One night a blizzard dumped another round of pass-blocking white and continued into the day. The trappers awoke in a cantankerous mood. They were anxious to cash in their winter's catch and have some rendezvous fun, but the snow kept coming. By midmorning, Yellow Beard and Colter had all that they could take. Grumbles of "we're outta meat" was all that it took to send them to their cave.

The thermometer would be in its bulb if we had one, Colter thought, as Yellow Beard and he crawled into the cave. Colter built a small fire. The light and warmth reflected from the walls and warmed the small space quickly. It lent a cheery atmosphere to the dankness.

They talked idly for a while until a lull in the conversation sent Colter to the mouth of the cave. He stood there and watched the massive snow flakes flitter-flutter down through the evergreen boughs. *How much longer will we be here? When will it quit snowing? Will I get me a trapping party?* Suddenly his heart filled with a sick feeling ~ it flooded out all these other thoughts. He had felt it before, every time he remembered how he had betrayed his daddy.

Yellow Beard was hunkered near the back of the cave. He had taken his necklace off and was admiring it in the light of their small fire. "U … h kershew!" His sneeze startled Colter. He whirled around on one heel realizing as he pivoted what the sound was and that it meant nothing. But Yellow Beard was fumbling with a beautiful-but-strange leather bag. It was made of some kind of opaque supple leather, and Yellow Beard was removing something from it. Colter wondered what a well-worn black walnut attached to a sinew string necklace could possibly be worth.

"Ah man!" Was all he could muster. Then he finally brought himself to ask, "Did you find that in here?"

Yellow Beard avoided the question; he rolled the black walnut around in his hand.

"This thing has a gold nugget inside it, but I cannot find the way to open the walnut. My father lifted it from a Comanche warrior who tried to kill him. He gave it to my mother to give to me on my tenth birthday, and I've had it ever since.

"Father left explicit instructions for me: 'only open it the way its maker intended.' I've tried to figure it out ever since. But I haven't had any luck … so far.

"I wear it round my neck, under my shirt. Mother told me it was my spiritual link between Father and me. Some men have seen this bag, but you're the only man that's ever seen the walnut necklace. Uh, you Colter … I trust. You and I have shed blood for each other! We are blood brothers. Here take a closer look." Yellow Beard shoved the pendent into Colter's hand. "While you're at it, see if you can find the secret to the way it opens."

Colter took the beautiful necklace and held it up to the light beam that came through the cave door. He rolled it around in his hand and admired the size of the smoothly worn but craggy walnut for a long while. He held his hand out and raised it up and down as if calculating the weight of the nut. He held it up to his ear, all the while rotating it and shaking it. Then he lowered it to his eyeball and squinted, giving it a close up look. "This thing sure is heavy. I give up on opening it … for now." He handed it back to Yellow Beard. "I bet if you ever find your daddy he knows how to open it."

"You've hit on what might be the secret link between Father and me. Any old codger could claim that the necklace had once belonged to him. But if the man I give it to knows how to open it ~ then I'll know that he is Father!" From that day, Yellow Beard didn't bother with trying to open the walnut.

Colter felt compelled to tell Yellow Beard about the money he had stolen from his dad and about his bet with William Sublette. He trusted Yellow Beard just like Yellow Beard trusted him. *Trusting him is not my problem; knowing how Yellow Beard thinks ... it is just so embarrassing,* Colter thought.

"There's something I've been wanting to tell you," Colter began. "When I ran away from home, it was because Daddy gave me an ultimatum. I could deliver a shipment of goods to his customer at Cantonment Gibson on the Grand River and bring him the money ~ or ~ be dismissed from the family. He said I had disgraced the family name because of my improper behavior with my lady friend. I was so hurt that when I delivered the goods and collected the money, I fled to St. Louis with Daddy's five thousand dollars. There is one more thing. I wanted to be a field captain of a trapping party, just like you are, so bad that I placed a thousand dollar wager with Milton Sublette: If I lasted one year and caught my share of beavers he would make me a field captain."

Yellow Beard thought about what Colter had told him for a long time. Finally the consequences of Colter's bet sank in. *He and Colter, as partners, would no longer be.* "You know I have my trapping party. You know you've met the requirements of your wager. You'll get your party! Then, you go your way … I go my way."

Colter's heart sank. He hadn't thought about that.

Colter and Yellow Beard knew if they barked to the tune of Sublette's orders, they would part and go their separate ways. There was no way around that ~ or was there? If there was, they couldn't think of it.

Finally the snow melt was sufficient for them to attempt the pass. Yellow Beard's trapping party would soon be on their way to the rendezvous.

~

"Two more days 'n' we're gonna shine!" Dunk's and Pug's voices echoed across the canyon and up the side of the mountain. Geezer's voice joined in with the echo. "Yep, we're gonna shine."

Yellow Beard and Colter felt the excitement mount ~ it was in the air. Rendezvous had been a long time coming. Winter had been hard, and the trappers needed a rest. Spirits were high as they headed to rendezvous, but they were soon to fall. There would be no merrymaking. There would be no spirits. The United States Congress had seen to that.

18

The beginning of the end to the rendezvous system of fur gathering and trading was in place. Whether Congress's new bill was intended for the boatmen or the Indians, it no longer mattered. The fall of 1832 through spring of 1833 was a time of turmoil; would there or would there not be any whisky at the 1833 rendezvous? Those were the questions.

Government inspections for whisky ~ under the direction of William Clark the superintendent of Indian affairs ~ had gotten off to a very nasty start at Fort Leavenworth in August 1832. Leclerc had gained passage with his two hundred fifty gallons of alcohol; whereas Chouteau never made it through with his fourteen hundred gallons. Furious at the inequity ~ Chouteau charged that there had been foul play. They both had held permits issued by William Clark allowing them both to transport whisky up the Missouri River. William Clark made all kind of wild accusations, Clark's interest in Leclerc's venture being one of them. At the very least the inspectors had failed to follow the letter of the law.

In 1833 there was no liquor to be had on the Missouri River.

The fur companies might have suspected that there would be uprisings due to the severe shortage of whisky. For some reason, known only to the fur companies, the central gathering place for 1833 rendezvous was within the confines of Fort Bonneville. For unknown reasons, by the trappers and Indians, they would camp along the Green River and Horse Creek.

When Milton Sublette and his trappers arrived at Fort Bonneville tired, hungry and thirsty, they expected a warm welcome from happy trappers, but that was not to be. People milled about, grumbling and scowling at each other about the lack of whisky. The Indians were cantankerous and not in the mood to trade their furs.

Milton Sublette pushed himself through the mob. He banged on the door leading into the room where his co-owners had assembled themselves. "It's Milt!" he heard someone holler, and the door swung open. They were weighing the situation: They only had a few gallons of raw whisky. There was an angry mob of whisky-starved Indians and trappers outside. What were they going to do? "Improvise!" someone said. Before the meeting was over, they had made a bunch of whisky from river water and whatever else they could scrounge. The concoction became known as "frontier whisky*."

The meeting adjourned; the field captains got liberal amounts of frontier whisky plus orders to strike camp on the Green River. Yellow Beard led his group about five miles down the Green River from its junction with Horse Creek.

~

The two hundred fifty gallons of alcohol turned into frontier whisky ~ as a result of Leclerc's monopoly ~ made him a fortune in one season. Accounts of frontier whisky selling for three dollars a pint and more were common, and who knows how much it sold for by the cup, which is the way most of the frontier whisky sold at the rendezvous.

The fur companies considered liquor the most important item they could bring to the rendezvous. They could convert it to frontier whisky and make a huge profit. For them to just roll over and play dead and give in to the government's wishes would cut their profits drastically. They would fight for their profits. They could trade trifling things such as beads, mirrors and trinkets to the Indians for their furs, but the Indians soon got enough of those. The only other thing the trappers had that the Indian wanted was guns. The trappers had rather trade frontier whisky to the Indians for their beaver pelts than guns. The drunkenness wore off, but the guns came back to haunt them.

Drastic measures were taken to obtain sufficient quantities of alcohol ~ not only to satisfy the demand for frontier whisky but to keep company profits high ~ that led to unethical practices by the fur companies. One practice was to dilute the whisky with water. When the fur companies began to dilute their alcohol, doing something to jack up the taste, as well as the kick it had, became a common practice. It was not uncommon to find in the dregs of a barrel of frontier whisky a cud of chewing tobacco or some hot red peppers or, in some cases, a rattlesnake head. Many times all three remained in the dregs at the bot-

*Actual recipes varied greatly. Tall tales varied even more. The following was reported to have plenty kick! 1 gallon of Whisky and 10 gallons of river water. Boil together 1 heaping handful of hot peppers and 1 pound black tabacker and sweeten with 1 pound black molasses. Dump that into a barrel and add 2 rattlesnake heads and/or beaver castoreum.

Note: the drunker they get the more water you can add.

tom of the barrel. After the fur companies put the whisky through their dilute and soup-up process, it became known as many things. Frontier whisky was what the fur companies called their concoction of death. The trappers called it fire water. The Indians probably coined the best name; they called it medicine water.

~

The runner came to Yellow Beard's camp bringing a rolled rawhide tied with sinew. He handed the roll to Yellow Beard and waited. Scratched inside with a piece of charcoal, Yellow Beard found Milton Sublette's words. "This is what Milton has to say: 'You, Colter and Yellow Beard: You shall make your appearance to the Rocky Mountain Tent before this noon. I expect your Promptness!' Then he signed his name to it."

Yellow Beard picked up a piece of charcoal from their campfire and handed it and the rawhide to Colter. "Write this: We accept your invitation to eat." After he wrote Yellow Beard's words Colter rolled the rawhide, tied it, and handed it to the runner. Colter speculated as to why the summons was for both Yellow Beard and him. *Could Milton be planning trickery and trying to renege from our bet?* He wondered.

Yellow Beard threw the door open; then Colter and he entered, unannounced.

"Don't you ever knock?" Milton scowled.

"No, but if you need to be hiding from someone, I'll start knocking." Yellow Beard kept a straight face.

Milton Sublette spoke with authority. "Colter you and Yellow Beard pull up you a bale of pelts and have a set." Milton left the room and returned with a plate of grub for each of them. "I gotta hunch you're hungry; mountain men never turn down grub." He set their plates down before them. They devoted their time to eating, and Milton let them eat in peace before he spoke again.

"I have a proposition for the both of you. It will fill my bet with you Colter, and I think Yellow Beard will like it as well. First … Yellow Beard, I want to congratulate you on one of the finest beaver harvests in recent years."

"You can give some of the credit for that to Colter. He is just as good a trapper as me!"

"I know that. Colter is a very good trapper. What makes your catch even harder for me to believe is that the beavers are getting more scarce up there in the Rockies every year.

"That brings us to the reason that I have summoned you here.

What is getting even more scarce than beaver is whisky. The United States government has cracked down on whisky getting to the Indians. Consequently, we can't find a brewer anywhere that will sell us whisky. The Mississippi River ~ there ain't a drop of whisky on her. It's the same thing with the Missouri and the Arkansas rivers; they ain't enough whisky on them to wet your whistle."

Milton took a long draw from his pipe.

"It's so bad that Mckenzie got a still, from friends on Red River he claimed, and tried to brew his own at Fort Union. He got caught, and they hauled him into Washington to explain. He made some silly excuse that he was experimenting with wild pears and berries, which no one believed. To save face, the American Fur Company fired him."

"Unh, I don't guess I have to tell you: Without whisky, the rendezvous system will collapse; and without the rendezvous system, the fur companies will collapse; and without the fur companies ~ you will collapse!" Milton Sublette let that thought breed in their minds while he knocked the spent ashes from his pipe and reloaded it.

"My partners and I have come up with an idea where, and how, we can get whisky. That River where Mckenzie claimed he got his still: She is kinda like a forgotten river; there ain't a lot known about her. She borders the United States on her south. Before the gosh awful Madrid earthquakes of 1811 that they had, she ran into the Mississippi River. All that's left connecting her with the Mississippi now is a dry riverbed that they call Old River. Now then, she runs with the Chaffeli River and runs into the Gulf of Mexico. Her name is Rouge River. Mckenzie called her Red River."

Milton is talking about the Rio Rojo, Yellow Beard thought.

"Fitzpatrick, Bridger, Fraeb, Gervais and me" ~ Milton stopped and lit his pipe ~ "we have arrived at what might be a solution to our dilemma. We want you and Colter to team up. You can pick your partners. We'll outfit you with what ever ya need. I'll have you some fine riverboats waiting for you where Old River intersects the Rouge River! Yellow Beard, you know the Rouge like you know your own self. We want the pair uh you to explore her under the pretese of finding us another source of beavers. What you're actually gonna be looking for is us some whisky.

"Colter if that will satisfy our bet ~ what with you sharing a party with Yellow Beard ~ and you all are successful, we'll cut you in for a share, say ten percent, of the profits. I have a hunch you'll make some real good money."

Yellow Beard jumped at the opportunity. *A chance to work the Red River again and go see my mother ... why not?*

Colter, while thrilled with the deal, had to negotiate a little. That was a trait he had inherited from his daddy.

"I'll uh … I'll think about it. I'll let you know in the morning, but I was kind of wanting a crew of my own." Colter hem hawed around, in hopes of drawing a better share of the profits.

"Unh, okay then … fifteen percent and that's final," Sublette shot back.

Colter recognized Milton's desperation, and he knew that Yellow Beard and he were their best bet for obtaining whisky from Red River.

"That's fifteen percent for Yellow Beard as well?" Colter countered.

"Unh, Fitzpatrick, Bridger, Fraeb, Gervais and me are gonna come in for eighty percent. I guess that leaves twenty fer you and Yellow Beard. Split it however you like. Take it or leave it."

Yellow Beard nervously fumbled with the opaque bag lying on his breast. He knew that Colter and he had gotten the best end of the deal, but he had to make sure.

"The plews and the whiskey, that's all you're interested in … right?" Yellow Beard asked.

"You got it … now you two get outta here and have some fun. You have got a long year ahead of you," Milton assured them.

Yellow Beard and Colter stepped out into the courtyard of the fort, and Yellow Beard cut down on Colter.

"Ya don't know the likes of Milton Sublette. In the morning his offer will have vanished. He doesn't like hesitations in the least bit. He says that a decision reached by hesitating is likely to get you kilt! I'm here to vouch for him ~ he is right!"

Colter ran back to Sublette's quarters, jerked the door open, and politely said, "We accept your offer, sir!"

"Get yourselves back in here then. We gotta shake on it. I never did like putting off till tomorrow what a man could do today!" Sublette grumbled. "You'll be operating under the name of the Red Exploration. Bring me all the whisky you can get your hands on, to the next rendezvous." Milton Sublette handed Yellow Beard a letter. "This is yours and Colter's orders. They give you authority to buy whisky on behalf of the Rocky Mountain Fur Company. I signed a certificate of deposit ~ it's in there to pay for the whisky ~ all you got to do is fill in the amount."

The three men shook hands. They had a deal.

~

Since the day Jac Colter received his mountain man duds he had thought of himself as Colter. He no longer thought of himself as Jacob Lilly or Jac or Jac Colter, just plain Colter. Upon hearing the name Colter mentioned by Milton Sublette ~ along with the names of James Fitzpatrick and Jim Bridger ~ he knew he wouldn't ever think of himself as Jacob Lilly anymore. Not even if he went home and made amends with his dad. Colter knew that this just might be his ticket to earn the five thousand dollars he owed his daddy.

Yellow Beard shuddered as he thought about what the future held. *I have a hunch I might be on the right track to finding my father now. He ain't up here in the Rockies chasing soft gold. Maybe he's somewhere around Santa Fe chasing real gold.*

~

Geezer met Yellow Beard and Colter on their way back to camp from their meeting with Milton Sublette. He had a look of concern that deepened the wrinkles in his forehead.

"While ya'll wuz gone, someone cum asnoopin' around. He said he wuz lookin' fer a feller by the name uv Jacob Lilly. He introduced hisself as Evert Hollman and he wuz a duded-up sort uv feller. He wuz a big man, and he had a funny lookin' big ol' ugly scar runnin' down the side uv his head. He looked like one uv them bounty hunters … yep he did!" Geezer's frown deepened.

"Uh, what do ya mean funny looking scar?" Yellow Beard asked.

"I don't rightly know. The nearest I could describe it, the feller looked as if he got run over by a red hot wagon wheel … yep he did!"

"Where did he go? What did you tell him? Did he say if he was coming back?" Colter threw the questions so fast that Geezer's jaw gapped open.

"Are ya through? Ya sure do be interested, if ya ain't Jacob Lilly. I don't know whar he wuz going. I don't know if he's acumin' back. I tolt 'im I didn't know a Jacob Lilly. I tolt 'im, besides if I did know a Jacob Lilly that it weren't none uh his business … nope I tolt 'im, it ain't none uh yer business!"

~

Colter left the task of choosing their partners to Yellow Beard. Yellow Beard knew from his past experience with the men which ones would stay sober and be closed-mouthed about their business and which ones weren't cantankerous. Yellow Beard wanted to take Geezer. He decided against it, though. He knew that Geezer had a tendency to indulge in frontier whisky. As far as cantankerous, that was Geezer's middle name. He had lost one good friend and trapper to Donnegan whisky, and he did not want to lose another one. Yellow Beard chose two trappers to take with them. Both were young and brave, quiet and reserved, and fast learners.

Barlow McKinsey would be their camp keeper. That meant his duty was to cook and keep the fire. He was a burly, big boned man, extremely agile and of swift mind and foot. His thick mop of black unruly hair and his wavy beard lent to his lumber jack appearance. *His jovial demeanor and his infectious down-from-the-belly laugh will take the edge off of the seriousness of this trip*, Yellow Beard thought. He could not resist the urge to chew on something and went about with a branch protruding through his thick wavy beard. Trickery of any sort was the thing Barlow lived for. He kept the Indian children as well as the grown men enthralled with his rope tricks and his shooting tricks. Barlow had been trapping a couple of years, and Yellow Beard had never seen him stumbling drunk ~ tipsy maybe ~ but never mad-dog drunk.

Ezekiel Netherly, on the other hand, came to rendezvous to get stumbling mad-dog drunk. He had been in Yellow Beard's party several times, and Yellow Beard knew he never touched whisky. Except during Rendezvous, that is, then look out! Zeke would be their mule wrangler. He was wiry, tall, and all bone and muscle. His face was leathery and in the middle of it was a long nose he could stuff into his lower lip. Zeke was quick and agile, and he boasted that it didn't make any difference from where or how hard anyone threw him; he always hit the ground on his feet. He bragged that he could stand with his feet flat on the ground and kick a person's hat off their head. Barlow attempted this feat once, but he landed flat on the ground instead of the hat. He never tried it again.

Zeke's pack mule, Dollar, unlike most mules displayed the same agile qualities as Zeke. Zeke delighted in teaching Dollar tricks, and one of their favorites was cockalorum. Zeke would stand with both feet flat on the ground then jump over Dollar's back. Then Zeke would stand humped over at the waist while Dollar jumped over him. Every chance they got, they performed their game of leapfrog for the children who delighted in seeing Dollar jump over Zeke.

~

When Colter learned that Barlow and Zeke were going to be their partners on the Red River exploration, he took a special interest in their performances. Colter, Barlow and Geezer had attended one of Zeke's and Dollar's performances, then had headed back to their camp. Just as they rounded the corner of Milton Sublet's quarters someone came out of Milton's door. Colter and he bumped headlong into each other, and the unsuspecting fellow went to the ground. Geezer recognized the man as Evert Hollman and ran to fetch Yellow Beard. Evert attempted to pick himself up but got his legs tangled and wallowed around a bit. Colter helped the man up then helped him brush himself off. Colter found himself staring into the icy-cold black eyes of scar-faced Evert Hollman!

"I am sorry, sir!" Colter said.

To the point and in a rudely spoken manner, the scar-faced man asked, "Are you Jacob Lilly?"

"Why should I tell you? I don't even know your name." Colter replied.

"I'm Evert Hollman," he said and shoved his pointed finger into Colter's chest. "I'll ask you one more time, are you Jacob Lilly?"

"What if I am? You clumsy maladroit galoot! Just what are you gonna do about it?" Colter hoped to taunt ugly Evert into challenging him.

Milton appeared from his quarters, and Geezer returned with Yellow Beard. They were just in time to hear ugly Evert's accusation.

"By golly, you are … Jacob Lilly!" Evert shoved his pointed finger deeper into Colter's chest, as if to accentuate his proclamation. "I … am taking you back to your pappy!"

"Unh … hold it a minute," Milton Sublette interrupted. "If Colter run away from home, he had a good reason."

"Sure enough!" Yellow Beard agreed.

Milton drew a deep drag from his tar-pot of a pipe and exhaled as he stepped into ugly Evert's face. "Beside that, he's my trapper now and you'll have to whoop the whole bunch of us to take him."

Evert choked so hard, his eyes bulged.

I have heard enough. It's time that I take a stand, Colter thought.

Before Evert could regain enough air to talk, Colter lit in on him.

"You think that I'm someone named Jacob Lilly, and you say you're taking me home to my pappy. Well, I ain't going without a fight. So … I take it you're challenging me to a fight, in which case I get to choose the medicine. We'll have us a first class wrestling match! If you win, I'll go with you. If I win, you'll tell whomever you think my pappy is that you couldn't find me!"

Evert Hollman was in a pickle ~ he didn't like hand-to-hand killing

~ he liked doing it clean, with a gun. He couldn't refuse to fight; now it was fight the whole bunch ~ or, fight Colter.

Wrestling ... what a grand idea, that is! Yellow Beard thought. He had seen Colter in action against an Indian warrior one time and then another time in a bout with a momma Grizzly.

Colter had wound up on the bruin's back and had choked the critter with his bare hands all the while hollering "Say uncle" until she turned blue in the face. When Colter turned her loose, she ran off into the woods with her tail ducked between her legs. *That's just what ugly Evert will do,* Yellow Beard thought. When the warrior dove at him, Colter turned a backward flip. The Indian grabbed thin air, and Colter kicked him in the head with both feet. *He can turn over in his own skin,* Yellow Beard thought.

Evert Hollman gave the appearance that he was as sneaky as a snake and as mean as a cornered Grizzly. He looked like he either was Lucifer or in cahoots with him.

Known fact was he killed for the dollar. His claim was that he had never met a man he wouldn't kill.

~

A ring clawed into the rock-strewn sand would serve as a visible boundary to hold the fighters in bounds. Empty whiskey barrels placed ringside would serve as betting tables. Preparations for the fight were complete.

Indians and white men alike had gathered from the far corners of the rendezvous. Milton Sublette had thrown open the gates to Fort Bonneville. *This will be a money maker,* he thought.

A man with a gravelly voice strolled through the crowds hollering, "Watch the big bounty hunter kill the mountain man ~ place yer bets now!" Yellow Beard and a few of Colter's closest friends gathered around the betting barrels to place their bets on Colter. Many of the mountain men had not heard about Colter's fighting abilities and placed their bets on Evert. It was not as though they were abandoning one of their own, a fellow mountain man; they were just betting to win the dollar.

Milton ordered that a full barrel of frontier whisky be brought ringside and sat on a bench. He stationed a barrel tender next to it.

"Yellow Beard, you're going to be the referee," Colter told him and informed him of the rules and asked him to announce them before the fight began.

Yellow Beard went to Evert Hollman's corner of the ring. "In this corner we have Scar face Evert … the challenger." He strutted over to Colter's corner. "In this corner we have one of our own … Jac the Ranter!"

The crowd roared. Colter held up a hand to try and quiet them.

Yellow Beard motioned for the two fighters to come to the center of the ring. He held up their hands. "Nothing is fair except what you brought into this ring with you!" He dropped their hands and announced to the crowd, "Now, we are gonna see us a fight!"

Evert scowled at Colter. "I'm gonna tear yer head off, ya little liver-bellied Lilly!"

"Let me quote to you what Mr. Robert C. Savage said: 'What counts most is not the size of the dog in the fight, it's the size of the fight in the dog.' You're a wimp … without your gun." Colter chortled.

"Enough … enough!" Yellow Beard screamed. "Ding-dong … ding-dong. Evert didn't realize there would be a ding dong to start the fight and just stood there.

Colter sped toward Evert. His body spun like a top, and he planted both feet squarely into Evert's jaw.

"Aaah!" Evert shrieked and went down.

Colter backed off. He gave Evert time.

Evert got his wonky legs back under himself and regained an upright position.

The crowd roared with laughter when they saw Evert's whopper-jawed face.

"Finish 'im off! Yep … finish 'im off, Colter!" Geezer squealed.

Colter's fans chanted: "Finish 'im off! Finish 'im! Finish 'im off, Colter!"

Colter saw what the crowd didn't see; Evert stood up with both hands full of sand.

Colter saw Evert lunging toward him, but before Colter could dodge out of the way, Evert unloaded two hands' full of sand into his eyes.

The crowd gasped; Evert was cheating!

Through his crystallized eyeballs, Colter saw the gnarly fist coming to put his lights out ~ wham***!

Colter stumbled backwards … and fell.

Evert pounced on him. Colter saw the grainy image of a big fist holding a rock, then he felt it grinding into his temple.

The crowd went silent ~ Evert was killing Colter ~ as they had bet that he would.

For the first time Colter realized Evert was going to kill him. He accepted the fact this fight was until death. *My death or his, that is the question*, he thought. His realization sent him into a wild frenzy. He flew into a wild spinning roll with such vehement force it would have loosed Evert from him ~ except that Evert was holding Colter's neck in a death grip. Colter bounced up from the ground onto his feet and brought Evert with him. He spun around within the grip of Evert's gnarly hands to bring himself face to face with Evert. Evert's hands burned the skin around his neck as he spun. He looked at Evert through his grainy dazed eyes. He clasped both of his hands together; with all the force he could muster, he swung the edge of them into Evert's Adam's apple. He felt Evert's windpipe collapse and heard Evert gasp … then wheeze. What Colter saw next would remain fixed in his brain for the rest of his life. Evert's face turned from a violent red to a putrid white; Evert's eyeballs bulged and glassed over. His face looked grainy like etched glass through Colter's sand-filled eyes. Evert released his grip and collapsed to the sand. It was over.

Colter looked up at the crowd. Everything appeared etched, and his eyes felt grainy. He jabbed at both eyes with clenched fists. He blinked tightly, trying to remove the gray-grainy film.

"Ya've whooped 'em! He's gone ta jine up with the Devil! Yep, that's whur he is gonna go!" Geezer pronounced his death and his eternity.

"What are you all gawking at? Go collect or pay your bets and git back to your whisky!" Yellow Beard demanded. His disgust for the attitude of the onlookers revealed a side of himself to Colter that he had not seen.

~

Colter lay and watched the twinkle of the distant stars while he tried to fall asleep. Visions of Evert's face and his bulged eyes kept dancing before him. The sand no longer grated against his eyeballs although the memory of Evert's etched ashy white face would grate on his conscience for a long time to come. Shortly before dawn, Colter's thoughts subsided and he slumbered in a restless sleep. The last thought on Colter's mind was that the coyotes had ceased to wail and the whippoorwills had ….

Colter woke suddenly and sat up. *Will there be another Evert, and if so when? If I know my pa, the question is not will there be ... but when will there be?*

Yellow Beard sounded the wake up call. "Wake up, wake up … whilst there's still some daylight left! Doesn't any-one want to go to Red River with me? Colter … come on now," he prodded.

"Ah, gimme a break. I gotta sleep it off," Colter grumbled.

"Did you go get drunk, Colter?"

"No, but I feel like I did!" He crawled out of his blanket yawning.

Barlow and Zeke fell out pronto. They were ready to travel, ready to see Red River. Barlow and Zeke, at this point, were just glad to get back in tune with nature.

Yellow Beard and Colter felt much anxiety about the year ahead. Thoughts of home filled them both although in different ways. Yellow Beard and Colter, as well as Barlow and Zeke, had become completely fed up with rendezvous socializing.

"Colter, you and me need to go see Moon Weaver." Yellow Beard recognized a puzzled look on Colter's face, as if he didn't remember who Moon Weaver was. "You know, she made your first mountain duds for you."

"I know. I was just trying to remember whether she was Flathead or Shoshoni. Man alive, I won't ever forget that fitting she gave me! Is she here? I haven't seen her." Colter had a surprised look on his face.

"I heard she's here. I haven't seen her either, but we can't go with-out seeing her. Barlow, you and Zeke be ready to travel to St. Louie when we get back."

Moon Weaver met them at the teepee flap with a little one on her hip.

"We hadn't seen you out and about, Moon Weaver," Yellow Beard said. "We're fixin' to head to St. Louie and wanted to tell you bye be-fore we left. Milton Sublette told me you were here."

"My little un, and my man, he's the jealous type ~ not to mention my dud makin', has kept me too busy fer me ta get 'round any this time."

Moon Weaver sounds regretful that she hasn't been able to socialize any, Colter thought.

"We need to go anyway. Yellow Beard's got the itch to get on our way," Colter explained.

"We're sorry if we caused you any trouble. We just wanted to say goodbye." Yellow Beard held up a hand.

~

Early the next morning, they gathered their belongings onto the mules and pulled out for the Red River. The trail back to St. Louis was well established now and would be the route they would take. Many of the frontiersmen had begun calling it the "Oregon Trail." Yellow Beard led the way and Colter followed him. Barlow and Zeke alternated bringing up the rear. The seventeenth of July was no time to be in the high-mountain deserts, and their every wish was to make it to the shade of the cottonwood trees that grew along the Sweetwater River.

It was midday before they stopped to chew jerky and rest.

After they ate, the sun warmed their full bellies. Barlow and Zeke quickly fell to snoring.

Colter leaned back against a big boulder.

"Uh kershew!" Yellow Beard slapped his hand over his nose.

Colter almost jumped out of his skin.

"You know, Colter, when Jinx and me came to St. Louis from Red River, we cut across to St. Louis from Paccawn Point. We left ol' Red River to her own doings. We sure saved a lot of time. We missed the Black Rock Bar and the Big Raft." He sneezed again.

"If we go down to the Mississippi River to where Red River used to run into her before the Madrid earthquakes, then follow Old River up to Red River ~ where Red River runs into the Chaffeli River ~ we're sure going to lose a lot of time. If we cut cross-land from here to Paccawn Point, we wouldn't have to put up with the Great Raft or the black rock bar." Yellow Beard made a good sounding case for taking the shortcut.

"You make me nervous, Yellow Beard. We have to go pick up the skiffs that Milton said he would have waiting for us at he junction of Old River and Red River." Colter fumbled with his ear lobe. "The way I look at it, we don't have a choice. "You're not thinking that we're not going to pick them up are you?"

"I guess we don't have a choice," Yellow Beard conceded. "But we're in a dilemma. I guess I better have a talk with Zeke 'fore long."

"What do you mean 'we're in a dilemma' and you better have a talk with Zeke?" Colter asked.

"I thought you were college smart, but if you ain't figured it out by now, then you ain't no smarter than me." Yellow Beard changed the subject.

~

They were worn and tattered after being on the trail over a month, but they would finally get some rest. They reached St. Louis midmorning, the third week of August, and held up just outside town, where a grove of large willows protruded almost down to the water's edge. Yellow Beard told Barlow and Zeke to strike camp. "There in the grove of willows but on top of the Mississippi River bank," he said. "Colter and me are going down to the dock to book passage down the Mississippi to Red River."

Barlow and Zeke dove into the chore of striking an extended camp in preparation for enjoying St. Louis for a few days.

"Barlow ya know there ain't neither one of us ever traveled richman style on a steamer!" Zeke said. Excitement filled his voice.

"Augh, I know it. I don't know why in tarnation we don't just walk ta Red River." Barlow spat shrivels from the stick he was chewing on.

Yellow Beard and Colter found that the dock was bustling with activity.

Paddlewheel steamers were everywhere; they sat in dock, they waited to dock, and they waited to leave dock. There were stern wheelers and side wheelers in every imaginable need of repair from shabby to well-kept lining the shores both above and below the wharf. There were large keelboats outfitted with living quarters and flat-bottom boats and canoes and you name it. Busy cargo handlers loaded and unloaded iron-wheeled carts along the stone wharf.

The streets were filled with their own kind of activity. Swinging doors were kept constantly swinging inward as patrons entered in search of relief for their desires; outward as patrons exited boozy legged or with smiles on their faces.

It took a while before they found a riverboat captain who would take their mules. When they found one, they signed on to go as far as Old River.

"It's a consternation why anyone would want to go to Old River," the purser said, scratching his head.

"How are we going to get our mules on one of them flat-bottom skiffs that we're getting when we get to Red River?" Colter asked Yellow Beard.

"Now you're beginning to get the idea … now you see our dilemma. I knew you would smarten up sooner or later, Colter. We have come shorthanded to handle two boats and our mules. We need two people in each boat and that doesn't leave anyone to handle the mules."

"We'll think of something." They made their way to the dry goods store to pick up some supplies.

Behind the counter was a weasel-looking sort of little fellow, but he seemed to have a handle on what he was doing.

"Have you got credit on your books for the Red Exploration? I'm Yellow Beard and this here is Colter. We're with the Rocky Mountain Fur Company, and Milton Sublette said we would have credit here."

"Pleased to meet you fellows. You can just call me Nary." The little man was looking in the ledger all the while. "Yep, here you are. Just help yourself to anything in the store."

They got a few new traps to replace the beyond-repair dilapidated ones they had. They also gathered up a twenty-five-pound bag of coffee beans, fifty pounds of flour, a slab of salt pork, a tin of horehound candy and twenty-five pounds of tobacco.

Yellow Beard asked the clerk to have their provisions delivered to the Mississippi Belle. He and Colter headed back to the grove of willows where they left Barlow and Zeke striking camp.

"I wonder what it would be like to sleep in a real bed again. Do you mind if I get me a bed at the City Hotel, Yellow Beard? Milton told me that William stayed there last year and that it was real fancy."

"It's your money." Yellow Beard laughed. "Just leave the floozies and the whisky alone! Early in the morning come to camp ready to board the Mississippi Belle."

Colter checked in at hotel and bought him a bath before going to his room. He lay on the soft goose-down mattress and reminisced about home, about his mother, about Annabelle. He began to get sleepy. His last thoughts were: *I share command of this trapping party with Yellow Beard, but somehow it feels as if Yellow Beard is totally in charge.*

~

They had been traveling a long time since they passed the Arkansas River, and Yellow Beard felt they should be getting near Old River. Way in the distance, Colter saw a wide gap in the vegetation on the west side of the Mississippi.

"Do you think that could be Old River?"

"Probably so," Yellow Beard said. "Red River must have been real big. Her old mouth there must have been a mile wide. Boy, those Madrid earthquakes back in 1811 and '12 must have been real shakers to make a river as big as Red River want to pull out."

Sure enough the purser came up to them and assured them that indeed was Old River they were seeing. "Your mules and your gear are being loaded onto a flatboat as we speak."

They overheard the purser mumbling to himself and shaking his head in disbelief as he walked away. "Why would anybody want off at the mouth of a dry river?"

The crew that was powering the flatboat did everything they could to propel the boat to shore. Some oared and some poled while still others paddled. They slowly inched their way to Old River.

~

"We're finally freed from all the gawking do-gooders and the wanna-bend-yer-ear city slickers," Zeke observed.

The mules, especially Dollar, acted equally relieved to be off the big boat and have their feet on solid ground once more.

August is a miserable time to be traveling on a river, Colter thought. I'll be glad when cooler nights set in. The days are too hot and the nights too full of mosquitoes. Better than traveling on land, though. The ticks are bleeding the mules, and the cottonmouth moccasins are dread awful in the river bottom sloughs.

The explorers followed the dry river bed as it meandered west. It was plain to see that Red River still used this route when she flooded. After they followed Old River for a few miles, they arrived at Red River. Where Old River and Red River intersected was a unique place. They could see that it had been a site of great upheaval in the past.

"Milton Sublette was correct in his assumption that Red River's old channel would be a good route to use to smuggle whisky off of Red River," Yellow Beard reminded Colter.

It was evident that before the Madrid quakes the now-dry river bed had been Red River's preferred course to the Mississippi River. It was further evident that the Atchafalaya River* ~ before the Madrid quakes ~ had been just a tributary of Red River but that she had been successful in her attempt to take Red River away from the Mississippi River.

"I found myself so infatuated with Madrid earthquake history back in college that I learned all there was to know about them," Colter said. Colter knew that Yellow Beard's inquisitive nature would force him to ask what he knew. He was fixing to have some fun out of Yellow

*pronounced as Chaffeli.

Beard.

Colter convinced Yellow Beard, so he thought, that what happened was, when the Madrid quake shook the living daylights out of the Mississippi River and she became so violent, Red River gave up on her and cut herself a new path to the ocean.

"It's for sure that no one would ever know, by any kind of deduction, what transpired here during the New Madrid earthquakes," Yellow Beard concluded.

Long silent minutes passed. Colter waited for Yellow Beard to ask him a question about the Madrid earthquakes.

Yellow Beard had sat down on a stump and leaned back against a cottonwood tree. He was in deep thought and ignored Colter. *Colter doesn't know all there is to know about the quakes. I got one up on him. I bet he doesn't know about Panther-Passing-Across! I bet they don't teach in his school what Indians know.*

Finally, Colter couldn't stand the wait any more.

"Don't you want to know about the quakes?"

Yellow Beard came out of his reverie and realized Colter had said something to him.

"Uh, what did you say?"

"I said don't you want to know all about the New Madrid earthquakes?"

"No … all you could tell me is what happened, and I can see some of that. I'm happy with just knowing how it happened I reckon!" Yellow Beard was having fun at Colter's expense.

"What do you mean, you know how it happened?" Now Colter was on the inquisitive side for a change.

Yellow Beard intentionally put a shocked-sounding tone to his voice. "You mean to tell me that you don't know the legend of *The-Panther-Passing-Across*?"

"No … but I'm all ears." Colter swallowed the hook.

Zeke and Barlow dragged in a big limb for the night's campfire and couldn't help overhearing that one of Yellow Beard's Indian tales was about to break out. They sat down on their hunkers and got ready.

> "It goes like this: It all began Wednesday, August 11, 1802.
>
> "Panther-Passing-Across knew it would require a great effort to get all the Indians from the land of the rising sun to join up with each other. He went to every single tribe and told them about a sign the Great Spirit would send in

the middle of the night. 'The sky will light up the same as when I was born,' Panther-Passing-Across said, 'and you will know I speak the truth. And when all the tribes join into one nation, the Great Spirit will cause the ground to shake, jugs to shatter, and rivers to run backwards. He will take away old lakes and make new lakes and cause trees to fall down without winds blowing them down. Then white man will fear and respect us.'"

Yellow Beard looked up. His partners were enjoying hearing the legend. Their slack mouths told the story. He had their full attention; he had their respect.

"On a day that you would call a December Sunday, Colter, back in aught nine, Panther-Passing-Across told his brother to go to the woods and make a bunch of sacred slabs. He described how to make them. Every one of them was supposed to be alike, and the brother was to make them out of red cedar. Panther-Passing-Across told him some things to carve on them and to put a bundle of red cedar sticks with each slab."

"Every tribe Panther-Passing-across went to, he gave them a slab and a bundle of sticks. Each cedar stick was for a new moon. When the new moon came, the keeper of the slab was supposed to throw away a stick. They were to do that until only one stick remained. As each new moon passed, Panther-Passing-Across threw away a stick from the bundles he hadn't handed out yet. His own tribe, the Seminoles, was last to get a bundle. The bundle Panther-Passing-Across handed them only had three sticks in it."

Yellow Beard looked into Colter's eyes.

"Twenty-nine moons after it all began, the tribes threw away a stick until they only had one stick left. The chiefs laid the last stick on the ground, took a piece of char from their fires and carefully marked it and cut it into thirty pieces. Every day after that they burned a piece of the red cedar stick just as the sun woke up. Every chief knew that in the night after the sixth stick was burned the Great Spirit would send a star shooting across the night sky to tell them he was guiding Panther-Passing-Across."

"The morning of the sixth day, the chief of every tribe threw his stick on the fire, and every Indian everywhere

> waited for dark to come. Under a cloudless sky the stars twinkled so bright it seemed you could pick a pocketful. The sixth day was coming to an end. Everywhere, thousands of eyes searched the stars."

"Augh, get on with it!" Colter complained. Yellow Beard knew Colter was about to bust a gut.

> "Just before midnight, it came. A bright star, like a ball of fire, shot across the sky. It hurt their eyes, like the sun, and it went faster than a ball out of your Henry, Colter. They knew the Great Spirit was telling Panther-Passing-Across what to say. Then each tribe began their trip, as Panther-Passing-Across had told them to do, to the place white man calls Detroit."

Yellow Beard glanced from Colter to Zeke and then to Barlow. He had them in a trance.

> "When the sun came up on the day before the thirtieth new moon, they were all in Detroit. Each chief had only one piece of the red cedar stick left. They could hardly wait for the night of the new moon. Finally full darkness set in and black hung all around the big campfire of the new Indian Nation. The last pieces of the red cedar sticks were pitched on the fire. Smoke rose up to meet the Great Spirit."

Yellow Beard fell silent. Colter started to speak, but Yellow Beard cut him off. "Nothing happened!"

"Augh, blast it, you mean you have went through this entire long story for nothing?" Colter protested.

"Hold on, Colter. It happened. Just let me figure out when." Yellow Beard resumed the legend.

> "Shortly after the middle-point of dark it happened. I think I heard a white man say it was at two thirty A.M. Monday, December 16."

Yellow Beard stomped his feet, and rumbling came from his chest.

> "Ugh, the earth shook! The middle of the Mississippi River busted open. Big bluffs tumbled down, and hills pushed up from the bottom of the river. Land that was dry flooded, and riverbeds went dry as a bone and left fish swimming on dry land. The mighty Mississippi turned around and flowed backwards."

Yellow Beard looked around. Everyone sat with their mouths gaped open and staring wide-eyed. "Hey," he hollered, startling everyone from their spellbound daze. "That is how it happened. The Great Spirit with the help of Panther-Passing-Across made it happen!"

~

"Looky there," Barlow said, pointing to a willow-covered sandbar just down from where Red River joined the Atchafalaya River. "Thar's 'em skiffs Sublette said he'd have fer you, Yellow Beard." Somebody had beached the two skiffs and tied them to one of the willow trees.

"Jest as sure as the sun sets in the west, Sublette has left the skiffs he promised ya," Zeke bragged.

"Milton Sublette has done us right!" Yellow Beard said. His satisfaction with the beautiful flat-bottom skiffs was apparent by the tone of his voice.

"Looky how long and sleek them boats are. They must be twenty feet long," Zeke observed.

"Their ends're shaller, and their middle is deep," Barlow noticed.

"That's their rake," Colter said.

"I guess you have a fancy name for them being wider at the top than they are at their bottom?" Yellow Beard prodded.

"I guess I do; that is called their flare." Colter smiled proudly.

"They sure are funny lookin', fat in the middle and skinny on each end," Barlow noted.

"Ah, that is their swell," Colter explained.

Zeke made his usual funny remark. "Man, you got a name fer ever'thing. Ya got one thing right, though. Them boats sure are swell."

"Milt Sublette sure done us right," Yellow Beard kept saying. "What does that printing say on the bow of them, Colter?"

"It says Red Exploration, and that is mine and your names burned into the bow of them," Colter answered. "One of them says Yellow Beard and the other one says Colter, and our names are in capital letters."

Yellow Beard let out a Yahoo! "Which one is mine, and what do you mean by capital letters?"

Colter pointed to the one on their near side. "That one is yours." Colter pulled at his ear lobe. He was trying to think of a way to explain to Yellow Beard what capital letters were. After a while, he said, "Capital letters are big letters." That seemed to satisfy Yellow Beard's curiosity.

After they transferred their cargo into the new boats and admired them for some time, Yellow Beard glanced toward Colter and winked. Then he asked Zeke flat out, "Uh, how are we going to get our mules into those boats?"

Zeke had a quick answer, as if he had been dwelling on the problem all along. "I ain't … how're ya'll gonna get yer mules in 'em?"

"We ain't; we're going to sell them," Colter chided.

"Not me; I ain't asellin' Dollar. Me and Dollar'll goes on the bank. I have been tolt Red River plays out 'fore ya get to Santa Fe. Me and Dollar'll needs each other then. I'd take ya'll's mules with me if ya'd like," Zeke volunteered. "I'll be the mule tender-to-er. I'd rather company with mules than the likes uv you three anyway."

Yellow Beard knew Red River played out before Santa Fe and they would need the mules then. "That's a solution that I ain't thought of. In fact, you and Barlow can be mule tenders, and if we get in a bind with the skiffs, Barlow can come to our rescue. One man can easily handle those skiffs even upstream.

"If Ya thinks ya need help with the skiffs, ya should uh thought uv the solution ta yer problem before we left rendezvous. Ya could've hired us a couple uh extra men." Zeke didn't look like he was going to budge, but finally he said, "Yeah, I'll share Barlow with ya."

Someone parted the willows and peeked out. "Reckon ya aren't gonna need no hep with the boats. One man kin take 'em ascattin' … even upstream ta boot."

"Come on out where we can see you," Yellow Beard ordered.

Wrinkled, weather-tanned and lanky, the someone stepped out of his hiding place. Yellow Beard surmised he was a fisherman, since the dried crust on the front of his tattered overalls appeared to be fish scum. The man asked to buy a mule from them.

"Whom might you be, and why were you hiding in those willows and spying on us?" Colter asked the raggle-taggle man.

"I wudn't aspyin'. I'd just walked up frum acheckin' my fishin' poles and heerd ya talking. I ez the fisherman what made them boats, and I wuz hopin' for uh easy way home."

"You still haven't answered Colter's question. What's your name and where is home?" Yellow Beard prodded.

"I ez tryin' ta get 'round ta that." The poor excuse for a clean man placed his forefinger against one nostril and blew hard, sending mucus flying. "I'm Fishy Fortner frum down on the Chaffeli River. I make uh livin' tyin' nets, buildin' boats, and acatchin' fish and sellin' em."

"You pointed downstream to the Chaffeli. Just how far is it down there to her?" Yellow Beard asked.

"Not so far's I can't walk if I hafta. Right here, where we're astandin' es where the mouth uv the Chaffeli use' ta be. Frum here upstream es Red River, and from here downstream es the Chaffeli, till she gets to the ocean. Now that ya know my hist'ry, what ez yer names, and what'cha gonna do with my perty boats?"

"I'm Yellow Beard, and the one there with the dark complexion and sandy hair is Colter. The brawny one is Barlow, and the tall one is Zeke. We're working for the Rocky Mountain Fur Company. Namely, we're the Red Exploration, and we're looking for beaver."

"Mr. Fishy, we ain't asellin' the mules. I guess you'll just have'ta make yer own tracks ta get ya home," Zeke said. Fishy nodded. He was used to delivering his fine boats and returning home on foot. But a mule would have been nice all the same.

"Before you go, Fishy … I have a question for you." Yellow Beard hoped Fishy might be able to help him.

"Sure enuf, fire 'way. I'll answer ya, if I can."

"In your dealings, have you ever heard of a trapper by the name of Bill Cooper?"

"Nope, can't say as ever I have." Fishy waved a hand and left, headed south, through the river bottom.

They spent two days at the junction of the Chaffeli and Red rivers but decided to spend one more night and leave early the next morning.

~

The Red River Expedition had been traveling up Red River three weeks, and the hot nights of August had given way to the cooler ones of September, but the days were sultry. Yellow Beard and Colter rounded a bend and heard the sound of voices. The small settlement was docile; a wagon drawn by a little mule coming down the miry street was the only evidence of life.

"Whoa!" the driver commanded as Yellow Beard approached. The man was sitting on the seat of the wagon, his blunderbuss in his lap.

"Where are we?" Yellow Beard asked.

"Natchitoches," the man said as his load of waterfowl began quavering. One especially large goose ~ apparently only wounded ~ caused the commotion. It was flouncing like a chicken with its head chopped off.

"The hunting must be good, mister," Yellow Beard remarked.

"Nah, huntin's off. Tis hard ta get more than a couple uh hundred a day now. I think the smallpox es hit 'em like it has the Injuns. Uh few years back a gent by the name uh Bill Cooper came through here and kilt four hundred geese in one evening."

"Sure enough! He's my father! Where'd he go?" Yellow Beard brightened.

"Don't rightly know; said they were headed ta Santa Fe."

Yellow Beard already knew that much, but it was good to hear the name Bill Cooper spoken by a stranger. He turned and walked back toward the river. *Smallpox, uh! Them white men won't ever get it! It's not the dying off, it's the ruthless killing!* The Red Expedition made camp in preparation to spend the night.

~

Two more weeks of easy traveling up the Red River after leaving the village had brought them to within eyesight of the "Great Raft." As far as the eye could see, Red River was jam-packed with logs and debris.

"Colter, what is that crazy contraption up ahead?" Yellow Beard asked.

"Man, I don't know what it is, but I can tell you what it's doing. It's eating that logjam."

"It can't be. Uh mechanical beaver, I ain't ever heard of such," Yellow Beard replied. "We're gonna camp right here. Barlow and Zeke need to catch up anyway. I gotta talk to someone and find out what that thing is."

Zeke and Barlow, along with the mules, arrived mid-afternoon. All of them sat around camp and watched the unbelievable machine eat logs. "Ain't it wonderful that we live in a time when such amazing things like a machine that can eat logjams exist!" Yellow Beard said.

In a little while, a couple of men left the rig and came ashore. They apparently intended to strike camp. Yellow Beard gave them time to get started then asked Colter, "Do you want to go with me and give the fellows a hand?"

"No. I see what I see, and that's good enough for me."

Yellow Beard gingerly approached the men to ask them if they needed some help.

He wished to impress upon them that he was not just an ordinary Indian; so he used his best English to introduce himself. He addressed the tall one who he assumed was in charge.

"Sir, I am Yellow Beard. I am in the employment of the Rocky Mountain Fur Company. I am the Field Commander of the Red Exploration. That is my men over there, and we are exploring Red River for new trapping territory."

"Well, I'm privileged to make your acquaintance, Mr. Yellow Beard. I'm Henry Shreve, and that's my steamboat out there. I call her my snag steamboat. I took a contract with the U. S. Government to remove that raft … she is an aberration to river travel. I mounted a big steam engine onto that barge, and she uses the logs in the logjam to generate power to winch more logs onto the barge. My men continually feed them into the throat of the gigantic firebox that fires the boiler. The more that they feed her, the more she wants. She just keeps inching her way into that big raft for more logs. I offer immediate employment for woodhawks. If you run into anyone who needs a job, send them to me, will you?"

"Uh, sure thing, I'll do it. That's quite a contrivance you have there, Mr. Shreve. How long's she been eatin' logs?"

"Nigh on to a month, and we're just getting started. It's probably gonna take us till the year '35 or so to get the job done," Henry speculated.

"Shame you won't be finished when we come back this way. The portage around this jam is not going to be fun. Well, I won't keep you talking. I need to get back to my men. Oh! One other thing, in your doings on Red River have you ever ran into a fellow by the name of Bill Cooper?"

Mr. Shreve scratched his head. "I can't say as I have. The name don't sound familiar."

"Thanks anyway. Nice meeting you. Catch you next time." Yellow Beard headed back to their camp.

~

With nighttime drawing nigh and the portage ahead, long and arduous, they struck camp. They built a fire and waited ~ there was not a wink of sleep ~ they just waited. The snag steamer's engine bellowed, the woodhawk's axes clanked, logs banged and bumped, and the crew barked orders at each other all night.

The Red Exploration was ready to travel at first light. They didn't have to get up; they were already up.

Yellow Beard instructed Barlow and Zeke to cut four long cedar poles. From them they fashioned two travoises to carry the boats around the raft. Yellow Beard and Colter hitched their mules to the travoises and turned the boats upside down on them. Along the way the mules took turns pulling the load. The mules that weren't pulling carried packs of supplies for the journey. The men dug a hole in the ground in which to cache the exploration's supplies that they needed to leave behind.

A well-worn trail by the side of Red River made by people portaging around was easy enough to follow. The Great Raft stretched on and on; one hundred fifty miles by some estimations, seventy-five miles by others, before Red River showed its face again.

"What if ya'll had've sold yer mules? Them boats have got ya'll's names writ on 'em. Barlow and me wouldn't uv helped ya tote em either," Zeke needled.

Six miserable days spent getting around the Great Raft called for a day of rest.

"Let's unload the supplies and unhitch the mules. We're gonna finish the day off here, under these beautiful cottonwood trees," Yellow Beard instructed. Zeke led Dollar and Squirt while Barlow led Yellow Beard's and his mules to a green grassy glade where he hobbled them. The men set up camp in the dappled shade provided by the surrounding cottonwoods.

"I'm gonna collect me the night's sleep that I lost listening to your mechanical beaver, Yellow Beard," Zeke said as he piled up under a tree.

~

The next day, Barlow and Zeke took the four mules and headed back to the cached supplies. Yellow Beard and Colter stayed behind. They planned to do a little prospecting and watch over the boats and their supplies. When Barlow and Zeke arrived back at the lower end of the giant raft, they retired for the day. The next morning, Barlow and Zeke dug out the cached supplies, loaded them onto the four mules, and headed back to the upper end of the Great Raft where Yellow Beard and Colter were waiting.

Yellow Beard and Colter had enjoyed the wait. They had spent some time prospecting for fur. They even killed a fat Elk and were busy jerking it over a smoldering pecanwood fire when Barlow and Zeke returned.

The Great Raft had made for a mighty lengthy delay ~ eighteen days to be exact. It was the first week in October, and the first frost of the season threatened as they plowed themselves deep into their blankets.

"In the mornin' we'll be atravelin' easy again," Barlow said, expelling a sigh of relief.

Colter, Yellow Beard and Zeke nodded in agreement.

20

The St. Louis-Santa Fe Trading Company, although a joint venture between Felipe and Pierre, had always operated on the premise that each division stood on its own merits. Pierre's St. Louis division was still strong as the breadwinner of the combined enterprise, but things were changing because of the new liquor laws.

The Santa Fe division continued to have serious troubles, which had been the case for nearly 20 years. Now it threatened financial ruin for the whole company, and the partners realized they needed to do something and quick.

"The Santa Fe division had no more chance than a boar shoat," Pierre conceded. A simple fact was there had never been an easy way to get to Santa Fe from New Orleans. Felipe tried to reach Santa Fe by traveling up Red River, as they originally planned. He ran up against overwhelming odds. Mother Nature drove the first peg in the company's coffin in 1811. She sent the New Madrid earthquakes.

The New Madrid quake had caused Red River to leave the Mississippi River. Only a dry river bed connected them in the quake's wake. Red River then joined up with the Atchafalaya River and they had made their way to the Gulf of Mexico. The mouth of the Atchafalaya was a giant mud hole of silt; that had settled out of the water, as the swift water of the rivers met the still waters of the Gulf of Mexico. Felipe's first obstacle was that he couldn't even find a way to get into Red River.

The Rio Grande, as a trade route to Santa Fe, was more impossible than Red River!

Every attempt that Felipe had made to establish a trade route between New Orleans and Santa Fe, South of Red River, had failed ~ for one reason or the other. The more Southern routes had failed because of two reasons. The first reason was; that those routes had taken them through the Comanches' trading grounds. The second reason was. Immigrant settlers from the United States had begun to spill over into the Mexican Province of Texas ~ as a result, all organized attempts to cross the Mexican territory of Texas met resistance from Mexican soldiers ~ they and Mexican soldiers were at each other's throats.

How to get from New Orleans to Santa Fe had remained the question to answer, for Felipe throughout his venture. He had come to the conclusion, that no viable way existed to do that. There wasn't anything else left to do; they dissolved their partnership. The St. Louis-Santa Fe Trading Company was no more.

Pierre held onto his old trading route between New Orleans and St. Louis. He changed the name of his company back to the Lilly Trading Company. Then he came face to face with a new problem: obtaining whisky. Company profits had taken a nosedive after the 1832 bill excluding liquor from being sold to the Indians. Whisky had become as scarce as hen's teeth. Pierre not only couldn't find whisky to take to St. Louis, he couldn't transport it there when he found it. What he needed was someone who knew Red River, someone who could guide him around its treachery and knew where the whisky stills were.

In a way Felipe was glad they had dissolved the old company. His son Juan and he began a new venture. They traded between Pierre Lilly in New Orleans on the one hand and his daddy in Veracruz on the other hand. Felipe and Juan named their new company The Sanchez and Son Trading Company. *We have a pleasant trade route, and the company is very profitable. What more could we ask?* Felipe thought. They relished the fact that they had no Indians and no Mexican soldiers and no logjams to contend with. They sailed leisurely along the coast between New Orleans and Veracruz ~ not a care in the world.

Felipe and Juan were making lots of easy money, and it began to break down Felipe's moral fiber; the more he got, the more he wanted. The profits grew, and Felipe became more and more unhappy ~ it was all too easy. He missed the excitement of the frontier. He missed the struggle, the fight and the raw excitement. Pierre wasn't helping matters.

~

Pierre pled his case. "We can get rich in just a few years smuggling whisky to the fur companies, Felipe, if you will only join me in my efforts. If we don't do it, someone else will."

"I know, but Juan and I are doing okay now, and smuggling is against the law. If the United States feels that the Indians shouldn't have whisky, who am I to deliver it to them anyway?" Felipe countered.

"Well, I'll tell you one thing. The United States has been so successful in drying up whisky production along the Mississippi, Missouri and Arkansas rivers, the poor trappers that need it can't get it! At the last rendezvous there was very little whisky and many dry throats. What little that skipped the search-and-seizure operations at Fort Leavenworth didn't hurt a thing. It wouldn't hurt if we smuggled just a tad through either." Pierre was extremely astute in what made Felipe tick. He knew Felipe could stomach, just a tad, the idea of smuggling more easily than he could their going in whole hog.

"Taking a small amount in wouldn't be so much like smuggling, I suppose. It would be more like we were taking enough whisky for the trappers and everyone, but not the Indians. They couldn't be much money, though, in such a small amount, do you think?" Felipe reasoned.

"I don't know about that. I've heard reports of a gallon of raw whisky being cut into ten gallons of river water. Then they soup it up a little bit and sell it for three to four dollars a pint or even a buck a cup." What Pierre didn't say was that was what it was selling for at rendezvous, but the fur companies would pay nowhere near that price.

Felipe's eyes lit up, but he didn't say anything.

Pierre knew he had Felipe hooked, or at least interested, in the idea. *Now all I have to do is make it sound easy.* Pierre began his pitch.

"Kenneth McKenzie ran the upper Missouri outfit for the American Fur Company ~ he tried to brew his own whisky ~ then he got caught and they let him go. After he got himself caught, the facts started to come out. He claimed that he got his still from some friends up on Red River. I have always known there were stills on the Red River, but they are so secret and off the beaten path they are being overlooked."

"There ain't anyone that has the experience with Red River that you do. I know that you and I are too old to go traipsing up the river; but that young Juan, now he could sniff them stills out and buy the whisky. Why, we can get richer than ye old Mint in Philadelphia." Pierre really gave Felipe a snow job.

"You know," Felipe began, "all these years we might have been missing the point about Red River's importance. We were consumed with getting to Santa Fe and with finding her treasures of gold and silver. We might have missed out on the real treasure, Red River herself and her whisky!" Felipe had not said so in so many words, but he had given in to Pierre!

~

Terisa learned that Felipe and Pierre planned to smuggle whisky to the fur companies, but this time she said nothing ~ this time she just brooded over the matter.

How could decent human beings poison other human beings? They know they are feeding them addictive poison, albeit it's to Indians! Against the wishes of the United States, against the law, and in the name of profit ~ how can they do it?

Terisa didn't have the desire to talk it out with Felipe, nor did she think that any good could come from it. They had had the greed conversation so many times before. She knew how obstinate he could be. Terisa had watched Felipe's greed consume him, and always before she had stopped him. Not this time. This time she quietly went her own way. She moved to Mexico City. Annabelle convinced Renee that they should move to Mexico City along with his mother.

"Your mother needs someone to look after her in her state of despair. Who better than you?" Annabelle pled.

It grieved Terisa every day that Felipe had chosen wealth over her. She could not bear to think of how he had openly violated her love for him. Seeing their fondness for each other wither, then turn to disdain, ripped her heart to smithereens. Their marriage ended in a bitter divorce.

Abner Lilly's law practice had grown into one of the most successful practices in New Orleans. It shocked him out of his mind when Felipe came to him. He had never thought he would be drawing up a bill of divorcement for his Uncle Felipe and his Aunt Terisa. It broke his heart when he had to do it.

"Only out of my love for the both of you will I do it, not for the money!" Abner told both of them as they sat on the other side of his desk.

Felipe knew even though Terisa never mentioned it, the problem she had with him was about the whisky smuggling. She had made it plain to him on many occasions that someday his greed for wealth would replace his love for her. *The sad thing is that we can't talk about it. If she would only talk, I might could convince her,* he thought

Felipe and Pierre went ahead with their plans to try and smuggle whisky off Red River. Felipe rationalized in his mind, *with the money we make, I can retire. Then I'll move to Mexico City and regain Terisa's love*.

~

Pierre had Abner draw up a contract that outlined the new venture, and both he and Felipe signed it. Preparations got underway to send Juan up Red River in search of a whisky still that would sell to them.

He was to leave immediately, but first he had to hire a guide.

The truth was Juan lacked the experience necessary to do the job Felipe and Pierre had for him to do. He hadn't ever been on Red River. He hadn't ever dealt with hostile Indians or with thugs like he would run into on Red River.

Their glaring mistake, though, was in letting him chose his own guide. He picked a boozy trapper who called himself Barney. He revealed to Juan that on Red River everyone knew him as Boozy Barney; that should have tipped Juan off, but it didn't. Pierre insisted if anyone can find whisky it would be a drunk.

The facts about Boozy Barney were that he had never been farther up Red River than the Great Raft and could not converse successfully with the Indians or anyone else, for that matter, due to his vaunty attitude.

His appearance was enough to make anyone want to fight. He wore tight-legged pants that were much too short. He had on a billowy shirt with lace around the cuffs and a dirty green beaver-fur top hat with a red feather in the brim.

Juan set forth on his exploration May 1, 1833. He and Barney left New Orleans and went to the mouth of the Atchafalaya River. They went up it to the Giant Raft on Red River. There they camped a few days and visited with Henry Shreve. They cached everything, except what they could carry on their backs, and began the portage around the logjam. They hardly got out of sight of Henry Shreve's camp.

The clues read that their ambush had come at the hands of a small raiding party. A small group of pretend Indians operated in the area and had been ambushing passersby. Indications were that they were the ones responsible. They had killed them, scalped them and robbed them, then left their arrows behind. Real Indians always took their arrows with them if they had time to retrieve them.

Felipe would not learn of his son's demise until July.

~

Pierre had retired from making the long voyages to St. Louis. His passion for the wild frontier faded to a memory in his mind. Maintaining the family estate was his passion now. He was always working in the yard ~ he cultivated beautiful roses, scraped the yard, and planted a vegetable garden ~ there was not a blade of grass in his landscape. The Lillys loved to entertain friends and guests and entertained on an almost nightly basis.

The day had been hot and humid, a typical July day. The evening provided the same kind of sticky humidity, the air almost too thick to breathe. *Every creature that can sweat is, even the snakes and the frogs,* Pierre thought. Pierre and Christine had retired to the rose garden where they were drinking tea and watching the hummingbirds work the trumpet vine that grew along the fence. Christine thumbed through the newspaper, reading the headlines.

"You know, Pierre, we're the two luckiest people in the world. We have everything that we ever hoped for. The mansion, wealth, success, and our health, what more could we ever wish for?" Christine was visibly happy, but she did have a wish. *I'm not going to bring up the only thing that I wish for, though.*

"Well, yeah, I guess," Pierre said.

Neither of them mentioned the only thing they had left to wish for. That wish always went unmentioned. They both longed to find Jacob and for the family to make amends. They had learned from the bounty hunters that Jacob had made a fine mountain man. All attempts to have him brought home, he had foiled and they had given up. If he ever came home now, it would be because he wanted to. They sat silently. *If Jacob and I could only go on an expedition up Red River, we could find the illusive Red River whisky. I know we could! I doubt Juan will be successful. He is too much of a city slicker,* Pierre thought.

"Juan should be back soon, don't you think?" Christine said.

"I 'spect so. We didn't send him all the way to Santa Fe to buy whisky. We just sent him to see if he could find a still on Red River. Do you remember when he left, honey?"

News from the rendezvous caught Christine's attention as she thumbed through the paper.

"Honey, did you read this account by Joe Meek of what happened at the rendezvous?"

"I reckon not … read it to me."

> "During the indulgence of these excesses, while at this rendezvous, there occurred one of those incidents of wilderness life which make the blood creep with horror. Twelve of the men were bitten by a mad wolf, which hung about the camp for two or three nights. Two of these were seized with madness in camp, sometime afterwards, and ran off into the mountains, where they perished. One was attacked by the paroxysm while on a hunt, when, throwing himself off his horse, he struggled and foamed at the mouth, gnashing his teeth, and barking like a wolf. Yet he

> retained consciousness enough to warn away his companions, who hastened in search of assistance; but when they returned, he was nowhere to be found. It was thought that he was seen a day or two afterwards, but no one could come up with him, so it was assumed he, too, perished.
> "At the time, however, immediately following the visit of the wolf to camp, Captain Stuart was admonishing Meek on the folly of his ways, telling him that the wolf might easily have bitten him, he was so drunk. 'It would have killed him, ~ sure, if it hadn't cured him!' said Meek."

"I sure hope that Jacob wasn't one of them that got bit!" Christine sighed.

"Probably not," Pierre said, "He's too mean for a mad wolf to bite him."

Two riders and their horses were coming down the long shady lane that led to the front gate. Giant magnolia trees cast their shadows along its length. The clip clop of the horses' hooves rang clearly, as the shod sorrel ponies cantered in and out of the shadows. The men, wearing military uniform, reined in their horses in front of the bench where Pierre and Christine sat. *Two soldiers could bear nothing but bad news. It's probably Jacob,* Pierre assumed.

"Sir, are you Felipe Sanchez?" one of the soldiers asked.

Pierre stood and saluted the officers. "No, sir, he is my brother-in-law. Maybe I can help you, though."

"Very well. I'll let you deliver this to Felipe Sanchez." He handed Pierre an official-looking sealed envelope. "It bears news of the death of Juan Sanchez."

Christine gasped and burst into tears.

"Certainly, sir," Pierre managed.

The horsemen rode down the lane and disappeared into the evening dusk.

Pierre put his arms around Christine and held her, all the while struggling with an anger boiling inside him. Finally, he could hold it back no longer.

"I'm going to break the news to Felipe and apprise him of the fact that our plans to smuggle whisky from Red River are off. Forgotten! Never will happen!"

~

Felipe said nothing for a long spell. His heart was broken. His only son was gone.

"See what greed can get you!" Felipe yelled into the winds. He wanted everyone to hear what he had to say.

"It cost me my son!" Felipe sobbed.

"It cost me my wife!" Tears ran down his checks like the waters of Red River at flood.

Felipe's heart only had room for one thought. *Now all I have is my worthless life!*

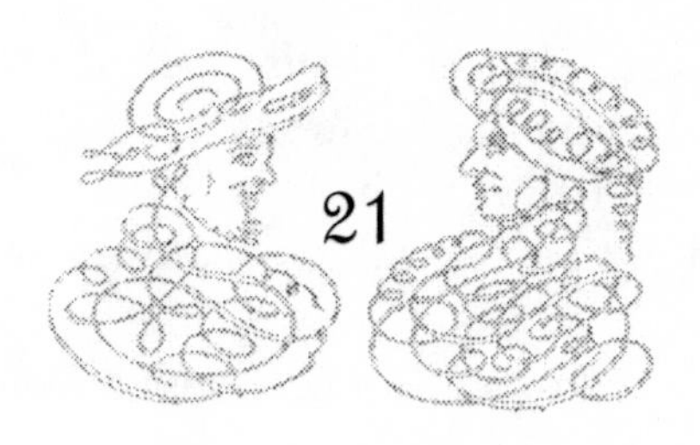

21

"We've been traveling north ever since we left the Great Raft. I know somewhere Red River'll turn west," Yellow Beard predicted.

"Yes, and it's been over a week since we cleared the great raft. I'm tired of north. I want to go west." Colter frowned.

A Gigantic rocky bluff loomed on the east side of the river. They had reached the spot. Red River was beginning a gradual curve to the left, toward the west.

Square in the middle of this big bend, Yellow Beard spotted a sign.

"Look, Colter. Somebody's marker ~ points up the bluff ~ what do you suppose it's for?" Yellow Beard pointed it out.

As they drew closer, Colter squinted. "Ah, it says: 'Fulton's whisky fer sale Cheap, by the pint.' Do you suppose we should check it out?"

"I ain't about to climb that steep bluff for a pint uh whisky. Besides pints uh whisky ain't what Sublette's looking for. If the reading said barrels, then maybe I'd go for it."

Upriver, about a mile from this bend, there were two rivers. One of them continued west and the other one veered north. The one headed west was slightly larger in size than the one going north. Yellow Beard and Colter studied both rivers for quite some time, neither of them sure which was Red River. They pulled ashore and waited on Barlow and Zeke to catch up with the mules. The two men arrived before nightfall.

"I'm tired uh going north, and I think Red River is, too. I bet that's her agoin' west," Barlow figured.

Yellow Beard and Colter agreed: The channel going west had to be Red River. Its water was red, and the river that came from the north had blue water.

Zeke voiced his opinion. "The river going west is a big river and the one going north is a little river." The name stuck. From that day on, the river that joined Red River just above Fulton's still became known as Little River.

The big sandbar that jutted out from Little River on its upstream side looked like a good campsite. They all agreed to camp there.

Willow leaves, small twigs and big limbs, bearing the gnaw marks of beaver, floated everywhere. Colter noted Little River in his log as a good place to trap, along with a crude hand-drawn map that showed the two rivers and the rock bluff. *Any time it's cold enough for fur to prime, this is a good place to trap*, he noted in the margin.

Yellow Beard was frying salt pork just as the last rays of light faded. Out of the corner of his eye, he saw a big alligator come from the willow-infested swamp behind them. She crawled out on the bank and made her way to the junction of Red and Little rivers. She came close enough to them that the firelight glistened from her wet mossy back.

Barlow, Zeke and Colter dove for the nearest saltcedar saplings and tried to shinny up them. Yellow Beard banged her on the head with his sizzling hot cast-iron skillet. He attempted to herd her away from the wildly gyrating sapling Zeke chose to shinny up. She snapped at Zeke's heels, her teeth clanked together.

"Uh, shew … Scat …." Yellow Beard turned the alligator away from Zeke, and she headed to the river. But for some unknown reason she turned and lunged toward Yellow Beard's face. He grabbed the skillet with both hands and slung it with all his might. The alligator saw the sizzling skillet come at her. She raised her head and opened her mouth. Her nostrils flared, and her eyelids slowly lowered to protect her eyes. Her teeth snapped together with a sound of enamel to cast iron. She commenced to slinging her head violently, back and forth ~ back and forth, in her attempt to separate yellow Beard from the skillet. Suddenly she realized the greasy sizzling hot skillet wasn't what she wanted. She dropped it and scampered away. They watched her enter the cool river water and roll over and over. She held her jaws open wide. *To cool her tongue*! Yellow Beard thought.

"I think the saltcedar saplin' that I chose ta climb would've helt me up, but I couldn't hold it steady enuf ta climb. Another thing I tried ta climb higher than it was!" Zeke shivered.

They all expressed relief that the incident was over. A sliver of the silver moon had risen over the towering trees of the riverbottom. It had been a full two hours since the alligator attack. Hunger pains reminded them that they hadn't eaten. Yellow Beard recovered the cold salt pork from the gritty sand. They swished boiling hot coffee, as strong as they could make it, around in their mouths to wash the cold-greasy-gritty-salt pork down.

Thinking that the big alligator might come back to her lair in the swamp, the same way she had gone to the river, kept much sleep from happening that night.

Unbeknownst to the prospectors, their camp at the black rock bar would prove to be more hair-raising than their Little River fiasco.

~

Barlow woke up with the sun blazing into his face. He crawled out of his blanket. *They must not uh got any more sleep than I did. They ain't anyone up an at 'em early*, he concluded.

Hunger finally prodded Yellow Beard awake, and he made sure the others followed. Yawns, stretches, and scratching were the first order of the day, but complaints of uneasy sleep came in a close second. Everyone agreed that fitful described the night of sleep they had. Everyone except Zeke, that is, who said his night's sleep was unfruitful. "I'm still tired," he complained. Barlow and Zeke and the mules pulled out of camp after they ate.

"Avoid that alligator swamp!" Yellow Beard hollered at their departing backsides.

"Don't sweat yerself over that," Barlow yelled back.

It was more than an hour before Colter and Yellow Beard got underway.

~

Even with the late start they arrived at the black rock bar an hour before sunset. "Look up ahead." Colter pointed to the shiny black chunks of rock that stretched haphazardly across Red River. Yellow Beard thought it best to cut the day's travels short and make camp.

"With the loss of sleep last night and that big blue-black bank in the north looking at us, I think that's a good bet," Colter agreed.

"We can put the boats into the high end of that black rock bar, there where it's flat, and camp in that little draw there by those big rocks," Yellow Beard instructed.

"The winds have been shifty all evening, and that bank has been building back there in the north. What little protection those big rocks give us will be welcome when the Norther hits us," Colter predicted.

When Barlow and Zeke arrived, the first thing Barlow noticed was there were no trees big enough for them to climb in case of alligators.

"There won't be any 'gators out here. They don't like for rocks to scratch their bellies," Yellow Beard kidded.

"Alligators like mud," Colter chimed in.

They crawled into their blankets, unsuspecting of what the night might bring.

Suspicion that a Norther would hit ~ or intuition about how to cope with it when it did ~ caused Yellow Beard and Colter to retire to the north side of the campfire. Barlow and Zeke unknowingly or unwittingly chose the south side of the fire for their beds. That put them in a position where the north wind would blow across the fire onto them and then continue across the river.

"We'll stay warmer than ya'll, 'cause the north wind'll be warmed by the fire before it gets to us," Zeke chided.

"I'd rather be cold than hot; someday it'll learn you," Yellow Beard warned.

The first Norther of the fall blew in with gale-force winds around midnight.

With each gust of wind, loose embers blew from the campfire and fizzled in the river water. The night air was growing colder, and the fire was dying down. Barlow and Zeke rolled closer to the fire for warmth. It was only a matter of time until an ember found their blankets. A severe gust sprayed live embers onto Barlow and Zeke. The winds fanned the sparks into smoldering hot spots. The two sleeping men were getting warm and rolled away from the fire.

The minute they rolled, the hot spots burst into flames. Engulfed in smoke and fire, they both rolled as furiously as they could into the icy water. The sound of frying flame and spewing smoke quickly gave way to screams and gasps for air. They tore themselves away from their drenched blankets and waded to the bank.

"What woke me up was the splashing and gasping that I heard when ya'll went into the frigid river water," Yellow Beard remembered.

"The sizzle is what I heard," Colter offered.

Yellow Beard and Colter went back to sleep and left them to build up the fire, thaw themselves out, and dry their bedding. It was in the wee hours of the morning before Barlow and Zeke bedded down again. This time they chose the north side of the fire. "My bed smells like a singed goose waiting to be plucked," Zeke complained. Barlow stifled a laugh.

Sleep was about to come when Zeke heard a deep-throated growl. Colter and Zeke sprang from their beds into a stand-up position. Yellow Beard recognized the sound even in his deepest sleep. He brought his Hawken rifle up with him when he rose to his feet. A white bear reprimanding her twin cubs for who knows what was equally as startled by the rising men as they were by her growl. She stretched to her full height on her hind legs and took giant steps right up to Zeke. Before he could react, the giant bruin swiped him with a forepaw and opened her mouth. She was aiming for his head.

Zeke muzzily remembered that bears fancied eating their prey alive. He shivered, tickling the she-bear's fancy even more.

Barlow watched in horror from just outside the firelight. *I must uv scared her when I left my covers 'n' come out here. I'm hepless. My Hawken is back in my covers.* All he could do was scream at the bruin. He did.

No one heard Barlow's screams. The resonate roar of the bear drowned them out. And if the giant white bear heard the screams, they had no effect. Yellow Beard couldn't fire his Hawken rifle, either, because when he looked down the barrel, all he could see was Zeke nestled in the bear's forelegs. Colter let out a blood-curdling scream and at the same time lunged onto the back of the frothing bear. He reached around the bear's massive head with his left arm, grabbed a handful of its long hair and hung on for dear life. With his right arm, he plunged his long, razor-sharp blade blindly into the bear's face. The blade found the bear's open mouth. A split-second later, Zeke's head would have been in there. The heavy cold steel blade buried into the scarlet flesh of the bear's palate. Colter felt her quiver and knew his blade found her brain. She slowly released her grip. Zeke fell to the ground and crawled on all fours so fast he skinned the hide from his knees on the sharp black rocks. The she-devil was unsteady on her feet now and flailed with her paws. Her attempts were futile. Try as hard as she could, she could not free the pestilence from her back. Colter twisted the blade and pulled it free, then plunged it in up to the hilt. Again and again he stabbed until Yellow Beard dragged him off the dead bear.

There was no more sleep to be had that night.

Colter skinned the bear by the light of the rising sun.

Yellow Beard rendered some of the bear's tallow over the campfire and set it aside to cool. He sorted through the bear's entrails and chose a nice big one that would make a good bag. He cut out a piece about a foot long and took it to the river where he washed it out thoroughly. Once the grease cooled, he packed it into the gut and tied off the ends.

Barlow and Zeke extracted the bear's toenails and rolled them up in a piece of rawhide for safekeeping.

"When we get home, Mother has got what it takes to put holes in them that you can put a sinew through. You can make yourselves a necklace," Yellow Beard explained.

They went looking, but the bear cubs were nowhere around.

"They're plenty old enuf ta make it on their own," Barlow told Zeke.

"I jest hope that when they grow up, I don't meet one uv 'em and it recognizes me and thinks that I was the one what killed its mammy," Zeke replied.

Yellow Beard and Barlow lay around camp all morning. They slept some but mostly just rested. They talked about the night's events, and Yellow Beard teased Barlow about the fire-in-their-bedding incident. They both had good laughs. The black rock bear incident wasn't a laughing matter. No one teased or laughed about that.

Zeke said that he was going to get some sleep if he ever quit shaking. "Right now, I gotta go pray to God and give him thanks for making that bear eat Colter's blade instead uh my head!" he said. He lay on his cover and thought about the last two nights. *Why on earth does ever critter seem ta wanta get ahold uh me? The 'gator or the bar, neither uv 'em wanted Barlow er Colter ... or Yellow Beard. I ain't askeered uv 'em any more 'en they are.* At last, sleep took him.

Colter was full of pent-up nervous energy, left over from his fight with the bear. There was no sleep in him nor any hurrahing. He worked on the beautiful white bear pelt. *I'm going to make me a sleeping robe that'll carry me through the Red River winter!* he decided.

He stretched the skin over a big rock and set to the tedious job of fleshing it. He cut away every piece of flesh and fat until the skin was nothing but rawhide. Next he made a paste from the bear's brains and the urine from its bladder. He put the brain-urine paste on the flesh side of the skin and thoroughly rubbed it in. After he admired the beautiful fur for a while, he made a lean-to over the fire and hung the pelt there to be smoke-cured.

Barlow roused out of his slumber. He stretched and yawned as usual. "Wonder what time uv day it's agettin' ta be?"

"Uh, it's 'bout time," Yellow Beard chided. "It's hi-noon. See there, you're standing on the shadow of yer head."

"What's that mean?" Barlow grumbled.

"When you can stand on the shadow of your head, it's the shortest that your shadow will be. From then on, the shadow of your head commences to get farther and farther from you, until it gets so far from you it disappears into the night." Yellow Beard educated them in the art of keeping time.

Barlow walked up the river bank in search of proper cooking wood.

That driftwood gives meat a punky taste. He could never describe to the rest of them just what kind of a taste that a punky taste was. Barlow returned with an armload of big splinters he had hacked from a pecan log that had drifted ashore during high water. He dragged some coals from the dying fire and placed a few small splinters on top of them. On knees and elbows, he blew into his teepee of splinters. Slowly the smoke increased until the fire could wait no longer. The teepee of splinters burst into flame.

"Wha'cha doin' thar, Barlow?" Zeke asked.

"I'm uh starvin' ta death. I'm gonna sizzle us up sum bear steaks. That is if'en anyone else is ahungered. Would ya go fetch me sum proper sizzlin' sticks, Zeke?"

Zeke left in search of good green hardwood. His mouth watered at the thought of roasted meat. He heard Barlow grumble something about his gut pinching his backbone. Shortly he returned with four good sticks and passed them around. By then Yellow Beard had cut four nice big juicy steaks from the bear's rump.

The fat dripped into the fire and caused the flames to leap higher and higher until they engulfed the sizzling steaks which browned in their own juices. The gentle breeze wafted the smell of the frying fat as it dripped on the glowing pecan-wood coals. Colter drooled when he opened his mouth to talk. "The smell is almost too good for me to bear."

"You'll have ta bear it; after all, it is bear," Zeke cracked.

Barlow spat shrivels from a stick he was chewing on. He took the chunks of meat off the fire and put them in a cast-iron pot.

They washed down the greasy bear steaks with boiled river-water coffee. Afterward they lolly-gagged around, until their stomachs settled. Zeke moved the mules to a new grazing spot and peeled them some cottonwood bark to eat. Barlow reloaded the camp into the boats. After the mules had sufficiently fed, Zeke and Barlow un-tethered them, and they left the black rock bar. Colter neatly rolled up his white bear pelt and left with Yellow Beard in the skiffs.

~

"The black rock bar was a piece of cake, Yellow Beard," Colter commented. "Didn't you say that we would lose time waiting for the river to rise before we could get past it?"

"Uh no, I said we were apt to lose time," Yellow Beard corrected. "The river is sure enough low all right. It's Fishy's boats that made it easy. I've never seen anything like them. The way he made them, they float in ankle-deep water even with a ton of cargo."

"We wouldn't have had any fun at all except for that ol' bruin that tried to eat Zeke and the fire-in-the-blankets incident," Colter said.

"Is bruins what bears are? I haven't ever heard them called that."

"Bruin was the name of the bear in *Reynard the Fox* by William Caxton, and ever since then bears have been called bruins," Colter said.

~

For the next couple of weeks, the weather settled down into its fall pattern. Every few days a fresh Norther would plummet down from Canada. The nights gradually grew colder and colder. The Canada geese were in their fall migration. As the prospectors sat around the campfire at night, they could hear the honkers go over. It was an awesome sight to see them flying in V-formation, silhouetted in front of the full moon, a wise old Gander leading the way.

"When the next good stream comes into Red River, Colter, maybe we ought to spend a few days trapping," Yellow Beard suggested.

"That sounds like a winner to me. I'm powerful tired of traveling and would like to spend a few days in the same spot. Looking back, we've made real good time; we left rendezvous the middle of July, and here it is just the end of October and we're only a couple of weeks from Bois d' Arc Creek," Colter figured.

Before the next main stream joined Red River, they received a pleasant surprise. Across on the south bank of the river, a body of water that looked like a long slough followed Red River.

"The way it parallels Red River and the way the vegetation is growing around it, I think that might be Paccawn Bayou," Yellow Beard speculated. "If it is, when we get on down the way it'll join back up with Red River again, but the water will be running into it from Red River. The land in the middle will be Paccawn Point." Yellow Beard brushed away a falling leaf. "If Jacob Black is still living there, we'll make an extended camp. We won't get out of there without losing at least a week. Another thing, after we leave Paccawn Point, I'll know what to expect. The Kiomitchie River is next after we leave Paccawn Point, and it's a bugger. That's where we lost Grizzly and Ketchum back in 1825. We want to be real careful around that nasty Kiomitchie!"

~

Yellow Beard and Colter guided the skiffs into the sandbar. Zeke and Barlow and the lathered mules came trotting out of the timber, rushing toward the reunion that was set to take place between Yellow

Beard and his old friend Jacob Black. Yellow Beard jumped out of his skiff just as Jacob Black grabbed his arm and pulled him into a full hug. Yellow Beard enjoyed seeing his old friend Jacob Black and Jacob Black he. Neither of them said anything for a long moment then they stood each other apart and studied each another. Jacob Black was the first to speak.

"Why, you old goat. That yellow, wiry, tangled up mat of a beard you got, I would have recognized you in tha dark. The only difference is last time I saw you, you were just a sprout of a kid."

"You've aged a little yourself. What happened to that black beard you had, grayed on you didn't it, and what's that shiny spot doing on top of your head without any hair on it?" They had much catching up to do and retired to Black's cabin. Colter joined them. Barlow and Zeke took the mules to Black's stable and went to the mercantile before they pitched camp down by the boats where they could watch over things.

Black was eyeing Colter steadily.

"Uh, forgive me, Jacob. This is Colter. Colter, this here is Mr. Jacob Black. All this land, Paccawn Point, belongs to him," Yellow Beard said.

"Did ya have any trouble following my directions to St. Louis?" Black asked.

"You give good directions. I had no trouble, easy as falling off a log," Yellow Beard assured him.

"Well, I am pleased ta make you acquaintance, Mr. Colter. Tell me Yellow Beard, what brings you and …?"

Colter butted in. "Yellow Beard and me are prospecting for … ah, for furs. We're working for the Rocky Mountain Fur Company."

Yellow Beard and Jacob Black held back from discussing Bill Cooper until the eve of their departure.

"Well, Yellow Beard, have you found your pa, or have you heard anything about him?" Black asked.

"Nary a word."

"How perturbing."

"I've given up on him being a trapper, and I'm on my way home. I hope Mother has heard from him … maybe he's there right now." Yellow Beard's heart quickened at the thought. "We'll be traveling come daybreak. We're going to prospect up the Kiomitchie River a bit. See if we can find the silver mines."

Yellow Beard and Colter were up just as the moon faded into the light of the rising sun. Colter said his fare-ye-wells to Black and went to gather up Barlow, Zeke and the mules. Yellow Beard, at his own insistence, paid the bill for the supplies Black had lent him so long ago.

It felt good to get underway again. Barlow and Zeke waded the mules across the shallow water to the north side of Red River. The last thing Colter saw of them, they had climbed the river bluff and disappeared in the canebrakes. True to Yellow Beard's prediction, they had lost the better part of a week, and even then Yellow Beard seemed reluctant to leave. Colter thought.

~

The boats made good time after they left Pecan Point, and things became more familiar to Yellow Beard with every passing mile.

He remembered how violent Red River's current was that day when Grizzly and Ketchum drowned. He could tell that he and Colter were nearing the place where the Kiomitchie ran into Red River. For several hours now, the river's current on the north side had gotten more and more swift.

"The Kiomitchie will enter soon," Yellow Beard predicted.

Of course the reason he is able to predict that is he remembers where the Kiamichi River runs into Red River, Colter thought.

Yellow Beard's prediction came true around the next bend. "Sure enough." Yellow Beard pointed to a beautiful stream that cut through an ancient grove of pecan trees and flowed into Red River.

Yellow Beard had to yell to be heard over the roiling water. "Us go into her abreast, and if either one of sees that we can't overcome the swift current, put in to the bank." Fishy's flat-bottom skiffs had amazed them time and time again, and this time was no exception. Yellow Beard and Colter stood up in their sterns and easily poled the skiffs through the swift current and into the calm waters of the Kiomitchie River.

They headed straight for the bank and made camp.

"When Barlow and Zeke get here with the mules, we'll all go across over there to that grove of pecan trees. We'll stay a few days and do us some trapping and prospecting." Yellow Beard's excitement showed. Trapping was in his blood, not to mention he thought Bill Cooper might be working the silver mines.

Colter and Yellow Beard built a fire and put coffee on to boil. Then they sat back and waited for Barlow and Zeke to arrive. When bedtime came and Barlow and Zeke still hadn't shown up, Colter stretched his ear lobe, and Yellow Beard knew he was nervous.

"What do you suppose is holding up Barlow and Zeke?" Colter asked Yellow Beard. He stretched at his other ear lobe. "I'm going to bed. Maybe they'll be here in the morning."

"I don't know what might be holding them up, but I'm with you, I'm going to bed, too." Yellow Beard crawled under his blanket. "In the morning we'll cross the Kiomitchie then make a more permanent camp. You can take Barlow or Zeke whichever one you prefer and I'll take the other one, and we'll catch us some beavers." Yellow Beard shut his eyes and relaxed his facial muscles.

"Sounds good to me. It's been too long since I took me a beaver." Colter's words fell on deaf ears. Yellow Beard had already started to snore.

In the morning, Barlow and Zeke were still no shows. Around mid-morning they straggled into camp ~ so beat, their tails were dragging between their legs.

"Where in tarnation have ya'll been?" Yellow Beard's concern showed.

"It's an awful long story. Do ya think we might get somethin' ta eat before we get into it?" Barlow pled.

"Help yourself. There's plenty left over for you to eat," Yellow Beard offered.

The eating slowed down a little bit and Barlow began to tell his story.

"Shortly after we left Paccawn Point, we wuz jumped by a band uv Indians. They wuz six or seven uv 'em, and they were all hooched up on whisky. They put up a real good fight ta be so drunk. Augh, did they ever fight!" Barlow put a bit of food into his mouth.

"And they wuz such young'uns," Zeke added.

"Yeah, we wuz in quite a predicament there." The wrinkles on Barlow's forehead deepened. "They were atryin' ta kill us and take the mules, and we couldn't stand the thoughts uh killin' one uv 'em. They wuz just pups." Barlow broke a stick from a bush and began to chew it into a toothbrush. "You tell 'em what you said, Zeke."

"I kept ahollerin' at 'em, askin' 'em how long they'd been weaned off uh their mammy. If anything it jest made 'em madder, though."

Barlow picked up where he left off. "Anyway, they kept us pinned the better part uv that day. Finally I got my shot. I put a galena ball across the top uh one uv 'em's head. It took hair and scorched a trench across his noggin, but it didn't kill him."

"It sure 'nuf made them pups skidoo!" Zeke observed. "That's 'nuf fer the baby Indian's battle. What's the plan, Yellow Beard?"

Yellow Beard pointed across Kiomitchie River. "Do ya'll see that paccawn grove over there? We're goin' to spend a few days over there and trap some beaver."

As it turned out beavers weren't very plentiful, and what few there were seemed trap wary.

They all liked their camp above all the others they had made since they left the Mississippi River. A herd of buffalo that lived in the area had kept the ground trampled clean to the point where there was no grass or underbrush.

They sat around camp and watched the sun go down. Squirrels harvesting their supper from the stark naked limbs of the pecan trees, backdropped by the setting sun, was a beautiful sight. The length of time it took between sunset and dark was all it took for everyone to go to sleep, except Colter. *The buffalo aided by the solid shade of the giant paccawn sure made us a perty camp.* Colter began to get dozey. *The snores of that tired and weary trio sure makes for horrible music*, he thought. Then he made it a quartet.

~

The cold January morning flushed the squirrels out in search of their breakfast. The first frost of fall had already knocked the leaves from the trees and exposed their bare branches. The exposed squirrels scampered from branch to branch and shook their bushy tails at the each other as they barked their chattering chants.

"Watch this shot." Barlow lined the .54 caliber Hawken's sights up on an unsuspecting squirrel. He gently squeezed the trigger. The powder exploded and blue smoke billowed out the end of the barrel. The galena ball from the Hawken smashed into the limb under the unsuspecting squirrel's head. Splinters of wood erupted ~ the squirrel fell to the ground, stone cold dead. "How's that?"

It was a well-known fact that Barlow loved to cook almost as much as he loved to eat. After he bagged a dozen or more of the pecan-fattened squirrels, he made his announcement.

"My mouth's awaterin' fer a good ol' squirrel stew." He began to bark orders. "One uv you go gather me a Indian turnip, and one uv you get the Dutch oven. One uv you crack me sum 'cons and one uv you get the cornmeal. Hey, one uv you stoke up the fire. We are gonna have a squirrel stew fer supper!"

"Ya might be good at barkin' squirrels, but you ain't no good at barkin' orders. You've barked five orders and they ain't but three uv us. What're you gonna do?" Zeke complained.

"Fer lands sakes," Barlow protested. "I've done barked the squirrels and now I'm gonna skin 'em and make 'em ready fer the pot, then I'm gonna cook 'em fer ya. Can't ya'll do more 'en one thing at a time?"

~

"I'm going up Kiomitchie," Yellow Beard announced. "The French call this Mine River because there's a big silver mine on the bank away up there." He pointed upstream. "The Indians have found silver on a little creek that dumps into the Kiomitchie about, what white man calls, three miles from here. My father may be there. I'll be back 'fore sun falls."

~

Barlow picked around on the squirrels for what seemed like hours getting all the hair off. Then he put some water in the Dutch oven and immersed the quartered squirrels in it. He slivered some Indian turnip into the concoction and threw in a double handful of pecan goodies. After the squirrels stewed about an hour or so, he removed the lid from the pot and poured a couple of handfuls of cornmeal into the pot. While he had the lid up, he waved his hand around through the rising steam a few times and wafted a little aroma toward the starved onlookers. After he replaced the lid he piled some red hot coals on top.

"It'll be 'bout an hour," Barlow announced.

They knew what Barlow wanted when he wafted the aroma in their direction ~ he was fishing for compliments ~ they would give him none of those.

"Is that an omen or a warning?" Colter gouged.

"Sometimes Barlow's grub ain't nothin' ta say Amen over," Zeke quipped.

"Jest ya'll keep it up, and I won't let ya have any uv Barlow's famous squirrel stew!" Barlow warned.

"We'll not peep nary anuther word," Zeke promised.

And no one did.

The stew was finally ready. Just as they began to eat, Colter looked up and saw a man and a boy, a grown boy, coming through the pecan grove.

"We got company."

Everyone made sure their guns were in reach as the approaching pair grew nearer.

"Hold your fire!" Yellow Beard announced. "This here is Stiller Johnson an' his son, Jeb."

"I'm Colter." Colter began to point as he introduced the others.

"That's Barlow and that's Zeke. What brings you, Stiller?"

Stiller Johnson pled their case with a halfhearted laugh. "We heard the shootin' and smelled the victuals. Main thing's we're hongry!"

Barlow took care of them.

"Find yersevs a tree ta lean back against and have a set. Ya'll are 'bout ta enjoy sum uv Barlow's perty near famous squirrel stew." Barlow's invitation was all it took. Stiller and Jeb fell in and made good hands at eating the stew. That ended the talk for the time being. They all filled their bellies. Barlow's stew was, now, world famous ~ their world that is.

It was November 12 by the time they pulled out of Kiomitchie River and headed up river toward Bois d' Arc Creek. Boggy River was a couple of days away and would be their next good rest.

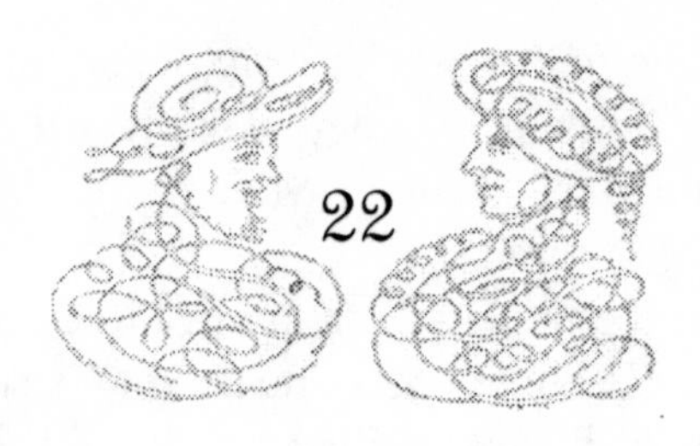

The Red River exploration got underway, and they didn't waste any time on the river. There was nothing between Kiomitchie River and Bois d' Arc Creek. *Nothing that is, that is more important to me than what waits for me at the Donnegans',* Yellow Beard thought.

Annalee was the one person in the world Yellow Beard wanted to see more than his mother and even more than his father. Annalee was all he could think about. *Colter ain't any help either. Ever' time I seem to get my thinking straightened out, he brings up his Annabelle back home and how she dumped him for his cousin.*

By late afternoon, the second day out of Kiomitchie, they had come a long way and needed a rest. There had been nothing of interest, as far as the eye was concerned, since they left Kiomitchie River. The winds were a different story. They were high out of the southwest and blew with a reckless abandon. They used the riverbed as a funnel and ground headlong down its channel into the eyes of Yellow Beard and Colter. Clouds of gritty sand billowed high into the air, poised like so many dragon heads.

"That's the Boggy River coming in there," Yellow Beard told Colter. "We call it Vazzures River; it has a soft miry bottom and its water is whitish, but it is well-tasted. You wanta stop early and spend a long night?"

"Yeah, I reckon the mules need a good rest." He answered.

"I was thinking that very thing, and our eyes could use a rest, too."

Neither of them would admit that the mules were fine, that it was the men who needed a rest. Barlow and Zeke caught up with them about an hour before sundown and voiced their approval of spending a long night and sleeping in the next morning. They wasted no time getting settled in and were enjoying the comforts of a warm fire. They were all yawning and about to doze.

"I'm alearnin' to love this here Red River," Zeke declared. "We have whooped her logjam, we have whooped her black rock bar, and we have whooped her Indians."

"Me too," Barlow said. "We survived her alligators and her white bears, and everything she could dish out."

"I use to think that all I ever wanted to be was a mountain man. It's fun being a river man, though." Colter added.

"Mountain men or river rats, it doesn't matter, we're the best there is," Zeke bragged.

The name stuck, and they began to think of themselves as river rats.

"If things go like we plan, we'll make a better and easier living than we ever did in the mountains, and on top of that I might find my father." Yellow Beard put in his two bits' worth.

"We're gonna make a lot of money too," Colter predicted.

~

The next five days, progress was fast. They traveled until almost dark and left before daylight every day. Finally Yellow Beard caught sight of the creek he had been looking for. Barlow and Zeke had beaten them to Bois d' Arc Creek, hobbled the mules, and got a fire blazing.

"We gonna hunker down here till the storm passes?" Zeke asked.

"No, it ain't over a couple of miles to the Donnegans'. We're gonna make it to there and hunker down in style," Yellow Beard boasted.

The kind of cold permeated the air that drove all the wildlife to seek shelter. Yellow Beard was no different. Visions of a dancing fire, crackling in the Donnegan fireplace and reflecting in Annalee's eyes, sent shivers down his spine. *My thinking about Annalee, warms the cockles of my heart, as the old timers would say*, he thought.

The last hundred yards was before them now. Yellow Beard had been damp all day and grimaced from the pain in his aching bones. The chill of the cold winter air had clutched at them all day. The smoke twining from the Donnegan chimney cured everything. Yellow Beard's aching pain gave way to the warmth of his excitement. There was something about the sound of his voice when he said, "The Donnegan girls" or something about seeing the smoke billowing from their fireplace that made him shiver deep inside. He knew not which nor could he explain it.

Annalee was the first one to see the boats coming.

"Guess what? There comes a boat, and it says Yellow Beard on the front of it!" Annalee screamed, running out the door with Eve-e right on her heels. Eve-e whispered under her breath to Annalee, "He has a man with him there in the boat behind him. Colter is the name on his boat."

"Yellow Beard, Yellow Beard, Yellow Beard. Oh! Yellow Beard." Annalee couldn't stop saying his name as she ran down the bluff and fell into his arms.

Colter and Eve-e found a way to make their own introductions. Eve-e felt right away that Colter had interests other than her. Maybe he had a girlfriend back home or maybe his interest lay in her daddy's whisky. She wasn't sure, except she knew he didn't have much interest in her. Colter's other interest was Annalee Donnegan ~ to him she was a spitting image of his first love, Annabelle. She looked like her. She giggled like her. She was flirty like her. Colter couldn't keep his eyes off her.

Roscoe Junior stood on the front porch, his thumbs hung in his suspenders, and watched his sisters greet the visitors. He hadn't seen Barlow and Zeke ride up on the mules and almost jumped through his skin when he heard strange voices.

"Where is yer pa, boy? We're here with Yellow Beard and Colter, and we need ta get the mules outta this blizzard," Barlow said, shivering.

Roscoe stepped out on the porch. "Did I hear you river rats right? Ya'll are here with Yellow Beard and Colter. Who's this Colter feller, and who are ya'll?"

"That's Barlow and I'm Zeke and ya see that man there," he pointed down the bluff toward Bois d' Arc Creek, "with that biggest girl? That's Colter," Zeke told him.

Roscoe shook his head. "Land sakes alive, 'em girls … I declare! Come on, them mules can stay in the barn tonight."

By that time, Roscoe Junior had hidden behind the woodbox to watch the goings on of his older sisters.

Gurdy announced her own brand of excitement when she stepped out on the front porch and banged on the dinner bell.

"Supper's ready! Wash up … and come and get it!" Gurdy never called twice. She didn't have to call twice that time either. All of a sudden Gurdy's small kitchen was full of hungry patrons.

The only complaint came from Roscoe Junior. "Momma, you scared me half-outta my wits when ya banged that bell so hard and right over my head."

"Laudy, I had to bang it doubly hard, seeing as how everyone was so preoccupied." Gurdy winked at Yellow Beard.

"Annalee, why don't you seat the guests?" Gurdy asked. The giant table was up to the task. It was at least twelve feet long and half again as wide. Having been fashioned from split green ash had caused it to warp a bit as it dried, but all its legs still touched the floor. Annalee placed Eve-e and Colter next to Yellow Beard and herself on the bench next to the wall. Roscoe claimed his spot at the head of the table, and Gurdy sat at its foot. Barlow, Zeke and Roscoe Junior held down the other bench. Set all around were big tin plates with spoons already in them.

"Junior, 'fore you set down, go fetch the big pot frum the fireplace, and I'll fetch the cornpone," Gurdy said.

"Are you sure that you got enough ta feed four extra hungry men that you wudn't countin' on?" Zeke asked.

"That's hunky-dory 'bout havin' extra men. Supper 'round here there is always aplenty. What's left is usually eat for breakfast. So, come mornin' I'll have to do cookin', but tonight, we eat right." Gurdy was right.

Gurdy set a skillet that was as big as a wagon wheel in the middle of the table. A buttery brown pone of cornbread filled the skillet.

Roscoe Junior set the number ten pot down beside the skillet. Gurdy stood up and squished her apron down between her and the table. "Gimmy yer plates." She fished out a big ham steak and scooped a big ladle of red beans, with enough pot-liquor to soak up a slab of cornpone, onto each person's plate. The plates made their appearance at the bean pot as fast as Gurdy could serve them until she finally picked up her own plate and helped herself.

"Okay, Roscoe. The blessin' needs done, 'cause we got company." Gurdy sat.

"Thank you, God, for 'em beans and that hog … Amen."

Everyone dove in.

Nobody said anything until everyone finished eating. Finally the silence gave way to scraping spoons against bare plates. Gurdy got up and went to the fireplace and fished out big sweet 'taters for everyone.

"I know ya'll have already eaten enough to flounder a mule, but here's somethin' ta top it off with." Gurdy doled them out. The mound of butter they had churned last night after supper disappeared before the 'taters did. The demand for breakfast butter would have the girls taking turns on the churn before bedtime.

"Roscoe, I have a question for you. Back in 1826, Jinx left me and told me he was coming here. He said that he was too old for the mountains anymore. Did he show up here? Where is he?" Yellow Beard could tell immediately that he had pried a bit too far.

"Don't go thar, Yellow Beard. He's gone. You're better off to jest let a sleepin' dog lie."

~

During the next few days, Yellow Beard and Annalee got reacquainted. Something was different, though. Yellow Beard couldn't put his finger on it, but something was different. When he had first arrived, Annalee couldn't keep her eyes off him, nor her hands. Now sometimes he caught her looking at Colter with a funny look in her eyes. It seemed like when she had the opportunity she picked at Colter, way too much. It wasn't like Yellow Beard had seen Colter take advantage of Annalee's flirtatious ways ~ he had not. *Once, I did see them look into one another's eyes, but then sometimes that's unavoidable*, he thought.

~

Roscoe took Yellow Beard and Colter on a grand tour of his operation. They went up Bois d' Arc Creek and saw Roscoe's black land cornfield. He had already broken up the ground and was ready for spring planting. From there Roscoe took them to the springs.

"Bois d' Arc springs is where we get all our water for the stills," he explained. "Its water is clearer than the sky and colder than the devil."

They followed a narrow trail around the south end of the rock bluff, up to the stills. Yellow Beard and Colter stood on the edge of the rock bluff and looked out over the creek bottom.

"The stench from the fermenting corn will almost take the hair from your nostrils," Yellow Beard commented.

The operation was more than impressive. Yellow Beard and Colter could not believe the amount of whisky Roscoe turned out. Neither could Roscoe believe he was about to add The Rocky Mountain Fur Company to his list of clients.

"I'll tell you what I'd like to do, Roscoe," Colter began. "I'm going on through with Yellow Beard to meet his folks. Yellow Beard and I are going west to look for his daddy and then we'll be coming back through here. I want to buy a few barrels of your whisky and take it with me to the 1834 Rendezvous. If Milton and his partners like what you make, they'll go under contract to take all that you can make. Does that sound like a deal?"

"Shucks yeah, it's a deal, Colter. I'll have the best I can brew waiting for you. By the way, Yellow Beard, I have some news about your daddy."

Yellow Beard didn't know how to take that statement. He hadn't ever, in all his life, heard of anyone having any news about his father.

"Really, what kind of news?" he asked.

"Back in the summer a man cum from a ranch out east uh Santa Fe somewhere. Rancho Bell he called it. It seemed that his boss had sent 'im ta buy sum uh my whisky."

"Yeah, go on!" Yellow Beard pushed.

Roscoe plowed his chaw out of his mouth with his forefinger and gave it a sling off Bois d' Arc springs bluff.

"He said his name was Lank. Anyways, Lank said, 'One day last spring this ol' man came riding into Rancho Bell with a Comanche war party hot on 'is tail. The old man had a cock-and-bull story about finding the Gran Quivira Gold mine hid right under the Comanches' noses. He said that every time he got close to it, the Comanche would attack him.' Lank said that the ol' man stayed 'round a few days, but got a case uv lockjaw when they tried ta talk to him 'bout the Gold mine. Then one day he left. Anyway I remembered that legend you told us of wacky pew …." Yellow Beard stopped him. "Roscoe, that's *The Legend of Weick Pah.*"

"Shucks yeah, anyway I remembered you saying your dad's Indian name was Gold Seeker. I just flat out ask Lank if the ol' man's name was Gold Seeker. He said, 'Naugh, it was Bill Cooper.'"

"That's him! That's my father ~ Bill Cooper! Did Lank say anything about what he looked like?" Yellow Beard could hardly stand still.

"Shucks naugh, he did say that he had the strangest hair, but I already knew what that meant."

"I don't know what he meant by that. Father had regular hair; it wasn't like mine. Now, Grandfather had hair like mine." Yellow Beard got a puzzled look on his face.

Yellow Beard was ready to go home. He knew he was on the right track now.

"Colter, have Barlow and Zeke to get ready. The river rats are pulling out first thing in the morning," Yellow Beard commanded.

Annalee begged Yellow Beard to take her with him.

"I can't take you with me, honey. I have to find my father, and I couldn't take you into Comanche Country and just dump you on my people. You have to understand. I'll be back soon, after I find what I'm lookin' for. Colter and I are going to Santa Fe and find Father. Then we're going to New Orleans for him to make amends with his pa. When we come back through, we'll have your Grandpa Stiller marry us. I hear he's real good at it." Yellow Beard laughed but Annalee didn't find it funny in the least. "I'll take you to New Orleans with me." *That seemed to satisfy Annalee,* Yellow Beard thought.

Yellow Beard watched as Annalee hugged Colter bye. He wondered what she had said when she tiptoed to whisper in Colter's ear. "Okay," he interrupted, "we got to be going."

Colter climbed into his boat and shoved it out into Bois d' Arc Creek.

Yellow Beard embraced Annalee and whispered "I love you" into her ear. He kissed her on the ear, sending shivers up and down her spine.

"You said you gotta go, honey." Annalee gently withdrew. Yellow Beard got into his boat, shoved it out into Bois d' Arc Creek, and took off to catch up with Colter.

I wonder why Annalee seemed to want to cut our kiss short ~ our good-bye short? I guess she's hurt because I have to leave so suddenly. He continued to think about Annalee for a long time. *Annalee's voice calling me honey will always warm the cockles of my heart.*

Yellow Beard had planned to winter over with the Donnegans, but now after receiving news about his father those plans changed. Annalee's standoffish attitude toward him left him with a cold feeling. It was the first week of December, and he wasn't the only thing that felt cold.

~

After they left the Donnegans', Yellow Beard spent more and more time by himself. There was a certain distance between Yellow Beard and him that worried Colter. *Is it jealousy over the way Annalee and I teased one another? Does Yellow Beard know how Annalee feels about me?* Colter wondered. Knowing how Yellow Beard held things in, he knew he would never know which was the case. *I would have thought that Yellow Beard would have been happy since he heard about his daddy, but he's not. Something is eating on him.*

Most nights after supper, Yellow Beard left and didn't come back until after everyone went to bed. On one occasion Colter followed him until he saw Yellow Beard sit down on the sandbar and lean back against a log. Yellow Beard took the necklace off and laid it in his lap. Colter watched him gaze up at the stars, never moving. It was like he was in a trance. Finally, Colter let him be and went back to camp.

~

Many days of hard travel had brought the Red Exploration to Yellow Beard's old stomping grounds. It had been twenty days since they left Bois d' Arc Creek and the Donnegans, and Yellow Beard had an even sourer taste in his mouth than he did the day he told Annalee bye. The thrill of spending the nigh at San Teodoro with the Taovaya Indians ~ of getting to see Jacques, his childhood playmate ~ raced Yellow Beard's heart.

Yellow Beard became deeply saddened to learn that Jacques was in the spirit world and that a lightning strike had taken him there.

He knew not to ask questions. He believed as did the Taovaya that a strike by lightning was an expression of outrage by the Great Spirit. Whether inflicted against man or beast or nature, a lightning strike was not something you questioned or talked about.

When they left, for some strange reason, Yellow Beard was different. Colter could not guess why; but Yellow Beard almost became Yellow Beard again. It was like a huge weight lifted from Yellow Beard's chest. He recovered from his sullen state, somewhat, and talked to them again. He revealed that he had dreamed the Great Spirit had called someone near and dear to him into the Spirit World.

"I was under the dread of going home, fearing Mother was the one in my dreams," Yellow Beard confided to Colter. Then Colter knew why he had been acting so strange, and he felt relieved that Yellow Beard was back to his old self. Yellow Beard had mixed emotions as they departed San Teodoro ~ he felt sadness because of the loss of Jacques, but he felt elation at being able to see his mother soon. They were almost to their winter camp and they traveled with renewed enthusiasm. Yellow Beard had returned to his former self, and Colter and he were on better terms.

They had been traveling all morning and the looks of things had been changing. By midday the steep river bluffs gave way to rolling hills that stretched as far as they eye could see.

The bottom-land hardwoods, pecans, walnuts, hickories, and oaks, had given way to mesquite and scrub brush. Giant Cottonwoods were still abundant ~ gone were the endless stretches of river bottom cane breaks. Separating the barren sand bars from the rolling hills ~ instead of the high bluffs they had become accustomed to ~ had grown a band of willow and dogwood, entwined with rattan and wild grape.

Barlow, Zeke and the mules wove their way forward. They alternated between traveling the sand bars and the brushwood swells. Several times during the morning they rode out to the water's edge and let the mules get a drink then visited with Yellow Beard and Colter.

Yellow Beard assured them that home was soon.

Barlow and Zeke traveled until dark overtook them. They stopped and tethered the mules in a grove of cottonwoods. They set up camp and built a fire where it would be visible to Yellow Beard and Colter from the river, and Barlow fixed supper. When Yellow Beard and Colter got there, they all sat down to a supper of jerky and a fresh pot of coffee.

"Jerky and coffee, man oh man, ya can't beat it unless ya got somethin' else ta eat," Zeke said.

"We'll get to the Wichita River sometime in the morning and winter there with my people," Yellow Beard assured them.

"It's 'bout time ta put up fer the winter," Barlow said. "We're too far into the dead uv winter to be atravelin', don't ya think?"

"That's fer sure," Zeke added. "My backside'd uh done friz plum off if it hadn't been for ol' Dollar akeepin' it warm."

Colter advised Barlow and Zeke:

"We're not fairing any too well out there in the bone-chilling wind and that icy fog that hangs on Red River, either."

"But yer asleepin' warm at night what with that white bear robe," Zeke said.

Yellow Beard didn't say anything. He knew his people would wrap them with warm buffalo robes and provide them with fur-lined moccasins.

Barlow and Zeke's mountain moccasins had held up pretty well. Yellow Beard's and Colter's had given up the ghost, though. They just couldn't take being soaked in Red River water day in and day out.

~

The sun was high overhead when Yellow Beard and Colter first saw the cone-shaped grass houses of the Wichita village.

The long ridge that played down between the Wichita River and Red River was all too familiar to Yellow Beard. *It looks just like it did the day that I left*, he thought.

Yellow Beard caught a glimpse of Barlow and Zeke moving through a break in the willows that grew along the edge of the sandbar. Yellow Beard waved his hat to catch Barlow's attention and motioned for Barlow and Zeke to come join them.

Yellow Beard pointed out the thatched huts along the ridge. "That's my home!" he yelled.

"Barlow, you and Zeke go on in with the mules and announce that Yellow Beard is coming," Yellow Beard said.

"How in tarnation are we gonna do that? Seeing as how we can't speak Wichita?" Barlow asked.

"Point to the sun, put your hand across your forehead, and pretend you're looking way off. My Wichita name is Son of Gold Seeker; they'll understand your signs. When you get their attention, point your finger out here toward us! We'll start on our way in when we see everyone come running down the river bluff to welcome us."

Yellow Beard watched through his spyglass.

Barlow and Zeke led the mules up the Wichita River bluff. Some of the ones who came to meet Barlow and Zeke Yellow Beard thought he recognized, but he wasn't sure.

Yellow Beard watched Barlow sign his message.

Was the gray-haired woman who ran toward Barlow his mother? He couldn't be sure. He saw the excitement build as Barlow turned and pointed in their direction. The gray-haired woman jumped up and down, and the reverberations of her voice echoed from the river banks. Son of Gold Seeker! Oh! Son of Gold Seeker.

Yellow Beard was sure now. That was his mother. *What has turned her hair gray? Has she worried about me?* he wondered.

Everyone dropped whatever it was they were doing and ran as fast as their legs could carry them to Red River.

Yellow Beard and Colter dragged the boats through the shallow water as fast as they could run. They splashed water and soaked themselves to the brim of their hats as their legs churned the water.

The gap between Dancing Waters and Yellow Beard shrank ~ then Dancing Waters had Yellow Beard in her arms.

"My baby … Oh! My baby!" she shrieked.

Yellow Beard was proud that Barlow, Zeke, and Colter couldn't understand the Wichita tongue.

Finally she turned him loose and stood him back where she could get a better look at him. "How long have you been traveling? You look so worn."

"I reckon about sixteen moons." He held a hand out toward his partners. "Mother, these are my best friends Colter, Barlow, and Zeke. We work for the Rocky Mountain Fur Company." *It would take too much explaining for me to tell her everything we're doing*, he thought. "We want to winter here if it's okay."

"You shouldn't ask such silly questions, Son of …. I mean … Yellow Beard. Go get your friends settled in with Jinx and Dancing Doe. They have three boys, and they all speak English. They'll fit in there.

Then you come home and tell me all about it. Did you find your father? Did you open the walnut? Go … then come tell me everything."

"No, Mother … to both questions. I do have some information about Father, though. I'll be back and we'll talk all night … just like we used to?"

"Do hurry!" Dancing Waters urged.

Leaving the mules in the pasture, Yellow Beard, with Colter, Barlow, and Zeke went to see Jinx and his family.

Yellow Beard announced their arrival. "Hey, you ol' drunken coot, guess who's come to see you?"

"Well, if it don't beat a hen apeckin' with a wooden bill. Come on in, Yellow Beard … if yer ears 're clean!"

That's Jinx aughright, always making funnies! Yellow Beard swept the door cover back and stepped inside. They grabbed each other's hand and tussled around a bit before Yellow Beard made introductions.

"Jinx, I was surprised to hear that you left the Donnegan whisky. What happened?" Yellow Beard asked.

"That's when I fell off the wagon. I ain't had a drop since. Roscoe thought me and Annalee was agettin' too friendly. Maybe so we wuz, 'cause I wuz always tanked up. One day Roscoe cum in and he put his ol' double-barrel shotgun ta my head then he gives me his ultimatum! That's what he called it, his ultimatum. Whatever that thing is."

"Ta give ya a wedding?" Zeke asked.

"Naugh, I'd uh gladly married the perty thang. Ferz I could tell, ta give me a send off!" Jinx laughed. Yellow Beard didn't. "Anyways, here I am, and I ain't had a drop in five years. Say, Yellow Beard, did you ever find your pa?"

"Not yet, but I have a real good lead. Matter of fact I have to go tell Mother about it, right now. I'll see you coots in the morning."

Yellow Beard took his time going to his mother's house. He wandered among the grass houses and reflected back to his childhood. He walked the familiar path to his Grandfather Ketox Runner's house. *Mother and I must talk; then I'll visit with Grandfather,* he thought. The dogs were not familiar with Yellow Beard's smell or his footsteps, and they yelped everywhere he went.

Yellow Beard stepped inside his mother's grass house. He watched her eyes light up and he felt the warmth of home. The feeling was the best thing he had felt in a long time. Her familiar voice asking him if he was hungry warmed him inside. Dancing Waters filled a gourd bowl with a creamy soup made of turtle meat and parched ground acorns, and handed it to him. Yellow Beard cupped the gourd in both hands and whiffed the tantalizing smell of his mother's home-cooking. He blew across the top, then sipped a taste. It had been too long.

"Mother, this is the best thing I've eaten since I left." Yellow Beard wasn't bragging.

She smiled. His compliment pleased her.

Yellow Beard finished eating the soup then he reached in his pocket and brought out something wrapped in parchment. "Here, Mother, I brought this for you from the Rendezvous."

She unwrapped it then rolled it around in her hands, with a puzzled look on her face.

"What is it?" Yellow Beard reached around Dancing Waters for the mirror and held it up to her face for her to look into. Dancing Waters jumped back in fright. "Where did that woman come from and who is she?"

"She is you, Mother. Don't be afraid. It's just a mirror. The mirror is showing you who you are," he explained.

Dancing Waters hugged Yellow Beard. She had a surprise for him, too. It was a beautiful pure white parfleche. She unrolled it and revealed a hand-crafted bow made from Bois d' Arc wood. This she handed to Yellow Beard. "I have been saving this for you, if you ever came back. Here, it is yours!" She smiled with pride.

"Thank you, Mother. I will make it mine, and it will go to the Great Spirit with me." He examined the bow carefully and held it up. It would make a fine hunting bow to show to his father. "Mother has a man ever stopped here by the name of Lank?"

Dancing Waters thought for a long time. "No, I don't believe so."

"He works for the Rancho Bell. His boss sent him to the Donnegans, a family on Bois d' Arc Creek down on Red River, to purchase whisky for him. Roscoe Donnegan is a good friend of mine, and he told me about Lank. Roscoe said Lank talked about a man whose name was Bill Cooper, how he'd come running into Rancho Bell one day with the Comanche hot on his trail. That Bill Cooper fellow had found the Gran Quivira Gold Mine. Anyway, according to Lank, Bill Cooper stayed there at the ranch a few days then left. I'm going to find Lank and get him to take me to Santa Fe. That's where Dad is, I know it!"

"Just remember your promise that you made to me before you left ~ you promised you would bring Gold Seeker to me," Dancing Waters reminded him.

"I do, Mother, and I will bring him to you. If he'll come. I don't know that I could force him."

"He will come. You will make him," Dancing Waters insisted.

"I couldn't ever figure out the secret of how the walnut opened. Colter and I spent at least a whole moon trying to figure out how its maker intended for it to open. There has been a little hole put in where the necklace goes in, and you can see gold down in there. Colter thinks that hole has something to do with how the walnut opens, and he is college-educated but he can't figure it out. Colter thinks that when I find my father he'll know how to open it, and that will tell me he is my father. He says that anyone could claim to have given the necklace to me, but the man who knows how to open it will be my father. He thinks the secret link between me and Father is that, and nothing inside could prove who my father is.

"Son, Colter is right."

~

Yellow Beard remembered back to the way that Annalee held onto Colter, then tiptoed to whisper something into his ear and the way they had picked on each other. Why hadn't Colter told him what Annalee whispered to him if it had been so innocent? Yellow Beard wondered. Those thoughts flip-flopped continually in his mind, and he began to read more and more into them, especially after he heard Jinx's story about the way Annalee had carried on with him. *I wish that I had taken Roscoe's advice and left well enough alone.*

He harbored jealousy in his heart, and it grew all winter long.

Yellow Beard made up his mind the day before they were to leave for Rancho Bell that he was not going to take Colter with him. He would take Barlow.

Zeke could go with Colter, to wherever it was that Colter wanted to go. To Annalee ~ or ~ to home!

"Colter, we have come to the end of our road," Yellow Beard informed him. "I'm leaving in the morning. Barlow's going with me. We're going to Rancho Bell. You and Zeke can have my boat. You'll need it to haul the Donnegan whisky to Rendezvous. Maybe our paths will cross again, my friend." Yellow Beard placed a firm hand on Colter's shoulder. "Go see your father, my brother, before it is too late!"

Colter couldn't say anything. He felt sick inside. He felt the tears whelping up inside. He turned away without letting Yellow Beard see his face and headed back toward Jinx's. "I'll see you in the morning … brother," he said, as casually as he could muster.

~

The next morning, Yellow Beard and Barlow packed their mules and headed up the featureless Red River sandbar, riding Wichita ponies. Yellow Beard felt for the scribbled map to Rancho Bell that he carried in his headband. It was still there.

Colter and Zeke loaded their belongings into the boats. They shoved them out into the river and let the current drift them along toward the Donnegans'.

Dancing Waters sat on the bank and watched them grow farther apart; *Until the distance between them became as much a part of their destiny as life itself*, she thought.

Yellow Beard and Colter waved furiously to each other one last time.

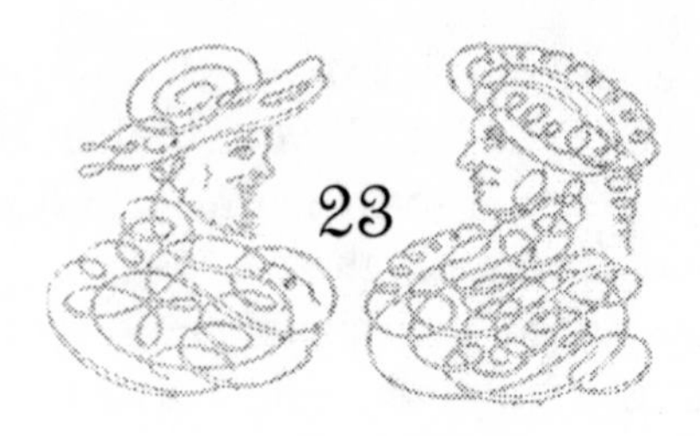

23

Yellow Beard's spirits were high. He had wintered good with his people. The new beginnings of spring had arrived. He had purpose in his reasoning, and for the first time in his life he had a real plan to find his father. He was at home on the plains; he had spent his childhood on their edge and he was more at ease than in the mountains.

Dancing Waters had given him new clothes. "When you go to Rancho Bell, you will need traditional Wichita clothes, not mountain man clothes." She had placed a new scalp-lock on his head. "Now, Nermernuh will recognize you." He wore a supple leather shirt, a loin cloth and leggings. He sat proud and tall on the back of his pony. He felt good.

Barlow was completely out of his environment, though, like a fish out of water. He was a mountain man, pure and simple ~ he didn't like the desert Yellow Beard had brought him into. Even in early spring the sandbars were hot. Loose sand swirled in the draft that seemed to follow the bed of the river, and it gritted up his eyeballs. Everything that grew seemed to attack him. Cockleburs, goatheads, devil claws and nettles of every description had thorns or claws that grabbed his flesh. Most of the time Yellow Beard and he traveled into the sun.

"I'd rather have the snow ashinin' in my eyes than that ball uv fire," Barlow complained.

Relentlessly, Yellow Beard carried them to the land of the setting sun. The choice of a decent campsite had become a matter of which cottonwood nestled beside what small hole of water would they light under when they couldn't pick their feet up anymore. Barlow longed to be with Colter and Zeke, back in the good life, headed down Red River.

"I'd rather be a river rat any day than a desert rat," he told Yellow Beard.

It was mid-afternoon and only the second day out when Yellow Beard and Barlow came upon a beautiful long grassy glade that looked as if it would be a perfect campsite. There was a giant old cottonwood tree in the middle of the glade. A gentle breeze blew through the tree's papery leaves, so they cast a dappled skittering shade onto the grass. Sweet spring water trickled from a cold spring down a little brook before it dumped itself into Red River. They had been traveling from get-up to can't-go, and they were both exhausted. Yellow Beard found this beautiful place too tempting to pass up.

"Strike Camp!" he hollered.

Barlow couldn't believe his ears. *Strike camp before dark? Who hollered that?* he wondered, although he knew it was Yellow Beard's voice. He struck camp before Yellow Beard could change his mind.

They removed the packs from their ponies and gave them a good rubdown. They showed their approval by running and making funny huffing noises.

Barlow sat down and leaned back against the gnarly bark of the cottonwood tree. In a few minutes he had slid down until his head was the only thing against the tree and began snoring. Not even the rattling sounds woke him. The rat-a-tat-tat … rat-a-tat-tat crept closer and closer. Then the sound stopped and waited for its prey to move.

Yellow Beard took the parfleche that held the Bois d' Arc bow his mother had given him from his pack and sat down on a big rock. He removed the bow and wiped its upper and lower limbs across his forehead and face, then wiped the handgrip across his nose.

Barlow roused, but he didn't move.

"What in tarnation are ya doin' to that thing?" he asked.

"I'm its first owner, and I'm making it my bow. It will have my oil to keep it limber. My people are known for our Bois d' Arc bows," Yellow Beard explained. "The Nermernuh come from miles around and want to trade for our bows."

"Ya keep talking 'bout the Nermernuh. Who are they, in my talk?" Barlow spat shrivels from the stick he was chewing on, but he didn't move his feet.

"The Nermernuh are the Comanche. Mother traded Maker of Bows for this bow and gave it to me before we left. He worked on it many moons. It is as slick as a rendezvous mirror. I would let you feel of it, but right now I have something that I have to do with it ~ just don't move!"

"What d'you mean … just don't move! What are ya fixin' ta do with that thang?"

"Do you see that Diamond Back Rattlesnake all coiled up there by your foot? Just don't move … don't say anything either!"

Fer cryin' out loud, why did I take my boots off? Barlow agonized.

Yellow Beard strung the sinew into one nock of the bow. Carefully he bent the bow until the sinew slid into the other nock.

It will take the string, but I haven't ever shot it, he thought. He placed the sinew into the nock of an arrow. "I guess I'll get a practice shot on that rattler's head," he said.

"What da ya mean, practice on 'is head? Can't you just get a stick 'n' kill 'im?"

"If either one of us move, that rattler will bite your big toe off."

"I ain't gonna move … just you hurry 'n' do it."

Barlow heard the rat-a-tat-tat. It was more than he could stand. He flinched.

Yellow Beard saw the muscles along the rattlesnake's body tense. He instantly changed his aim to compensate. His lead was perfect. The arrow caught the striking snake's head, dead center, and pinned it to the ground.

"What a shot! How'd ya do that? You shot 'im right in mid-air, in the middle uv his strike!"

"That was nothing. If you had shot as many varmints with a bow as I have, you could do it, too." Yellow Beard skinned the snake and offered the rattlers to Barlow to remember the snake by. Barlow didn't want to remember the snake. He also refused to eat any of the rattlesnake jerky, despite the claims Yellow Beard made that it was delicious.

When daylight came, they got back to their same routine of traveling until dark but after a few days they made camp early in order to harvest some food.

"When the sun goes down, there'll be some jack rabbits come out over there and prance around on that grass by the water. You'll eat one of them, won't you?" Yellow Beard licked his lips.

"Now I can eat sizzled rabbit. I might eat some rattlesnake jerky if ya hadn't ett it up frum me. What's wrong with my Hawken agettin' one uv 'em rabbits?"

"We're in Comancheria now, the land of the Comanche. We do as they do. We not shoot little rabbit with big Hawken. Do you know what Comanche means? It means anyone who wants to fight me all the time."

Barlow got the point.

"We should reach the Palo Duro Canyon tomorrow;" Yellow Beard predicted, "then when Red River comes out of the canyon, she is the Palo Duro Creek. From there, water will be scarce till we reach the Canadian River. You can use your Hawken against buffalo in the canyon, or we'll be eating dog. The jerky is all gone."

"What in tarnation do ya mean eatin' dog? I ain't gonna eat no dog!" Barlow spat.

"Prairie dog--they make a good soup. They've got some fat on them. A man will dry up and blow away if antelope and jackrabbit is all he eats."

~

The river bluffs rose higher and higher. "We're in the Palo Duro Canyon. We can use your ol' Hawken to get us a buffalo now," Yellow Beard reminded Barlow. In some places the canyon walls seemed like they were a thousand feet straight up. They had Red River trapped in their clutches.

Yellow Beard had heard stories all his life about the colored rock of the canyon walls. None of the stories had done the walls justice. *Instead of naming this the canyon of hard wood, they should have named it the canyon of many colors*, Yellow Beard thought. Bright layers of orange, red, yellow, maroon, and white rocks stretched in bands, like an endless rainbow.

The Prairie Dog Town Fork of Red River cut a path for about sixty miles, meandering from wall to wall through the canyon. The canyon floor was rich and grew a wide variety of plants, including grass, prickly pear and yucca, mesquite, juniper and saltcedar. The towering cottonwoods, willows and junipers leaned over the waterway ~ their branches hanging in the water ~ as if to guide the current through their reflections. Wild game was plentiful. The canyon walls provided shelter from the winter winds, and there was food and water. It wasn't a great mystery why the Comanche lived here.

Barlow and his Hawken proved to be a deadly combination and soon had a nice fat yearling lying on the ground. The two men struck camp right on the spot and ate their fill of sizzled buffalo steaks before spending the night jerking a big hind quarter. Yellow Beard washed the buffalo's paunch out thoroughly and rolled it up to use later for transporting water.

~

The Palo Duro Creek had just become a dry gulch and now they were on rations. "There is one more water hole on this creek fit to drink out of. We'll fill our buffalo paunch with water there, but it'll have to do us till we get to the Canadian River," Yellow Beard warned.

The combination of the dry sandy stream bed and the overhead sun made them proud of the water in the buffalo paunch. They were in their third day now since leaving the water hole. Yellow Beard knew that the only water they would have for the next few days would be what they had brought with them. *Unless, that is, one of those spring cloudbursts waters us,* Yellow Beard thought.

The sun had gotten low by the time they struck camp. They camped under the only cottonwood tree they had seen for miles. *And that we're likely to see for miles more,* Yellow Beard thought. It was in a dry gulch, and other than a few dead fallen limbs, there was no firewood around. Barlow managed to wrangle a couple of pieces of bark from the ol' cottonwood tree for the mules to chew on. It must not have been very good because they wasted very little time chewing on it. Yellow Beard and Barlow chewed on buffalo jerky, but with very little water to wash it down, with they soon got their fill.

Yellow Beard pulled Ketox Runner's rough map from his headband to refresh his memory. He studied it a long time before he spoke. "When we can't follow this dry gulch anymore, we strike a due-north, till we come to the Canadian River."

"Then what?"

"Before your 'then what,' we've got about three more days of travel without much water. That's what. We'll have to go sparingly with our buffalo paunch water. Once we reach the Canadian River, we're home free as far as water. Then what we'll do is head up it to the Rancho Bell."

Yellow Beard and Barlow were traveling by daybreak. With two thirsty souls and two thirsty beasts to share the water, it played out by the second night. The third day they spent without water.

Late in that evening, they began to see a dark bank in the distant north. Before sundown they could tell it was a treeline. It would be well after dark before they reached the Canadian River, but the thought of striking camp before they got to the Canadian, never entered their mind. The moon had risen and the stars were bright when they reached the cool waters of the Canadian River and stopped for the night.

Yellow Beard read from his map: "Grandfather said, 'The second day of travel into the Canadian current, keep a watch out to where the sun sets. You will get a glimpse of a big adobe hacienda high on a bluff. It overlooks the Canadian River bottom. It will be Rancho Bell's headquarters.' That's all of the map. I guess we're close."

~

Yellow Beard took a sharp rock from the river and scraped the bark from a big tree on the bank. The mules and ponies were happy, and they were happy. They had made it to water and had dined sufficiently. What more could they want?

They followed the river closely not knowing if they could see the house from any other vantage point. When they finally caught a glimpse of the adobe dwelling, it shocked them how far they would have to climb and how steep the bluff was that led up to the place. They all four, man and beast, were panting by the time they ascended the long steep bluff.

Yellow Beard handed his reins to Barlow, stepped up onto the verandah, and knocked on the door.

A dainty little gray-haired Mexican woman came to the door.

"Lank … please," Yellow Beard said.

The lady held a finger up, winked, and turned to go get Lank, Yellow Beard assumed. She returned in a few moments with a stately looking older man.

"You want Lank?" he asked.

"Uh, yes, sir. Does he work here?"

"Yes, he works for me. His name is Lankston."

He doesn't volunteer much, Yellow Beard thought.

"Sir, I am Yellow Beard and a friend of mine, Roscoe Donnegan, said I might could get Lank to help me find my father."

"The Donnegan whisky brewer? Yeah, I know him. I am Don Pablo Montoya. I own Rancho Bell, and if your father is Bill Cooper, then I suspect Lankston can help you. Are you up to no good?"

"Sir, we're not to cause trouble. I just want to find my father," Yellow Beard assured him.

"Lankston lives down yonder, on the creek, in that little adobe. You being a friend of the Donnegans and since Bill Cooper's your daddy, go on down there and talk to him. Tell him that I said it would be all right."

Yellow Beard and Barlow mounted up. They led the mules in the direction Montoya had pointed out. When they came to the little adobe bunkhouse, they tied the ponies, hobbled the mules, and proceeded to rouse Lank. Yellow Beard ducked under the low stoop and knocked on the door facing.

"Come on in, the door's open," a voice said from inside.

Just as Yellow Beard had envisioned Lank looking ~ Lank looked. He was tall, thin and wiry with burnished leathery skin. A warm compassionate smile spread all the way across Lank's face. His smile carried the corners of his mouth into a bristling mustache. Lank's eyes, unlike most ranch hands Yellow Beard had met, were warm and compassionate as well.

He was lying across a bunk-style bed, his boots on. One look told Yellow Beard that Lank very rarely if ever took his hat off, either. At first, Lank's head appeared snow white and hairless. On second glance, Yellow Beard saw the jagged incision made by a stone-bladed knife. It made his butt pucker. When Lank caught a person giving his head a second glance, he liked to enforce their visual image. "I can't leave my hat off too long. The air gettin' to my scar makes it ooze!" Hardly any one glanced at the wound the third time. Lank's dirty worn hat hung on the back of a straight chair. The broken straws in the shape of a horse's hoofprint revealed Lank's passion … breaking broncos.

"What brings ya?" Lank inquired.

"Roscoe Donnegan …."

Lank broke in and stopped Yellow Beard's sentence. "Well, I wouldn't've give a plug uh tabacker for the thought uv him ~ Roscoe Donnegan ~ Well, how is the ol' whisky brewin' river rat adoin'?"

"The last that I knew, he was doing fine. In fact, the way that he brings me to you is that he told me you know something about my father, Bill Cooper. Know him?"

"Bill Cooper's your father? He never mentioned himself ahavin' a son."

"I bet he mentioned my mother … Dancing Waters?"

That convinced Lank that Yellow Beard was for real.

"Yeah, Bill Cooper talked about Dancing Waters all the time."

"Well, let me tell ya the real reason I went ta see Roscoe. Somehow, I got me a soft spot for your pappy. I let 'im hook me into takin' care uv his whisky needs. He told me not ta mention his name to the Donnegans. So I made up that cock-and-bull story about buying whisky for my boss."

"Where is Father? Can I see him?" Yellow Beard was anxious.

"Well, yeah, I can take ya to his place, but he might not be there. He goes off to his imaginary gold mine and doesn't come back till the Comanches run 'im back. He owns a spread over on the Pecos River outside of Puerto de Luna. He thinks the Blue Hole waters'll cure 'im. I'll take ya to him. I need ta check on 'im anyway. I'm the only friend in the world he's got, and if I tell 'im you're his son, he'ul believe me."

"There's no need for you to tell him." Yellow Beard sensed he was in the presence of someone he could trust. He pulled the necklace from his shirt and began to tell Lank its history.

"Father gave this to Dancing Waters when he left her, and he told her to give it to me on my tenth birthday. He told her it would guide me to him. Father will know I'm his son when he sees this necklace. By the way, what did you mean when you said that he thinks the Blue Hole waters will cure him? Is he sick?"

"Well, yeah, in the head. We'll leave first thing in the mornin', but I'm awarnin' ya, you ain't gonna like what yer gonna see. Ya'll can sleep there in the floor if ya want."

"I ain't use ta sleepin' under a roof," Barlow said, declining. "You can stay here if ya wanta, Yellow Beard. I'm gonna go to the river."

"Thank you, though." Yellow Beard agreed with Barlow. "We'll be back up here by daylight, raring to go."

Yellow Beard and Barlow gathered up a big pile of firewood. The night air made Yellow Beard shiver deep inside. He sat silently, chewing on a piece of jerky and contemplating what the morrow would bring. Barlow chewed on an elm stick.

"You know, it's an awful thing that Father got himself scalped by them Comanche. I just wonder how Mother will take seeing Father's head butchered like Lank's was!" Yellow Beard's voice trembled. He was nervous inside. His guts were quavering from his anticipation of seeing his father ~ or ~ from his fear that his father would reject him. He knew not which.

"What makes you think your pappy got scalped?"

"Lank said Father was sick with his head. That can't mean but one thing: He's been scalped!"

~

They left early the next morning and were two days getting to Blue Hole. They asked several of the patrons of the healing waters and found that Bill Cooper had not been there, at least not recently. They crossed the Pecos, climbed the bluff, and started down the long lane toward Bill Cooper's adobe house. Yellow Beard, followed by Lank and Barlow, single-filed up to the porch steps. Yellow Beard handed Barlow his reins and made his way to the door. He rapped his knuckles against it.

No answer came.

He rapped again, harder. Still no answer. Yellow Beard's heart sank.

Lank reached around Yellow Beard, twisted the brass door knob, and cracked the door open.

Those words that Yellow Beard had said, "go see your father, my brother ~ before it is too late," and the tone in which he'd said them, haunted Colter. Every waking moment ~ until his journey ended ~ he ran those words over and over in his mind.

Colter came to accept that there was nothing that had happened between him and Annalee to cause Yellow Beard to part ways with him.

Yellow Beard in his wisdom knew that he shouldn't drag me all over the world in search of his father, Colter thought. *Yellow Beard knew how important it was for me to go home and make amends with my own father. He did it for me.*

~

Colter and Zeke saw each other around the campfire. Their travel arrangement ~ their two mules and two skiffs ~ kept them separated during the day, though. Colter soon discovered that he could drift along with the current and keep up with Zeke. After that, the only time he exerted himself to paddle was when he needed to overcome the current. He had gotten so lazy, the only time he paddled was when he wanted to get somewhere special.

Colter lay in one of the skiffs and twiddled his fingers in the water, while the other skiff drifted along with him. They had been going down the river for days and were still a couple of days from the Donnegans', and he wanted to spend some time there. *I don't quite understand why. Maybe I want to find out what Annalee had in mind when she whispered in my ear. I can still feel her words, "Will I see you again?" tickling my ear.*

Colter and Zeke had agreed to spend the last night before Bois d' Arc Creek at Blue River.

When Colter came out of his Annalee daydreams, Blue River was passing him by. He grabbed the oars and shoved their blades into the water. That sent the skiffs toward the down-river side of Blue River's mouth. There Zeke was, with a camp already struck and the mules hobbled, lying there on the blue-grayish flint stones that lined the river doing some daydreaming of his own. *She's called Blue River 'cause 'er water's so clear and good drinkin',* Zeke mused.

Colter tied the skiffs up high just in case of a flood.

"Man, you sure wuz in a hurry ta miss the campsite. I betcha you wuz daydreaming, wudn't ya?" Zeke prodded.

"Yeah, I guess I was."

Zeke had been there awhile. He had already killed their supper, a fat young deer, and was busy sizzling chunks of meat and drying jerky. Colter pulled up a log and sat down beside the fire. They both relaxed there, absorbed by their own thoughts until their supper began to char.

"Looky there!" Zeke broke the silence. They grabbed for the sticks and rescued their supper just before it burst into flames.

After supper Colter and Zeke threw a few traps over their backs and headed up Blue River. They had been catching a few beavers every night, and by the time they reached the Donnegans' they hoped to have enough to buy some things they needed. They got back to camp just as dusk gave way to dark. They lay on their blankets and listened to goose music. The spring migration back to north country was in full swing.

"It's a strange thang why God made us where we could run like a deer and swim like a fish and didn't make us where we could fly like a goose, ain't it?" Zeke marveled.

"Yeah, I guess, but you can forget it. Man has tried everything he could think of to make himself fly, and it ain't gonna happen."

"I wonder if they ever found Yellow Beard's pappy."

"I wouldn't know. I was wondering if Roscoe has my whisky ready."

"We'll know 'bout yer whisky tomorrow, but we may never know 'bout Bill Cooper … do ya reckon?"

"Yeah, I bet when Yellow Beard winds up his business, he's liable to come on down." Colter yawned.

The night chill set in, and Colter and Zeke scrunched down in their blankets. Now, they both were yawning.

"I wouldn't count on it, Colter. He ain't never had a family 'fore. And then there's that thing with you and Annalee."

"What do you mean, thing with Annalee and me? She's Yellow Beard's woman."

"Everyone could see that Annalee had an eye fer you. I guess you think that Yellow Beard never noticed."

"Well maybe she did." Colter didn't want to admit it to Zeke. He sure hoped she had an eye for him, though.

~

The reception the Donnegans gave Colter and Zeke was cold to say the least. The Donnegans had expected Yellow Beard and Barlow to be with them. Colter had some quick explaining to do. He quickly set the record straight by telling them that they had decided to separate. "Yellow Beard went to Rancho Bell and took Barlow with him. I brought Zeke with me to take Milton Sublette's whisky to Rendezvous. Yellow Beard and I will get back together, there at the rendezvous," he assured them.

"In the morning we'll load the boats. I rigged a block and tackle ta let the barrels down the Bois d' Arc Springs bluff and right onto the boats." Roscoe spoke with pride.

"Barrels … load the boats with barrels? Man them are skiffs. How much whisky do you have for me, anyway?" The mention of barrels shocked Colter. He had expected a barrel, maybe two, of whisky.

"Shucks, I got ya ten barrels full, in charred oak! You said Fishy made them boats. Ya ain't got no sweat."

Milton Sublette said for me to buy all that I could buy, Colter thought.

"I got more than that, but I don't know if them little boats'll haul it. Shucks, ya would need a keelboat if ya was gonna take it all.

"If Milton likes this batch, I will bring a keelboat as soon as rendezvous is over, and we'll haul off all that you have."

Colter's brain began to sum up the profits. Three hundred gallons at five dollars, that's fifteen hundred dollars cost. Then Sublette will mix one gallon with ten gallons of water, and that'll make three thousand gallons. That'll be twenty-four thousand pints at three dollars a pint. *Whew man, that's a lot of profit. That's at least seven thousand my share!* he thought.

After supper, Colter and Annalee went for a walk down to the big bur oak tree. The giant of a tree overlooked the creek bottom, and Roscoe had hung a swing built for two from one of its limbs. They sat in the swing and looked out across the creek for a long time, while Colter thought of just how to say what he wanted to say.

"I thought I made it clear to you, Annalee, when we were here before. I would not take a fancy to you as long as you were Yellow Beard's girl."

"Yellow Beard knows that I love you. I don't love him … I told him that. I want to be your girl."

Colter knew how he felt about Annalee, and now he had heard

from her how she felt about him.

For the next several days Colter weighed his options in his mind. *I could take Sublette's whisky to the rendezvous and collect my share of the profits, then go home and settle with Daddy. Of course, if I did that, I would have to leave Annalee here. I couldn't take her to the rendezvous.*

Or ~ he thought, *I could take the whisky to the Mississippi and sell it for whatever I could get. That would not be enough to settle up with Daddy. Then I could go home and pay Daddy whatever I got and offer to pay the balance later. If I did that, I could take Annalee with me.*

The take-Annalee option sounds best, but then there is something else I have to face if I take that option. Colter shuddered at the price he had paid for absconding with his daddy's money. *Should I compound the injustice and make off with Milton Sublette's whisky,* he asked himself. Yellow Beard's voice raced across his brain. *"Go see your father, my Brother ~ before it is too late!"*

"You're worryin' over somethin' that you have no control over. You will do what you hafta do, when you hafta do it," Annalee said.

Colter made up his mind. They would leave first light in the morning, and 'they' would be Zeke, Annalee, and him.

He and Annalee swung silently with their arms around each other and watched the sun melt into the horizon. The dying light brought a chill to the air that caused Annalee to shiver. She snuggled deeper into Colter's arms. "Honey, do you have to go so soon? I cannot stand the thoughts of waiting another year to see you."

The spring mating calls of the whippoorwills echoed along the creek bottom. The wavering wails of wolves in season rose to greet the rising moon. Flitting lightning bugs flashed their throbbing beacons in hopes of finding a mate. Colter felt the urgency of the moment. He tenderly placed his hand on Annalee's face and looked into her eyes. "Annalee … will you marry me?"

"Yes! … Oh, yes!" Annalee said. "We can get Daddy to vow us."

"Yeah, until we can get a real preacher to marry us." They talked for a long time, making plans for their future.

They left the swing and, with their arms around each other's waists, strolled up the bluff. When they approached the porch, they saw Roscoe's silhouette through the window. He bent over and puffed his cheeks and blew out the grease lamp. Annalee grabbed for the raw-hide door handle and thrust Colter into the pitch black room in front of her.

It was too late, but they screamed it anyway. "Wait! Don't blow the lamp out yet!"

Roscoe re-lit the lamp. Its warm soft glow gradually filled the room.

Eve-e and Roscoe Junior had rushed to the loft railing and peered down. Gurdy hurried to Roscoe's side and took hold of his arm.

"What's happened?" Gurdy uttered in a panicked voice. "Has one uh you got copperhead bit?"

"Naugh … a copperhead didn't bite one of us. The love bug bit us! Colter and I are gettin' married!" Annalee's eyes glimmered.

Roscoe and Gurdy hooked arms and cut a dido across the floor.

"Pa will you vow us?" Annalee pleaded in an I-know-you-will tone of voice.

"Shucks yeah … you know I will. Zeke, fetch that crock frum the woodbox."

Zeke had not said a word. He was too busy mulling over what Colter had in mind. *Are we gonna take a woman ta the rendezvous? Is he gonna marry her, then leave her here? Are we gonna take 'er to his mammy and pappy 'fore we can go ta the rendezvous?* Zeke suddenly felt precarious. *I won't have 'is botheration for long.* He grabbed the jug from the woodbox, uncorked it and tipped it up. He re-corked it and went back inside.

"Take ya a big swig, Zeke, then hand 'er to me." Zeke made it two in a row. Then Roscoe drank a big swig and passed the jug to Colter. Colter had not had a drink of anything since that frontier whisky made him so sick at his first rendezvous. He wasn't sure he could even get past the smell. Colter turned the crock up, all the time thinking *If I'm going to take Roscoe's daughter, then I gotta take his whisky.* To Colter's amazement it went down easy.

By three O'clock in the morning, Roscoe was ready to do the vowing and Colter was ready to get hitched. They couldn't find the womenfolk anywhere, though. They finally located them up in the loft fast asleep. By then the men were too drunk to climb the ladder, so they hollered, whistled and blew the dog horn until they woke the women up.

"Get down here, girls! We're fixin' ta have a weddin' tanight!" Roscoe hollered.

"Laudy, that wuz loud enough to wake the devil. We'll be down thar in a minute." Gurdy called from the loft.

By then Zeke didn't care whom Colter took along on the rest of the trip or where they went. Matter of fact, he thought, *I may even find me a woman ta takes along.*

Roscoe performed the ceremony just in time; just as he said, "I pronounce you man and wife," they all passed out.

Annalee, with the help of Eve-e, Junior and Gurdy, dragged the men out on the front porch and left them there to sober up on their own.

"I won't ever forget this weddin' night!" Annalee vowed as she followed Eve-e up the ladder to the loft.

Her heart leaped out of her chest when she heard Colter. She looked over the rail and there he stood. He held on to both sides of the door frame and yelled up to her, "This un wuz fer me … hun. When I get you ho-ho-home ta Naugh Leans … I ul throw one uh these, uh, wingdings fer you!"

~

The Donnegan visit had taken a long time, and it was the end of April before they pulled out into Red River from Bois d' Arc Creek. Zeke put Colter and Annalee on notice. "When we get ta the Mississippi, I'm aleavin' you two love birds, and I'm agonna go ta the rendezvous."

What should have taken them a week of travel had taken two weeks. Between Colter's and Annalee's dilly-dallying around and Zeke's not wanting to run off and leave them, they were getting nowhere fast. The instant they rounded the big bend and he saw the sign-post at Pecan Point, Colter recognized that a change had taken place. Two Bois d' Arc poles standing out of the sand supported a huge Bois d' Arc cross member. From the cross member a sign hung that read: Paccawn Point Plantation - Robert Hamilton owner.

"Jacob Black said something about selling out and moving west. I guess he did it," Colter said.

Carpenters were fast at work building a plantation house on the bluff above Red River. Colter and Annalee walked up the trail that led to the site. A distinguished man riding a well-manicured horse approached from that direction. He reigned up in front of them. "I'm Robert Hamilton," he said. "What brings you? Paccawn Point is no longer a place of trade. I bought Jacob Black out in January. I'm going to grow cotton for gun cotton*. Who knows, I may even start making my on gun cotton."

"We're not looking to trade, sir. My name is Colter, and I'm the proprietor of the Red River Transport Company. We're waiting on Hen-

*As early as 1813, nitrocellulose, gun cotton, was being made from raw cotton.

ry Shreve to get the Giant Raft cleared out of Red River. We plan to transport goods between Bois d' Arc Creek and the Mississippi River with my sternwheeler. Maybe I could be of assistance to Paccawn Point Plantation, sir."

"What is it with the woman?" Robert Hamilton asked.

"Sir, forgive me. Mr. Hamilton this is Annalee, my wife. Annalee is part of the reason I'm here. I came to take Annalee Donnegan to be my wife, and now I'm taking her home."

"Roscoe Donnegan, the whisky brewer's daughter? I heard he had two beautiful daughters, and I'm proud to meet one of them."

"If you think she's pretty now, just wait till I get her home and get her all primped up."

"Looks like your little boats are loaded to the gills."

"This is a trial run for the Rocky Mountain Fur Company. They hired me to transport a shipment of Donnegan whisky to the upcoming rendezvous. Next run I'll be bringing my sternwheeler," Colter bragged.

The mention of a contract with the Rocky Mountain Fur Company and of bringing a sternwheeler up Red River got Robert Hamilton's attention. That was big talk, and Robert Hamilton had big plans.

"I have a scout, Zeke, riding shoreline with a couple of mules. Have you seen him, sir?"

"No, I haven't. Why don't you and your beautiful Annalee join my family and me for the night. If Zeke expected you to camp at Paccawn Point, he'll find you. Tie your boats to my signpost and come on up when you get ready." Robert turned his horse around and rode back to the construction site.

"Colter, you talk so perty, when we get ta Naugh Leans, I want ta go ta school 'n' learn ta talk perty."

"Well, okay, but it is not Naugh Leans. It is New Orleans." Colter pronounced New Orleans slowly for her.

"That's what you called it last night. You said when we got ta 'Naugh Leans' you wuz gonna give me a wingding."

"Maybe I did. I was pretty drunk."

Annalee determined that she was going to pronounce New Orleans right, and she practiced every chance she got. She wanted to surprise Colter when she got it right.

"Naugh Oleans," she said, making the O with her lips. *New Oleans, that's better,* she thought. *New Orleans ~ I finally got it right!* She squealed in delight.

~

After they left Pecan Point, Colter heard the mules whinny at night, but he and Annalee hadn't seen hide nor hair of Zeke or the mules.

"Why does Zeke strike a separate camp?" she asked.

"Zeke is either embarrassed by our carrying on, or he's being considerate."

Colter and Annalee arrived at the Great Raft with the sun still three hands high. They struck camp, and Colter went hunting for supper meat. He returned with a big back strap from a buffalo calf, a large bundle of poke, and a whole passel of wild onions.

By the time Zeke, Dollar, and Squirt arrived, sunset had happened. Setting the table was happening although the table was only the top of a whisky barrel.

After they finished eating, Zeke wiped his sleeve across his greasy mouth and grinned.

"That Annalee uv yourn can sure cook that poke sallet. That pone uh fried cornbread with them green onions in it, that was the best vituals I ever had. Yer momma did ya right, ateachin' ya how ta cook, woman."

Colter and Zeke sat around the campfire and planned how to make the portage, while Annalee cleaned up the dishes. *It ain't agonna be fun totin' ten barrels full uv whisky and two boats around the raft*, Zeke thought.

"I wonder if Henry Shreve will still let us borrow his carts. He told Yellow Beard last year that when we got ready to make the portage on our way back, to come get a couple of his carts," Colter remembered. "Me and Annalee will take the mules and go get the carts, I don't want to leave Annalee here by herself to guard the whisky."

"Won't work!" Zeke advised. "Dollar dudn't work fer nobody but me. Dollar and I stay together. You got no choice, Colter ~ Annalee can guard the whisky by 'ersef ~ else her and Squirt can go with Dollar and Me."

Colter thought for a long time. Then he realized the choice must be Annalee's. "Annalee, what do you want to do?"

"I hep Daddy fight Indians off all the time. I guess I could fight thirsty varmints off just as easy. Besides that, travelin' is tiring. If I stayed here, I could get me sum rest. Load up me a Hawken with a load uh coarse river sand, and I'll take my chances here," she decided.

When Colter and Zeke left, Annalee was still snoring. Colter kissed her on the cheek, but she never roused. The eastern sky had just begun to get a blush of pink as Zeke, Colter, Dollar, and Squirt started down the trail through the cane break. There was no way for Colter and Annalee to know that by the time Colter got back, their whole world would turn upside down.

25

Bill Cooper sat at a small table, his back to the door, slumped forward with his head on the table. In front of him an empty cup kept company with a wide-mouth crock jug of Donnegan whisky.

"Come on, Barlow, us let Yellow Beard and Bill have their time. We're going to Puerto de Luna, Yellow Beard. We'ul be back 'fore dark," Lank announced.

Yellow Beard glanced around the room. *Why are all the black walnut hulls littering the floor?* he wondered. Two very wrinkled and yellowed newspaper clippings hung from the adobe wall, fastened there by a thorn pierced through them. Hanging beside them pierced by another locust thorn was a black walnut necklace just like the one Yellow Beard had on. *Had Daddy found a cache of gold or had he killed another warrior? Had the warrior scalped him?*

Yellow Beard walked around the table and forced himself to glance at his father's head. *The Comanches hadn't scalped him!* He felt relieved. *His hair ... it is strange!* He shivered.

Yellow Beard suddenly remembered what Lank had told Roscoe about Bill Cooper's hair. *Roscoe and I missed the point. We thought he meant strange like mine.*

Bill Cooper's hair was colorless ~ not white, not gray, just colorless. Yellow Beard knew why.

"Bill …," Yellow Beard whispered, "Bill Cooper … wake up."

Bill lifted his head. He looked at Yellow Beard through glazed crazy eyes. He blinked as if to clear them. "Rev thirsty … would ya poor me 'nother drink … Pa?"

"I ain't your Pa! I am your son!" Yellow Beard felt exasperation and pity in one flood of emotions. "I'm Yellow Beard!"

"Rev doesn't have a Yellow Beard son."

It dawned on Yellow Beard that his father would not know the name Yellow Beard. "I am your son! I am Son of Gold Seeker!"

Yellow Beard removed the necklace from his neck and handed it to Bill.

Bill cuddled it in his hands and cocked his head to one side then looked at Yellow Beard like he may remember.

"You gave that to Dancing Waters to give to me when I turned ten years old. Do you remember?" Yellow Beard pleaded.

Bill's eyes lit up at the mention of Dancing Waters.

"I couldn't ever open that walnut. You left instructions for me. You said to only open the walnut the way its maker intended. I couldn't ever figure it out."

"You find Gran Quivira, too?" Bill asked. Bill's eyes twinkled, like a kid up to mischief, as he laid the walnut on the table. He reached over and picked up the crock and raised it carefully, Yellow Beard supposed in order to take a drink. Then he crashed it down on the walnut. Hulls flew in all directions. A big gold nugget spun around until it came to rest in front of Yellow Beard.

"That's the way the maker wants walnuts opened!" Bill Cooper said. He rustled around in his pocket and brought out his own walnut, along with an impressive gold nugget that bore the wrinkled impressions of the inside of a walnut hull.

Father has found the secret cache of Gran Quivira! Yellow Beard laughed out loud. *Lank thinks it is just a cock-and-bull story made up by a crazy old man.*

He placed his walnut on the table and crashed the jug down on it. The walnut busted into smithereens. There was nothing left on the table but an oily spot left from the walnut goodie.

"Holy Jumpin' Jehosaphat! You my son! Dancing Waters your mother? Would you please take Rev to Dancing Waters? You can have my walnuts; they all I got."

"Yeah, I take you to Dancing Waters. Where are your walnuts?"

"In the wide-mouth Donnegan crocks. If Rev sleep now, then will you take me home to Dancing Waters … Pa?" Bill Cooper seemed to beg.

Yellow Beard didn't have the heart to argue the point about him not being Rev's pa.

"Yes Father, sleep now."

"Holy Jumpin' Jehosaphat! Don't ever call me your father. God your Father ~ me just plain Rev!" He closed his eyes and settled into a deep sleep.

Uh, Yellow Beard thought, *he doesn't want me to call him father, that's for sure, and I ain't calling him Rev, that's for sure too. I guess I'll call him daddy, like the white man does.*

While Bill Cooper slept, Yellow Beard went to the stable and picked out two of Bill's best horses. He found a large leather bear-skin rug on the tack-room wall. It would make a perfect pack for Daddy's belongings. He removed it from the wall and went back into the house. He lay the bear skin out on the floor and emptied the walnuts into the middle of it. On top of that, he placed all of Bill's personal belongings and folded the bear skin into a large bundle suitable for transporting on the back of a horse.

Lank and Barlow returned earlier than they had promised. It was a long time before dark.

"I understand now what you mean about Daddy being sick in the head. Sometime he knows I am his son and he wants me to take him home to Dancing Waters, which Barlow and I will do. Other times he thinks he's someone named Rev, and he thinks that I'm his pa," Yellow Beard told Lank.

"Fightin' with them Comanches all these years has done somethin' awful to him!" Lank surmised.

Yellow Beard knew the awful things Comanche warriors did. The things that caused a man's hair to go colorless. Lank doesn't realize it, but there are worse things than losing your scalp, Yellow Beard thought. Yellow Beard removed the newspaper articles from the wall, folded them neatly, and put them in his shirt. He took the walnut necklace down from its place on the wall and hung it around his own neck That will replace mine that Daddy busted.

"We aught ta wait till mornin' to head back," Lank suggested.

The trip home will be slower. Daddy will require a lot of rest, plenty of water, and more than Jerky to eat. The trip home will be the best time of all to dry Daddy out. Yellow Beard realized. He got up and gathered up all the Donnegan whisky that he could find and carried it out to the back stoop where he poured it out on the ground.

It was dusky dark when a painted pony trotted by Bill Cooper's porch and over to the corral. Yellow Beard looked outside just in time to see a tall form followed by a mane of long black hair disappear into the stable. The woman knew something was wrong and busted through the door in an angry mood. "What goes here?" she demanded. Her angry voice woke Bill Cooper, and he began to holler. "Will-O-Willow, you're back!"

"Is he stuttering, or is that your name?" Yellow Beard asked her.

"Will-O-Willow is my name. What goes on here?"

"What is it to you?"

"I belong here. Why are you here?"

Something doesn't add up, Yellow Beard thought. *Daddy is so old, and she's so young. She can't be his woman. She is so beautiful and as tall as I am. What does she mean, she belongs here?*

"He's my daddy, and I've come to take him home," Yellow Beard answered.

"No, no, no! He save my life. You take him, then you take me. I belong to him." She came out from behind her back with a pistol aimed straight at Yellow Beard's belly. "I take care of him!" she shouted. "You leave, now. Pistol say that Will-O means it!" She glanced at Lank and Barlow and saw that Lank had his own pistol drawn on Bill Cooper's head.

"You lay your pistol down, woman, or I kill him!" Lank said smoothly.

She laid her pistol on the floor. "We talk this out."

Will-O stirred Yellow Beard's feelings. She was so agile; in one graceful swoop she had laid the pistol down and then stood tall and straight. *She stirs me like Annalee never did, never could and never would. Annalee plays on everyone else's whims ~ Will-O makes her own whims!* he thought.

Yellow Beard and Will-O talked it out all right, all night long. Yellow Beard made it clear the next morning that Will-O had agreed to come along as Bill's Guardian Angel. He didn't tell them, though, that she had become his Angel too.

~

The next several days getting back to Lank's house were the most trying. Bill constantly begged for whisky. They spent the night with Lank, then headed down the Canadian River. It was the end of May when they reached the tree Yellow Beard had blazed on the way up, they left the Canadian River and headed south. They held a more easterly heading going back. He wanted to be sure that they intersected the Palo Duro Creek and didn't go around the west end of it. Bill Cooper really got excited when they passed through the Palo Duro Canyon. Yellow Beard could tell he knew he would soon be home. Bill Cooper was making the trip to the Wichita River fine, in spite of getting cold at night. Will-O was constantly caring for him. When he shivered, she covered him or built up the fire. If he had a bad dream, which was several times a night, she soothed him down. When he cried for whisky, she cried, too.

The long trip home showed on Yellow Beard and Barlow more than on Bill Cooper or Will-O. When a nightmare came on, he would jump out of his blanket screaming. His 'Holy Jumpin' Jehosaphat' screams were something no one could get used to. If that weren't enough, he would tear out through the woods in his drawers and Yellow Beard would have to chase him down and bring him back. On top of that he would take spells of plowing through all the gear, searching and begging for Donnegan whisky.

Yellow Beard and Will-O spent many waking hours fretting over the care of Bill. They learned each other's desires and fears, and they shared one another's thoughts. *Finally the Great Spirit sent me someone*, Yellow Beard realized. *Finally the Great Spirit sent me someone,* Will-O concluded. They fell in love.

They camped on the Pease River a month to the day after leaving Lank's, and Yellow Beard knew they were nearing home. His heart beat fast as he wondered what his mother's reaction would be to his father's sickness of the head.

~

Dancing Waters had a very restless night. She woke up several times feeling someone was standing in the doorway. Once, she fell into an awful dream. Someone kept beckoning for her help. She searched the river bottom in desperation and in vain. Then she woke in a fit of exhaustion, panting for air. She opened her eyes and lay on her buffalo rug watching the room fill with color as the break of day washed the black away. *Finally it's getting daylight*, she thought. Something, a feeling of anxiety, drew her to Red River. *Maybe it was my horrible dream.* She sat on the big rock at the mouth of the Wichita River, the place where she went when troubled. She watched the featureless sandbar that stretched toward Santa Fe. Midmorning came and went, and Dancing Waters continued to watch. By mid-afternoon her eyes and mind locked together in a trance. She saw everything at once and nothing in particular, and her thoughts blurred into fuzzy visions. Yet, she watched and waited.

Half the sun had sunk below the horizon. The remaining half ~ instead of a blinding yellow ~ appeared to be oversized and orange and was easy to look at. A black speck grew larger as it approached from the direction of the horizon. It danced in the mirage that lay across the sandbar. Then as the speck got closer, it suddenly became two, then three, then more. They danced in the mirage. The specks finally danced their way into Dancing Waters' daydreams. *Yellow Beard and Barlow!*

I knew they should be back! Dancing Waters thought, finally recognizing them.

Dancing Waters stood up and held her hands over her eyes to block the sun, so she could study the approaching travelers better. She could see four animals abreast. Yellow Beard and Barlow were riding two of them. She peered harder. Gold Seeker has got to be with them! Her heart raced. Where was Gold Seeker? At last she spotted him. He was on a travois trailing behind one of the mules. Her mind flooded with questions. *Why? Is he wounded? Is he gone?*

Dancing Waters ran to greet them. She fell on her knees beside the travois and looked into Bill Cooper's eyes.

Bill opened his eyes, but they were cloudy, wild and crazy.

"Oh! Gold Seeker, I missed you!" she cried. Dancing Waters kissed him on the forehead.

That did it.

"Holy Jumpin' Jehosaphat, if it ain't Dancing Waters!" Bill screamed, jumping up. It took all the strength he had left, but he threw his arms around Dancing Waters. She saw Gold Seeker's joy. She watched his joy paint understanding into his cloudy crazy eyes. He never called himself Rev or called Yellow Beard Pa from that day hence.

"Mother, now that you have the excitement out of you, seeing Gold Seeker and all, there's someone I want you to meet. This is Will-O-Willow, and Will-O, that is what I call her, this is my mother. I'll tell you all about how we met later, Mother, but for now, all you need to know is that the Great Spirit has joined us together."

She beamed a smile at Will-O and put an arm around Bill's shoulders. "Let's get him inside then. I'm anxious to hear all about my new daughter."

Someday I'll be Grandma! she thought happily.

When they arrived at Dancing Waters' house, Yellow Beard took Bill's pack inside, then he and Barlow helped Gold Seeker off the travois and into the house.

Barlow took the animals to pasture before heading off to Jinxes and Dancing Doe's house. He didn't think he would, but he had really missed Little Feather. He could hardly wait to see her.

Yellow Beard lay Gold Seeker down on a buffalo rug.

Dancing Waters made a batch of turtle soup and visited with Will-O.

~

Barlow was happy for the time being. He had developed a special friendship with Jinx and Dancing Doe's daughter, Little Feather. Barlow knew the rest of the summer and the winter belonged to them. He began his family, living among the Wichita Indians.

~

Dancing Waters had never been happier in her life. She had Gold Seeker back ~ what more could she ask for? On top of that, Yellow Beard was home and had taken a woman. She couldn't wait to hold a baby again. Gold Seeker, under Dancing Waters' fine care, regained some of his composure. It was only temporary, though.

Gold Seeker broke his last walnut and never found another gold nugget!

26

Colter and Zeke wound their way through a big thicket of dogwoods. They knew they were close.

"Havin' ta spend only one night on the trail'll make the portage much easier. Now, if Shreve'll only loan us sum carts, we'll have the great raft 'hind us in no time," Zeke said.

"If I have to, I'll trade him whisky," Colter said. "It's gonna take a lot longer going back, though, with carts to drag."

Suddenly they burst out of the thicket and into a clearing. They found themselves right in front of Henry Shreve's camp.

Shreve's snag steamer had been busy. It had eaten more than half the Great Raft. His assault on this huge logjam that clogged Red River was serious. Shreve's workers had also widened and cleared the trail around the giant obstacle. That would make the portage a lot easier. The end of the raft was now in sight, both figuratively and literally.

Shreve's crew was still hard at it, and while they had made lots of progress, there was still much work to do. Shreve assured Colter that they were on schedule and the Great Raft would cease to exist by the spring of 1836. Colter's idea was, even if the job wasn't complete when they came back with the sternwheeler, they could camp onboard and wait.

"Mr. Shreve … uh, last year you said you might loan us a couple of carts to portage our things with when we returned. We could sure use them now." Colter didn't want to sound demanding.

They walked to the wagon yard as they talked.

"Yeah I did, and you can. Since you're making it my business, how much and what do you have to portage?"

"Two boats, ten barrels of whisky and personal effects for three," Colter said.

"For three … which one don't you have, the Indian or the big lumberjack?"

"Yellow Beard and Barlow," Zeke said. "We don't have either uv 'em. He's got 'im a woman." Zeke pointed at Colter and winked.

"Ain't that sweet. I betcha you're all tuckered out. Haven't been gettin' much sleep, have you?" Shreve teased until Colter turned scarlet then changed the subject. "With only a couple of carts you'll be all year! Will your mules double team? If they will, you can take that wagon."

"Naugh, they can't double team. That little Squirt ud work Dollar ta death." Zeke balked.

Colter eyed the big freight wagon parked in the wagon yard with an idea in his mind.

"Have you got the team that it takes to pull that big freight wagon?" Colter asked.

"Yeah, I sure do. I got four big Drafts that can pull that wagon loaded with galena* straight up a mountain."

"I'll tell you what I'm prepared to do, Mr. Shreve. I'll give you a gallon of the finest whisky that you ever sipped for the use of that wagon and team for one trip around the Great Raft."

"Donnegan whisky … is it?" Shreve asked.

"Don't ya know it. Jest as sure es yer name's Henry Shreve it is," Zeke pledged.

"Throw in a gallon for my men and you got yourself a deal, Mr. Colter. You boys just help yourselves. The harness is there in that shed, and the Drafts are in that makeshift corral. I gotta get back to the snag steamer."

They left Shreve's camp before noon. They were riding in the freight wagon with four of the biggest horses they had ever seen pulling it and ol' Dollar and Squirt trailing along behind them. Zeke was singing his own made up words: "We got the world by the tail now"; and Colter was whistling a tune to them.

"Just look at Ol' Dollar," Zeke said. "He's agrinnin' frum ear ta ear 'cause he doesn't have ta pull no cart."

Annalee was anxious for Colter to get back so she could tell him her news. *I am gonna turn his world upside down*, she thought.

When Colter showed up, she was overrunning with joy and couldn't shut up.

"The hoot owls ahootin' and the whippoorwills awailin' didn't bother me none; but then, there was an ol' panther that kept caterwauling out in the cane break. He kept getting closer and closer ~ now that bothered me! Honey, I ain't had a wink uh shuteye since ya left! On top of that, those skeeters and the nasty gnats and the seed ticks are tryin' ta

*Lead ore.

carry me off. I'm sure glad ta see ya'll got a big wagon and enuf team ta pull 'er. We can portage everything at once, and I won't have to stay here one more night by myself!

"The best thing in the world, though, is I have been so sick uv a mornings. I've been athrowin' my toenails up." Her face was shining with delight.

Colter had the most puzzling look on his face. *What could be so wonderful about being sick in the morning?* he thought.

She saw his puzzlement. "I'm with child!" She watched his puzzlement turn to shock. *I could knock him over with a feather*, she thought and smiled to herself.

~

The six days it had taken the year before to make the portage around the great raft were cut to two this time for Colter and Zeke. Colter, Annalee and Zeke soon got back into the routine they had before the Great Raft interrupted it. They camped at the end of the day in close proximity to the river. Zeke continued to give them their space. He kept within hearing range of them but out of sight. Annalee cooked for all of them, and the men brought home the meat for her. The only difference in things was her morning sickness and her craving for the tart taste of Sheep Sorrel. Annalee continued to have morning sickness ~ something they were proud of ~ the timing couldn't have been worse, though.

The boats drifted leisurely along with the flow of Red River's current. Colter and Roscoe had placed the barrels, five in each boat, crossways and on their sides. Colter and Annalee reclined on top of them and watched the scenery slide by.

It was late in the day during the second half of the waning moon. Colter and Annalee had arrived ahead of Zeke and had struck camp at the junction of Old River. Colter felt under the weather and just sat and stared up Red River. Zeke arrived a short time later, all out of sorts. It was apparent to Annalee that Colter and Zeke were having trouble dealing with their fate, the fate that controlled their future.

"You both are pouting around here like it was yer last day on earth. Ya'll had better come out of it 'fore ya step on one another's bottom lip," she told them. They laughed but got down to the serious business of figuring out what to do next.

"Just how are we gonna get the whisky down Old River? It's dry." Zeke said. "Them barrels are way too heavy fer a travois. Are ya gonna roll 'em? If you have a plan, I'll stay on and hep you; otherwise, in the mornin' Ol' Dollar and me are goin' ta the Mississippi River to catch uh paddlewheeler ta St. Louis. I'm way too late ta make it to rendezvous; so I'll stay in St. Louis and come fall I'll catch a trappin' party to the mountains."

"Here's the way I see it, Zeke. We could never roll all of these barrels of whisky to the Mississippi. The barrels are already on the boats. I reckon we can take them down the Chaffeli, then up the coast to the Mississippi River. I can take the boats right to Daddy's warehouse on the wharf. I'll figure out how to get them to Milton Sublette from there. You tell him, when you see him, that his whisky is on the way."

That made sense to Zeke, so he accepted Colter's reasoning. "I'll go first thing in the morning."

Colter and Zeke shook hands, and Zeke hugged Annalee bye. "It's been good," Zeke said.

"Sure enough has. Maybe Yellow Beard and Barlow and you and me can do it again sometime!" Colter hollered to Zeke as he rode out of sight.

Zeke and Ol' Dollar disappeared into the rising sun. All that remained were memories of Zeke and his voice as it echoed between the river banks. "Name 'im after me!"

"We will!" they hollered in unison.

"You know, Annalee, this place right here is where we're gonna come back to and build us an outpost. If we had a rig like Henry Shreve's, it wouldn't be any problem to sneak the whisky over to the Mississippi at night ~ then sneak it to St. Louis. When we get home, Daddy is either going to kill me or he is going to team up with me. If he teams up with me, he'll help me buy a sternwheeler to haul whisky from your daddy's to right here! This will be the Colter-Yellow Beard outpost."

~

Colter and Annalee left the junction of Old River and Red River and headed down the Atchafalaya River. It was mid-June and the days were warm and sunny. They were slowly drifting along on the lazy river ~ they had been since mid-day. The slow current and a gentle breeze in their faces slowed their progress. The constant slap-slap-slap of ripples against the front of the boat had lulled Colter into his own little world of garbled thoughts. *The baby is sure showing now. I sure would like to see Fishy. Surely Pierre wouldn't kill his own grandson's father! How will I recognize Fishy's place? By the time we get home, Annalee will really be showing. I wonder if I could sell Fishy some whisky? Annalee and I need some clean clothes before we go home.* That was his last thought. Annalee had been snoring awhile. Now, Colter joined her.

The two boats drifted down the Atchafalaya River ~ minding their own business ~ with no one in control of the direction they chose to travel. Since no one seemed to care, they decided to drift farther and farther apart. They stretched against the long rope that held them tethered together; until the excess of it begun to play out between them. That allowed them to drift farther apart. If one or the other of the boats didn't change directions the rope was going to snag a big cypress tree that grew up out of the river. Neither boat changed direction ~ their master was asleep. They chose opposing sides of the cypress in their downstream journey and dragged the rope toward the tree. The boats went gliding by the cypress tree a full twenty-five feet apart. The center of the rope snagged and quickly tightened, drawing the boats toward each other on a collision course.

Several yards downstream of the big cypress, the two craft were only inches apart. Wham! The two boats struck side to side. They rocked enough that the barrels crashed toward each other. Awakened rudely, Colter grabbed Annalee's arm and threw her overboard. His quick action to keep her from being crushed between the whisky barrels saved her life. He stood up, teeter-tottering on one foot, and took a nose dive into the water himself. He lunged toward the boat, grabbed it, and pulled himself over the side, then helped Annalee back into the boat.

"Look, Colter, there's a man there on the bank with something bad wrong with him." Annalee pointed.

The man flounced around on the ground, kicking both legs as if he was running, while holding his sides, which ached from laughing. Colter grabbed a paddle, unwound the boats from the cypress tree, and paddled toward the dock. By then the fellow had composed himself and waved for them to come on in.

"It's Fishy, Annalee, the man who built our boats!"

There was a big sign on the bank that if they had been doing anything but sleeping they could not have missed it. The sign read: Fishy's Boats, Hoop-nets and Fish.

"Fishy, we ain't got long to stay. I want you to meet my wife … Annalee. Annalee, this is Fishy Fortner. I wanted to tell you, too, that you make the best boats that I have ever seen. These two have been all the way up to the Wichita River and back."

"We're on our way …."

Annalee stopped Colter. “Let me,” she said. “We’re on our way to New Orleans so I can meet Colter’s mother and daddy, Mr. Fishy.”

Wow! Colter thought. *Annalee must have been studying the way I talk.*

“Fishy, could I interest you in some of the smoothest whisky you ever put down your gullet? I am selling it for twenty dollars a gallon.”

“Would it be sum uv that Donnegan whisky?” Fishy asked.

“It so happens that it would be. And, on top of that, I am Roscoe’s Donnegan’s daughter,” Annalee said proudly.

“Yeah, I’ll take five gallons if you’ll take fish fer it.” Fishy tried never to pay cash for anything.

“Can’t do it. Annalee and I need money to buy us some new clothes with, before she meets Mother and Daddy. It will have to be cash.” Colter drove a hard bargain.

“Well, in that case if I can hep you kids out, give me ten gallons!” Fishy’s eyes beamed.

They left Fishy’s place, whistling and singing and with money in their pockets.

“We have enough money to get a slip at the wharf, where no one will bother our cargo,” Colter noted. “We can rent us a room and buy us a bath; then we can get something to eat and buy some new clothes; and we’ll still have money left.”

“Can we buy somethin’ ta eat, that somebody else has cooked, in one uv those places were people go to do that sort of thing?” Annalee asked wistfully. “I’ve read about it, but I ain’t never did it.”

“Sure, honey, we can do that.” *She sure is back-woodsy*, Colter thought. “Then you and me are going to pay Pierre and Christine Lilly a visit.”

~

Colter could not believe how beautiful Annalee was in her new silk dress. She had chosen a natural color silk. She had taken her hair out of the bun that had always remained hidden under her bonnet. Her long curls flowed over her shoulders and were hanging to her waist. They were the same color as her dress and had the same intense sheen she wore on her face ~ the blush of pregnancy. The moonlight danced in Annalee’s eyes as they walked up the lane that led to the Lilly mansion. He had never seen eyes the color of milk chocolate. Annalee’s were, and they were the most beautiful he knew he had ever seen.

Annalee had never seen a clean-shaven man with a fresh haircut and wearing city clothes. Colter’s coal-black hair contrasted with his powder-blue puffy-sleeved shirt. She shivered with excitement. *I can't believe what a difference clean can make in a man. Our baby can't help being beautiful*, she thought.

Colter and Annalee walked up the steps between the big columns of the Lilly mansion. *This is too fancy for me,* Annalee thought. Colter looked into her eyes with anticipation and gave her a look of, oh well, here we are. He picked up the brass ring ~ she saw his hand tremble ~ and struck it against the brass striker plate.

They waited.

The thumping sound is his heart beating, Annalee thought. The dog quit wagging its tail against the porch column and came up to sniff Colter's leg. "Ol' Butch, you're still here. I thought you'd have died by now."

Annalee caught a glimpse of someone through the isinglass side panel of the door.

"He's coming!" Annalee said, and jiggle-danced and squeezed Colter's arm in her excitement.

The door opened. "Yes, may I help you?" asked the little Chinese fellow.

"We're here to see Pierre and Christine Lilly," Colter said.

"They are gathered in the parlor. Follow me." The little man turned toward the parlor.

Colter looked at Annalee with surprise ~ *were they expecting us ~ gathered in the parlor, for what?* His puzzlement showed.

The door-keeper swung the door to the parlor open, and there Colter's mother was; her face turned pale pink. Then she wilted and fell prostrate at her own feet.

Annalee knelt beside Christine and tried to revive her. Abner walked up at that moment, and Colter greeted him. Abner, too, paled. "Not you, too, Brother," Colter said.

In a few minutes, Christine regained her composure and with Annalee's help stood up.

"Mother, I want you and Abner to meet my wife ~ Annalee Donnegan Colter."

Everything hit her at once ~ the last name Colter, the new wife, the baby ~ it was too much for Christine. She did a repeat performance.

Annalee ministered to Christine for the second time. Meanwhile, Abner clued Colter in as to what was going on.

"Father is on his deathbed, and we have gathered the family. How is it that you just happened in?"

Colter's legs became wonky and he almost joined his mother on the floor; but he managed to hold himself together. *Go see your father, my brother, before it is too late!* flashed through Colter's thoughts.

I cannot tell Mother now that I've changed my name, Colter thought.

Christine roused from her faint. "Thank God you're here, Jacob. Your father has been begging for you. Go on in and see him while Annalee and I get acquainted."

Colter looked into Pierre's eyes and knew his father's light was fading.

Pierre held his heavy eyelids open although it took a great effort.

"Son …." Colter put his forefinger over Pierre's lips. "Daddy, I've come home to repay you the money that I owe you and to beg your forgiveness!"

"Jacob … I don't care about the money. You did no more than I did, when I ran away from home back in Ireland and came to America. Just stay with me, Jacob."

I will, Daddy. I'll be right here by your side as long as you need me."

Colter sat by his dad's side the remainder of the night. Pierre faded in and out of consciousness. Once, he whispered, "Jacob, are you still there?"

"Yes, Daddy, I'll not leave you."

Colter didn't have the heart to tell Pierre Lilly his name was no longer Lilly. That now his name was Jac Colter.

Late in the evening of the second day, Pierre whispered, "Get Abner and Christine." Pierre held their hands for a moment ~ his grip relaxed ~ then he went home.

~

Christine wanted more than anything for Colter to take back the family name. She nagged at every opportunity. *At least the family name, his given name; he can do anything he wants to with that. He should at least take back the family name,* she thought.

Colter Lilly ~ that sounds silly. Colter is who I am ~ I can't change that. Colter had always hated the name of Jacob and couldn't bring himself to be Colter Lilly.

They will just have to accept me as Jac Colter, he decided.

The End

ABOUT THE AUTHOR

The alignment of the stars – No – Red River shaped my destiny. My dad and mother accompanied by his brother and sister-in-law, Uncle Earl and Aunt Dovie, had gone fishing on Red River. I remember the story well. "The year was 1940, and the best I can remember it was September," Dad would begin. "We threw our pallets on the sandbar. Your mother and Dovie built sandcastles while Earl and I caught fish for supper. After supper we searched the skies for the Little Dipper and watched the moon rise." Nine months later, July 11, 1941, I made my debut. Since that humble beginning long, long ago I have felt drawn to Red River like a divining rod drawn to water.

It took me a long time to create a way to make a living from Red River. In 1986 I began to design and build furniture using dogwood hoops like Dad had used in his fishnets. By 1998 I had perfected my designs, and that year I was recipient of the Texas Forestry Association's annual "*Award of Merit for Architectural Excellence in Wood Design.*"

I got caught up in Red River history. As you might suspect after reading *Treasure River*, I became obsessed with Red River. I became one of her people; I became her most astute scholar. In 2002, I hung up my hammer and picked up the pen, then embarked on a 16-day 400-mile canoe trip down Red River. My goal: to interview people along the river; to study her history and tell her story.

I come to you neither with a list of published books nor great accomplishments in the academic or literary world. I come inviting you into my world; the world of *Treasure River* where we can become river people together – if only for a little while.

The silvery sands of time sift between my fingers. With each escaping grain I taste the salty tears of the Indian losing his way of life, I feel the strife experienced in taming the Wild West, and I hear the screech of the eagle … soaring. As the last grain tumbles to the ground, I remember from whence we came.

Go to redriverscholar.com for the Wildwood Dean story.